CW01394628

FIRST LADY

FIRST LADY

T. Novan
And
Blayne Cooper

First Lady

Copyright © 2003 by Blayne Cooper & T. Novan

All rights reserved. No part of this publication may be reproduced, transmitted in any form or by any means, electronic or mechanical, including photocopy, recording, or any information storage and retrieval system, without permission in writing from the publisher. The characters herein are fictional and any resemblance to a real person, living or dead, is purely coincidental.

eBook ISBN 978-0-9969734-2-7
Print ISBN 978-0-9969734-3-4

9 8 7 6 5 4 3 2 1

Fourth Edition

Published by T. Novan
8210 Bultaco Trail, Mechanicsville, VA 23111
Printed and bound in the United States of America

ACKNOWLEDGMENTS

Alison Carpenter, Barbara Davies, Nancy J. Ashmore and Judith Kuwatch—your assistance was invaluable. To the many friends who offered encouragement, suggestions, and good advice—you continue to be appreciated. Finally, we would be remiss if we didn't mention the many readers who stalked us relentlessly after reading *Madam President* and asked for more. Most of all, this story is for you.

— T. Novan & Blayne Cooper

DEDICATION

For everyone who waited so patiently for this novel, thanks for hanging in there with us. You're the greatest!

—*T. Novan*

You'd think someone who spends so much time laboring over the right words could come up with something more creative than telling her spouse "I love you and thank you." And yet, as in our life together, in simplicity I find beauty and perfection.

—*Blayne Cooper*

JANUARY 2022

Sunday, January 2nd

The silence was deafening, broken only by the inordinately loud ticking of the wall-mounted clock.

Dr. Rothschild turned to the President, his mouth set in a grim line. "I'm afraid... well, there's nothing more I can do, Madam President." He exhaled wearily. "I'm sorry."

Devlyn Marlowe crossed sweater-clad arms over her chest and lifted a single dark eyebrow at the sheepish, but still defiant, patient. "Are you happy now?"

A blonde head shook.

Dev's gaze softened. "Honey, it won't hurt." Her lips twitched a little, but with effort, she held her smile at bay. "Be my big girl and let the doctor do his job."

"Nuh huh."

Dev sighed. This was not the way she wanted to spend her Sunday morning, but desperate times called for desperate measures. "He's the best in the business!"

"No." Said between clenched teeth, which was hard to do considering how woozy the patient was. "No. No. No. No. No. No. No. No. No."

"When you're finished you can have..." the doctor cast a desperate glance at his nurse, who was straightening the tray of instruments that hadn't been touched yet.

She blinked a few times, realizing that he was actually addressing her. "Ummm...a balloon?"

There were three children in the room, but none of their eyes lit up like Aaron Marlowe's.

"Not for you," his brother said, jabbing an elbow into Aaron's midsection.

As any self-respecting five-year-old would do, Aaron kicked Christopher's foot in retaliation.

"Ouch!"

"Boys." The warning in Dev's voice was clear.

Ashley Marlowe, the oldest of the children, stepped forward and put a small hand on Lauren's arm. "It's only a filling." She didn't have any of those. She didn't even know anyone who did. But her mother had assured her it was common in the "olden days" and no big deal. "You can be brave. I know it."

Lauren Strayer, the President's biographer and fiancée, smiled warmly at the dark-haired girl who so closely resembled her mother. Of course, the action caused a long string of drool to drip from the corner of her mouth. She couldn't feel lips, gums, or most of her tongue, but that didn't matter. Jesus Christ himself could step down from the mount, but if he held a dental drill in one hand Lauren was going to run in the opposite direction. That's just the way it was. And no fancy dentist, with his high-tech laser equipment, was going to change that. Inwardly, she cursed her own fear, knowing that it had been more than a year since her last appointment and that she had probably made things worse for herself.

"Eww!" Christopher and Aaron chorused when they caught sight of the drool. Then they laughed and pointed.

Lauren shot Devlyn a look of pure ice for bringing the children along to her appointment.

Devlyn shrugged one shoulder, correctly interpreting the die-die-die look Lauren was giving her. "Sorry, I had to play dirty." Of course, she wasn't sorry at all, but it sounded good. This was for Lauren's own good, no matter how much her lover fought it. "I love you too much to let you become a toothless old hag." A beat. "Before your time."

"Why you—" Lauren began to sit up, intent on killing Devlyn then and there, and thus delaying the replacement of an old filling for twenty to life, but Ashley blocked her way. The sudden movement caused Lauren's small, wire-rimmed glasses to end up hanging crookedly from her face.

The nurse deftly plucked them off and set them on the tray alongside the instruments so they wouldn't get broken, giving Lauren a reproachful look for being so much trouble.

Chuckling at Lauren, Devlyn jumped back a step, just in case she got a second wind.

Lauren closed her eyes in the hope that the room would stop spinning. She was allergic to the super-strength topical numbing agent applied for most dental work. That left her two choices: an old-fashioned shot of Novocain or gas. She'd passed out cold the last time someone came close to her with a needle, so gas it was. "If I wasn't so stoned, you'd be in deep trouble," she murmured.

"Fine. Fine." Devlyn lifted her hands in resignation. "I'm giving up."

The dentist, his nurse, Lauren, and the Secret Service agent standing unobtrusively in front of the window all gaped at Dev and said in unison, "You are?"

Dev nodded. *Sorry, sweetheart.* "I sure am. Go to it, kids."

Like von Trapp family clones, the children lined up by age and size and stood before Lauren, who broke into a rousing, drooling chorus of "Edelweiss" before they could even say a word.

Dev covered her mouth with her hand, but her shoulders still shook with silent laughter.

Realizing that nobody was singing but her and that the gas she'd been gulping down only moments before like there was no tomorrow was just a *teensy* bit more potent than the last stuff they'd had to special order for her back home in Tennessee, Lauren quieted. Fair brows drew together. "Party poopers."

Ashley, the children's spokesperson, looked at her future stepmother with serious brown eyes. "If you won't stop fighting the dentist and let him do his job, then how can you expect us to?"

Aaron and Christopher nodded their agreement.

Lauren gasped and pointed a shaking finger at Devlyn. "That's... why, that's *horrible*! You trained them to say that," she accused, more drool leaking onto the blue paper bib around her neck.

"Did it work?" Dev asked.

Lauren looked back at the three little conspiring monsters before her, whom she loved with all her heart. *Crap.* She sighed and grumbled, "Yes, it worked."

The children cheered.

"But I need more gas." Lauren turned pleading eyes on Devlyn and the tall woman's demeanor changed instantly, all traces of teasing vanishing before her next heartbeat. Lauren wasn't joking; she was truly afraid.

Dev took a step closer to Dr. Rothschild and pinned him with a serious stare. "Can she have more and still be okay?"

"Define okay."

"Alive."

"She can have more."

This time it was Lauren who cheered, scaring the nurse so badly that she backed into the tray of instruments and sent them clattering to the floor. The woman mumbled something to Lauren, who mumbled something back, only twice as loudly.

Christopher looked at his mother in confusion. "Mom, what's a Nazi?"

Dev shook her head. It was going to be a long morning.

Lauren, in a pair of worn jeans and a sweatshirt, sat in front of her computer. She stared intently at the wide, crystal clear screen. Finally, she sighed. "File close." She tapped her finger on the desk as she thought. "Open file name: Marlowe twenty ten to twenty fifteen."

The sound was turned off, so silently and dutifully, the small machine obeyed her voice commands.

Lauren found her place at the bottom of a plain text document and began to type, her fingers moving in a steady blur. But after only a few moments, her fingers paused over the keyboard. She frowned and took off her glasses to rub tired gray eyes. "Close file. Open story notes file: Marlowe." The screen before her flashed and changed. "Deactivate keyboard."

Gremlin, her chubby pug, recognized the command as his opportunity for some attention, since his own canine partner, Princess, was sleeping at the other end of the bed and paying him no mind whatsoever. He jumped down from his spot squarely in the center of Lauren's tall bed and lazily walked to his mistress.

Lauren looked down at the animal with a small smile. She could see the gears in Gremlin's head turning.

He looked up at her lap and the jump he'd have to make and then promptly dropped down on top of Lauren's feet. "Slug," she said affectionately, reaching down to scratch Gremlin's short, coarse fur. "Let's see if I can remember how to use this fancy new machine Devlyn bought me for Christmas." She'd been resisting it over the past few weeks, but knew if she put it off much longer it would hurt Dev's feelings.

Gremlin let out a low growl at the mention of the President's name.

Lauren snorted. "That's what I love about you, Gremlin, consistency." She reached for a thick manual on her desk and quickly found the voice command she wanted. "Activate dictation."

"Ready when you are," appeared at the top of her screen for several seconds, then disappeared.

Lauren nodded a little, obnoxiously pleased with herself for getting this far. She tossed the manual back on her desk and steepled her fingers. Then she began to speak, pouring her thoughts out into space and into her computer's memory.

"The hardest part of this story is not telling who Devlyn is. I know who she is. Or at least I know her better than anyone else on earth doing this job would. I've given up hope of really capturing her in a single book. But she's easy to know and easier to love, and what I'll be able to share will be enough for the outside world. But I can't approach this story the way I have my other biographies. I'm not disinterested. I'm way over-the-top-in-love interested.

"I've already deleted five times as much text as I've kept, especially when it comes to the "Marlowe For President: A Voice for the People" campaign. I feel like my being out of the country for most of her campaign is really hurting my ability to chronicle that part of her story. Sure, I can read the papers, interview people, and talk to Devlyn herself, but I didn't 'live' those last few years with the rest of America. I didn't 'feel' it like the rest of America did. Up to that point, and after that point, I'm fine. I think. Though putting her term or, God help me, two terms in office into some sort of historical perspective is going to be a challenge. Too many people are still walking around with their mouths hanging open, not believing that it happened at all, much less understanding how or why.

"The first female president. That makes Devlyn the most powerful, and probably most famous, woman in American history. Sorry, Jackie and Marilyn. And I haven't even touched on her being the first open lesbian to take a stand squarely in the center of the world political stage. Sure, there've been a lot of actresses and singers who did, but never a woman politician at anywhere near her level of success. Though I think of Canadian

Prime Minister Martin Allaire coming out of the closet after his male lover died... what, eight or nine years ago? It wasn't quite the same because he was already in office when he made the announcement, but it still paved the way."

Lauren sighed deeply.

"It makes me sick to think about what happened to him and, God knows, I don't need another reason to worry for Devlyn. I've got enough already. We've come so far in just a single generation, but there is still so much hate. It wasn't even a Canadian who stabbed Allaire, but an American. Anyway.

"Certainly the social and economic revolution spurred by the recession of two thousand eight set the stage for the Emancipation Party's rise to power. But how does a party that nobody had ever heard of twenty years ago elect a president? How did the Republican and Democratic Parties lose so much that they allowed this to happen? Isn't that beyond the scope of this book? Do I care? I've never had to write so much back history before. Will readers buy it simply because it actually happened or will they require more? I'm not—"

A gentle knock on the door interrupted Lauren. She looked at the screen and nervously licked her lips, unsure of how to preserve her work. "Save file," she said, and "Saved," flashed at the top of the screen before disappearing. She silently uttered a little prayer of thanks. "Close file. Activate screensaver."

"Coming," she called, hearing another knock at her door. She extracted her socked feet from beneath Gremlin's warm belly, missing his warmth instantly as she jogged across the floor. Lauren opened the door to find a Secret Service agent standing there with a thick envelope in his hand.

"Ms. Strayer," he greeted her cordially.

Lauren smiled at him. His short, nearly military haircut, clean-shaven face, and dark suit would have given away his job had the writer not known exactly who he was. "Hello, Jeff."

"I have something for you that came special delivery, and something from the President as well."

Lauren took the large envelope, a little startled by its weight. The label read "Starlight Publishing." Her brow creased. She wasn't expecting a manuscript back.

"And these are from the President." The young man couldn't suppress his grin when he reached into his blazer pocket and pulled out two Hershey Bars.

Lauren laughed, but happily took the chocolate. "And was there a message with this important presidential delivery?"

"There was." Jeff blushed a little.

Lauren's eyebrows jumped. "Well?"

"Umm… she umm… She said to tell you she was sorry for playing dirty." He peered down uncertainly at Lauren. "And that you'd know what she meant."

Lauren's eyes narrowed as she remembered. "I most certainly do know what she meant. I was supposed to have an appointment to get my hair trimmed and somehow the driver, who I didn't want in the first place I might add, ended up taking me to the dentist! And then—"

"Ma'am?"

"Uh, yes."

"That's more information than I really needed."

Lauren's mouth clicked shut. She winced. "Oh. Sorry, Jeff." She squeezed his arm and her gaze softened. "I know I keep telling you and you keep ignoring me, but you can call me Lauren, you know. I've known you for nearly a year already."

"I know, Ms. Strayer. Thank you."

Lauren rolled her eyes. Why did she bother? "Thanks for the goodies."

Jeff bit his lower lip in a gesture that Lauren found oddly adolescent for a man with a fully loaded Glock Forty strapped to his side. "I'm supposed to report back to the President and tell her if she and the children are forgiven."

Lauren sucked in a surprised breath. "What is she talking about? The children never needed to be forgiven. Could you ask them if they'd like to come over to my room and… I dunno, do kid things?"

"Yes, ma'am." He rocked back on his heels and decided to be bold. "And the President? Can she come over and play?"

Lauren laughed, thinking that his choice of words was perfect. "Of course, Jeff."

He looked relieved.

Lauren lifted her chin a little. "As soon as she comes and apologizes on her own."

A wide grin split his face.

Lauren blinked for a few seconds, surprised by his reaction, until realization dawned. "What time did you pick?"

"Pick? I'm not sure I understand, Ms. Strayer," he lied, glancing down at his wristwatch uncertainly.

"Uh huh." Lauren pursed her lips. "In the pool," she prodded, gesturing with one hand. "What time are Devlyn and I supposed to make up today and how much will you win if you're right?"

Jeff's face turned bright red. "Umm…"

"Don't bullshit me, Jeff. I've had a recent dental experience. After the way Devlyn tricked me, killing you would be anticlimactic."

"I have three-thirty and I'll win seventy-five dollars," he admitted sheepishly.

"Cheapsters," Lauren snorted. She'd made two-hundred-and-forty dollars the week before when she correctly selected the exact moment during Devlyn's meeting with the Secretary of Defense when that little vein in the President's forehead would pop out, signaling doom for whomever the tall woman was talking to.

Lauren checked her watch, then looked back up at Jeff. She wasn't exactly mad at Dev, she decided, more like supremely annoyed. It was two forty-five. "Give the children their message now, please. And you can tell Devlyn to stop by in about," she grinned and slapped Jeff on the back, "oh, forty-five minutes or so. Dinner's on me."

Thursday, January 13ᵗʰ

Dev tossed for the thousandth time; sleep, apparently, was not on her agenda for tonight. She rolled over to face Lauren's side of the bed. It was cold and empty. A little sheepishly, she grabbed the pillow Lauren normally used and tried to connect with her absent partner. But her linens had been freshly changed and all she could detect was the faint scent of the fabric softener, which smelled good certainly, but not like her longed-for companion.

She sat up and then swung her feet over the edge of the bed, pushing them into her slippers as she reached for her robe. Sighing, she padded to the window and gazed out at the moon that hung low and full in the sky. "You're pitiful, Marlowe." She closed her eyes and let her forehead rest gently against the cold glass, feeling foolish and lonely. "She's only been gone for ten days." And that meant four more until she'd be home.

Devlyn opened tired eyes and looked out at the gently falling snow. A thick blanket covered the ground, looking clean and pristine, and she smiled, thinking that her kids and Lauren would love to go out and make a snowman.

Dev wondered if she would go insane before the writer returned home from her business trip. She knew that Lauren couldn't spend all her time in Washington. The younger woman needed to conduct interviews in Ohio and several other states before flying to New York to deal with her publisher. Still, Dev had hated to see her go and had felt a little unsettled since she'd been gone.

To need someone this much was as discomfiting as it was wonderful. Even when she and Samantha were married, the irresistible first Mrs. Marlowe could go on a trip, which she frequently did, and Dev had always managed just fine. *Maybe it's just because I'm older now. I get all sentimental.* But somehow, Devlyn knew that wasn't the whole truth.

With Samantha, so much of Dev's focus was on herself, her career, what she wanted, how she felt, and the bright future that Sam and the children would share in. On many levels, Dev realized that she'd been rather selfish with Samantha; Lauren didn't let her get away with any of that. This time they each had their own ambitions and expectations, and somehow Dev found herself much more comfortable with that. Despite her role as the most powerful person on the planet, she didn't feel that she eclipsed Lauren. She had met her match and it was a relief.

That didn't mean, however, that she liked being separated.

"Shit," Dev mumbled, pushing off from the window and returning to the bed. She yanked up her pillow and left her room, wandering down the hall to Lauren's room in her pajamas. The Secret Service agents at each end of the hall pretended not to notice as a disheveled Dev quietly walked past the portraits of previous presidents and an antique settee.

Trying the knob on Lauren's apartment, she found it unlocked. No matter how much she'd prodded, Lauren had insisted on keeping her own separate quarters. It had been controversial when Lauren moved into the White House to observe the President for her work on Dev's biography. Now, however, the press was having a field day over the two women living in the same house, a house owned by the taxpayers, while being engaged. Lauren had insisted on not adding fuel to the fire by officially moving into the Presidential living quarters, though Devlyn suspected that Lauren's motives for wanting her own space were far simpler than that. Life with a boisterous family, for someone who was generally a quiet, independent person, was still a lot to take. Even after a year at the White House, Lauren needed her privacy.

Devlyn stepped inside the large room. It was mostly dark, and it took a moment for her eyes to adjust to the bluish light streaming through the window. She took a deep, comforting breath. The room held traces of Lauren's perfume. Her gaze flicked under the bed. She waited to hear a familiar growl before she remembered that Gremlin and his lady love, Princess, a prize-winning Pomeranian that Devlyn inherited from her mother when the show dog was knocked up by the randy Gremlin, were sleeping with the children while Lauren was away.

Dev ambled across the floor and pushed off her slippers as she crawled into bed, snuggling up to Lauren's pillow and tossing her own to the side. "Yup. Pitiful," she murmured, letting the familiar scents wash over her. "Ahhh… Much better." She closed her eyes to give her exhausted brain some much-needed rest.

It was bad enough that Lauren was out of town and Dev felt like a spoiled child denied her favorite toy, but the State of the Union address was only a few days away, and the President was, as her father would say, "As nervous as a long-tailed cat in a room full of rocking chairs." Because there was no way to deliver a realistic address only a few weeks after taking office, she had dispensed with the State of the Union address in her inaugural year, as many presidents before her had done.

But this year the address not only was expected, it had been in the planning stages since late November. In just a few days, she would take that walk into the Capitol, where both Houses of Congress and the nation would wait to hear what she had to say. She almost wished that President Wilson hadn't revived the practice of the president actually delivering the speech and that she could use Thomas Jefferson's method of having clerks read it to both Houses independently. Then she wished she had back the time that she had wasted learning tidbits of information that were better suited for Trivial Pursuit than real life. A wry smile curled her lips. *At least I usually win.*

It wasn't as if she hadn't done this sort of thing before. Every year, she had delivered the State of the State address to the citizens of Ohio. But as Governor, she wasn't standing before the entire world when she spoke. And she'd never, ever, had a year like she'd just had.

There had been a bombing of civilian targets by a violent anti-government militia. Dev's move to quash the group had been bold and decisive, but not without loss of life. In her mind at least, it had not been one of her shining moments.

There had been an assassination attempt that had very nearly claimed her life and was still the source of sporadic nightmares and physical pain. If it weren't for the support of her closest friend and political ally, chief of staff David McMillian, and Lauren, Dev wasn't sure she would have made it through the months of rehabilitation, both mental and physical.

Then there was the on-again-off-again turmoil that surrounded Lauren's presence in her life. Her own party had nearly deserted her when what started as a business relationship with Lauren had deepened and turned decidedly romantic. Lauren, however, wasn't ready to quit as Dev's biographer and Starlight Publishing had saved the day by buying out the party's contract for Lauren's services.

Now, she was trying to juggle a new relationship and three children, while running a nation. *God, no wonder I'm tired.*

Dev's first year in office had been a roller coaster, and there were days when she felt like she was going to be thrown from her seat. President Truman had said, "Being president is like riding a tiger," and Dev couldn't agree more. She made sure to count her fingers every night to see that none had been bitten off.

It was no wonder the dream started the way it did.

Dev was in her office pouring over the speech she was about to give. David was pacing nervously around her office, while various aides made sure she knew exactly which points needed to be stressed and which should be glossed over.

"Would you sit down?" Dev growled in David's direction. "You're making me a nervous wreck."

The tall, red-haired man grumbled and took a seat. He began chewing at his thick mustache in a way that Devlyn usually found endearing. At the moment, however, it was just plain annoying. When Dev looked closer, she realized he was also wearing a feather boa and a ridiculous hat. "I don't care if they are in style, David. Get rid of it; you look hideous."

The scene shifted; suddenly she was standing in the Capitol, outside the massive doors, waiting for the Sergeant at Arms to make the formal announcement of her arrival. Dev twitched at her skirt, wishing she'd selected a pair of trousers instead. As she stared at the doors, a small panel slid open and a very mis-chievous set of green eyes stared at her before asking, "Are you a good witch or a bad witch?"

"What?" Dev felt the panic rising in her chest.

The voice was impatient. "Are you a good witch or a bad witch?"

"Umm…" Dev stood dumbstruck, trying to figure out how to answer this question. "Depends on what day it is and if I'm PMSing," she finally said, taking a step forward. She was late; she didn't have time for this nonsense. "Now, let me in."

"Bad witch," the voice squeaked as the panel slammed shut and the eyes disappeared.

Dev looked around the hallway where she was waiting; it was empty, except for small wind-up monkeys, which skittered around the polished marble floor as they played their cymbals and drums. She tried to shake the vision, but they only got bigger as they came at her. Just as she felt she was about to be attacked by the mechanical monsters, the doors flew open and she stum-bled into a room full of laughing people. People laughing at her.

"Aw, shit," she muttered as she fought to maintain her bal-ance. "This is my worst nightmare."

Somewhere in the back of her mind she realized that indeed this was a nightmare, and she watched with fascination as face after face in her dream shifted and changed, morphing into an entirely new person each time. They were all there; everyone who had ever meant anything to her. Her parents, her children, Lauren, her staff, everyone. Very soon they all became a blur and the room felt like it was spinning out of control. Colors flashed as the spinning got worse and voices blurred into a sin-gle white noise that nearly drove Dev to her knees.

Suddenly, the spinning stopped and there was but a single, hauntingly familiar voice. "Dev?"

The tall woman spun around to find Samantha standing a few feet away wearing a beautiful, flowing gown made of white silk. She was an angel, and the sight of her brought tears to Dev's eyes.

Her throat felt dry and her tongue heavy. "Samantha?" She took a hesitant step forward.

"Why, Dev?" Samantha's eyes held the bewilderment of a child, but her warm voice was all woman.

"Why what?" Dev tried to step closer to the radiant vision of her deceased wife, but her feet felt as though they were encased in cement.

"Why are you leaving me?"

A sudden stabbing pain in Dev's chest made it hard to breathe. "I'm not leaving you. I love you."

"Then why are you marrying her?" Samantha pointed and Dev looked over her own shoulder to find Lauren standing behind her.

Lauren was wearing a pair of faded jeans, no shoes or socks, and a soft white cotton shirt. Her wavy, shoulder-length hair was slightly mussed from running her fingers through it, and she had a pencil tucked above her ear the way she did when she was working. She smiled gently at Dev, the action creasing the skin around her eyes and making Dev's heart feel as though it might burst.

"Dev?" Samantha's smooth voice prodded.

"I, I, I..." Dev sputtered and shook her head, trying to clear it. She didn't know what to say. She told herself this was just a dream, then watched with a slightly open mouth as Samantha floated over to Lauren and hovered next to her. The two loves of her life stood very close to each other, but not touching. Dev looked for it, but couldn't see any animosity between them.

"It's all right, Devlyn," Lauren drawled gently. Her eyes shone with understanding and love. "No matter what, you can tell us the truth."

Dev nodded and shifted her attention to Samantha. "No matter how much I love you... loved you... you're gone, Sam." Her smile was bittersweet. "I'm marrying Lauren because I need to get on with my life and because I love her. She's my future."

The words were still hanging in the air when Lauren vanished into thin air and Samantha began to morph into Louis Henry, the teenage boy who had tried to assassinate her. Dev watched in horror as he raised his gun and pointed it at her head. Her heart leapt into her throat. She tried to move, but her feet were still rooted firmly to the ground. The sounds of gunshots exploded in her head, so loudly they hurt. Her hands flew to her ears, and then the scene changed again.

Dev was now standing before the joint session of Congress. The expectant, somewhat impatient look on everyone's face made it clear she had been saying something, but for the life of her she couldn't remember what. She glanced around the huge gallery and felt a cold sweat across her upper lip. Her pulse began to thump wildly in her ears as the moment stretched on endlessly. Finally, in a near panic, she shouted, "I quit!"

Dev shot up in bed. She was twisted in the sweaty covers and breathing hard. She knew instantly that she'd been dreaming. "Jesus Christ on a crutch." After a moment of carefully sorting through the mental jumble, she was able to sigh in relief and even smile a little ruefully. "I'm cracking up."

She started to settle back into Lauren's bed when she realized she wasn't alone. Glancing behind her, she discovered that Aaron had found his way there too. She smiled and lay back next to her son, who curled up against his mother without ever waking. *Guess I'm not the only one missing Lauren.*

It was close to four in the morning when Lauren opened the door to her room, carrying her computer case and a small travel bag. Closing the door behind her, she was just about to flip on the light when she saw several lumps in her bed. She nearly screamed, but one lump in particular looked familiar. Setting down her luggage, she carefully crossed the room.

Devlyn, Christopher, and Aaron were practically lying in a pile on her bed, with Dev on the bottom. Ashley was resting crossways along the headboard with one leg on Christopher's head and her arm on Aaron's head. The eight-year-old was in her pink footie-pajamas and snoring nearly as loudly as Devlyn.

The Marlowes' sleeping arrangements reminded Lauren of the puglies, Gremlin's half-pugs, all of them such ugly puppies that Dev had cleverly given them away as "gifts" to her ex-friends and staff. But instead of a pile of canines, it was a pile of people, their limbs braided together and contorted bodies twisted around each other. Lauren questioned briefly how Chris could breathe with his sister's leg draped over his face.

A smile worked its way across her face as she took in the scene. She marveled for the millionth time how she had lucked across an entire family who loved her. A little guiltily, she realized that it had been two days since she'd called Devlyn, but far longer since she'd talked to any of the kids. Before the Marlowe children, she'd never given parenthood a second thought. Then, without her knowing quite how, they'd wormed their way into her heart to stay. Only she wasn't as good at showing that yet as she wanted to be. She would work to change that, she promised herself. They deserved that. *No more trips this long, not alone at least. My publisher and everyone else can just go to hell.*

Lauren stripped off her coat and clothes, slipping into a pair of thick sweat pants and a well-worn University of Tennessee T-shirt. She yawned and looked longingly at her bed. It was king-sized, but everyone was lying at such odd angles she didn't see a spot where she could fit in. Suddenly, she caught a glint of light as it reflected off Dev's eyes. *Damn, she's beautiful*, Lauren's mind whispered, everything else forgotten for a moment.

"You're home early." Dev's voice was rough with sleep.

Lauren walked around to where her lover was lying and pushed back a shock of dark hair to kiss her on the forehead, then she moved down and brushed her lips against Devlyn's, humming into the sweet but brief contact. "I was missing you guys like crazy," she whispered. "After the first few days I realized I was a hopeless case, so I worked extra long so I could finish early. I didn't want to say anything in case I couldn't pull it off." She gazed down fondly at Dev and quietly said, "I'm sorry."

"S'okay," Dev replied. She rolled over and pushed Christopher, and before Lauren's eyes the pile of children shifted dramatically, but no one woke up. Dev opened her arms and Lauren eagerly fitted herself into the space that had been created just for her.

When their bodies touched, both women sighed.

"I'm so happy to be home," Lauren said quietly, her eyes already closing. "I missed you all."

"Not me," Dev answered, feeling Lauren's lips curl into a smile against the sensitive skin of her neck. "I didn't miss you at all. Same with the kids. We hardly knew you were gone."

"I can see that," Lauren chuckled weakly, Dev's words barely penetrating her tired brain.

"Welcome home, sweetheart."

But a warm puff of air and Lauren's gentle snore were Dev's only answer.

Friday, January 14th

Dev sat behind her desk in the Oval Office while Lauren perched on one of the room's two couches. The television news, with the sound so low it could barely be made out, was playing in the background, and the three-dimensional image of an anchorman hovered near the door. They had already had their first two meetings, and now the women were enjoying a quiet breakfast together. Almost. The food had been delivered a half-hour ago and was still sitting untouched on the table while both women worked in their respective spots, Lauren compiling notes on what she'd observed and Devlyn reviewing several documents from the Secretary of Homeland Defense.

The smell of bacon was finally too much for Lauren to ignore. She set down the hand-held computer as she contemplated what she could safely eat considering she'd stopped working out with Devlyn in the mornings several weeks ago. The answer was nothing, so she promptly disregarded that conclusion and thought about something else.

"Devlyn, your mother is going to kill us for foisting the wedding plans on her."

"My mother will love it." Dev signed her name again, wishing she had taken David up on his offer to get her a stamp for the less important documents. But no, she had to be a "President of the People" who signed every scrap of paper that came across her desk. *I think David only listens to me on things like this to torture me. He knows he knows best!* "By the way, after we get married, you get to sign off on all the kids' report cards."

Lauren stared at Dev. "What?"

"Never mind." She signed her name for the last time and stood up, taking a deep breath. "Come on, sweetheart, let's eat. I'm starved and I've got another meeting in less than a half hour."

Lauren joined Devlyn at the serving table. Once the coffee was poured and they were back on one of the sofas, Dev gave the voice command to increase the volume of the newscast. "Ooo, look who's getting a spot on the news." She gestured as Lauren's face appeared on the screen above a coat rack.

"Terrific," Lauren mumbled around a mouthful of eggs. "I saw them when I ran into Geoffrey yesterday." Her expression darkened. "Assholes." Her short relationship with the media had already been a stormy one. "I should have figured a camera was on me."

"You can never safely pick your nose again."

"I would never!" She laughed, and then winked. "At least in public. But the Republican Party Chairman doesn't let the cameras stop him."

"Why do you think I avoid shaking his hand?"

The television picture shifted to a shot of Lauren walking alongside the Vice President.

"You need to get him out more, Devlyn. Half of America doesn't even believe that Vice President Geoffrey Vincent actually exists. Late night television is saying he's really just a good-looking blowup doll."

Dev burst out laughing. "Brenda must love that one. Rubber-hubby."

Lauren chuckled, but sobered quickly, thinking of why exactly Geoff had to move around so much. The thought of the assassination attempt on Devlyn usually made her physically ill.

Dev patted her hand but didn't say anything.

A still shot of Lauren appeared over the anchorman's right shoulder.

"Presidential fiancée Lauren Strayer's decision to primarily take public rather than government transportation has been called 'insane' by security specialists and 'incredible' by the public.

"White House pollsters are smiling over Ms. Strayer's recent jump in popularity. It seems her refusal to strictly adhere to White House protocol has endeared her to working-class America as well as young voters."

"Television off." The image disappeared. "Well, well," Dev teased Lauren, nudging her with her elbow. "They didn't mention you living here in sin with me. Will wonders never cease? Keep it up and they'll give you my job."

"As if I'd want your job. Trailing around after you all day is exhausting enough. Being you would kill me. Besides, then I'd technically be sleeping with myself and doing things to myself that would make me go blind or grow hair on my palms. And I'm just not up for that. I'll keep my job, thanks."

Dev hastily swallowed her mouthful of coffee so she wouldn't lose it laughing. "Chicken."

Lauren waved her fork at Dev. "Where do you think these eggs came from?"

Dev smiled just as she heard a single knock on her inner office door, and David entered. His gaze stopped on Lauren and his feet ground to a halt. "Oh, I'm sorry, Lauren. I didn't know you'd be here. I thought you were out of town."

"Got back early." She gestured to the couch across from where she and Dev were sitting. "Come have some coffee with us. How's Beth?"

He made a face and loosened his tie. "Mad at me for something, and I can't figure out what." He handed Devlyn a stack of papers before pouring a cup of steaming coffee and sitting down with a groan. "Did you know I'm as dumb as a bag of dirt?"

"I've always suspected," Dev answered as she looked at the papers. "What's this?"

"Your speech for the United Steelworkers of America. You're going to Detroit today."

She looked at Lauren and shrugged. "I am?"

"You are."

"And when was this decided?"

"Last week."

"Shit." She tossed the papers onto the coffee table. "I tell ya, if Liza doesn't get off vacation soon I'm going to lose my mind. That temp who is taking her place is worthless."

David frowned. "Why didn't you say anything? Do you want me to get you another one?"

Lauren gave Dev a knowing look as she spoke to David. "Don't bother. If it's not Liza, she still won't be happy."

"Gotcha." David nodded. "Sorry, Chief, but Detroit it is. You leave at eleven-thirty, but should be home before your munchkins are in bed."

"Great." Dev looked at Lauren with round, innocent eyes. "I guess you get to call Mom by yourself."

Lauren's jaw dropped. "Devlyn!"

Dev lifted her hand. "Honey, what can I do? She's insisting on this call and I'm going to be in Detroit. I asked the temp to clear my schedule for the call, but clearly she missed it somehow." Dark eyebrows drew together in consternation. "You know, I don't think my mom likes talking about the wedding with Michael Oaks." More than once Devlyn had considered firing her personal aide, turned social secretary, because of his poor people skills. But he was good at what he did and had proven himself time and again, earning her trust, if not her friendship.

"Can you blame her?" Lauren glared at David. "You did this just to get her out of this phone call, didn't you?"

David blinked slowly. "Would I do something like that?"

Lauren tapped her coffee mug with her fingernail impatiently. "Yes."

"Okay, I would. But this time, I didn't. It's been on her tentative schedule for a couple of weeks."

Lauren shot them both looks that sent shivers down their spines. "I hate you both."

"Then solve the problem by telling Mom we're eloping." Dev chuckled as she buttered her toast.

"I'd elope with you in a heartbeat, Devlyn," Lauren shot back. "But there is no way on God's green earth I am telling that to Janet Marlowe. You've heard the Princess Diana speech, haven't you?"

Dev rolled her eyes. Had she?

"How she watched it on television in the wee hours of the morning, entranced. The dress, the pageantry… blah… blah… blah."

David grunted in a gesture that Devlyn figured was as close to sympathy as she was going to get from her dear friend. Beth's mother had talked Beth into powder blue tuxedos for his wedding. The memory of those ruffled sleeves still made him slightly ill. "Thanks for the coffee." He stood up. "I'll see you later."

"Thanks so much, buddy." Dev threw a wadded-up napkin at her friend as he fled her office. Then she took Lauren's hand. "I'm sorry you have to do this alone. Mom's probably peeved that we haven't talked to her about any of the details yet." There was no "probably" about it. Dev's father had warned her a few days ago.

"We don't know any!"

"I know that," Dev replied reasonably. "And you know that. Now you just have to tell my mother that. What can I do to make it up to you?"

Lauren sighed as she looked into guilt-ridden eyes. "I'm sorry. I guess your job makes it impossible to make this small and simple, huh?" It was a rhetorical question, but Dev nodded anyway.

Lauren melted under Dev's gaze. "You're lucky I'm so in love with you."

Dev smiled, recognizing Lauren's surrender. "I know."

"I'll try to be more understanding. And I'll call your mom this afternoon as planned, don't worry."

"Thank you," she said sincerely, knowing that Janet loved Lauren completely and that the younger woman would be subject to far less grief than she herself would.

"But if you want to bring me back a present from Detroit, I won't complain."

"Sure. I can probably get a Chevy in my suitcase." Devlyn leaned forward and kissed Lauren.

"Devlyn?" she muttered against soft lips.

"Mmm?" Dev kissed her again.

"Make it a red 'Vette."

Lauren looked at the phone on her desk, contemplating the device as she held her head between her hands. Finally she sighed, "Call Janet Marlowe."

The phone rang three times and then Janet's hologram appeared. "Hello, sweetheart." She smiled fondly, the motion creasing the skin around her mouth and eyes. "How is my favorite daughter-in-law-to-be today?"

Lauren's smile was wan. "Well, I'm here." She paused, not wanting to deliver the news, but seeing no way around it. "Which is more than I can say about that good-for-nothing Devlyn."

Janet glanced around with narrowed eyes. "Lord help me. That girl will be the death of me yet! What has Devil done now? Do I need to come over there?"

Lauren laughed. The image of the President's mother storming into the White House with a wooden spoon in her hand, ready to strike, was an image she wouldn't soon forget. If there were one person in the world who could do it, it would be Janet Marlowe. "No, you don't need to come over. Devlyn had to go to Detroit today. That's why she's not here."

Janet frowned at the look on Lauren's face. "We'll manage without her, dear. How much help do you think she was really going to be anyway? And when she ends up wearing a light pink 'poofy' dress she won't be able to say a single word about it. Not one."

Janet grinned and Lauren's eyes widened a little. It was an evil little grin that reminded her very much of someone she loved. *Oh, boy.*

"I'm assuming we have a date to work with." It wasn't really a question, but Janet's tone was more gently prodding than angry.

"That's the good news."

Janet waited, but Lauren just looked at her, not saying another word. After a few oddly silent moments Janet said, "Um, dear, usually when someone says there's good news, that means there's bad news to go along with it."

"That is the way it usually goes, isn't it?" Lauren chewed on her lower lip and girded her mental loins. "The bad news is that we only have six months to put the wedding together. But with Devlyn's schedule it's the only good time. I swear," she blurted out. Six months sounded like plenty of time to her, but Michael Oaks had nearly had a stroke when she told him the date they'd selected. She chuckled inwardly, admitting that that part had been sort of fun.

Janet snorted. "Don't worry about it. I've already gotten calls from every wedding planner on the planet. All we need to do is decide which one to use. Then I'll have a little more help," her blue eyes twinkled, "and I won't have to hurt you and Devlyn, who I just know are going to try to leave all the details to me."

She's not angry. Thank God. Lauren felt relief course through her body. "I love you" she heard herself say. It was as though the words were coming from someone else's mouth, but as soon as she heard them, she knew they were true. *Wow.*

Dev's mother laughed softly and smiled. "I know, honey. I love you too. Don't you worry about a thing; these things have a way of working out."

Or not, Lauren thought.

"Are you two going to be home next week so I can come visit and get the ball rolling?"

Lauren's eyes brightened. "Absolutely. Devlyn will be in and out, but we might be able to corner her for ten or fifteen minutes."

Janet nodded smartly, the motion bouncing her thick salt-and-pepper-colored hair. "I'll make all the arrangements and see you next week." She gazed intently at the younger woman. "Lauren, I mean it when I say you shouldn't worry. I know people are making a terrible fuss, and I'm one of them. But things will be all right. You'll see."

Lauren felt a lump develop in her throat. "Thanks, Janet. I wonder if Devlyn knows how lucky she truly is."

"Of course not!" Janet scoffed. "But don't worry, honey." She winked at Lauren. "I'm not above reminding her."

Friday, January 21st

Dev sat in the padded lounge chair, watching indulgently as David and Christopher did their best to fend off the splashing of Beth, Ashley, and Aaron. It was a losing battle, but they were having a great time so that's all that mattered. She glanced over at Lauren, who was sitting near the back wall of the pool area, on the videophone with Wayne, her New York publishing agent. Dev could tell by Lauren's jerky hand motions and her frequent frowns that something was going on with one of her books. She hoped it wasn't the biography.

She's been under too much stress lately, Dev worried silently. Ever since they announced their engagement, the press had been unrelenting, hounding her for interviews, stalking her for photos. *This is supposed to be her home, not a trussed-up prison.* Tiny lines of tension around Dev's eyes eased a little when Lauren laughed heartily at something Wayne said, the sweet sound carrying above the children's squeals of delight.

On Dev's swimsuit-covered belly sat a stack of papers Liza had given her to review before tomorrow's seven-thirty a.m. meetings with eleven Emancipation Party governors, who were in Washington for several rounds of party meetings that would last the entire weekend. Today was also David's birthday. They hadn't had time to celebrate last year, when the haze of confusion that surrounded her taking office put every other part of their lives on hold for a while. This year, however, she was bound and determined to do something to mark the occasion. And a family swim was just what the doctor ordered.

Gremlin was sitting in his own lounge chair, watching the pool festivities and wearing a pair of sunglasses that Ashley had slipped onto his face. The ugly, white dog with black face and ears was as happy as could be, occasionally turning to Devlyn and giving her a short growl, before turning back to people he apparently preferred. The President found the sight as ridiculous as she did disconcerting. She half-expected the disobedient beast to demand a margarita to go with the bowl of doggy biscuits Christopher had placed within handy reach of the mutt.

A barbeque in the dead of winter, consisting of grilled burgers, hot dogs, and chicken breasts, and salads with all the fixings, had been served up buffet style and Lauren, the Marlowes and the McMillians all had slightly bloated bellies as a testament to their appreciation of the feast. The children were running and splashing and screaming. Dev herself felt like rolling over and taking a nap, and she wondered for the hundredth time what it was about food that revved her children up as if they were on speed.

She used the pen in her hand to scratch her temple as she forced herself to at least try to scan the papers in her hands. *Only a year ago you were a governor yourself, Dev. Take this seriously.* Then, Ashley executed a perfect cannonball into the pool and Dev sighed. *Or else get up two hours early and do it then.* Decision made, she tucked her papers under her lounge chair and got up, intent on trying her own cannon ball. She was sure she'd be a little rusty, but either way, she was bound to make a helluva splash.

As she passed by the far door, she heard a knock. Dev pulled open the door to see Emma standing there looking like the proper nanny, a stack of towels in hand. "What took you so long, Emma? David and Lauren nearly cleared out all the hot dogs."

"I'm crushed," Emma said flatly, though her hazel eyes twinkled.

"I knew you would be." Dev's gaze strayed down to the stout woman's dress. "Where's your suit?"

Emma smacked Dev's arm. "You know good and well this body is not going to be seen in a bathing suit."

"Aww… Emma." She lowered her voice. "Beth hardly has a perfect figure and she's in the pool right now."

Emma glanced at Beth, who had Ashley riding on her shoulders. The George Washington University professor was big-boned and wide-hipped to begin with and on top of that enjoyed good food and better beer. She waded through the water, oblivious to the thirty-five pounds she needed to lose to look truly good in a swimsuit. Emma crossed her arms over her ample chest. "That's all well and good. But I'm not a young woman, Devlyn Marlowe."

Dev's eyebrows jumped. She turned her head and cupped her hands around her mouth to yell, "Hey, Beth. Emma says you're a young woman."

Beth stopped her path through the shallow end and gave Emma a beaming smile. "Thanks!" she exclaimed happily. "Seems I'm the only one of the women here who could be torn away from work long enough to play. Are you going to fix that, Emma?"

"Not in this lifetime," Emma answered easily. Emma gestured to the children, who were laughing and carrying on with David and Beth in the pool.

Beth shook her head, nearly sending Ashley toppling into the water. "Go get your woman off that darn phone, Dev. It's Friday night, for God's sake."

"Yeah, yeah. I'm going," Dev muttered absently as she indicated that Emma should take her chair. "She gets another five minutes." This said loud enough so that Lauren could hear her. The younger woman nodded and winked at Dev, telling her silently that she was nearly finished.

Emma plopped down with a groan and gave serious thought to taking her shoes off and showing her feet to the world. "Everyone will be properly worn out tonight."

Christopher and Aaron jumped out of the pool and grabbed a pair of super-soaker squirt guns. Then they jumped back in right next to David, drenching him from both sides.

Dev smiled fondly at her boys. "No doubt. They've been romping for the last hour."

"I was talking about David and Beth," Emma clarified with a grin.

"Oh. Them too."

David climbed out of the pool and haphazardly ran a towel over his body before dripping his way over to Dev and Emma. He was panting, and his ruddy skin had taken on a deeper glow. "Do those kids ever quit?" He scrubbed his thick rusty-colored hair with the end of his towel.

"No." Dev shook her head in wonder. "They've got more energy than all of us combined." She reached out and patted her friend's arm, waiting for him to make eye contact before saying, "Happy birthday, David."

David gave her a genuine smile, then a hug, as much to get her wet as to show his affection. "Thanks, Devil. It's nice to spend it with you guys. Beth is taking me out later, but this... well, this is great." He shook his head at the sparkling water. "I can't believe we haven't done this before."

"No kidding," Dev agreed wistfully. Living in the White House was a lot like living in Disney World but never having time go on all the really cool rides. The children enjoyed the magnificent living quarters far more than she did.

David used the towel on his ears. "Are you sure the office won't explode without us?"

"No, but when it explodes they'll just rebuild and there'll be twice as much work on Monday."

David groaned. "No kidding. Have I—?" Then he paused, distracted by Lauren's frustrated voice.

"I don't care!" Lauren said, clearly back in the middle of something with Wayne. "They can't do that, can they?"

David gestured to Lauren with his chin, a crease forming on his forehead. "What's up with her?"

Dev kicked off her shoes and adjusted the straps of her suit. "I'm not sure. But whatever it is, it's not good."

"If the papers would give the poor girl a break, she'd be all right," Emma sympathized with a sigh. "She hasn't been out of the house all week."

"Excuse me for a second," Dev gave David a parting pat. "I'm going to go make sure she's okay."

Dev could hear Wayne promising that he'd "try" and then Lauren ended the call. The smaller woman met Dev half way and, without warning, flung herself into Dev's waiting arms.

"Whoa," Dev squeaked, glad that she was standing on one of the few dry spots left.

"Stop the world." Lauren buried her face in Devlyn's neck. "I want to get off." Long arms tightened around her and she let out a sigh of pure relief, sinking into Devlyn's warm body.

"Tell me what's wrong, sweetheart." Dev pressed her lips to Lauren's hair, breathing in the light scent of her shampoo.

Lauren whimpered. "The very first book I wrote was when I was young and incredibly stupid."

Dev drew in a breath to speak.

"Not a word," Lauren warned, giving Dev's throat a playful bite and feeling the body pressed tightly to hers shake with silent laughter. "I was still in college and I signed a rotten contract with a small publisher and I pretty much forgot all about it after the book didn't sell well."

Dev frowned. "You're unhappy about poor book sales ten years after the fact?"

"Nuh uh." Lauren shook her head. "My old publisher contacted Wayne, looking for an address for Lauren Gallagher." It was the pen name Lauren used for her fiction, and thus far Wayne had been successful in hiding the link between Lauren Gallagher, reclusive, moderately successful fiction writer, and Lauren Strayer, respected biographer. "Seems my old publisher has sold my story to a movie studio."

"That's great!" Dev grabbed Lauren by the shoulders and took a step backward to examine her face. She winced at the dour expression that met her. "Or not."

"It's... well..." Lauren's face turned bright red and suddenly she couldn't meet Dev's gaze.

Dev blinked. "C'mon, whatever it is, it can't be that bad," she lied.

Lauren closed her eyes and exhaled. "The movie company that bought the book is known for its... well... for producing," she lowered her voice, "adult films."

Dev's eyes widened. "Porn?" she blurted out loudly.

"Shhh! Jesus." Lauren looked around self-consciously as Dev burst out laughing.

"Oh, God. You're kidding?"

Lauren's eyes flew open, then turned to dangerous slits. "Do I look like I'm kidding, Madam President?" And with a stiff push, she sent Devlyn careening backwards into the pool.

Dev shot up out of the water sputtering and coughing. "Puh. Bah." She spat out a mouthful of water.

"Do it again! Do it again!" Aaron cried gleefully, thinking he'd never seen anything so wonderful as his mother soaking wet and her hair hanging over her eyes.

Dev thrust her chin into the air and arched a slender black eyebrow at Lauren, who returned the challenging gesture, placing her hands on her hips for good measure. She stuck her hand out to Christopher. "Weapon." The boy dutifully handed his mother his squirt gun.

Ashley sloshed over to the edge, plucked Aaron's gun from his hands, and tossed it up to Lauren. "I'm on your team!" she yelled.

"Hey!" Aaron complained, shooting his big sister an evil glare.

"Me too," Beth chorused, scurrying to put herself as far away from Devlyn as possible.

Aaron pulled his chubby body out of the pool and ran over to the bucket containing their arsenal to hunt for another weapon. "I'm with Mom!" The boy pulled out an enormous squirt gun with an empty tank nearly the size of his head. He fumbled with the big gun, his wet hands slipping on the plastic handle. "Will you help me fill it, Lauren?"

Lauren looked at Dev and smiled lovingly, her eyes glittering with happiness. Then she turned her attention back to Aaron. "Sure, honey." She called time took off her glasses and set them on a stack of fluffy, turquoise beach towels, then scooted over to fill her and Aaron's guns, while those who weren't packing heat scrambled to the bucket to remedy that problem. Even Emma joined in. She knew better than to be caught empty-handed when battle lust took over the Marlowes and company.

In the age of biological, chemical, and nuclear weapons, a war to the death raged inside the White House. Only this one was fought with chlorinated water, laughter, and the occasional sloppy kiss when someone was captured by the opposing team.

FEBRUARY 2022

Friday, February 11ᵗʰ

Beth McMillian shifted from one foot to the other as she peered around Lauren to see what she was looking at. "Dev would go bananas if she knew we were doing this," she murmured as she waved away a sales clerk.

Lauren nodded absently as she lifted a silk robe from the rack and examined it with a discerning eye. She was ignoring the cloying, nearly overpowering scent of perfume from the counter nearby, determined not to let the budding headache from the combinations of odors ruin her time.

She and her then husband Judd had stopped exchanging Valentine's Day gifts after they'd married. Judd had informed her seriously that he didn't need a made-up holiday to tell her he loved her or to buy her a gift. He wouldn't have married her if he didn't love her. So why should Hallmark put him on a schedule? And she'd readily agreed, mostly because she found herself with little interest in picking anything out for him.

The mixture of butterflies and anticipation that was brewing in Lauren's belly for this Valentine's Day made it crystal clear to her that she and Judd had been full of shit.

What color? The holiday calls for red, I think. But…

"Ooo… Nice." Lauren spied another robe and pulled it off the hanger, fingering the cool silk with her fingers. *With those gorgeous eyes, how can I pass up blue?*

"Lauren?"

"Hmm…" *Black is nice too. This robe will be short on her and that color against her skin would look so…* She swallowed. *Oh, my.*

Beth put her hands on her ample hips. "Are you even listening to me?"

"Yes." Lauren nodded, but her attention remained on the rack. "You're getting ready to moan and complain about the lack of agents following my every move as I try to shop in peace."

"Well, you have to admit you are—"

Lauren draped the blue robe over her arm and tossed the black one over the rack as she turned to face her friend. The look on her face caused Beth to blink and shuffle her and Lauren's jackets, which she had obligingly held so Lauren could dig through the lacy unmentionables in the store. The movement caused her brown curls to bob wildly.

"Just what *exactly* do I have to admit?"

Beth's brown eyes widened a touch. *Uh oh.* "Umm… well—"

"That I'm here without security?" A pale brow arched.

"Now, Lauren—"

"Don't you 'now Lauren' me." Her voice was low and edged with irritation. "Just what am I to believe he is? Hmm?" Lauren shot her arm out sideways and pointed to a Secret Service man who was standing about fifteen feet away and trying quite unsuccessfully to blend into the background. "Or her." Lauren's arm shifted to a woman in a dark suit who visibly cringed when she realized what had just happened.

"Lauren!" Beth grabbed Lauren's arm and forced it down. "Are you crazy or something? Don't point them out! They're supposed to be…"

"Hiding from me?"

Beth opened her mouth and then abruptly closed it. She had the good grace to blush when she realized Lauren not only knew about the protection that shadowed her when she thought she was sneaking out of the White House, but she also knew that Beth knew. "Protecting you."

"I don't need protecting."

"Yes, you do," Beth shot back just as stubbornly. There was a long moment of silence that was finally broken by Beth saying, "You don't want it, but you need it, Lauren. You do. It's a dangerous world."

Lauren held her breath for a moment before exhaling raggedly. She knew Beth was making a veiled reference to the assassination attempt on Dev. "You're fighting dirty, Beth."

"You're too important to lose too, Lauren. I'll fight dirty if I have to, at least on this. Besides, I'm rarely if ever wrong. Just ask David."

Both women exchanged weak smiles, then Beth sighed. "Don't kill Dev for this. She's just worried for you. It's not as though you left her much choice."

"It's not as though she left me any choice either." Lauren turned around and began to replace the black robe on its hanger, her eyebrows drawn together. Her voice dropped to a whisper. "I can't be under lock and key every second, Beth. I'll go crazy."

"I know." Beth put her hand on Lauren's shoulder, feeling the warm fleece of her sweater beneath her palm. "Look, I know you and Dev have gone round and round on this, but since announcing your engagement certain things stopped being optional. Security for you is one of them. I'm sorry. This comes with the territory. You know that."

Lauren made a face. "Knowing it and accepting it are two different things." She squared her shoulders. "I understand that I'm more recognizable than I was a few months ago."

Beth's lips quirked. "No, really?" She lifted her hand and flicked her finger at the bill of the baseball cap Lauren was wearing in an effort to disguise herself.

Lauren blew out a breath and knocked away Beth's teasing fingers. "You're not helping."

"Sure I am. I'm telling you the truth." Beth, however, didn't think it was necessary to mention the agent lurking at the entrance to the shop as well as the one hovering near her car to make sure it wasn't tampered with that Lauren had apparently missed. She firmly believed there was such a thing as too much honesty.

"No one's even noticed me," Lauren asserted lamely. *Like she's gonna buy that.*

Beth snorted. "Sell it to someone who's buying, Lauren."
See?

"We've been in the store for thirty minutes. Big Burly," Beth gestured to the male agent, who more closely resembled a mountain than a man, "and Bad Ass," this time she gestured to the female agent, who had a predatory expression permanently plastered on her face, "have discreetly kept at least ten people from coming up to you. I think the poor saleswoman has nearly been shot three times without knowing it."

"Is that really their names, 'Burly' and 'Bad Ass'? They sound like characters in a buddy novel." Her tone became speculative. "I could write that."

"Lauren," Beth said impatiently. "Do not make me stamp my foot. My mother stamped her foot and I refuse to go there."

Lauren smiled. "All right. All right." She waved a hand in surrender. "But I do understand more than you realize." They began walking toward the cash register, with the agents trailing discreetly. "Especially after…" she licked her lips and swallowed hard as she usually did when mentioning it, "Devlyn's shooting."

Beth's gaze softened as she regarded her friend. Lauren really was trying. She'd been through an almost unimaginable life change over the past year, and Beth reluctantly gave her credit for always doing the most prudent thing when the children or Dev were involved. Her track record when it came to decisions involving herself, however, wasn't nearly as good. And, Beth admitted, it wasn't like she could truly relate. She didn't know what it was like not to be able to run over to a convenience store without turning it into a major production. Or how a simple baseball game or theater tickets now took weeks of planning.

Lauren wanted to make Beth understand. "I knew we wouldn't be alone today." Her eyes pleaded with her friend, who she knew damn well wouldn't give her quarter. "This was sort of private, Beth." Her cheeks flushed pink. "It's our first Valentine's since... well, you know."

Beth grinned cheekily. She most certainly did know, along with everyone else on the planet. "And you didn't want to be watched as you bought your girlfriend sexy undies?" She gestured to the robe in Lauren's hands. "That's really nice, by the way."

Lauren scowled as her temper flared. Sometimes she felt as though she was smack dab in the center of a pressure cooker. "This trip wasn't the Secret Service's business!"

"Do you really believe that?"

Lauren crossed her arms over her chest. "Would I have said it if I didn't?"

Beth rolled her eyes. "Does your need for privacy overrule everyone else's needs? Devlyn loves you and you will have protection one way or the other." She paused and turned toward the perfume counter. "Does it have to smell like they wax the floor with cougar piss and ox musk? Yuck!" She turned back, but despite the non sequitur her face was very serious. "When those agents are forced to sneak around to protect you, they aren't doing their job the way they are trained to. They aren't private security, Lauren. Or even CIA or Office of Homeland Security agents, trained to fight in the shadows. They're Secret Service, who will literally put their body between yours and a bullet if they're able. Their lives are put in greater danger by protecting you on *your* terms," she said flatly. "Stop fighting the inevitable."

Lauren blinked. In a few short sentences Beth had distilled the issue into something she couldn't… wouldn't ignore and put her in her place to boot. The very thought of one of those men or women risking their lives for hers made her sick to her stomach as it was. *Why isn't she on Devlyn's staff?* "Shit."

Beth's expression was a little smug, knowing that she'd won this round. With Lauren, victory was rare. "Exactly."

"Be my chief of staff," Lauren said suddenly.

Beth stopped walking and stared. "Huh?"

"Be my chief of staff," Lauren repeated. "Michael Oaks and Devlyn both insist that as First Lady I'll need one. I didn't know there was such a thing. I guess it's the equivalent of David's job only for the President's other half."

Beth blinked a few times, wondering if she could really do that.

"You're not only my best friend, well, besides Devlyn, of course. But you're smart and know the ropes, Beth. I'm going to need help and I trust you. That's more than I can say for ninety-nine percent of Washington." Politics, Lauren had learned long ago, could be a very nasty business. "I could use your wisdom on a permanent basis."

"Is that an age crack?" Beth asked with faux annoyance. At forty-one, she had a solid decade on her friend.

"Basically." Lauren laughed.

Beth's mind was racing, and she was fast warming up to the possibility of really doing this.

Lauren recognized the gleam in the shorter woman's eyes. It wasn't that long ago that she herself had been offered the opportunity of a lifetime and everything had changed.

"What about my teaching position?"

Lauren chewed her lip. Beth was a respected professor of history at Georgetown and as much as she wanted her for this and believed that she'd be perfect for the position, Lauren would never ask her to permanently give up something she loved so much.

"How about a sabbatical? Or a leave of absence? The university would have to be stupid to let you go completely if they could avoid it." She winked and offered wryly, "I could have Devlyn sic the IRS on them until they comply?"

Beth burst out laughing. "No need for that. I… well… maybe I could lighten my load to just one course a semester and still do this?"

Lauren nodded quickly. She'd take Beth on any terms she could get. "Anything."

Now Beth was getting excited and it was starting to bubble over. Her dark eyes twinkled, and Lauren knew she had her. "I'll have to talk to David about it."

"Of course." *Yes!* Lauren grinned wildly. She set her purchase onto the countertop and after a moment's deliberation snagged a gold gift bag covered in tiny red hearts from the display near the register. She sucked at wrapping things. The card, however, was something she wanted to make herself. She began rooting around in her leather purse for her wallet, but Beth beat her to the punch, shoving a MasterCard at the ebony-skinned sales associate. Lauren could pay her back later.

The woman gasped as she took in Lauren. "Aren't you—?"

"No," Beth blurted, cutting off Lauren before she could even open her mouth. "She's not. I know she looks like it. But look closer, you'll see what I mean."

The woman surveyed Lauren critically as she took Beth's credit card. "Sorry, you're right."

"She is?" Lauren asked, bewildered.

"Oh, yeah. Lauren Strayer is way skinnier. No offense, ma'am," she added quickly, not wanting to lose the sale.

Lauren's gray eyes turned to slits as she glared at Beth, who looked like she was about ready to sink into the linoleum. "Oh, Beth?" she drawled in a singsong voice.

Beth gulped. "Yes?"

"You're fired."

Monday, February 14th

Dev rolled her shoulders, humming in pleasure when she felt her spine and neck crack and move back into proper alignment. It was eight-thirty p.m. She was bone-tired and all she really wanted to do was call it a night and go to bed early, but she knew she still had something very important to take care of. It had been on her mind all day, and much to her private embarrassment, Dev felt a little like a high schooler with her first crush. *God, I hope she likes it. What if she doesn't like it?*

With slightly trembling hands, she took the two boxes from her desk drawer and headed out of the office. She laughed a little, realizing she was making herself crazy for nothing. Glancing at the clock, she frowned, knowing she'd missed dinner with the family and that the kids would already be in bed.

That meant Lauren would be in her room working or in the kitchen playing cards with whichever agents or staff members had drifted there over the course of the evening. Dev smiled a little and shook her head as she exited the Oval Office. That discovery had been a bit of a surprise. Devlyn had overheard Amy, one of the agents who was permanently assigned to the Marlowe children, complaining about the seventy-five dollars she'd lost to Lauren that week and the six pounds she'd put on since they started playing cards in the kitchen near all that food.

Dev stopped at Liza's office and rapped on the doorframe. Two agents, who shadowed the President's movements through the White House, stopped too, staying well back to remain as unobtrusive as possible. Her personal assistant worked nearly as late as she did. "Liza?"

The reed-thin young woman glanced up quickly from her computer. "Oh, Madam President, I'm sorry I didn't hear—"

"No worries." Dev was quick to assure her. "Everything's fine. Go home and have some fun tonight." Dev winked. "That's an order."

"Are you knocking off early yourself, Madam President?" That didn't happen very often and Liza knew it. But today was special. She bit back a grin.

"I'm going back to the residence for the evening. It's umm," she blushed slightly, "Valentine's Day, you know."

"I know. I have a late date."

Dev let out a relieved breath; glad it wasn't just her. Liza looked excited too. "And I have a couple of surprises for Lauren." She absently fingered the small boxes in her hand. "I want to give them to her before it gets too much later."

She nodded at her boss. "Yes, ma'am. I'll see you in the morning."

"I'll be here."

Devlyn walked down the hallway with increased speed. As tired as she was, the thought of spending the rest of the night with Lauren was giving her renewed energy. She entered the Executive Quarters and quickly checked the children, finding them sound asleep. They looked so peaceful and quiet. Life, she decided at that moment, was very, very good.

Her next stop was her own room, where she changed from her skirt, blouse, and proper shoes into something far more comfortable. Donning a pair of jeans and a heavy-weight, tan-colored polo shirt that Lauren had given her for Christmas, she ran a brush through her dark hair, the dry air causing it to crackle as she brought it to order. She remained in socked feet, retrieved the gifts that she'd tossed on her bed as she dressed, and began padding down the hall.

Knocking softly on the door, she suddenly worried that Lauren might have given up on her for the evening. But when the door opened her face broke into a radiant smile. Worries forgotten. "Hiya, beautiful."

Lauren wore an answering smile of her own. She was beginning to wonder if Devlyn had forgotten about the holiday completely. "Sweet talker." Casually, she leaned against the doorway. "Care to come in?" Lauren stepped back.

"Love to." Dev entered the room and waited for the sound of the door clicking shut before she turned to face her fiancée. She drew in a deep breath. "I'm sorry it's so late."

"It is late," Lauren allowed softly. "But I love you anyway." She stepped forward and wrapped her arms around Dev's neck. "I was really hoping to see you tonight." She leaned forward and placed a gentle kiss on her partner's throat, smiling when she felt Dev shiver at the contact.

Dev swallowed, a little amazed at how undone she could become over a simple kiss. "How could I not come see you?" she finally muttered. "It's Valentine's Day."

"I—" Lauren's words were cut off when Devlyn ducked her head and captured her lips in an insistent but tender kiss that quickly became passionate.

Dev's assault continued until she was treated to a throaty moan by Lauren and felt her companion melt into her arms. "I love you," she told her, punctuating each word with a nearly chaste kiss to Lauren's cheeks and nose.

Lauren blinked slowly. Her heart was beating double time and her libido was enthusiastically doing a happy dance. "I believe you."

Chuckling, Dev brushed her thumb over Lauren's lips. "I can't wait to be married to you."

"Me too." *Married to a woman. To the President of the United States. To Devlyn. God, who would have thought?* Blonde brows contracted slightly as she considered their current position. "But it will be different how exactly?"

"I won't have to come to an entirely different room to see you."

Lauren laughed softly as she held Dev close. "I like my room. But you know darn well that I spend most nights in your bed as it is." She shook her head at Dev's pout. "It won't be forever, Devlyn. But this arrangement keeps the press from shredding you."

"No, it doesn't."

"Devlyn," Lauren warned playfully. She was not going to get into this discussion again.

"Sorry." Dev stepped back and reached into her pocket. She pulled out two carefully wrapped jewelry cases and offered them both to Lauren with a hopeful look on her face. "Happy Valentine's Day."

The writer shook her head, correctly guessing that the boxes contained gifts that were far more extravagant than those she could give Devlyn in return. "You're going to spoil me."

"I hope so." Dev followed Lauren to one of the two sofas that flanked a cherry wood coffee table. Proudly displayed on the table were the two dozen fragrant, very fresh, blood red roses the President had ordered that morning. Dev grunted her approval. "The White House florist does a hell of a job."

"They're beautiful as always." Lauren leaned over and inhaled a deep nose-full of their spicy, gentle scent. "Mmm…" She sat next to Dev and shook the smaller of the two boxes next to her ear.

Dev rolled her eyes and grinned. "Just open them already."

"Don't rush me. I like the anticipation." She slipped her nail under the tape and lifted the flap, going at a snail's pace just to tease Devlyn. It was a method of playful torture each employed with the other in a variety of scenarios that often included the bedroom.

"You're making me crazy!"

"Well, duh." Lauren winked. "Good crazy or bad crazy?"

"Yes." Dev watched as Lauren opened the small box to reveal a pair of solitaire diamond earrings.

Lauren's eyes widened a little as the stones glittered elegantly in the soft light of her room. *Jesus.* "Oh, Devlyn, they're beautiful."

Devlyn was glad she was sitting because her knees went watery with relief. "I'm glad you like them." She gestured with her chin toward the other package. "This one is just a little something to go with them."

The second box revealed a diamond tennis bracelet. Lauren looked to her fiancée. "You shouldn't have."

"Sure I should have. I love you. You deserve beautiful things."

"I love you too." Lauren removed the bracelet and wrapped it around her wrist. "It's beautiful, Devlyn." She held it up and the light caught the precious stones, causing them to sparkle happily and both women to smile in frank appreciation. "Thank you."

"You're welcome."

She carefully put on the bracelet and placed the other piece of jewelry back in the box, setting it on the table. "I have something for you too. It's not quite as grand as this, but—"

"I love it already," Dev told her sincerely.

Inexplicably, Lauren felt her throat close at the simple words. She nodded a few times, then pushed to her feet. She pointed at Dev. "Can you stay here for a moment? I'll call you when I'm ready."

"But—"

"Hush and wait for me to call you. No peeking."

Dev huffed. "Fine. Waiting right here."

Lauren headed for the bathroom and Dev sighed. Her sitting still on the sofa lasted all of one minute before she was on her feet pacing around the room. She stopped her restless roaming when she spotted two new photographs on Lauren's desk. Photography was a hobby Lauren took seriously, many of her photographs ending up in the biographies she penned. And she was just as likely to follow Dev around with an old-fashioned thirty-five-millimeter camera as she was with a pen or recorder.

Dev lifted one of the new, silver-framed photos, the metal feeling cool against her hand. It was a close-up black-and-white shot of her sitting at her desk in the Oval Office as she gazed down at a stack of papers. One hand was pushing her obsidian hair from her face while the other was tightly clenching a fountain pen. Her expression was that of a serious, very intense woman puzzling something out. Dev wasn't sure if she liked the photo or not. It was almost disconcerting the way the lens and Lauren had captured her completely, the picture easily conveying emotion she was aware ran close to the surface.

The second picture was completely different and Dev recognized the scene instantly. It had been shot right after she and Lauren had announced their engagement to her children. After dinner they'd all adjourned to the family room to watch a movie together, and what began as a tickle from Ashley devolved into a free-for-all. She hadn't remembered Lauren taking the photograph, but the wonderful feeling that pulsed happily through her veins that day was still very fresh in her mind.

She brushed the tips of her fingers over the frame and smiled. The mutual, if sometimes awkward, love affair Lauren and her children shared warmed her heart.

"Devlyn?"

Dev's head snapped up at the sound of her name. She saw a naked arm snake out behind the bedroom door and set a gold gift bag on the floor. Then the arm disappeared.

Devlyn quickly crossed the room, and with a smile on her face, she pulled her gift from the bag. The silk robe was a deep, midnight blue and the fabric slid against her fingers. Hoping this was what Lauren had in mind, she quickly shed her clothes and slipped into the robe, groaning a little under her breath as the cool silk caressed warm, naked skin and sensitive nipples that already ached in anticipation of what was behind the bathroom door. "Ohhh." The robe's billowing sleeves were very full and three-quarter length, and the hem stopped well above mid-thigh.

"Devlyn?"

That soft southern drawl from behind the door caused Dev to lick her lips nervously. "Yes?" she croaked, rolling her eyes at herself. She could hear the smile in Lauren's voice as she spoke.

"Are you going to stand out there all night?"

"Uh… No. Of course not." Dev kicked her discarded clothes out of the way and reached for the door handle. She stopped with her hand still in the air and wiped her damp palms on her robe.

The sight on the other side of the door took her breath away.

The room was illuminated with soft candlelight, and a steaming bubble bath half-filled a large tub. Champagne was chilling in a bucket, and best of all, Lauren was sitting on the edge of the tub, dressed in a black negligee with matching sheer black robe. Dev's mouth dropped open, but somehow she still had to fight to keep from swallowing her own tongue.

Lauren's eyes twinkled happily at her lover's reaction. She resisted the urge to run over to Devlyn and run her hands across that smooth silky... skin. *Breathe, Lauren.*

"Aren't you cold?" Dev managed to croak out as she took a slightly wobbly step forward. *Dressed like that,* her mind finished.

"You decide." Lauren crooked her finger at Devlyn, then stood, giving Dev a full view of her outfit, or more precisely, her lack of outfit.

Oh, my God. Devlyn was sure her heart, or possibly her head, was going to explode before she made it across the large bathroom. Lauren Strayer was undeniably the most beautiful woman she had ever seen. Her heart began to race.

"You're beautiful," Dev whispered as she ran her eyes all over Lauren's body like a hot bath.

The beauty of Lauren's choice of attire was, in actuality, that it didn't reveal much at all. It merely hinted at the treasures that lay beneath. The younger woman knew she had just put a match to what promised to be a short, but explosive, fuse.

"I'm glad you like it, Devlyn. I thought you would," Lauren said quietly, a hint of a smile playing around the edges of her lips. Moving away from Dev just as the President reached her, she began to pour a glass of very cold champagne. The room was hazy with steam from the bath and cool droplets developed on the champagne flute, falling to the ground silently. "Here, I think you might need this." With the grace of a cat on the hunt, she moved back to Devlyn and offered her a drink.

"Most definitely." Dev took the glass and drained it, never taking her eyes off Lauren. She licked her lips lightly when she was finished. "Thanks." Eyes still locked with Lauren's, she set down the flute on a small wooden table next to the bath. "I want you."

Lauren's eyes fluttered closed as she gathered her wits. "You do?" she managed, her pulse visible on the pale skin at her throat.

Dev's eyes darkened. "I do." She reached out and barely touched Lauren's shoulder, her fingers grazing Lauren's skin through the sheer material. "You're driving me crazy."

"You said that before," Lauren answered amused, her stomach muscles contracting from her own desire. "Good crazy or bad crazy?"

"You said that before too," Dev breathed, leaning in and kissing a wet trail from Lauren's cheek to her shoulder. She uncovered the skin with a simple brush of her hand while she distracted Lauren with gentle kisses.

"Devlyn…" Lauren moaned, her eyes closing as fire erupted deep in her guts and spread lower.

"Mmm?" Her lips never left Lauren's skin.

"I, I." Lauren swallowed hard as she tried to focus on what she wanted to say. "I drew you a bath."

"What bath?" Dev hummed at the taste of Lauren's skin.

"I don't know," Lauren said fuzzily, her hands sinking into soft hair as she pulled Dev closer, completely giving up the idea of rational thought.

Devlyn dropped to her knees, hitting the slick tiles with a loud thump. Long fingers traveled up Lauren's belly, skimming her breast on the way to the strap of her negligee. She lowered it slowly, reverently, a kiss finding its way to every new inch of exposed skin. The delicate material and Dev's hot tongue slid down Lauren's skin like warm butter, causing her to shiver and gasp as her arousal built to a nearly painful pitch.

"I'm keeping you. You are so perfect," Dev muttered against the soft skin of Lauren's breast. "Thank you, this is exactly what I needed."

Lauren's knees threatened to give way as Dev began to suckle in earnest. "God!" If it weren't for Dev's hands, which moved to the small of Lauren's back, holding her steady, she would have melted into a puddle on the floor.

"Bed," Dev whispered hotly. "Or I'm having you right here, right now."

Lauren wasn't aware of much more than Dev's teasing tongue and ardent lips until she felt the coolness of the bedspread against her back and the wet heat of Dev's skin as she climbed on top of her. Lauren's own hands had been mostly idle, but the temptation was too great not to reach out and take what was being so freely offered. She ran her palms over Dev's back, then used them to guide Dev's mouth to hers for another devastating, probing kiss.

Tongues collided as groans filled the quiet room. They both lost track of the time, kissing and touching well into the night.

While her lover was distracted with a particularly intense exchange, Lauren reached between them, her hand sliding down along smooth skin and soft flesh. She moaned her approval when she reached her goal.

Dev had been a wonderfully patient lover with her, allowing her time and space to work through her inexperience when it came to loving another woman. Sometimes, to Lauren's frustration, Devlyn could be too patient. But once Lauren understood that was just Dev's natural state of being, that she was truly free to experiment, or much to Dev's delight take the lead, her imagination grew wings. Tonight, for example, Lauren Strayer's patience had come to an end. She wanted Devlyn and she wanted her now.

And she was going to have her.

Devlyn was panting now, her skin slick with perspiration and condensation from the steamy bathroom and her own arousal. "Oh, Lauren…" she gritted out, the power of their lovemaking washing over her like a tidal wave, leaving her shaking in its wake, her body convulsing powerfully as she buried her face against Lauren's salty-tasting neck.

Lauren's hands slipped from between their bodies, and she began a gentle massage as she waited for Devlyn to recover. She knew she wouldn't have to wait long.

The taller woman groaned loudly when strong fingers dug into tired shoulder muscles. "God, I am so keeping you."

Lauren laughed. "Were you thinking of getting rid of me?" Dev's quick movement onto all fours above her caused her to jump in surprise. "Yeow!" Transfixed, she watched the sensual sway of Devlyn's breasts as she spoke.

"I am never getting rid of you," Dev growled, lowering her head and carefully taking a painfully sensitive nipple between white teeth and tugging gently.

Lauren nearly exploded off the bed. "Jesus Christ, Devlyn," she hissed, her head thrown back in rapture, hands flying to the bed and tangling themselves on the damp bedspread. "Yes!"

Dev's mouth found swollen, sensitive flesh and Lauren came hard, her heart threatening to pound out of her chest as she moaned out her release in a steady stream of unintelligible words. Her own chest heaving, Dev crawled up Lauren's body, kissing as she went and wrapping her arms tightly around Lauren's torso as she pillowed her head on soft breasts.

"Any chance of sleeping in tomorrow?" Lauren asked quietly after a long time, a sleepy, sated smile curling her lips. She already knew the answer. She asked it almost every time they'd just finished making love, the desire to snuggle against Devlyn, savoring every blessed second for hours on end, nearly overwhelming.

"Actually, yes." Dev sighed and spared a thought for the candles that were probably gutted by now and were threatening to burn down the White House. But there was no chance she was moving from this spot, even if she could, which she wasn't so sure about. She gave the voice-command to activate Lauren's phone and asked housekeeping to come and extinguish the candles and drain the tub, making it clear they were to use the service entrance to the bathroom that would leave them undisturbed. She also took the time to order breakfast in bed.

When Dev disconnected the call, Lauren said, "Now I know I'm dreaming. Breakfast in bed on a weekday? And you said eight a.m.? Sweet Mother of God, am I dying but I just don't know it yet so I'm getting the royal treatment?"

Devlyn chuckled. "I'm taking the day off tomorrow, as much as I can, and I'm spending it with you and the kids."

"Now I know I'm dying." She tugged on a lock of dark hair. "You're really taking a weekday off?"

"Really."

Lauren felt Dev nod.

"I've been really busting my butt these last couple of weeks. How many times in the last two or three weeks have I had dinner with you and the kids?"

"Twice."

"Exactly." Devlyn paused to place a kiss on the soft skin above Lauren's breasts. "I have barely spent any time with you at all. An hour or so here and there just isn't cutting it. Hell, I don't even know how Ashley is doing in school."

"She's doing just fine. We're getting an A in English now."

"That's my girls." She squawked when Lauren gave her a teasing pinch. Lauren was turning into a wonderful mother and it was happening so gradually that she wasn't even aware of it. Devlyn, however, was loving every moment of it. "Happy Valentine's Day. I love my robe."

"Mmm...you looked great it in, but even better out of it." Lauren cracked open an eye. "Where is it anyway?"

"I have no earthly idea." Dev lifted up a very disheveled head and peered at Lauren's face. "Do you want me to go find it?"

Lauren snuggled deeper into the mattress, tugging Dev down with her. "Not on your life," she said seconds before they both tumbled into some very well deserved sleep.

Monday, February 28th

Dev sat in her private office, reading over some documents that David needed her opinion on by the end of the day. After hearing how enthusiastic about it the boys were, Lauren had agreed to endure the security and media circus and take the children to the Museum of Natural History for the afternoon.

The boys had heard about the new dinosaur bones exhibit from their friends at school, and Dev was afraid that if they didn't go soon they were going to combust. Ashley hadn't been nearly so excited about going to look at "dumb old bones," but a promise by Lauren to take her to the Native American exhibit made the entire trip worthwhile in the little girl's eyes.

Devlyn glanced at the clock. They were actually due back any moment.

A soft knock at the door brought her head up from her documents. "Come in."

Jane opened the door and gave Devlyn a huge grin. "You have a very special visitor."

Devlyn sighed and tossed the pen she'd been restlessly twirling between her fingers onto the papers in front of her. "Unless it's the paperwork fairy…"

"No, but almost as good." Jane stepped to the side, and a woman with long blonde hair pulled back in a stylish braid stuck her head 'round the door.

"Hey, Stinky, you got a minute for an old sister-in-law?"

"Sarah!" Dev came out of her chair as if her pants had caught fire. "Damn, woman, where did you come from?" She bolted from behind her desk, biting back a grimace at the pain that flared in her hip. After long hours at her desk she would still feel the effects of being shot. Dev pulled Sarah into a full body bear hug, lifting her off the ground despite the fact that she was nearly as tall as Devlyn.

The embrace lasted for several long emotional seconds before Dev gently cleared her throat.

Reluctantly, Sarah pulled away. "I've been in Argentina, actually." Sarah took a step back, giving Devlyn an appreciative look accompanied by a low whistle that caused the President's cheeks to grow warm. "You look wonderful." There was a wistful note to her voice that the other woman missed completely. "Just as wonderful as I remember."

"So do you." Dev shook her head. "All grown up. Every time I see you I still can't believe you're not that skinny little kid with braces and skinned knees. When did you get into town? What are you doing here?"

Sarah chuckled and took a seat on a couch near the fireplace. "Easy, one at a time. My God." Her wide-eyed gaze flitted eagerly from one surface to the next. "I can't believe I'm in the Oval Office and that you're the President. The *President!* Jesus, Dev."

Devlyn plopped on the sofa next to her, leaning close and bumping shoulders with her. "No kidding. I haven't stopped pinching myself yet."

"I'll take over that task if you need someone." Sarah's fingers shaped claw-pincers and Dev laughed.

"What are you doing now, Sarah? You're not still in school?"

Sarah gaped. "That was years ago. God, has it been that long? I worked odd jobs for a few magazines before catching a break and accepting a position with *World Traveler Digest* two years ago." They were known for their photographic pictorials.

"Impressive. You know, Lauren has traveled extensively for her work. You two would have a lot in common," Dev said enthusiastically, beaming proudly for the both of them.

I wondered how long it would take her to mention her. Sarah ignored Dev's comment. "I'm on assignment here in the city, and I thought I'd stop by and say hello and see the kids, if that's all right." She laid her hand on Dev's thigh.

Dev put her own hand on top of Sarah's and squeezed gently. "All right? I've missed you, Pee Wee." Her gaze softened. Sarah had been only ten years old when her sister Samantha had wed Devlyn. And for many years after, she was a constant fixture in the Marlowe household. For Dev, only child, her young sister-in-law was the closest thing to a sibling she ever had. "Of course it's all right. The kids have missed you in their lives. Pictures and recordings just aren't the same."

Sarah looked away but left her hand where it was. "I know," she said softly.

Dev kicked her long legs out in front of her. "In fact, the kids and Lauren are due back soon. How about if we sneak back to the residence and rustle up some lunch before they get here?"

"Sounds great."

But neither woman moved.

Sarah continued to stare straight ahead, gazing into the embers in the fireplace while Dev openly observed her, struck again by how much Sarah Turner resembled Samantha. The nose was a little different, not quite as delicate in its slope, but the dark blonde hair and cornflower-blue eyes were so similar it was eerie. Even her voice made Dev shiver a little.

For the first time the silence between them was decidedly uncomfortable. It was Sarah who broke it first. She sighed. "I didn't handle Sam's death very well."

Dev suddenly felt as though a weight was pressing against her chest. Some types of pain would never completely go away. "None of us did."

Sarah sighed again. "But I should have tried to stick it out for you and the kids. Mom and Dad were already gone, and then Sam too." Her chin quivered a little. "I just—"

"Shh…" Devlyn pressed a tender kiss against Samantha's cheek. "I know."

Sarah turned back to Dev and gently grasped a lock of hair. She couldn't meet her eyes. "No grays yet?" Her attempt to move to safer ground was painfully obvious. "Or is Ms. Clairol on the payroll?" she joked weakly, running her fingers through Dev's silky strands, not seeming to notice what she was doing.

"It really is okay, Sarah." The tightness in her chest was making it hard to speak. But this was something that needed to be said. "We all needed time. Some of us more than others. I love you. And I'd wait a hundred years if that's what you needed."

Sarah gathered her courage and glanced up at Dev. Those soulful blue eyes had always been her undoing. She'd spent years envying the relationship Samantha had with Devlyn. And years more mourning the loss of someone irreplaceable in her life. But her sister wasn't here anymore. And if Samantha's death taught her anything, it was that life was short and that sometimes you didn't get second chances.

Sarah lifted her palm and cupped Dev's cheek. She could see tears shimmering there and watched compassionately as several finally spilled over. With her thumb, she brushed one away. Then, on impulse, she leaned in and removed the second with her lips. Before she could lose her nerve or think about what she was doing, she ducked her head and kissed Devlyn softly on the mouth.

It began as chaste, and for a second or two Devlyn was frozen. She didn't return the kiss, she didn't move at all, unsure how to interpret what was happening. This was *Sarah*, for God's sake!

Then two things happened simultaneously. The door to the Oval Office opened, and Sarah moaned lightly as she leaned forward and tried to deepen the kiss.

Devlyn grasped Sarah's hands firmly and pushed her away. "Sarah—" She looked up at Sarah's face, but the younger woman's attention was elsewhere.

Sarah's eyes were riveted on the door and two very shocked women: Beth and Lauren.

Dev's head snapped around. "Lauren." *Uh oh.* She jumped to her feet, nearly knocking Sarah off the couch. "I didn't expect you and the kids for a while."

Lauren's lips thinned and she was surprised that the words came out as evenly as they did, considering her mind was reeling. "I can see that." *No. No. No. I did not just see that! Devlyn loves me! She's not like Judd.* But even the possibility that she'd been wrong about Devlyn's feelings for her was suddenly too much to bear.

The pressure-cooker of emotion that Lauren had been living in bubbled dangerously close to the surface.

"I'm so sorry, Dev," Sarah told the President. "I know you wanted to sneak back to the residence before they got home."

Lauren and Dev's eyebrows nearly popped off their foreheads.

"Sarah!" Devlyn screeched. "That's not what I meant." She chanced a glance at Lauren. *Oh, fuck.*

Lauren looked at Devlyn as though seeing her for the first time. "You really said that, Devlyn?" she said, hearing the catch in her voice.

"Well... I..." She threw her hands in the air. "It's not what it looks like." *Christ!* Dev was starting to panic and didn't know what else to say. So like any savvy politician, she stayed quiet, carefully choosing and discarding words. In this instance, however, her silence spoke louder than her words ever could. The cold mask that dropped over Lauren's face caused Dev's heart to pound and she suddenly realized her error. "Lauren, please... It's not what you think."

Lauren willed her hands to stop shaking. "I think I walked in here and caught you two kissing. Are you saying I saw differently?"

Devlyn swallowed hard. "Yes. No. I mean, sort of. Shit!"

The tension in the room skyrocketed.

Beth dropped her face into her hands. She could hear Devlyn's mental mantra of 'ohshitohshitohshit' from where she was standing.

Sarah stood as gracefully as was possible considering her off kilter position on the sofa and waltzed across the room, offering her hand to Lauren.

Lauren's heartbeat was thundering in her ears, while one thought chanted mercilessly in her head. *She's gorgeous and she looks exactly like Samantha!*

When it appeared that Lauren was too stunned to acknowledge Sarah at all, Sarah addressed Beth. "Long time no see, Beth."

Beth ground her teeth together, giving Devlyn, who looked like a drunken deer caught in the headlights, a dirty look of her own. Then she focused on Sarah. *What the hell have you done, Sarah?* "It has been a while, Sarah. I see your acne cleared up."

Sarah? The girl from the family pictures? Acne? Lauren marveled. Sarah looked like a fashion model. And Lauren hated her with an intensity that would melt solid steel.

Sarah turned to Lauren. "And you are?" She knew damn well who she was.

"That's my—" Dev began.

"Don't!" Lauren interrupted, her face turning an angry red as her hurt and anger mixed. "I can speak for myself."

Dev's mouth clicked closed.

Lauren took a calming breath. "I'm Lauren Strayer." Hard gray eyes trained themselves on Devlyn. "The President's biographer."

Dev's stomach dropped twelve stories.

Lauren's hands were shaking. Humiliated and torn between dissolving into tears and murder, she quickly tucked them under her arms. *This has to be wrong, but I saw it with my own eyes. My own eyes! That was no sisterly kiss.* "I'm going to leave now," she ground out, feeling as though she was going to throw up.

Devlyn panicked. "For God's sake, Lauren! It wasn't—"

Lauren turned on her heels and marched out of the Oval Office on slightly wobbly legs, leaving the trio of stunned woman behind her.

For a second Dev wasn't sure what to do, then she bolted for the door.

"Dev," Beth began softly, "I wouldn't."

Devlyn looked at Beth with an expression so heartbroken it brought tears to Beth's eyes. "But I *have* to go and fix things." Dev's shout rattled the pictures on the wall, then it dropped to a whisper. "She doesn't understand." *This is not happening.* She lifted her jaw a little, daring Beth not to believe her. "It wasn't what it looked like. I would never do that to Lauren. I'd die first."

Sarah closed her eyes as Dev's words pierced her heart. *Damn.*

Beth shook her head quickly. "Don't do it, Dev. She needs to cool off or—"

Dev's jaw worked silently. She had no choice. "I won't risk losing her by doing nothing." *She'll understand once I talk to her. I know it.* But memories of Lauren's words about Judd's infidelity haunted her. *"I won't live that way again. Ever."*

Beth watched as Devlyn disappeared into the outer office and with a tremulous voice asked Jane which direction Lauren had headed. Then she was gone.

Beth whirled around and pinned Sarah with a withering glare. She marched up to the younger woman and grabbed her by the shirt, dragging her over to the sofa where she roughly pushed her down. "Talk," she demanded. "And don't you lie, Sarah Turner. Devlyn might not have noticed the crush you've had on her since you were old enough to know what one was. But she's the only one who didn't."

Sarah swallowed hard. "Devlyn didn't do anything either." Her eyes conveyed a mixture of fear and anguish. "I think I really messed up, Beth."

Beth groaned. *I knew it. Thank, God.* "You'd better hope that Dev can convince Lauren of the same thing, Sarah. Or I wouldn't want to be you," she said grimly, meaning every word.

MARCH 2022

Tuesday, March 1ˢᵗ

Lauren sat on a bench in Rock Creek Park, soaking in the sounds of the night: the wind rattling dry branches, the faint but sharp cracking of sticks, and the rustling of old leaves and rocks as a small animal or two scurried through the woods around her. The morning sun was still several hours away and soft moonlight bathed her in a muted, ethereal glow as she tucked her chilled hands into the soft pockets of her leather coat. Small patches of snow still dotted the brown grass, though the temperature was well into the forties.

Removing one hand from its warm haven, she gave Gremlin—who was lying next to her on the bench with his head resting on her thigh, sound asleep—a scratch behind the ears. While she wasn't exactly at peace, she was far more centered than when she'd briskly walked into the park the evening before. She hadn't cried, plotted anyone's murder, or contemplated the devastating thought of life without Devlyn for several hours. This was, she decided, something she needed very much. To be alone.

Not the "alone" she'd experienced since becoming engaged to the most famous woman on the planet. But really, actually *alone*. Unless you counted Gremlin, which she didn't. No paparazzi. No milling aides or secretaries. No agents with guns, grim faces, and annoying protocol. Just her. Funny thing was, despite wanting it so badly, she still felt a little lonely. Lauren dropped her face into her hands. "What is wrong with me?"

She let out a deep breath as her mind replayed her hasty retreat from the White House. She had known that Devlyn would come looking for her and had purposely hid in the kitchen for a few moments before going back to her quarters and packing an overnight bag. Talking to Devlyn just then would have been dangerous. Too dangerous. Because, in all likelihood, it would have been for the last time. She was *that* angry and hurt and that stressed.

But the last few hours of solitude had given her a little of the perspective that she'd lacked earlier. Lauren was honest enough with herself to admit that she hadn't been fair to Devlyn when she refused her the opportunity to explain. But her blood had been boiling, and like a wounded animal she longed to lash out, to savagely inflict pain in a misguided attempt at self-defense.

She was glad now that she'd been able to escape. Glad that she'd seen David on the way out of the White House and told him in no uncertain terms that if she was followed she wouldn't be coming back. Ever. She hadn't meant that, not even then, when her heart felt so raw she could hardly breathe. She didn't really believe Devlyn would cheat on her. But her heart had lied to her before, hadn't it? "Damn."

Lauren sucked in a deep breath and tilted her head skyward, her cheeks long dry of the tears she'd shed earlier. The faint sound of crunching wood chips in the distance caused her to turn her head and peer intently through the darkness.

Instantly awake, Gremlin jumped down from the bench and began to growl into the night, baring his tiny crooked teeth in an impressive show of ferocity.

Lauren felt her pulse pick up a little as she belatedly realized that it wasn't safe to be sitting in the middle of a very wooded, very secluded park at three a.m. Then she sprang to her feet, standing behind Gremlin as a single figure emerged from the shadows. Her fists clenched and unclenched as she glanced behind her, prepared to run if she needed to. Her heart began to pound and a rush of adrenaline sang through her blood. *How stupid am I?* she berated herself. *I'm gonna get myself killed!*

"Who is it?" Lauren asked, hearing her voice shake a little.

The figure moved closer. "Lauren?"

The blonde woman nearly collapsed in a heap when the familiar voice washed over her. "Devlyn?" *It can't be.*

Dev stepped closer, giving the still snarling Gremlin a disgusted glance. "You know who I am, dog. See?" Devlyn bent down in front of Gremlin so he could see her face. Once he did, however, he continued to bark and growl even louder. "Stupid mutt," Dev grumbled, moving a step backwards when Gremlin's snaggle-toothed mouth began snapping open and closed. A tiny part of her, however, was glad the worthless canine was so fiercely protecting Lauren. *She'll let him do that,* Devlyn thought enviously, *but not me.*

"Gremlin…" Lauren warned in a soft, but firm, voice. Her gaze never strayed from Devlyn.

The small beast quieted instantly, but kept a wary eye on his mistress' lover.

Dev sniggered inwardly, enjoying the tiny victory while she could.

"How did you find me?" Lauren asked, not masking her surprise and making no move to sit down or cross the ten feet or so that separated her from the other woman.

Gremlin trotted over to Lauren and plopped down on her feet, already bored.

Dev sighed, her eyes showing her longing to embrace Lauren but also the fear that she would be turned away if she tried. *At least she's still talking to me. That's something.* She swallowed, knowing she had to tell the truth, but dreading saying the words. "I spoke to all of the agents assigned to you." She didn't mention that she'd called half of them out of bed to come to the White House to be grilled by her when her initial searching couldn't turn up Lauren. "And this was one of the places they told me you like to come sometimes." She was suddenly struck by the thought that they'd never been here together.

"Mmm…" Dejected, Lauren nodded. She gave Gremlin a gentle nudge and he moved off her feet, allowing her to pad back to the bench and sit down heavily. "Why are you here, Devlyn?"

Her voice was so quiet it was almost swept away by the breeze.

Devlyn's stomach churned. She felt as if she were in some bad movie where someone else scripted the predictable lines and she was being swept away by the drama of the scene, scared and out of control. *I'm here because I love you. I'm here to explain. I'm here because I'm afraid this life will be too much for you and you'll leave me bleeding and broken and desperately alone.*

"You know why I'm here," she said, trying to keep her resentment and fear from her voice. "May I sit down?" She indicated the bench next to Lauren.

Lauren gave a quick nod, scooting over a little when Gremlin jumped up next to her and snuggled up to her thigh to stay warm.

"Is it safe?" Dev asked, not really caring what the answer was. She would have sat next to Lauren if a crocodile, instead of merely the ugliest dog on earth, had been resting his face in her lap. "You haven't been holding my picture in front of him and training him to kill, have you?"

Lauren's first instinct was to smile and she didn't try to fight it, though the gesture was half-hearted at best. "No attack training. He won't even fetch when I ask him, much less anything more strenuous." An image of Dev and Sarah kissing flashed through her mind and she felt a little sick. She turned away from Dev, unwilling to look at her as she released a heavy breath.

Dev's heart clenched when Lauren looked away, and she felt tears fill her eyes. She blinked them back and sat down with a weary groan. With a single hand she rubbed her tired, stinging eyes, wishing she could start the entire day over again. Then she tucked her hand back into the pocket of her long woolen coat. It was the coldest part of the night and an oppressive dampness was overtaking the air.

She had combed the park looking for Lauren for nearly three hours and had run across four sleeping homeless people, two of whom were children. She made a mental note to do something about them. The wheels of government turned too slowly for her taste, but she could help two specific kids in the cold, if she put her mind to it. There had been a pair of young lovers on a blanket, who were... well, she didn't stay around long enough to see *exactly* what they were doing, but their moans and the steam rising off their barely-blanket-covered bodies left little to the imagination. There was a harmless jogger and then finally came a man who was singing "Some Enchanted Evening" at the top of his lungs to his unfortunate paramour, who also happened to be an oak tree. God, she missed Ohio.

Lauren's head swiveled sideways as she realized something. She looked over the tops of her glasses, behind Dev and into the woods around them. Seeing nothing, she squinted as she gazed down the narrow path from which Devlyn had emerged. "You're alone," she whispered. "Or do I just not see them?"

Dev knew this wasn't what they needed to talk about. But now that she was here she found herself in no hurry to tackle the tough stuff. That would be hard enough without diving right in. She shook her head, not needing to ask to whom Lauren was referring. "I told them to wait by the car." Though she'd checked in with the Secret Service every few minutes and moved the car no less than six times so they would never be more than a moment or two away.

Lauren's eyes widened. She looked at Dev again, realizing that, except for a few days at Janet and Frank's farm in Ohio, she'd never been outdoors and alone with Dev. It seemed odd and disconcertingly intimate after the events of the day. "David must be having a fit."

Dev studied her shoes. "Umm..."

Lauren cocked her head sideways, recognizing that tone. "What?"

"I don't think he's speaking to me right now," Dev admitted a little sheepishly, cringing.

"Why? If he should be angry with anyone, it's me. God, what I said to him."

"He's not mad at you."

Lauren gave Dev a look.

"Okay, he is mad at you. At us both. He didn't want me looking for you, and when I told him I was doing it anyway, well, things got out of hand."

Lauren took off her glasses and stuffed them into her pocket—a light fog was settling over the park and they were steaming up. "And then?" she prodded.

"And then I fired him."

"What!" Lauren's voice was so loud it nearly woke Gremlin. Nearly. "It's not safe for you to be out alone. It's not the same for me, Devlyn. The shooting—"

"He's not the boss of me," Devlyn stated, hoping it didn't sound as childish to Lauren's ears as it did her own.

Lauren stretched out her feet and stared into the trees with unseeing eyes. "We're quite a pair, aren't we?"

"Are we?" Dev forced the words out. "A pair?"

The air between them crackled with tension.

Lauren took a shaky breath. "I'm not sure anymore, Devlyn." She turned her head and the women locked eyes. *It didn't hurt this badly with Judd,* her mind cried. *Not even close.* "We need to talk about Sarah."

Dev ran a hand through her hair, praying she'd do a better job of explaining this now than she had earlier. She was well aware that this might be her only chance, and frankly, that thought pissed her off nearly as much as Lauren's lack of faith in her. "We do." She drew in a deep breath. "Nothing happened between Sarah and me." There. The simple truth was always best.

The flashing of gray eyes was visible even in the moonlight.

Dev quickly held up her hand. "I know what you saw. But that was her kissing me, not the other way around."

"She forced you?" The incredulous tinge to Lauren's voice let Dev know how unlikely she considered that prospect.

Dev looked horrified. "Of course not!" She lowered her voice.

"She's not like that. She's a good person."

Lauren ground her teeth together. "You're defending her, even now. There is no defense for that. You're engaged to *me*!"

"Just because Samantha is gone, it doesn't mean I don't consider Sarah my sister."

"Sister!" Lauren's face turned a deep shade of red, and the anger that had been simmering since she left the White House exploded to the forefront. "And here I thought I was from the South. Christ on a crutch! What the hell kind of sister kisses you like that?"

"I don't know," Dev said between clenched teeth, shifting around so she was fully facing Lauren. "It's never happened before. And it will never happen again."

"She kissed you?"

Dev lifted her jaw a little. "Yes."

"That kiss didn't look like too much of a hardship, Devlyn. I have eyes. She's a beautiful woman and even if she started it, you weren't trying to stop her."

Devlyn opened her mouth, then closed it. She felt her ire rise along with one of Lauren's eyebrows. "Don't you do that. Don't you dare keep acting like I have something to hide! I am not the one who cheated on you and yet I already feel like shit and am so scared I can't see straight. I. Didn't. Do. Anything. Wrong!"

"I saw it." Lauren shook her head quickly, remembering all the times her genuine inquiries with Judd had been met by lies. And how it was just easier to believe than to be bothered to dig for the truth. How she didn't *care* enough to dig. She spent a long moment, letting the past rear its ugly head… and bite her. Then some of her rational mind kicked in. What she had with Dev was worlds away from what she'd known before. And this time, she decided, she did care enough to fight tooth and nail.

"You think I'm not scared and sick too?" Lauren informed her hotly. "I spent the first hour away from the White House hanging over a motel toilet. I *want* to believe you, but you're making it so hard!" The words came out in a steady stream, like a dam had finally burst. "You're acting guilty. And she's beautiful and looks exactly like your dead wife." Lauren's throat closed. "The one you still love," she managed to get out, ashamed of her bitterness toward a dead woman.

"Lauren…"

Lauren shook her head. "Please don't say it. I know Samantha is your past. But that woman in your office isn't. I saw what I saw,

Devlyn. Give me more so I can convince my head of what my heart is screaming," she begged, soft gray eyes glistening in the moonlight.

"Ugh!" With a slightly shaky hand, Dev rubbed her forehead briskly. "When she kissed me, I didn't know what to do. We had been talking about Sam and she touched my face and I wasn't expecting it, and…" She lifted one hand and then let it fall helplessly. "I've never been kissed by her before. I wasn't even sure it wasn't innocent until she tried to—"

"Inspect your tonsils with her tongue?" Lauren snapped, closing her eyes and turning as she angrily swiped at her tears.

"Something like that," Dev grumbled, fighting back the desperate feeling that had been gnawing at her guts all afternoon. "As soon as I knew what was happening, I moved to stop it and you walked in."

Lauren swallowed hard, replaying the events in her mind and trying to focus on what'd she actually seen and not the wild surge of jealousy and betrayal she'd felt upon seeing. "Is… Is this the first time that's happened?"

"How can you even ask me that!"

"How can I not!"

The park went silent, save for their slightly rough breathing, the breeze in the trees, and Gremlin's gravelly snores.

"Do you love me?" Devlyn finally asked, her heart in her throat.

Lauren let out a shuddering breath, her own heart suddenly pounding. *Do I love her?* her mind gasped. *God.*

Dev reached out and brushed away Lauren's hot tears, leaving her hand there to cup a chilled cheek. She brushed her thumb over soft skin.

"You know I do," Lauren finally whispered raggedly, eyes closed tight, "more than anything or anyone."

"Then stop this before it goes any farther," she pleaded, knowing this went beyond a simple misunderstanding of a kiss. But to get to those issues, they had to successfully traverse this minefield. Dev didn't know what she would do if they couldn't. "Believe in me." She looked deeply in Lauren's eyes, willing her to have faith in what they shared.

Lauren bit her lower lip. "Do you know what you're asking?" she whispered, her voice tight with emotion. "To believe you more than my own eyes?" But she found herself wanting to do just that. With devastating certainty, her heart knew why she was frightened beyond reason.

Blindly trusting Dev wasn't difficult. It was, in fact too, too easy.

"Trust me." Dev felt Lauren lean into her touch, hot tears rolling down the back of her hand. "You can always believe in me. I will never, ever, do to you what Judd did to you. You and the kids are my family, and I love you." Devlyn blinked a few times, clearing her eyes of her own tears. "Please," she whispered brokenly, desperation creeping back into her voice.

Lauren's breathing hitched and Devlyn's plea forced her to open her eyes and look at her. She couldn't stop herself. That was all it took. She didn't know how she ended up in the older woman's arms, but there she was, Dev's hands gently stroking her wavy pale hair, her body heat seeping into her cold skin, her heartbeat thundering wildly and visibly in the fair skin of her throat. "What am... what am I doing? I'm so sorry," Lauren mumbled, her lips against Dev's chilled cheek.

Dev tightened her hold on Lauren, a single tear blazing a path down her cheek. "Me too." *Thank you, God.* She felt a little lightheaded and wasn't sure if it was from relief or the death grip that Lauren had on her. Either way, she welcomed the sensation. "Me too," she repeated, pressing her lips against Lauren's cheek. "I'll talk to Sarah. I'll work it all out, you'll see. She knows I love you Lauren. *Everyone* knows I love you. I'm not sure what she was thinking."

Lauren sniffed. "I love you too. I'm sorry." Dazedly, she blinked a few times. "I'm not thinking straight. I—"

"I know." Devlyn felt Gremlin milling around at their feet. "I should have paid more attention to you, to Sarah, to Beth, who warned me that you were under too much pressure weeks ago."

Lauren felt warm puffs of air against her hair as Dev spoke.

"She told me that Sarah's had a crush on me for years." A dark head shook in disbelief. "I never knew... I promise. Hell, I should have paid more attention to everybody."

"You're busy," Lauren murmured quietly, nuzzling as close as humanly possible to Devlyn.

"Not too busy for that. I can't be."

Lauren pulled back, and both women wiped gently at each other's faces. "Devlyn, I think I need a vacation to regroup," she admitted tiredly. "Since we announced our engagement, I feel like things have been spinning out of control."

Dev nodded thoughtfully. "With us?"

"No," Lauren promised fiercely. "You and the kids and Beth and David, you're what's solid in my life. It's everything else right now. The press. My mother's death. My father's rejection. The book. I haven't written a thing in nearly a month. I need some time."

Dev sighed inwardly. She was afraid of this. "We can postpone the wedding." *Please just don't say cancel it.*

Lauren smiled sadly, reading the worry on Dev's face as easily as if it were her own. On impulse, she leaned in and kissed her soundly, feeling Dev's surprised squawk more than hearing it. "Not on your life, Madam President," she whispered against soft, moist lips as she leaned back just a hair. "Nobody is taking that from us. I want to marry you. I just need to get used to the demands that go along with being your… your…" She looked at Devlyn in question. "Wife?" She didn't much like the term when Judd had used it to introduce her. It had never felt right.

Dev grinned. Sometimes she forgot that Lauren's relationships had been exclusively with men. "If you like. Or some people say spouse or partner?"

Lauren smiled, that last one ringing unfamiliar but pleasant chords deep within her. "I like that. But I don't mind the other either. So long as you're my wife too."

Dev nodded enthusiastically. This was more like them. Talking things through. Working things out. Her stomach finally settled down and she felt mortally tired.

"I'm not willing to let other people take our happiness from us, Devlyn. I just need to get my head on straight to face the battles. I don't know how you do it." There was genuine awe in her voice.

"Would a couple of weeks in Tennessee help?"

Lauren blinked. "God, no!" There was nothing for her there. She hadn't been home since her mother's funeral the year before, hadn't called her father and invited him to the wedding, though she'd stood staring at the phone more times than she could count. She couldn't face him cruelly dismissing her again by hanging up before she'd even said why she was calling. Her mother's suicide and her relationship with Devlyn had, she admitted sadly, killed what little relationship she had with her father. She wondered briefly if anything so terribly broken could be repaired and how a parent's love for his child could be so conditional.

"All right." Dev considered the possibilities, then gave voice to the most logical one. "My parents' place? Mom was coming out here next week anyway. You could go there instead."

Lauren's eyes lit up at the thought. It was so peaceful there. "God, that would be wonderful. Do you think they'd mind?"

"Don't be silly. They'll be thrilled. They love you." Devlyn grasped her hand and threaded their fingers together. She took a deep breath, knowing what she had to do and already shuffling through mental contingency plans. There had to be another way. "Okay. I'll make arrangements to cancel my trip and—"

"Don't."

Startled and hurt, Dev scrambled for something to say. "I'll still give you some time alone. I meant that," she clarified quickly, not wanting to Lauren to think she was smothering her. "I just thought—"

"I'm going to be fine," Lauren soothed, "and your trip is too important to miss." She smiled encouragingly. "Go, Devlyn. Save the world and all that. I'll be here when you get back."

Dev pulled her into a rough embrace again, her eyes fluttering closed. Lauren did understand. "It's not saving the world... but I do..." She exhaled slowly. "You're sure?"

"I'm sure." Lauren reached up and tucked a lock of blowing hair behind Dev's ear. She'd had enough of the difficult stuff for one evening. "Now, how long do we have before the army comes marching through this park?"

"Has it been ten minutes yet?"

Lauren's eyes went round. "Yes!"

"Then we're fine because they gave me twenty."

Lauren let out an explosive breath. "Funny."

"But," Dev leaned forward a little, taking Lauren with her, "we should be going."

They stood, each a little wobbly from the emotional strain of the day. The President wrapped a long arm around Lauren's shoulders as they walked, Gremlin trailing lazily behind them.

"You need to apologize to David," Lauren reminded Devlyn gently. *And so do I.*

"I will."

Lauren glanced up at Dev as they walked, concern etched over her tired features. "Do you think you'll get him back?"

"Huh?"

Blonde brows pulled together. "You said you fired him. Do you think you can get him back? I can talk to Beth and we can—"

Devlyn waved her off. "David isn't going anywhere, Lauren. He knows I can't run the damn country without him. He's going to make me beg and plead and apologize, of course. All of which I owe him. But after that, he'll be back." A wry smile touched her lips. "I fired him four times in the month after Samantha died and once when I didn't make it to the hospital on time to see Chris be born."

"Was that his fault?" Lauren asked, guiding them down a small set of wooden steps. "About Chris?"

"Nah. We were both working on a last minute piece of legislation and had turned off our pagers so we wouldn't be disturbed. Chris came two weeks early and Samantha's labor was so short... I should have..." She shook her head a little. "Well, I just wasn't thinking is all. David and I made up though. We always do. He's a gracious man and I'm good at groveling." Dev smiled at Lauren's muffled snort. "He's quit a few times too over the years. So the situation has been reversed. We started in politics together about," she let out a low whistle, "about a million years ago. I... I don't know that I'd want to do this without him."

"You're lucky he's your best friend."

Dev stopped walking and gently grasped Lauren's chin, lifting it a little to force eye contact. "He's my right hand and I love him, but you're my best friend," she corrected, her eyes showing her devotion.

Lauren leaned her head against Dev's shoulder. She sighed happily, her heart greedily absorbing the words. "You're mine too, Devlyn." *And I need to trust you all the way. Or this will never work. And, God, how I want it to work.*

"Then I guess I am lucky."

They walked for another moment or two until they came to a clearing that was dotted with picnic tables.

"'Some enchanted evening!'" a man sang freely, his voice loud and proud. His clothes were in tatters but his sparse, black hair was slicked back neatly, befitting the importance of his courting. "'When you find your true love.'"

"'When you hear her call you, across a crowded room,'" Lauren crooned along, causing the man to turn and Devlyn to burst out laughing. "'An' somehow you know, you know even then, that somewhere you'll see her again and again!'"

"Hey!" he protested indignantly, planting himself in front of the oak tree as if to shield his ladylove from the view of unwanted strangers. "There should be a law against interrupting a man's love song."

"You're right," Lauren called over her shoulder. "Let me see what I can do." She glanced over at Dev and winked. "I know people."

Monday, March 7th

Dev looked at the itinerary Liza had handed her before the woman scooted out the door. The President was seated in her office behind her massive antique desk, barefoot, her pumps hidden behind it. She chewed her bottom lip as she read over the schedule of her trip to Scotland for the World Economic Summit. It would be held in Edinburgh this year. Still reading, she pushed to her feet and reluctantly wiggled tired feet into her shoes.

She poked her head out of her office and smiled at Liza, whose nose was buried in Dev's calendar, and Jane, who was sorting through a stack of correspondence.

"Your next appointment is a video-conference with Vice President Vincent in four minutes, Madam President," Liza bit off, "and thirty seconds."

"Thank you, Liza. Where are my golf clubs?"

Liza's eyebrows jumped as she scrambled for an answer. "Umm... I didn't know you played golf, Madam President."

"She doesn't," Jane mumbled. "What was your last game? Fifty-five over par for nine holes?" Dev scowled, but Jane continued undaunted. "You remember, the last game you played before you ordered me to donate your clubs to a charity auction."

"Oh. Right." Dev really did detest the sport and only played to placate her father, who was the most avid golfer on the planet. A wry smile curved her lips as she recalled the obscenely expensive golf "clinic" given by Tiger Woods that her father had enrolled her in during the summer of her senior year in college. Meeting Tiger had been a treat. But thousands of dollars later her golf game had still sucked. To this day, Tiger refused to acknowledge she'd been to one of his camps.

She sighed, knowing that her father would love a chance to play at St Andrews and that her attendance at the conference was more for show than substance. Her advisors would be doing the bulk of the work. "Liza, would you please find me a set of clubs? I'm taking my dad to Scotland with me and I'll be humiliating myself on the golf course so we can spend some time together. If they stop taking my picture for more than five minutes, I'm sure we'll find the time to play at some point."

Liza breezed through several screens on her handheld computer. "You won't have to *find* time, Madam President. You're already scheduled for a round of golf with the First Minister MacBheath and his wife on Sunday."

Wonderful. An audience. Dev scratched her forehead and sighed. "Who scheduled that?"

"Michael Oaks," Jane said. "He insisted, saying all politicians golfed at least well enough to have their picture taken at the club house. I tried to tell him…" Her voice trailed off.

Dev groaned. There was no way for him to know she couldn't golf… at all. But still, the arrogant shit should have listened to Jane. "Make those a magic set of clubs, Liza. Please."

"One that can actually hit the ball," Jane murmured, still not looking up from her work.

"I heard that!" Dev blurted. "I can hit the ball!"

"Of course you can," Jane replied automatically, in her normal, placid voice. "I heard you did it once in two thousand three. Too bad no one took a photograph."

Dev narrowed her eyes at the older woman.

"I'll order those clubs, Madam President," Liza said dutifully, trying hard not to laugh.

Dev took a step closer to her long-time secretary and friend. "Jane?"

"Yes, Tiger… err…." she gulped at the look on Dev's face, "Madam President?"

Liza didn't know what to think and her eyes widened a little as she glanced nervously between Jane and the President.

Stony-faced, Jane and Dev glared at each other for several long seconds before neither woman could hold the line and they both burst out laughing.

Liza exhaled in relief then blinked stupidly as she watched the bare-

ly veiled and undeniably rude gesture Dev made to Jane before returning to her office, but leaving the door open. "Buh…." Liza scrubbed
her face. "Did she just…?"

"I can't be sure, but I think she did!" Jane laughed. "I'm going to
tell Janet on her," she said in a raised voice, smiling triumphantly when
she heard Dev's gasped "Uh oh."

Dev was just rising from her chair to head back to her quarters for
the day when there was a gentle knock on the door that led from David's office to her own. "Come in."

The tall man lifted his hands to forestall Dev before she could even
get out a greeting.

Dev felt her heart rate pick up a little. That was always a bad sign.
Very bad.

"Don't kill me," he warned her seriously. "I had nothing to do with
it."

She licked her lips and braced herself. The kids were in bed, right?
Yes, she remembered, Chris and Aaron had phoned her to say goodnight. Ashley was already asleep. But what about Lauren? *Where is
she?* They'd spoken on the phone only an hour ago. *She looked fine,
but… What if it's raining or snowing in Ohio? What if…?* A knot
formed in her stomach. "What?"

"I just heard through the grapevine that your mom has hired Toby
Yagasuki to design your wedding dress."

Dev closed her eyes and let out a ragged breath, a little amazed at
how quickly she could get carried away.

"Hey." David looked concerned. "Are you all right?" He reached
out and grabbed Dev's hand, noticing a chill.

Dev gave him a quick nod and moved quickly to safer ground.
"Would the grapevine happen to be named Beth?"

David gave her hand a squeeze, then dropped it. "I refuse to divulge
my sources. 'Operation: Wed Dev' is highly sensitive. You don't have
the security clearance," he teased.

"Why would I care about who Mom—? Oh, God!" Her jaw
dropped. "Is Toby Yagasuki that little Japanese queen with big bouncy
hair?"

David winced at the blunt, but apt, description.

"He does everything in mint and lime green. I saw him interviewed on television after the last Oscars." A panicked look crossed her face. "No way!"

"Sorry, Dev. The grapevine never lies, unless it's about who used the end of the toilet paper last and didn't put on the new roll." He loosened his tie as he took a seat in one of the armchairs in front of Dev's desk, grunting in satisfaction. "The chairs in my office aren't this comfortable."

"Who cares about chairs? I'm the one who is going to look like a piece of Key Lime pie! Things can be 'all about you' when I'm finished with things being 'all about me.'"

David made a dismissive gesture. "Suck it up and be a man about it."

Playfully, Dev kicked at David's shin. "I'm not a man!"

"I know." He shrugged. "But I couldn't think of anything else to say."

Dev leaned against the front of her desk, a bewildered look on her face. First golf and now this? How many humiliations would come to pass in a single day?

David chuckled, not-so-secretly enjoying the nonplussed look on Dev's face. "If the Secretary of Defense needs a new advisor on surgical strikes, I nominate your mother. She's vicious."

Dev whimpered. "It's going to be a huge circus, isn't it?"

"Ringling Brothers, and everyone else in the entertainment industry, have already made an offer to provide… entertainment, I guess."

"My cousins will already be there. That's my quota of freaks for the day."

David laughed. "No, no. Not freaks. It was a legitimate offer and one we're considering."

"What is it?" Dev's voice was wary as she pushed off from the desk and plopped down in the chair next to David's.

"Releasing two thousand doves dressed in tiny tuxedos from a fake cake while the national anthem is blaring over the loudspeakers."

Dev's eyes bugged out. "What!" David sniggered evilly and Dev realized she was being played. *God, I knew I was going to pay for firing him.* "Don't do that to me, damn it. My heart can't take it. I believed you."

"The part about the designer was true."

"Christ."

"Beth says you should see your mom, Devil. She's having a ball."

Dev sighed. "I know. And because of that I'm going to bite my tongue and know that someday I'll end up in daughter heaven. Samantha and I got married in front of a justice of the peace. I thought Mom was going to have a litter of kittens when we told her."

David shook his head and leaned forward, placing his elbows on his knees as he stretched out his tired back. "I remember. Oh, Lord, do I remember. Do you know she called me and chewed me out for letting you do that." He snorted. "Like I could have stopped you. I took hell for *years* over that." He relaxed back in the comfortable chair and considered stealing it for his office. "What about Lauren?"

"A civil service. Apparently, she didn't feel comfortable in front of a minister, and Judd was just cheap."

David laughed.

"Mom is making up for missed opportunities now, isn't she? You do realize that this would still be a circus, even if I weren't President."

"Just keep telling yourself that this will be your last wedding and you'll make it through."

Dev's jaw worked for a moment, her eyes dropping to the painfully clean carpet. "I want to. God, do I want to. But I can't," she admitted quietly. "I said that when I married Sam."

David mentally kicked himself. "Oh, damn, Dev. I'm sorry. I didn't mean to…"

"It's okay. You know," she paused, wondering how much she wanted to say, even to David. "I've been thinking a lot about Sam lately."

"It's only natural."

"Maybe it's because I'm older," Dev speculated out loud. "Or maybe it's because I never thought there would be someone after Samantha died." She shook her head slowly and then glanced up at her friend. "Is it wrong for me to feel like I love Lauren more than I loved Sam?"

"I don't think so." He smiled reassuringly. "I don't think you love Lauren more. I just think you love her differently." *She's more your equal, my friend. She challenges you in ways Samantha couldn't.*

"I do," Dev agreed, wanting to believe it as much as David apparently did. *It's just different,* she told herself. *Not more or less. Oh, Sam.*

"So," Dev slapped her knees and forced the maudlin thoughts from her mind. She'd have enough time alone with them in bed tonight. "Do you think Beth and Lauren are having a good time with my mother? I think sending them both down there was a good idea."

"It was and they are. When did you talk to Lauren last?"

"An hour ago. I heard from her just about the time the little traitors were going to bed."

David laughed at Dev's reference to the children who had chosen to accompany Lauren to Ohio rather than going to Scotland with her. They were on a weeklong break from their classes. "Be glad they love Lauren so much."

A bright smile split Dev's face. "I am." She felt a happy warmth fill her belly. "You have no idea how good it makes me feel to see them with her. They adore her, and she's so much better with them than she realizes." Dev shook her head in amusement. "You should have heard her the other day trying to explain the birds and the bees to Aaron. It was priceless."

David's rusty-red eyebrows drew together; was Aaron getting that big already? "Why was she doing that?"

"He asked," Dev said simply. She got up, kicked her shoes against the wall and trudged over to a table holding a carafe of strong coffee. "We were having dinner and out of the blue Aaron asks how many babies Lauren and I will be having after we're married."

David's eyes went a little round.

"Not *if*, but how many."

"Oh, boy." David joined Dev, filling his own cup with steaming brew. Then they both plopped down on the sofa and stretched their feet out in front of them. "And what did you say?" he finally asked, interestedly.

"I didn't say anything. I was too busy laughing at the look on Lauren's face. Lauren on the other hand, tried to explain to him that we didn't know if we would." Dev took a sip of her coffee, lost in her thoughts for a moment as she wondered if perhaps Lauren had wanted to say no, but didn't, only because they hadn't really talked about having more children themselves. "Then Aaron asked why we wouldn't and it went downhill from there."

David ran his finger over the rim of his cup, carefully considering his next question. He drew in a deep breath. "Dev?"

"Mmm?"

"Umm, I was wondering." He shifted uncomfortably, fully aware that this was something they'd consciously avoided talking about over the years. But since the assassination attempt on Dev and her engagement, a day hadn't passed where he hadn't thought of it. "When you and Lauren get married, what happens to custody of the kids?"

"Huh?" Dev looked at him as though he were crazy.

"No." He shook his head briskly, feeling incredibly awkward. "What I meant to say is, if something should happen to you... and I don't think it's going to, mind you. But on the horrible chance that it did, Beth and I were supposed to get custody. Now..." He looked away, his teeth busily gnawing at his long mustache.

"I haven't talked to Lauren about this yet. But she would be their mother just as I am." Dev's tone had cooled considerably. "I would want her to have custody, of course. And you and Beth would be in line in the unlikely event that something happened to both Lauren and me."

David stared at the bright flag behind Dev's desk. "I see."

Dev's eyes softened as she set her cup on the coffee table. "David—"

"It's okay." He felt a little angry at himself for even asking. "I was just wondering."

"You know that I think you and Beth would be wonderful parents. I know you love the kids and are prepared to take them if necessary. But—"

"I know." He waved her off, not wanting to press it further. At least not today. But he couldn't help but add, "I do have a special interest in the munchkins." His gaze strayed to the photo of Lauren and the kids displayed proudly on Dev's desk, and a tendril of envy threatened him.

Dev's chest began to tighten. What was happening here? "Do you want to tell the kids, David?"

"No!" David's eyes widened and he nearly shot up off the sofa, before he realized he was right on the verge of overreacting. "No," he repeated as he sat back. "We had an agreement, Devlyn. I intend to stick to it." His grip on his cup tightened. "Unless it's a matter of medical necessity, we won't tell the kids I'm their... father, donor, whatever. Being Uncle David is quite sufficient. Beth and I just don't want to lose them from our lives."

Dev relaxed a little but still felt unsettled. She managed to give David a slightly scolding look. "You know better than that, David. I keep my promises too. You'll never be out of their lives. No matter what."

"What does Lauren have to say about this?" He finally turned to face Devlyn.

Dev blinked stupidly. "I... well... I don't know."

"Huh?"

"She doesn't know about you being their father."

"Shit, Dev!" David nearly spilled his coffee. "Are you insane?"

Dev wrinkled her face in dismay. "It hasn't come up. And this was something we agreed to keep between ourselves." She was starting to get annoyed. "God, until you mentioned it just now, I hadn't even thought of it in years, David. Besides, we did this long before I even met Lauren. She loves the children and she thinks you and Beth walk on water. I'm sure she'll find the entire arrangement perfectly logical," Dev pronounced firmly, her voice exuding confidence.

"I'm sure she'll think you didn't trust her enough to tell her," David corrected. "Samantha put up with that crap, let you decide what was important enough to share and what wasn't, make all the big decisions. I doubt that Lauren will."

"It wasn't like that, and you know it," Dev snapped, her eyes flashing a warning to David. He was going too far. But now a tiny part of Dev was beginning to worry about Lauren's reaction. "We'll talk about it eventually, and the rest is a private matter between us."

Wisely, David backed off. Neither one spoke for few moments as they intentionally allowed their tempers to cool. He tapped the rim of his mug as an old memory flashed behind his eyes. "Do you remember what Beth's first question was?"

"You mean when Samantha and I told her we wanted you to be the donor?" She relaxed into her seat again.

David nodded. "That's the one."

Dev tilted her head back and looked at the sculpted ceiling. She would have to explain this to Lauren too, no doubt. "She wanted to know if we were going to sleep together."

Dev's chief of staff smiled a bittersweet smile at the memory of that very intense, very emotion-filled late night talk. "And of course that was right on the heels of your so-called 'rebellious period' where you got a motorcycle just because."

"I was never very good at being rebellious," Dev conceded ruefully.

"No," David smiled in remembrance, "you weren't. Except for the way you feel about women, you've always played by the rules, Devil."

"And those rules are changing." The pride in her voice was unmistakable. In a single generation so much had changed about the public's attitude toward homosexuals. And she knew it was largely due to people like her, who lived their lives the way their hearts told them was right and somehow achieved their dreams in spite of people's petty prejudices.

"When you drove up on that motorcycle, Beth thought you had lost your mind. *Then* you come to her asking for a sperm donation."

"I'm surprised she didn't try to have me committed. I was scared to death to ride the silly thing but too embarrassed to admit it to Samantha, so I did it anyway. I was young and stupid." She spared a wistful smile for her younger self. "But I knew I wanted a family sometime. And those little suckers hold up pretty well in the freezer." She gave him a nudge with her shoulder and he laughed quietly.

"I think she always felt a little odd about me having children with two other women." He took another sip of coffee, deciding Dev didn't need to know that he and Beth had been trying unsuccessfully to have their own for the past several years. Some things were too private even for the closest of friends. "Then she was there when Chris was born and those doubts seemed to disappear. I mean, she loves Ashley and has since the day she was born, but when she actually got to be the first person to hold him... I could have fathered a dozen children for you and she wouldn't have cared."

Dev fingered the slightly scratchy material of her navy, wool trousers. "I couldn't be the first to hold him. I'm glad it was Beth. She was really there for me and Samantha that night."

A knock on the door interrupted their trip down memory lane. "Come in."

Liza took a step into the office, trying not to yawn. It was nearly eight at night. "Michael Oaks to see you, Madam President."

Dev and David traded unhappy looks. "Thank you, Liza. Please tell him to come in."

"Yes, ma'am." Liza began to back out.

"And, Liza?"

She stopped dead in her tracks, her attention riveted on Dev. "Ma'am?"

"Go home."

For once, she didn't argue. "Thank you, Madam President. Good night. And goodnight to you, Mr. McMillian."

"Night," David and Dev chorused.

Liza waved Michael Oaks in and he closed the door behind himself before issuing a polite greeting. Young, ambitious, and disgustingly good at his job, Social Secretary Michael Oaks was one of the least popular members of Devlyn's staff.

"Madam President, David, good evening." He hesitated for a moment as he forced himself to say her name. "Strayer was supposed to fax me a copy of the guest list for the wedding and she hasn't done it yet."

Dev bit her lips to keep from taking his head off over his attitude toward Lauren. To put it simply, her lover and Michael hated each other and not even the President could end the little, though continuous, war between them. He was, Dev decided, just annoyingly anal, persnickety, and pompous. All qualities that didn't mix well with Lauren... or anyone else who would stand up to the arrogant man.

"Mike." Devlyn called him Mike because it annoyed him the same way his distaste for Lauren annoyed her. "She's only been in Ohio for two days. This trip is mostly a vacation. Give her a break, will you? Besides, my mother hasn't even gotten the first draft of the list done yet, and I'll bet fifty bucks she's still adding people to it."

Michael scratched the side of his neatly coifed Afro, a gesture both Dev and David recognized as one he made only when he was frustrated beyond words. They both suppressed grins.

He puffed out his slender chest. "Ma'am, I really need that report."

Dev rolled her eyes. "First, it's not a report. It's a guest list for our wedding. And who will be there for the most important day of my life is important to me. So I'm not rushing anybody when it comes to it. Second," she got up and walked slowly toward him, her posture and tone sending out a strong warning. "You will address the future First Lady as Ms. Strayer unless she gives you permission to do otherwise. Understand?"

"I don't think *Lauren* would give it either, do you, Dev?" David asked blithely.

"No. I don't think she would. You'll get the list when you get it."

Michael squared his shoulders and replanted his feet, intending to stand his ground, even if it was just a little. When was the President going to realize he really did know what was best in these matters? Leaving important details to her flamboyant mother and bitchy fiancée was a recipe for disaster. "Ma'am, you don't understand—"

Before another word could escape his lips, David sprang off the couch. "Excuse me, Michael. What part of 'you'll get it when you get it' didn't you understand?"

Michael fought the urge to take a step backwards. "Sir?"

"The President's statement was crystal clear."

Michael sighed inwardly. He was a man who believed in picking his battles. And he'd just decided that he wasn't going to pick this one.

He knew his appointment more than three years ago to the then Governor of Ohio had been a political favor. But sometimes being a Republican in an Emancipation Party administration that was very Democrat friendly was more than he could bear. He felt like a noble among liberal peasants.

"I'm sorry, David," Michael began. "But we don't have much time to put this wedding together, and the more time that's frivolously—"

David grabbed Michael by the arm of his perfectly pressed, gray suit and escorted him to the door. Dev had managed to rush around them to open the door. She was afraid that David might send Michael right through it without bothering with that small detail. What had gotten into him tonight? "Out. Get out!" He let go of Michael's arm and gave him a little shove when it appeared his feet were glued to the ground.

David pointed at Michael as he spoke to Jane. "If he tries to get back in here, have Security shoot him. The President is busy for the rest of the night."

Jane nodded and gave Michael a dirty look before making a shooing motion to send him on his way, watching as he gave his suit coat an indignant tug and stomped away.

That young man is trouble, Jane thought, as she rose and clicked off her desk lamp. The door to the President's office slammed and she wondered what had riled the usually gentle David McMillian. "The Ides of March are upon us," she said ominously as she retrieved her coat and began to walk down the darkened hallway.

Thursday, March 10th

A single dark eyebrow jumped as Dev watched her father line up his putt. She looked to David with an evil expression that caused her friend to shake his head emphatically. Her grin grew wider, and in turn, David shook his head even more frantically. "No!" he mouthed silently.

Just as her father ended his abbreviated swing, she sighed loudly. The ball missed the cup by two inches, and Frank turned around to bestow a murderous glare on his only child. "Not nice, Devil."

"I did nothing," she protested, raising her hands in innocence.

"Right," her father grumbled as he stepped back and allowed David to prepare his shot.

"Sheesh, don't blame me if you're not good at golf." Dev plucked a bottle of water from the golf cart and took a healthy drink. "I was just standing here behaving myself."

"Uh huh." He sneered a little as she handed him the water. "You know, by my calculations, you're about thirty over par."

"Hush." She looked aghast that he would bring up such a thing. "I don't know why you drag me out for this. You know I'm not any good."

"You can't be good at everything, sweetheart." He smiled as Dev scowled. "This keeps you honest."

"Hell, I'm not good at a lot of things," David chimed in as he plucked his ball from the cup. "Just ask Beth."

Dev moved over to her ball, which was just on this side of the green, and for several seconds regarded the putt she knew she would never make.

Just as her club made contact with the ball, Frank asked loudly, "So when are you and Lauren planning children?"

The ball rolled well off the putting green, then down a steep slope. "Shit." She glanced up at her father. "What? Have you been talking to Aaron?"

"Of course. He is my favorite grandson," Frank reminded her reproachfully. "Along with Christopher, my other favorite grandson."

Dev huffed as she retrieved her ball, sticking it into the pocket of her pants. "I am not shooting it again." She marched over to the cart and took a seat.

Frank chuckled as he sank the putt he had missed. "Watch it, Dev. The press will get a picture of you pouting."

"I don't care," she answered as she crossed her arms over her chest, grateful that the First Minister had begged off today and wasn't around to witness her humiliation first-hand. Of course it would be in all the papers in the morning. She groaned inwardly.

David and Frank both burst out laughing as they climbed in the cart and headed to the next hole, with a small caravan of press and Secret Service following just out of earshot.

Dev glanced sideways at her father, who was driving. "Why did you ask that?"

"Seemed like a logical question, Devil. I know you always wanted lots of kids. And I wasn't aware that had changed."

Dev examined her putter with exaggerated interest. "Yeah, well, I'm not sure Lauren wants lots of kids. I think she thinks that the three we have are plenty."

David shifted uncomfortably, wishing he wasn't here for this particular conversation.

"You haven't talked about it?" Frank asked, his tone more surprised than scolding.

"No." She set down her putter and began picking at a clump of dirt attached to one of her cleats. *"Why not, Devlyn?" comes next.*

"Why not, Devlyn?"

She looked at him sharply, annoyance written clearly on her face. Then she glanced back at David, who pulled his golf cap down over his eyes.

"Dad, sometimes, when you love someone, you just go with what you've got."

"Bullshit." He looked at her sternly. "You never know until you ask. Your mother and I didn't raise you to run away from things."

"Dad…" she warned.

"No, now listen to me, Devil. You're not going to be President forever; you're going to go back to at least a semi-private life eventually. Why should you give up on the things that you've wanted your entire life because you're marrying Lauren?"

"Because that's how equitable partnerships go, Dad."

"Don't lecture me about partnerships, young lady. I've been married for over forty-two years."

"Yes, sir." Devlyn was instantly contrite.

Frank sighed and patted Dev's leg. "I don't mean to push, honey. I just hate to see you abandon something that was important to you without even trying for it."

Dev resisted rolling her eyes. "We have three kids. I'm sure that is plenty for Lauren."

"Or are you just afraid of what her answer will be if you do ask?"

Dev groaned. "You're like a dog with a bone."

Frank let out a low growl, and David chuckled despite himself.

"God," she dropped her face in her hands. "Has anyone ever told you you're a pain?"

"Yes. Several times," he answered as he slowed the cart and then turned toward her and pinned her with intense eyes. "I nearly lost you last year. All I could do was sit back and watch you recover from being shot. I watched you. I watched Lauren. And I could see it then, the way you two were falling for each other. The way she worried about you. Then I looked at my grandchildren." He swallowed hard and took her hand. "Sam's death was hard enough for all of us. Losing you would have…" He stopped and shook his head. "Just make sure you talk to Lauren. I want you and Lauren both to have everything you want in life, sweetheart."

She nodded, trying to understand what he was saying. "We'll talk, Dad. I promise. But no guarantees."

"Of course not." He lifted his chin a little, pushing back the morbid thoughts. "Deciding to stop with the wonderful grandbabies I have now is one thing. But let it be a decision you *both* make. Give Lauren enough credit to at least include her in it." He pressed the gas pedal on the cart and they began to buzz along again. The air smelled fresh and cool, tinged with the green scent of wet grass. "Besides, I think Lauren would make really cute babies."

"Hey, what about me?" Dev blurted. "I make pretty good looking kids too, ya know."

"Yeah." David sat up straight now, finally willing to wade into the conversation. "But you're getting a little long in the tooth there, Dev. It won't be long before you go through 'the change.'"

She snatched the cap her father was wearing, which only served to complete his hideous golfing outfit of blue-and-green-plaid pants and a pink shirt, and beat David with it, knowing that cameras behind them were probably clicking madly, but not caring a bit. "You are so fired."

David grabbed the hat and grinned. "So what's new?" He gently placed the cap back on Frank's head. "You're going to have to do better than that before I get worried."

The cart stopped and they climbed out. As they picked their drivers, Frank placed his hand on Dev's shoulder and gave it a squeeze. "I know I sound like I'm butting in, a task I usually and very happily leave to your mother."

"It's okay, Dad, truly." Devlyn knew her father had wanted more children but that her birth had been exceptionally difficult on her mother, who was warned that another childbirth would be life-threatening.

"Are you happy, Devil?" The answer was painfully obvious, but he felt like it was his fatherly duty to ask every once in a while anyway.

Dev beamed. "You have no idea."

"Can your old man make one more observation?"

"Could I stop you?"

"No."

"Didn't think so."

"I do have an idea, because when I watch you with Lauren and I see the way you look at her," he paused, blushing slightly. "It's the same way I still look at your mother, even after all these years."

"I've got it that bad, huh?" Dev's eyes twinkled happily.

"You've got it in spades."

"Good."

Frank winked and gestured toward the green, where David was waiting patiently. "Shall we, Madam President?"

"Sure, I can handle another five holes of humiliation." Dev leaned up and kissed her father's cheek. He smelled of Old Spice, and she smiled as the scent so familiar from childhood tickled her nose.

As they walked she looked up to the press following them and waved; the faint sound of cameras clicking made her shake her head. "I'm glad my ability to be President isn't impaired by my inability to play golf." She leaned on the club, standing side-by-side with Frank, unintentionally creating a memorable photo op while David swung his club.

Friday, March 11th

It was well after midnight and Lauren had had such a wonderful day of not doing much of anything at all that she was now wide awake and in search of a cup of coffee. After a year of living with a self-proclaimed coffee addict, she found herself craving the tasty brew nearly as much as Devlyn did.

She'd spent five days in the cabin on the Marlowes' property all alone, enjoying the peace and solitude and trying to work her way back to a healthy state of mind. She didn't work on Dev's biography or even on the installment in her Adrienne Nash fiction series that she and

Devlyn were supposed to do together, but never seemed to have enough time for. Instead, she wrote bad poetry that caused her to burst out laughing when she read it out loud, read trashy paperback romances, ate popcorn for breakfast, and daydreamed to her heart's content. It was a much needed respite in a life that had somehow spun out of her control, and she was at last able to spend a good long while remembering the good things in her life and being thankful for them.

In her pajamas and a robe, Lauren padded slowly down the stairs of the main house that led into the Marlowe kitchen. The lights were off, but the soft moonlight streaming through the windows allowed her to see where she was going. The wooden floors were cold on her bare feet, and she spared a brief, wistful thought for the pair of toasty sweat socks that she knew she had stashed in the dresser upstairs. The house was large and well appointed by any standards, but held a warmth of character that the White House couldn't match in her eyes. She was glad that Devlyn had grown up here, where love flowed like a river, filling things up. Things here were so bright and hopeful.

When she closed her eyes and thought of the small, working class house where she grew up in Nashville and where her father still lived, one word came to mind... dark. In every way. Her mother had suffered from migraines and debilitating bouts of depression, and the shades at the Strayer house were always drawn tightly together, blocking out the light. *And everything else.*

"Oh, Mama," she sighed. "Please let it be that you finally found the peace you craved." She closed her eyes, feeling the familiar ache in her stomach that accompanied thoughts of her mother. Anna Strayer's suicide had been on her mind a lot lately as she fought with her own seeming inability to get a handle on the media and political frenzy that accompanied her engagement to Devlyn. After spending her entire adult life as a professional observer, she found being under such maddening, intense scrutiny more than she could bear at times.

Lauren fiddled with the coffee maker on the kitchen counter, letting out a small, satisfied grunt when she found that the aromatic grounds were already neatly in place, waiting to be brewed. She pushed the "on" button, her mind still on her mother. "Maybe I need to go to the doctor?"

"Are you not feeling well, dear?"

Lauren whirled around at the unexpected voice, inadvertently startling the speaker as much as herself.

"Oh," Janet gasped, then smiled in apology. She was wearing a thin, red plaid robe and brown suede slippers. She also didn't look like she'd been to bed yet. "I didn't mean to frighten you."

Lauren let out a slow breath, her heart pounding so furiously that she was a little dizzy. "No," she chuckled a little sheepishly. "It's all right. I just wasn't expecting anyone."

"I heard footsteps."

Lauren moved away from the counter, the motion bringing the scent of coffee to Janet. She smiled fondly. "You have been spending too much time with my daughter, I see." She made a face. "I never could drink the stuff. Too bitter. I prefer tea with milk and sugar, I'm afraid."

A shy smiled twitched at Lauren's lips. "Even though she's turned me into a hopeless addict, my time with Devlyn is well spent."

Janet grinned broadly. Love was such a beautiful thing it made her want to cry. "I imagine it is." She wove her arm through Lauren's and led her to a small breakfast table. "Here." From the deep front pocket of her robe she pulled out a pair of heavy gray socks. "I thought you might need these. The floors are cold at night."

Lauren's face lit up. "Oooo... yes, please. You always seem to know. Are you a witch or something?" Happily, she took the socks and sat down. Tugging them on, she sighed as her toes instantly warmed.

"Depends on who you ask, dear." Janet sat down across from Lauren. Her blue eyes twinkled and unerringly reminded Lauren very much of a shorter, older, salt-and-pepper-haired version of Devlyn. "I have my moments."

Lauren reached across the small table and took her hand, absorbing the warmth and strength of Janet's grasp. She briefly focused her attention on Janet's hands, thinking that, despite the fact that Janet Marlowe was a very attractive woman, it was true what people said. The face might lie, but the hands always reveal a woman's real age.

The older woman's gaze softened. She remembered looking at her own mother's and grandmother's hands with just the same expression. *God, where have the years gone?* "How was the cabin?"

"Mmm..." Lauren looked up from their linked hands. "Good, I think," she said a little hesitantly. "I'm... I'm not sure what Devlyn told you."

Janet's eyebrows lifted. "She told me that you needed a place to relax."

Lauren swallowed, ashamed. "That's all?"

Janet sighed. "That's all, honey. Although I did have an interesting talk with Sarah Turner, who called me last week and told me that she wouldn't be coming to the wedding."

Janet's expression turned slightly sour and Lauren wondered why. She didn't have to wonder long. "That girl has always been a handful, and it hasn't helped that Devlyn is such a babe in the woods."

Lauren snorted. "Babe in the woods? The woman who I've personally seen stare down the most powerful men and women in the world and either win them over or scare the crap out of them, depending on what she was trying to do? *That* woman?"

"That would be the one." Janet patted Lauren's hand and stood, making her way back to the coffeepot. "Surely you know that you're far more experienced in matters of the heart than Devlyn," she chided gently. "Dev married her first love with nothing more than a few random dates under her belt for experience." She pulled two mugs out of the cabinet and set a kettle of water to boil, spooning some sugar into her mug and reaching into the refrigerator for the milk. The bright refrigerator light illuminated her profile, causing the silver streaks in her hair to nearly glow.

"I was…" Lauren shrugged. "I was a little surprised when she told me she didn't have much experience." An understatement and she knew it. "But she was with Samantha for years." *And it's not like I've ever had a successful relationship for nearly that long.*

"Yes," Janet allowed, "she was. But she learned how to handle *Samantha* in that time. And that's about all. When it comes to other women, including you… well, as I said, she's a babe in the woods. When it comes to politics, she's as savvy as a fox. When it comes to love…"

"She believes that everyone else is as honest and straightforward as she is."

Janet nodded. "Exactly. Which is why Sarah threw her for such a loop."

Lauren glanced up, surprised.

"Sarah told me what happened," Janet confirmed, pouring a splash of milk into her cup and then putting the milk back into the fridge.

"I… Janet." Lauren tugged on her lower lip with her teeth for a moment, gathering her courage. "After seeing Sarah and Devlyn… It was hard for me to believe nothing was going on," she admitted, chagrined. "I should have trusted her more."

"Mmm…" Janet was noncommittal. "I don't know. You're being pretty hard on yourself. Only a fool doesn't look before she leaps."

"But I already leapt when I proposed to Devlyn. Isn't it a little late to be looking now?"

"Isn't it a little late for Devlyn to be being kissed by other women?" Janet answered reasonably, pulling a bag of lemon herbal tea from a box and placing it into her cup. She poured the steaming water over it, mingling the scent of citrus with the aroma of coffee.

"You both made it through this, Lauren." She turned to face the blonde woman. "And in the end that's what counts. Not the arguments or compromises that happened along the way." She laughed softly, the melodic sound making her seem much younger. "I can't tell you how many times Frank and I have wrestled through things over the years. But we're still together and still in love."

Lauren shifted in her chair and regarded Janet curiously as she filled both their mugs. "You and Dr. Marlowe," she backtracked at Janet's stern look, "you and *Frank* are very different people." She imagined there were many times when the mild Frank and fiery Janet clashed.

"Like you and Devlyn," Janet pointed out, retaking her seat at the table and passing over Lauren's steaming mug.

Lauren smiled her thanks. They sat in silence for a few moments, enjoying each other's company and the fragrant liquids that slid down their throats and warmed their bellies. A gust of wind rattled the kitchen window and both women turned toward the sound.

Janet gently cleared her throat, treading very carefully into unknown waters. "You mentioned a doctor before. Are you ill?"

Lauren wasn't expecting that, thinking that she'd successfully dodged that bullet earlier. Before she could stop them, tears filled her eyes. "I don't know," she whispered.

"Oh, honey." Janet leaned forward a little, searching Lauren's down-turned face. "What is it?"

Lauren swallowed a few times before speaking. "I haven't been handling stress very well lately." There. Starting was always the hard part. "I've been getting frustrated or upset far more than I should and… and it's made me think of Mama."

Janet was still terribly at sea, but sensed this was something very important to the younger woman. "Devlyn explained that your mother passed away last year. I was truly sorry to hear that."

Lauren nodded mutely.

"There are still times that I miss my mother." Janet lifted her tea bag and watched it drain into her mug before dunking it again. "When something good or bad happens, I still find myself anxious to tell her, and it's been nearly ten years since she died."

Pale brows furrowed deeply as Lauren thought. "That hasn't happened to me once, I'm ashamed to say. We," she sighed, "we didn't have a very good relationship. We never did really." How could she capture a lifetime of disappointment and hurt in a few words? A contemplative look crossed her face. "She loved me the best she knew how, but she was always so remote, just out of reach, I don't feel like I ever knew her at all."

Suddenly, Janet's choice of words replayed themselves in her mind. *Passed away...* "Janet, didn't Devlyn tell you what happened with my mother?"

"Well…" she paused as she thought back. "She said that your mother had been ill and had passed away. Other than that—"

"She hung herself," Lauren said softly. There was a resigned, flat quality to her voice that caused a shiver to race down Janet's spine.

"Oh, God." For a moment Janet was shocked into silence as the unexpected words soaked in. "I'm so sorry. You and your poor father," she uttered quietly. "How horrible." Then her eyes widened briefly, but she firmly clamped down on herself, not wanting her reaction to cause Lauren to withdraw. *Oh, no.* "You haven't been thinking of—"

"No," Lauren interrupted instantly, still managing to read Janet's alarm. "I would never do anything like that. I haven't even considered it. I swear."

Janet let out a shaky breath. "Thank goodness." She slumped back in her chair. "You had me concerned there for a moment." She set down her cup and took Lauren's hand again. "Then what's this about doctors and things reminding you of your mother?"

A pained look crossed Lauren's face. "Mama couldn't handle stress. Obviously. She never could, even when I was a child. If I caught a cold or twisted an ankle, she'd look at me with such a helpless expression that it would break my heart. Even when intellectually she knew what to do, emotionally she couldn't handle it. She would just go into her bedroom, lock the door, and stay there." *Sometimes for days.* Lauren drew in a breath, memories clouding normally bright eyes. "I would hear her crying and Daddy would insist that I leave her be, that she was dealing with things in her own way."

Janet's heart ached for Lauren, and she felt a wave of anger for the child who had to grow up under such impossible circumstances and the woman who would always carry the scars.

"But she wasn't dealing with anything," Lauren continued bravely. It was easier to talk to Janet than she thought it would be. On some level, easier than Devlyn, who sometimes couldn't repress her own anger and outrage over Lauren's long-dead past. In those situations Lauren found herself wanting to comfort Devlyn more than to continue their conversation. She hadn't consciously planned it, Lauren admitted to herself, but she and Janet had some time alone together now and she needed to talk. Especially after the solitude of the cabin had allowed her to put some things into perspective.

"Mama was hiding from the world." Lauren braced herself for the hardest part. "And lately… umm… I've been wanting to do the same thing." She glanced at Janet's face, worried, half-expecting to see pity or disgust, but finding only empathy and love. She let out the breath she'd been holding.

"I see," Janet said slowly. She thought for a moment before saying anything else, but when she did speak, it was with a quiet certainty. "Did your maternal grandmother or father commit suicide as well?"

Lauren blinked. "I… uh… No." She shook her head. "Grandma had a heart attack when I was four and Grandpa was killed in Vietnam."

Janet absorbed that information. "Was your mother hounded day and night by reporters?"

Lauren's eyes widened a touch. "Of course not."

"And was her every move regulated, scheduled, and guarded with men and women with guns?"

Lauren shook her head, a tiny smile twitching at her lips. It was impossibly easy to love Janet. "No. But—"

"And in the span of less than a year did she go from being someone who could walk down the street in peace to someone whose face was plastered on half the magazines at the newsstand?"

Lauren's eyes softened as she looked at Janet. Devlyn's mother would champion her, just as the younger Marlowe would. "No." She gave Janet a watery smile full of affection. "I guess she didn't."

"And I'm assuming she didn't have three rambunctious children pop into her life all at once, needing from her every bit of the love and attention they could get from a second parent. Or…" Janet gave her a curious look, "and forgive me if I'm out of line here, but I do know that you were married to a man and then divorced. Is Devlyn the first woman you've had a relationship with?"

Mutely, Lauren nodded, squirming a little in her chair. "First and last, I hope."

Janet smiled sagely. "And was this a revelation for you last year? Your interest in women?" she inquired gently.

"Not completely new, no." Lauren fiddled with her mug, feeling her face heat and hoping this wasn't going to lead to a discussion about sex. "But it wasn't something I let myself think about much either. And certainly nothing I'd ever acted on."

"Mmm… Hmm…" Janet tapped the tabletop with her index finger. "So on top of everything else, last year you acknowledged another facet of your sexual orientation for the first time when you fell in love with my daughter?"

Lauren's mouth worked for a few seconds, but no sound came out. She watched as Janet lifted her chin in silent triumph. "I guess I did. God, it's a wonder I'm not in the booby hatch, isn't it?" she muttered in awe. Had all that happened in only a year?

Janet chuckled. "Basically." Then her expression grew more serious. "Please don't think that I don't believe your mother had real problems, dear. It's clear that she must have been fighting horrible demons. But I don't think, because there are times you need to regroup or you want to push the world away for a while, that you're anything but normal and healthy." Her voice strengthened. "You've earned the right to pull back and take a deep breath when you need to." She stared directly into Lauren's eyes. "Don't deny yourself, honey, or think you're crazy for needing it." She patted Lauren's hand before releasing it. "Had I been in your shoes, I would have snapped weeks ago. And outright killed that annoying man, Michael Oaks."

A small laugh forced its way from Lauren's throat. "No, you wouldn't," she told her with a raised eyebrow.

"Oh, you'd be surprised." A feral look flickered over Janet's face before being replaced by her usual, pleasantly neutral expression. She glanced at Lauren's nearly empty mug. "A refill?"

Lauren shook her head and sighed, feeling a good portion of the unbearable weight that had been crushing her shoulders begin to ease.

Janet took a long swallow of tea.

"Janet," she held her tongue until Devlyn's mother had her eyes fastened on her before speaking. "I don't want you to think that Devlyn or the children have been a hardship. They haven't," Lauren promised emphatically. "I love them all with all my heart. They aren't what I ever thought I'd have in my life, and still, they're the best things in it."

"I know that, honey," Janet answered kindly, understanding more than the younger woman would have ever suspected. *Maybe it will help...* "Have I ever told you how I met Frank?"

Lauren started a little at the change in subject. "No." She cocked her head eagerly and a slow smile spread over her face. "But I'd love to hear."

"I was working the late shift at an ice cream parlor when he walked in."

"Ooo, my fantasy job," Lauren said dreamily. "But only if I could quit after I got full."

They both laughed softly.

"Trust me, it wasn't that glamorous." She gave her a conspiratorial wink. "Though I did gain seven pounds before I had the sense to quit. Anyway, I was set to run away from college the next day."

Lauren's forehead wrinkled. "With Frank?"

Janet flashed Lauren a wicked smile. "With Brian Webber."

Ooo... Lauren's interest was piqued. "Oh, my."

Janet grinned nostalgically. "I haven't said that name in years." She sighed. "He was a wild and handsome boy, with long, untamed blonde hair and a guitar always strapped to his back. He had a peace symbol tattooed on his shoulder and wore nothing but those floppy leather sandals all year long. Even in the snow, the goof."

Lauren stifled a giggle.

But Janet giggled a little herself, something Lauren had never seen her do before. She was charmed.

"He was a songwriter who was going to change the world with his music." Janet lowered her voice a little, as though Brian might actually hear her. She wrinkled her nose. "Though he wasn't that good." Her voice returned to normal. "We met on campus at Ohio State after he'd given a free concert on the grass in front of the student union."

"Were you in love with him?"

Janet considered the question thoughtfully, thinking that Brian deserved at least that much. "I was in 'lust' with him," she finally confided. "But it wasn't the same as what I came to feel for Frank. Brian fascinated me beyond reason, igniting my imagination. And God was he good in bed." She fanned herself. "He made love to me as though the world was ending." She winked at Lauren, who was now sporting a blush so pronounced that it was visible, even in the dim light. "Don't worry, dear. I'll spare you the gory details so your head doesn't explode."

"Thanks," Lauren croaked, swallowing hard.

Janet waved a dismissive hand. "Nothing as pedestrian as marriage and children would do for us. We had a different, daring life planned. One that didn't even remotely resemble the ordinary middle class family I'd been raised in or the upper middle-class existence I was supposed to aspire to. I wasn't just going to break away from that tired old mold. I was going to explode from it."

Enthralled, Lauren waited for her to continue as Janet gathered her thoughts. A far off look crossed the older woman's face and then she smiled.

"I was just about to close the shop for the evening and was thinking about what I would pack and how I would explain to my poor parents what I was about to do, when a tall, slim, dark-haired man strode into the shop. His pants—not jeans, as we all wore in those days, but cotton trousers—were neatly pressed and his shoes were so shiny I could see the reflection of the ice cream case in them when I peered down at them."

"Frank?" The description, except for the dark hair, which had turned a snowy-white with the passage of time, was still a very apt one.

Janet nearly swooned as she said, "He had the most beautiful blue-green eyes I had ever seen, and when I looked up from what I was doing I actually gasped."

Delighted, Lauren laughed. "And you fell instantly in love?"

"Hardly!" Janet contradicted, excitement lighting her eyes. "After I managed to peel myself away from those beautiful eyes, I asked him, rather rudely, I might add, what kind of ice cream he wanted. I was anxious to leave and meet Brian, you see." Janet crossed her arms over her chest. "You'll never guess what kind of ice cream he ordered."

An enormous grin split Lauren's face. "Sure I can. The same kind that Devlyn prefers. Vanilla."

"Vanilla," Janet confirmed, wrinkling her nose. "We had one hundred and one flavors in that store and that's what he ordered. I looked at his wholesome clothes and neat haircut and considered his dull choice of ice cream and actually smirked."

"Uh oh."

"'Uh oh' is right," Janet informed her blithely. "He spent the next ten minutes explaining to me why vanilla was the perfect choice and one that would never be subject to fads or go out of style. It was, he told me in that that deep voice of his, a timeless classic."

"And what did you say?"

Mischievously, Janet chuckled. "I said so was my granny's girdle, but that didn't mean I wanted one."

Lauren shook her head, easily picturing the words coming from a young, polite, yet feisty Janet Peabody. If Janet had mellowed over time, what must she have been like in her youth.

"But I was lying," the smaller woman said ruefully, "because by the time Frank had finished his dissertation on ice cream, darn it if I didn't actually believe him. He helped me close up that night and offered to drive me back to my dorm so I wouldn't have to take the bus. In the car, I told him about Brian and our plans and how I would write my parents and tell them after we'd gone."

"Had Brian met your parents?" Lauren pulled her feet up into her chair and wrapped her arms around her knees, hugging them to her as she listened intently.

"Of course not," Janet scoffed. "Simply the thought of doing so terrified him. I also knew they would hate him, so I didn't press it, though it did make me more uncomfortable than I wanted to admit at the time. Frank sneered at that, saying that any man worth his salt would *want* to be a part of my family and would spend his entire life, if need be, convincing them that he loved their daughter and was right for her." Janet got up and pulled a tin of cookies from the cabinet. She popped the lid and took out one, passing the tin to Lauren before easing back into her chair.

Lauren reached inside, plucked out a cookie, and took a bite; and all the while her eyes were riveted on Janet.

"Then I dared him to put his money where his mouth was." Janet crunched the cookie, catching the crumbs in her cupped hand.

Lauren's eyes went round. "You what?"

"I told him if he was so keen on meeting people's parents that he could drive me to Cincinnati that night and meet mine."

Lauren's nose wrinkled as a genuine smile curved her lips. "And he did."

"And he did." Janet put the lid back on the cookie tin. Her expression turned wry. "Of course, my parents adored Frank, and in no time, when I looked into those beautiful eyes of his, I felt the same way."

Lauren sighed happily.

"I called Brian and told him I wasn't going anywhere." Janet looked at Lauren and smiled gently. "I was never going to marry or have a child, you see. So Frank and Devlyn... well, they aren't what I ever thought I'd have in my life, and still, they're the best things in it."

Lauren's own words echoed back at her, and she sucked in a surprised breath as the story came full circle.

"Sometimes the best things in life aren't what you expect them to be, Lauren. But that doesn't mean they can't work out." Janet stood and bent to place a delicate kiss on Lauren's forehead. She rested her warm palm on Lauren's cheek. "I know you're under enormous pressure right now. But being part of this family means you're never alone unless you want to be. We love you and are here whenever you need us." She allowed her hand to drop from Lauren's face after a loving pat. "Now, dear, I'm off to bed. I promised to take Ashley horseback riding in the morning."

Janet took a few steps toward the stairs, hearing Lauren sniff a few times.

"Janet?"

The older woman turned around and cocked her head toward Lauren. "Yes?"

"Can..." Lauren licked her lips as her stomach did a nervous flip. "Can I..." She swallowed. "Can I call you Mom? I mean, it can be after the wedding, if you want," she finished in a rush, surprised to see tears shining in Janet's eyes and a tremulous smile shaping her lips.

She crossed the room again and pulled Lauren's head to her chest, giving her a strong hug that Lauren sank into with almost shameful relief. "I would love that, honey. And you can call me that right now. No ceremony will change how I feel about you."

Lauren smiled against Janet's robe. "Thanks, Mom," she said softly. It felt strange and thrilling and she spared her own mother a melancholy thought, hoping that she would be happy that a long absent piece of her daughter's life had finally found its way home.

Janet sniffed and wiped at her eyes, then reached down and gave Lauren's side a playful pinch.

Lauren squeaked, eyes round with mock outrage.

"It's bedtime," Janet directed in her most motherly voice.

Lauren nodded and wiped at her own eyes as she stood.

Janet took her hand as they made their way to the stairs.

"Jan...Mom?"

"Mmm?"

Lauren suddenly felt exhausted, as though she'd climbed an enormous hill and was standing at the top, looking down the other side. "Thanks."

APRIL 2022

Wednesday, April 6th

It was late, the lights were dimmed, and Devlyn and Lauren were reclining comfortably on Dev's bed. A light spring rain pelted the White House, its uneven pitter-patter joining the muted clicking of Lauren's typing. The writer was diligently working on her laptop, the light from the screen reflecting off the small lenses of her silver, wire-framed glasses, while Devlyn was re-reading one of Lauren's Adrian Nash books, trying to unwind from an impossibly long day of meetings.

"You know," Dev said, closing the book with a satisfied sigh, "this is my favorite of yours."

Lauren smiled but kept typing. She was clad in a pair of lightweight silk pajamas and slippers and was very comfortable. The fire in the fireplace was nothing more than a uneven pile of glowing orange embers, but the room still held the faint scent of hickory, which Lauren found oddly relaxing. "You say that about whichever book you're reading."

Dev's forehead creased, and she looked at the book as though seeing it for the first time. "I do?"

"Uh huh."

"Oh." Dev set the book on the nightstand, fluffed her pillow, and began to fiddle with the bedspread.

Lauren looked up from the screen, her fingers pausing over the keys. She tried not to sound exasperated. "Why don't you try some television?"

"Do I have a television in here?" Curious, Dev glanced around her room.

"You'd think you'd know what's in your own bedroom, you work-aholic." The light from the computer reflected off white teeth as she smiled.

"*You're* in my bedroom." Dev pinched her, causing her to laugh and squirm. "And you should talk." Her laughter was even louder than Lauren's as the younger woman nearly wiggled off the bed. "Who's working at nearly midnight?"

Lauren didn't bother answering the rhetorical question. She smiled fondly at Dev and gave long dark hair an affectionate tug before extending her arm and pointing. "The TV is in that case, honey. Give me a few minutes and I'll be finished." A slow, sexy smile crept across her face and her voice dropped an octave. "And then we can do something else to occupy you until you're ready to sleep."

Dev felt the words all the way to her toes. She grinned wildly, not noticing that Lauren had begun to type again. "Now you're talking." Eagerly, Dev began to work the buttons on her pajamas, nearly tearing one of the more stubborn ones off in her haste. "Stupid, pain in the—"

Lauren glanced sideways and her fingers froze on the keyboard, her mouth suddenly going dry. Her eyes traced the gentle swell of Devlyn's naked breast. *Sweet Jesus.* She swallowed hard, very aware of her body's instant, pulsing response. She groaned, but reluctantly, she reached out and stilled Dev's hands.

Dev looked up with an innocent, slightly harried expression that nearly caused Lauren to burst out laughing. "What? I'm going as fast I can."

Unexpectedly, Lauren leaned over and kissed Devlyn on the mouth with brief but sincere passion.

Dev moaned at the feeling of warm, silken lips against hers. "Mmm... Hey, why are you stopping?"

Lauren eyed Dev dreamily. *Good question.* She barely resisted the urge to toss her computer on the floor and attack Dev's pajama top herself. With her teeth. "I need a few more minutes to finish, honey." Quite without her permission, one of her hands wandered over to Dev and began to softly stroke the silky skin of her collarbone. "It has to go to Wayne in the morning. I promised him." She sighed wistfully. "And if you get naked in this bed with me, I am done for the night." Gray eyes twinkled. "At least with work."

Dev's expression turned smug. "Well," she tried to look modest, but didn't quite manage it, "in that case..."

"You'll watch TV for a little while." It was more a statement than a question. Not waiting for an answer, she gave the voice command for the television and the cabinet across the room opened to expose an older model fifty-two-inch screen. "Just fifteen more minutes, okay?" She patted Dev's leg.

"Where's the remote? I hate the voice command."

"Top drawer of the nightstand," Lauren informed her absently, her eyes already back on the computer screen, a tiny crease in her forehead letting Dev know she was trying to concentrate on something.

Dev retrieved the remote and climbed back into bed. At a speed faster than Lauren knew the television would work, she began changing the channels, pausing occasionally when something caught her eye. She listened to an infomercial for a moment, then pursed her mouth and touched her upper lip with a fingertip.

"Hey, Lauren?"

"Mm?"

"Do I have unwanted facial hair that I was unaware I even had?" Dev asked seriously.

Lauren turned to Dev and pulled her glasses off. She stared at her as though she were an alien. Then she heard the announcer selling a miracle cream. "Yes. Lots."

Dev scowled. "Ha. Ha." She changed the channel.

"Welcome to this very special live version of the Gary Kramer show. And I'm your host, Garreeeeeee Kramer! Tonight's topic: Is She or Isn't She?"

Dev snickered. "God, I can't believe this show is still on. You'd think he would have run out of nutcases and hillbillies to pay to come on the show."

The studio audience went wild, hooting and hollering and chanting Gary's name over and over

"Gary Kramer is a freak," Lauren muttered. "And his trashy talk show guests are bigger freaks." She began searching her computer directory for a particular file.

A curtain went up showing the darkened outline of men on bar stools. Their backs were to the camera.

"I'd like to introduce Billy Ward, former student at Nashville's John Overton High School."

"Hey," Lauren's eyes lifted, "I went to John Overton." Pale brows furrowed. "And I knew Billy. Damn, don't tell me he's dating his sister or something. He was a sweet guy."

A light came on over the first man's head. He was in his early thirties with sandy-brown hair and soulful brown eyes. The audience cheered, and he gave them a nervous wave.

"Billy, let's get right to tonight's sizzling hot topic. You know the question on all of America's minds. Lauren Strayer, lesbian? Is she or isn't she?"

Once again the audience burst into applause, some shouting yes and some shouting no, a few going as far as to boo, giving her wild thumbs down.

Lauren's jaw dropped. "Oh, my God!"

The private phone rang and Devlyn snatched it up as the lights above Lauren's former lovers, including ex-husband Judd, lit up the sound stage. "If this is anyone other than David, go away."

"Are you watching—?" David heard a loud crash, and string of obscenities that would have made the Seventh Fleet collectively blush. "Never mind."

Lauren flew out of bed, sending her computer clattering to the floor. She marched up to the television and poked her finger right into Man Number Three's chest. "I never slept with you, you sorry son of a bitch!" she roared. "I wouldn't even kiss you!"

Dev heard Beth shout from somewhere behind David, "Tell Lauren that if she slept with Number Three, I quit."

Dev winced at the lurid shade of purple coloring Lauren's face. "You guys had better get over here. And David?"

"Yeah?"

"Bring Valium."

"For you or Lauren."

"Yes."

Twenty minutes later David, Beth, and Dev were all on the President's bed, watching the broadcast. Billy had just finished pronouncing—in a deep Southern accent and with a good dose of indignation—that if Lauren Strayer was a homo, then so was he.

Lauren paced the room like a caged beast, her hands a blur of agitated movement. The words: prom night, Budweiser, pickup truck, and cherry were still viciously whizzing around in her head. She wasn't close to her family. But she couldn't help but think, *Jesus H. Christ, Daddy is going to see this!*

"Sweetheart, if you don't calm down something important is going to burst. It's not," Dev glanced helplessly at Beth and David, "*that* bad."

"It is, Devlyn," Lauren vowed in all seriousness. "It's *that* bad."

Beth eyed Billy speculatively. "That first guy is cute for a high school boyfriend. And he really seems to like you. At least he doesn't look like he was on the chess team or anything."

"Hey!" David glared at his wife. "I was on the chess team."

Beth smiled placidly at David. "Yes, dear, you were." She turned back to Lauren. "Where'd you park the pickup when you did it?"

Lauren sneered at her chief of staff, who was enjoying this way too much. "None of your God da—"

"Beth, behave," Dev growled as she got off the bed and caught up to Lauren. She put a calming hand on her arm. "Relax." She wrinkled her nose. "Budweiser?"

Gray eyes narrowed. "*My* house didn't have a wine cellar."

"Next up is Carter Simpson, University of Tennessee graduate and part owner of Rocky's Tools in Memphis. How can you shed some light on the subject, Carter?"

Carter was beefy and tall and looked uncomfortable in his navy blue sport coat and tie. "Huh? I thought you paid me to come talk about sex." He scratched his square jaw, and several women in the audience began to swoon. When he smiled, deep dimples dotted his ruddy cheeks.

Beth burst out laughing. "He's beautiful, Lauren. Too bad, the lights are on but nobody's home."

Dev looked at him with a discerning eye. "He's not so great," she said unconvincingly. "Did you really sleep with him?" Part of Dev hoped that all these men were fakes. Even Judd. That wasn't realistic, of course. But if she was going to delude herself, why not go all the way?

"Ugh," Lauren groaned and nodded miserably. She rubbed her face. Could this get any worse?

Dev glanced back at Carter and rolled her eyes. "So what if he's good looking? It's not like he's… oh, I don't know... the *President*!"

David and Beth laughed. Sometimes Dev was so touchy.

"He was really sweet, Devlyn," Lauren scolded. "We just didn't have anything in common except for—"

"Fantastic, tongue-wagging, sweat-sliding, hip-grinding, sweet-mother-of-God-if-I-died-now-I'd-die-happy, all-American sex!" Carter finished proudly. He looked a little overheated and had to wrestle loose the tie that circled his thick neck.

All the other men looked at Carter with wide eyes just as they cut to a commercial break.

Lauren shrugged one shoulder and admitted weakly, "I came out of my shell in college with Carter."

"Wow," David mumbled from the bed as he reached over for a glass of water on the nightstand. After drinking it down, he pressed the glass to his forehead. "Sometimes the First Amendment just sucks. Can I sleep with you, Lauren?" he blurted, unable to resist.

Beth choked on her drink, then smacked David in the back of the head. Of course that didn't stop her from asking, "Me too?" Which earned her a playful slap from her husband in return. "Ouch." Beth laughed, rubbing her head.

"If I can't, you can't," David insisted, leaning in and kissing his wife soundly. "Besides, I couldn't stand the competition."

"Me neither," Beth agreed happily, kissing him back.

"All right, that's enough," Dev bit back a laugh, then masked the command with a smile, though it was clear she was serious. "Don't make me separate you two troublemakers."

"Killjoy," David mumbled. "First we don't get to see Lauren's tattoo, now this."

"Yeah," Beth echoed solemnly. "What he said."

Dev focused on Lauren, who was staring at the television images, still in shock. "Lauren, are you okay?"

Lauren stuck out her tongue at Beth and David, then addressed Devlyn. "No, I'm not okay," she whined, praying Carter wouldn't remember that time they did it under the bleachers at half time. "Can't we assassinate them or something?"

"Your old boyfriends?" Dev looked surprised, then slightly pleased by the notion.

"No," Lauren corrected with an arch look thrown in the general direction of Dev's bed, "David and Beth."

Dev sighed and opened her arms, an invitation for Lauren to take refuge. "'Fraid not. But don't think I haven't considered it."

Lauren was too agitated to stop moving, and a flash of hurt flickered across Dev's face when her lover didn't come over to the bed. The sight stopped Lauren's pacing cold, and she walked over to the bed and took Dev's hand and gently kissed her knuckles.

The commercial ended and Carter began talking again. At the words "tied up" Dev's bedroom went absolutely silent.

Lauren whimpered. This actually rivaled her mother walking into her bedroom when she was fourteen at the exact same moment that she'd finally gotten up the nerve to try masturbation for the first time. Only now the room was more crowded. *Kill me now, God. Please.*

Tied up. Well, well, well. Dev looked from the TV to Lauren and back again three times before squeaking, "Really?"

"Even then he worked at a hardware store part-time," Lauren said, as if that explained everything.

Beth was now laughing so hard she was in danger of falling off the bed. "I'm gonna wet my pants," she howled. "I know it."

"At least we know what to get them for Christmas," David said seriously. He looked at Beth and they both said, "duct tape" at the same time before dissolving into twin fits of laughter.

Carter proclaimed Lauren as hetero as… Well, he couldn't come up with an actual analogy. But he swore the sex was great and that while they were under the bleachers her eyes hadn't roamed over to the cheerleaders even once.

Dev started to say something and then her mouth clicked shut and she took a seat in a chair. "Tied up?" She looked at David and Beth, who were finally starting to calm down. "I tell ya, Lauren, you may be too wild for my white bread tastes." She gave Lauren a very serious look. "Are we talking tape or rope or chains?"

Lauren was well aware that she was being tweaked. She tilted her chin upward with an indignant grunt and crossed her arms over her chest, petulantly refusing to answer.

"There's still more men to go," Beth reminded Dev helpfully. "Let's wait and see."

It was now Man Number Three's turn.

As soon as the camera panned sideways, Lauren crowed, "I did *not* sleep with him!" Beseeching eyes begged her friends to believe her. "He was a freshman when I was a senior for God's sake. He helped me on a chemistry final and I went on one," she held up her index finger, "single, pity date with him. That's it!"

"Did you pass the exam?" David snorted from the bed where he was reclining as though he owned the joint, his back against the headboard.

"Yes," Lauren snapped, as she mentally eviscerated the man on television. "You're in deep trouble, nerd boy," she shouted to the image. "I know people with guns and bombs, who aren't afraid to use them."

Nerd boy, better known to some as Wendell Fleshman, spent most of his fifteen minutes of fame bragging about his and Lauren's torrid love affair.

Beth asked Lauren, "Did you ever get poked with that pocket protector while you were doing it? That could have been messy. Of course, he probably carried sanitary wipes around in his back pocket."

"Doesn't everyone?" David said, winking at Beth.

Lauren ground her teeth together.

Gary Kramer thrust his microphone in Wendell's face, "Did you ever once see a sign that Lauren was attracted to women?" He leaned closer to Wendell. "Anything. Anything at all that was a hint of what was to come? The public has a right to know."

Wendell thought for a moment and then nodded his head. "Yes. Yes, I did."

David, Beth, and Dev all leaned forward in anticipation.

Even Lauren took a step closer to the TV.

"One night after studying, we went out for a Coke."

Three sets of eyes swung toward Lauren.

The blonde woman nodded reluctantly. "It wasn't a date, though," she corrected carefully. "My apartment didn't have air-conditioning and it was a million degrees outside. We were boiling and needed a break."

Wendell let out a contemplative breath. "When we got to the convenience store, there was another girl there; she was in our chemistry class too."

"Shirley," Wendell announced, with Lauren whispering the name right along with him as the past came rushing back to her.

"Shirley was twenty-five cents short for the Coke she wanted to buy and Lauren ran up to the counter and offered Shirley a quarter." Wendell paused, well aware that the studio audience was hanging on his every word. "And then they both smiled at each other." He shrugged and adjusted his heavy-framed glasses. "And I knew."

"Knew what?" the host prompted breathlessly.

The camera zoomed in on Wendell. "Knew there was *something* there."

"That's it?" Gary asked, doing his best to hide his disappointment. His show hadn't paid all this money to hear about lingering smiles.

"That's it."

The audience groaned, let down by the pedestrian encounter. But Lauren blinked stupidly. "I can't believe it," she said quietly. "He's right."

Beth blinked at her friend. "He is?"

Lauren nodded. "I wasn't thinking about kissing her or anything romantic. The thought never entered... well, it never entered my conscious mind at least. But she was really interesting and pretty and had the greatest laugh. And I remember thinking that wouldn't it be wonderful if we ran into each other again sometime before school let out."

This time the pang of jealousy nailed Devlyn right in her heart. "And did you?" she finally got out, surprised that this would affect her so. She wasn't a jealous person, but perhaps when it came to Lauren, all bets were off. "Run into each other?"

Lauren smiled wistfully, completely unaware of the look on her own face. "Nope. I graduated a month later. And I was already dating Judd by that time. Unlike Wendell, however, Judd sucked at chemistry."

The President sighed and murmured, "He sucked at a lot of things."

Judd looked as though he wanted to blend into the background. Billy, Carter, and Wendell all looked relaxed and happy. He couldn't understand how they could be enjoying this.

Billy made a comment about Lauren's talent for a particular sexual act, much to the dismay of the other men, and Dev's face turned to stone. "I feel an audit coming on for you, big mouth. Hope you know a good tax lawyer."

Gary Kramer got his note cards mixed up and decided to wing it as he spoke to Judd. "Ah, the illustrious Mr. Strayer."

Everyone in the President's bedroom winced, including Lauren. Judd had always hated that with a passion.

"That's Radison," Judd ground out, his hands shaping into white-knuckled fists.

"Sorry," Gary continued blithely. "You, more than anyone, would know the answer to our question. After all, you were married to the woman. Is Lauren truly a lesbian? Or is she simply using President Marlowe for the power and prestige?"

"Yeah, this is really prestigious," Lauren said, her face twisting into a sour expression. "Especially at this very moment."

"Maybe she likes men and women. Why don't you just ask Lauren?" Judd suggested reasonably, his self-disgust leaking into his words. With every passing second he looked more and more like he wanted to bolt from the studio.

The President of the United States' eyes burned holes into her television.

Judd threw a loathing-filled glance at Wendell. "For the record, there is no way she slept with you, Wendell. So just give it up."

"Thank you!" Lauren shouted, throwing her hands in the air. "Finally."

Gary tried to get a few more details out of Judd and grew angry when the architect refused to give up anything juicy. "Did Lauren like to be on top or on the bottom?" he tried to toss in casually and catch Judd off guard.

The audience went wild, hooting and screaming.

Judd just glared.

"Don't you do it, Judd," Lauren warned as she bit the inside of her cheek. "Not a word."

"Top or bottom?" Gary persisted. "Top or bottom?" He motioned the camera closer. "Top or bottom?" Closer still the camera came and Judd began to sweat. "Top or bottom?"

"Top!" Judd screamed, unable to take the pressure for another second. "There. Are you happy?"

"You spineless shit." Lauren sighed.

Carter's thick eyebrows pulled together. "Not with me."

"I would have thought she'd be afraid that a Paul-fucking-Bunyan-ape like you would crush her," Judd shouted, any semblance of calm flying out the window.

Carter jumped out of his seat and several large staff hands had to restrain him.

Gary smiled happily. "After this break, we have a final, surprise guest and a vote from our panelists."

"All good things must eventually come to an end." Beth sat up and padded across the room to Lauren, who was looking out the window. "It really isn't so bad, Lauren," she whispered.

"And if it were your sex life up for public discussion?"

"I wouldn't be handling it as well as you are," Beth said cheerfully. "But it's not me. Thank God."

Lauren ran a nervous hand through wavy blonde hair. "It's almost over," she said as much to herself as Beth. "I can take it."

"Of course you can." Beth glanced over her shoulder and then back at Lauren, lowering her voice further. "Who is the special guest? Any idea?"

Lauren nodded. "Oh, yeah. They've done a pretty good job at hunting down people. So I'm expecting they didn't miss Man Number Five from my past."

"Oooo, is this man worth all the mystery?"

Lauren shrugged, hearing the music for the Gary Kramer Show begin again. "You tell me. C'mon." They moved over to the bed and sat next to their respective mates. Lauren, burrowed into Dev's embrace, letting out a deep breath. *It's almost over*, she told herself.

"Welcome back, ladies and gentlemen." Over the host's shoulder, Judd, with a stark white bandage taped over his nose, was clearly visible. "Before our last guest, we've asked the men on stage to rate their sexual experiences with the future First Lady on a scale from one to five."

"Jesus Christ!" Lauren exploded. "That's not fair!"

Billy held up a card that proudly proclaimed a four.

Carter flipped up his card and showed an eleven. Again, everyone gaped at him, causing him to exclaim, "What?" a little defensively.

David looked back over at Lauren. "Are you sure I can't—"

"David…" Dev warned in a low voice.

Wendell held up a three, and Billy hit Wendell over the head with his card.

Lauren rolled her eyes.

Judd turned his card over very slowly, looking as though he wanted to die. His read a three.

"Don't worry about him, Lauren." Beth snorted. "You weren't getting any higher if he wanted to go home to his current wife tonight."

"Smart man," David pronounced knowingly.

The audience cheered and Gary Kramer eased back into the scene. "And now for our final guest. A man from the lovely country of Ireland."

Lauren shook her head. *How in the world did they find you, Alex?*

A devastatingly handsome man in tight jeans, boots, and a faded denim shirt swaggered on stage. "This is a live television program, right?" he asked in a thick brogue.

"Yes."

"Good. Because I just have two things to say. First off, Lauren, love, I hope you're sending me a weddin' invitation." He blew a kiss into the camera and Lauren's face broke into a huge smile. "Second… Ireland forever!" And with that, Alex began ranting about the English and hostile occupations and a host of other things until he was bodily dragged off stage.

The show ended in chaos and Lauren took the remote from Dev's lifeless hand. She turned off the television, casting the room into the muted light from a single lamp.

Dev licked her lips before speaking. "You never told me that one of your lovers was a black man."

"I didn't think it was important," Lauren said honestly, though she knew her father would go into cardiac arrest if he heard. "Is it?"

David and Dev shared a look. "David—?"

David lifted a hand. "I'll talk to Press Secretary Allen in the morning so we can head off any hillbilly fallout."

Tuesday, April 19th

Dev slept peacefully, her arms wrapped tightly around Lauren, who had her face buried in her pillow and was snoring gently. When the alarm sounded, Dev was up like a shot with Lauren close behind.

Lauren's heart instantly leapt into her throat. She hated that damn alarm; it only signaled horrible things.

Dev slipped quickly into the sweats that had been tossed at the side of the bed and hastily pulled her sleep-wrinkled T-shirt out of the waistband, cinching the drawstrings.

Lauren, still partly in a daze, stumbled a little as she moved for her robe. She grabbed it and brought it back with her to bed so she could slip it over her pajamas if need be.

Dev retrieved a pair of socks from the dresser, plopped down on the floor and put them on while giving a voice command. "Videophone, cue on my location." The lens of the videophone dutifully shifted to where Dev was sitting, putting the bed containing Lauren well out of sight. "Marlowe, access code delta six, omega three, six, five, seven, gamma…." She rattled off a long list of numbers and letters before ordering the alarm to cease.

Lauren watched as a video feed, which was still a lifeless blue square, appeared above the small desk in the corner of the room. She reached for the nightstand and, out of habit, sleepily slipped on her glasses, amazed that Dev could remember all those priority codes when it seemed the world was about to crash down around them.

Dev stood and moved to the chair at the desk, the camera following her as the feed from the Situation Room flared to life. "What's going on?"

"Madam President," a young Air Force officer, who looked exceptionally pale, addressed her, "Freedom Six is down."

Freedom Six…Freedom Six… Mini-spy sub, her brain reminded her. Full of hardware. Dev's eyes widened as the news sank in. "Fuck!" Dev exploded as she pulled a large black box from a hidden compartment in her desk. She lifted the box and allowed its sensor to scan her retina for identification purposes. The lock opened with a quiet snap. "How long?"

"Five minutes, ma'am. Advisors are on their way here now and—"

"So am I." She pulled two files from the case and reset the lock before tucking it away. "I'll be there in three." She considered several calls she needed to make. "Scratch that. Make it fifteen. End call."

The link went dead, and Dev ran a hand through her disheveled hair as she padded quickly for the door. She paused, backtracked, and gave Lauren a kiss on the cheek. "Go back to bed." She cupped her chin with a gentle hand. "You have to sit this one out. It's highly classified."

Lauren opened her mouth, then closed it. She knew she shouldn't be asking, but, with a gulp, she did it anyway. "Are we okay here? Should we get ready to—?"

"No." Dev cringed inwardly. *Stupid.* She sighed and let her hand drop from Lauren's warm skin. "I should have said that before so you wouldn't be frightened." Her gaze softened. "You and the children are fine, I promise."

Lauren let out a relieved breath.

"I'll be back when I can," the taller woman whispered softly, smoothing the comforter over Lauren's thighs.

Lauren nodded, watching in wonder as Devlyn transformed herself from President of the United States to lover and back again, all in the blink of an eye.

Dev dashed out the door. Lauren waited until it closed, before sitting down at the desk and opening her computer. She suddenly had the urge to work on Devlyn's biography.

Dev entered the Situation Room, alert eyes scanning an interior filled with men and women pulling up various maps and information and speaking in hushed, grave tones. "Where are they?" she asked, bringing all eyes to her and a host of military personnel scrambling to their feet, their chairs scraping loudly against the floor.

"Attennnntion!" someone called out, briskly.

"At ease," she responded automatically. "Where?"

The Secretary of the Navy crossed the room, his puffy eyes still holding traces of sleep at their corners. "They are currently in the Gulf of Oman, off the coast of Iran, Madam President."

"And exactly how in the hell did they end up there? Their—?"

Before Dev could finish, the door opened. More staff members entered, including the Joint Chiefs, all five of them looking ragged. They obviously didn't respond any better than Dev to being yanked out of bed at two in the morning. Behind them came the directors of the CIA, Homeland Defense, and the National Security Agency, with David bringing up the rear.

"In my office, ladies and gentleman," Dev ordered and watched as they all filed in ahead of her. She took David by the arm and whispered in his ear. "We've got big problems here, David. Freedom Six is apparently trapped in the Gulf of Oman."

"Oh, my God." David's shoulders sagged. There was a long pause. "Do you want me to call him?"

Dev's stomach was in knots as she considered his question. "Let's wait and see exactly what we're dealing with first."

David discreetly patted her arm, very aware of the deep lines of tension on her face. "I'll be ready if you need me."

"I know you will, David." She reached out and squeezed his hand, then let go, her posture straightening and her voice taking on its normal volume and timbre. "Is everyone else on their way in?"

David tapped a small computer in his hand. "Two still haven't checked in. Their E.T.A. is six and five minutes respectively."

Dev nodded grimly and gestured for David to go into the office ahead of her, then followed, the thick wooden door closing and locking behind them.

The light in the room was dim as, twenty minutes later, the Secretary of the Navy was pointing to a location on a holomap. "This is where Freedom Six is trapped, Madam President. For reasons still unknown, their navigation system malfunctioned as they were leaving the Arabian Sea sometime last night. By the time the system went back on line, they found themselves in the Gulf of Oman."

"Once they were able, why didn't they get the hell out of there?" She threw her hands in the air. "They've got half a billion dollars of spy equipment on board."

"They tried, Madam President, but the Gulf of Oman is prone to eddies. They got caught in one and have run aground."

Dev rubbed her forehead and leaned against a table. "So they're stuck like a tractor in the mud?"

The man ground his teeth together, not liking the comparison of one of the Navy's finest, multi-million dollar vessels with a John Deere. "Unfortunately, ma'am, yes. They're stuck."

"Christ." Dev glanced around at a room full of somber faces. "So tell me, is there any way to get them out of there?"

"Not without serious risk to any vessel we send in. As you're well aware, we currently have hostile relations with nearly every country in that region. If we send in a rescue team, we risk making ourselves known to our enemies."

Dev pushed off the desk and moved toe to toe with the older man. He was tall, slim, distinguished-looking, with a head of short silver hair and a small, neatly trimmed mustache. He reminded her vaguely of her father. "I'll need a full briefing on those risks, Secretary Krenshaw."

"Yes, ma'am."

"And Jerry?"

He glanced at her in question.

"I want as many specifics as we've got time for. Educate me."

Unconsciously, he squared his shoulders. "Yes, Madam President."

Dev began to pace, thinking out loud. "Freedom Six has six crew members aboard, correct?"

Several men and women were nodding, but it was the director of the CIA who spoke. "Yes, ma'am. Four members of the Navy and two of our own people." Her expression grew even more sober. "Including the Vice President's nephew."

"I know," Dev acknowledged quietly.

"M... M... Madam President?" A short, muscular airman handed Devlyn a piece of paper. His face was bright red and Devlyn realized that he was new to his assignment and this was the first time he'd spoken to her.

"Relax," she said under her breath, allowing a very small smile to cross her face. Normally, she would have taken a moment to speak with the man and introduce herself as a person and not just a title. At the moment, however, she only had time to say, "Good job."

Such a tiny thing made such a big difference. The airman's color improved before her eyes. "Thank you, ma'am." Beaming, he stepped away, disappearing into the crowd of milling people that filled the room as Dev read the note.

And her stomach dropped.

"Shit!" Groaning loud enough to garner everyone's attention, Devlyn crushed the paper in her hand, her knuckles white.

David was instantly at her side. "Madam President?"

"Freedom Six has been detected." She handed the wadded up paper to David, her chest feeling tight.

David smoothed the paper against his thigh and passed it along si-lently, as the appropriate personnel glanced at its contents. There was a flickering of light as new maps and charts materialized in the air around the room's walls, circling them in neon.

A low murmur washed over the room, and the tension increased ten-fold.

"Ma'am?" The Secretary of the Navy laid a gentle hand on her arm. "We can't risk that technology being captured."

Dev turned her eyes to David. "Call Geoff and get him over here."

David drew in a ragged breath. "Right away." His voice broke.

While she waited for the Vice President to arrive, Devlyn went into her office and shut the door, closing out the sounds of computer key-strokes and the low rumble of voices. She clicked on the light over her desk, which cast her face in an eerie glow. She pored over the reports, several of them having just been received from Freedom Six's own crew over secure communication channels. She read them as many times as it took, until she felt she had as firm a grasp as time allowed on the dilemma at hand.

The boat was trapped on a rocky ledge and was without sufficient power to move, the propulsion system damaged beyond immediate re-pair.

Situation serious. Unable to extract. No casualties. Advise immedi-ately.

God, give me strength. She scribbled a quick note and opened her office door. A communications officer was waiting there. "Send that and let me know as soon as you have a response."

"Understood, ma'am." The young woman looked at the note. *Un-derstand situation. All options being considered. Hold tight. D. Mar-lowe.* "Right away, Madam President."

David moved around the young woman and gazed at Dev compas-sionately. "Geoff's here."

Dev swallowed hard. "Bring him to the Oval Office to wait. I'll be right in."

David's eyes cast downward. It was times like these that he was very glad he maintained a behind-the-scenes role, forsaking the visible power for something more suited to his personality. *And at least one level higher on the rungs of Hell.* "Yes, ma'am."

Dev called the Secretary of the Navy into her Situation Room office and shut the door behind her. When she emerged two minutes later, she looked pale.

She strode through the Situation Room and out into the hallway on her way to the Oval Office, hating every single step she was taking. And dreading what was to come. *No option,* her mind whispered. *It has to be done.* She stood outside the door for a long second. Then she sighed and entered.

Geoff was standing, looking out the window over the Ellipse and out to Constitution Avenue. He had one hand resting on the back of Dev's chair. When he heard the door close, he turned to her. "It must be serious for you to have called me over here in the middle of the night." He was dressed casually, and Devlyn could see a garment bag containing a suit draped over one of the sofas.

"It is serious, Geoff." She gestured to the couch. "Come on, have a seat."

Geoff deserved the direct approach, not that there was time for much else. She drew in a deep breath, her ribs expanding fully. "Freedom Six is trapped in the Gulf of Oman. There is no way to do a rescue. Hostile vessels are in the area and closing in on Freedom Six as we speak."

The blood drained from his face. "Oh, my God. My nephew is an equipment ensign on Freedom Six."

Dev's hands shaped into fists, but her voice remained calm. "I know, Geoff. That's why I called you." She hesitated and looked deeply into her old friend's eyes, wondering briefly if she might throw up. "We have to destroy that boat. We can't risk it being captured. If the equipment on board were captured, it would change the balance of power in the Middle East."

Geoff blinked at her, staring in disbelief. "He's only twenty-five years old."

Dev closed her eyes. "I know. I hate this, Geoff. I can't tell you how much I hate this. But we don't have a choice."

"Don't." He stood and looked down at her. "There has to be another way. Have we even tried a rescue?"

Dev shook her head. "Our nearest vessel is over two hours away. The next closest is one of Britain's and that's three hours out. We don't have that kind of time."

"Damn it, Dev!" He scrubbed his face wildly. "What about intercepting the enemy vessel to keep it from reaching Freedom Six?"

"Geoff," she said gently. "In fifteen minutes that submarine will be in enemy hands. We can't intercept. There's no time and it would be an unprovoked attack. Freedom Six isn't in international waters, Geoff."

Geoff fell back onto the sofa next to Dev. "Christ." He looked to her with watery eyes. "An escape pod or hatch or something for the crew?"

Dev gave a quick shake of her head.

"There's no other way?"

Her expression softened. "I swear there's not."

He nodded, resigned to the facts as tears began rolling down his cheeks.

Dev moved off the sofa and knelt in front of him. He was close to breaking apart. "Geoff, they've been maintaining radio silence, but I think they deserve the right to hear this from me directly, so I'm going to order a link established. We'll do our best to scramble it. Would you like a chance to talk to your nephew?"

"Yeah." He pulled himself from his chair and rubbed his eyes, suddenly looking far older than his years. "Let's go."

Back in the Situation Room, everyone watched as they entered and took seats at the head of the table. Dev hit the button on the communications console at her fingers. "Open a visual link with Freedom Six."

There were murmurs among the collected staff, but within seconds the link flared to life and the captain nodded to the President. "Madam President." He looked haggard, his skin a ghostly gray in the sub's emergency lights.

"Captain, I am afraid I don't have good news."

He nodded, swallowing hard. "We have been preparing for that, ma'am."

Dev gritted her teeth, forcing back the tears she could feel coming. "We have no choice," she whispered harshly, hearing several discreet sniffs from somewhere behind her.

The captain looked away, remaining silent for several long seconds. When he turned back to her, his cheeks were wet. "We would like to send a transmission for you to give to our families."

"I'll deliver them personally," Dev swore fervently, her emotions threatening to surface. "The bravery of you and your crew in the face of the impossible is astounding, Captain."

The captain sighed heavily. "We've transmitted as much data as possible to help in determining what went wrong."

Dev nodded. "Is Ensign McQuire present? The Vice President would like to speak with him."

"Of course."

The image shifted to a young man who could have been Geoff's son. "Mr. Vice President," he greeted weakly, doing his best to smile bravely, though his chin was noticeably quivering.

"Jack," the man's voice cracked, and Devlyn stood and rubbed his back gently, not giving a damn what it looked like. "I wanted... wanted to tell you, I love you."

For a moment it didn't look like the ensign was going to hold it together long enough to respond. Finally, he whispered, "I love you too, Uncle Geoff. Please ta... take care of Mom for me."

"You know I will." A pained pause. "If there was any other way—"

"I know," he answered bleakly.

An aide stepped close to her and let her know that all information had been received from the boat and they were prepared to take the next, inevitable step.

"Ensign McQuire, Jack, I need to speak to the captain." *I'm sorry.*

"Yes, ma'am."

Dev firmed her jaw. "Captain, I can do this remotely from here, or you and I can enter the codes together."

"This boat and her crew are my responsibility. I'll set the codes from my end."

David handed a black envelope to Dev, and she cracked the seal. A trickle of sweat rolled down her back, causing an involuntary shiver to wash over her. As she slid the key card and the destruct codes from it, the captain was doing the same thing aboard the submarine. "I'm ready when you are, ma'am." She could hear the Lord's Prayer being recited somewhere behind the captain, and several people in the Situation Room joined in the barest of whispered voices.

Dev glanced sideways at Geoff with watery eyes. "Do you want to leave?"

He shook his head curtly. "No. I'm staying."

"All right," she whispered, laying everything out in front of her and reading the card. Through force of will alone, she managed to keep her hand from shaking as she picked up the key card and swiped it through the console in front of her. "Enter six, three, seven, three, five, seven, six."

The image of the captain could be seen punching in the numbers as directed. "Destruct protocol in place," he told her dutifully.

Dev stared at the man in something close to awe. "I don't know what to say to you or your crew."

He sniffed once. "There's nothing to say, Madam President."

"Thank you, Captain." Dev's jaw silently worked for a few seconds. It felt as though ten men were standing on her chest. "God bless."

A computer-generated voice began a count down. "Destruct sequence initiated."

"In five," Dev's voice cracked as she laid her hand on the button that she herself was required to push. She quickly made a fist, trying to wipe the sweat from her fingers. "Four, three, two..." As she said "One" she pressed the red button and the link went dead.

Dev closed her eyes and concentrated on her breathing. She felt a little light-headed, but appeared the very picture of calm, contemplative leadership.

The entire room was silent for more than two minutes, each person's breathing sounding unusually loud in the quiet room. Finally the Secretary of the Navy handed her a piece of paper. "The boat is destroyed, ma'am."

It was two hours before dawn by the time Devlyn made her way back to her quarters. She'd cleared her calendar for the following morning and left word with David that she wanted to visit the houses of each of the now-deceased servicemen as soon as possible and that the press was not to be informed about the trips.

She slowly pushed open her bedroom door, glad to see Lauren had decided to stay. The younger woman was lying in an uncomfortable position, her glasses still on, her small computer perched on her chest as she slumbered.

Dev used her feet to push off her shoes, then sat down heavily in a red wingback chair near the bed, staring at Lauren with dull eyes as she watched her partner's chest rise and fall with each peaceful breath. She tried to focus on the woman in front of her, but the night's events were still too raw to be pushed from the forefront of her mind, no matter how much she tried.

"Destruct sequence initiated." Stop it! *"Please ta... take care of Mom for me."* Her eyes began to burn. *"In five, four, three..."* STOP IT! She leaned forward, her elbows on her knees and brought her palms to her eyes, feeling her breathing hitch. *I'm sorry. God, I'm so sorry.*

"Devlyn," came the sleep-husky voice. Lauren struggled to sit up in bed, temporarily confused at waking up alone but in the President's room. She pushed her small laptop onto the floor. "Darlin'?"

Dev glanced up at Lauren in agony.

Lauren scrambled out of bed and dropped to her knees in front of the other woman, gently brushing her knuckles against Dev's cheek as she worriedly searched her face. "What's wrong?" The bolt of worry that lanced through her was nearly enough to make her dizzy. She'd never seen Dev look quite so undone.

The softly spoken words so full of concern did it. The tears that had been brutally pushed back all night rushed forward with a vengeance. Dev's breathing hitched again and she began to cry.

"C'mere." Shoving down her own panic, Lauren stood and led Dev back to the bed by one hand. She quickly adjusted a pillow and then climbed in, silently asking her lover to join her with a pat on the bed next to her.

Dev eagerly complied, lying down with her head on Lauren's chest and feeling strong arms wrap themselves around her in silent support. "I'm… I'm sorry, I didn't mean—"

"Shh…" Lauren admonished gently, her heart aching for her friend. "You don't have to apologize for this." She kissed the top of Dev's head.

It took a long time for the tears to slow, then stop, as the exhaustion that always follows a good cry began to take over. Lauren whispered words of reassurance and comfort the entire time, one hand gently tracing Dev's back in a calming motion. Finally, the sky began to take on the faintest hint of pale purple and she knew, without looking at the clock, that it would be dawn in a few moments. "Do you want to talk about it?" Lauren asked in a low voice, punctuating her question with a soft kiss near Dev's ear.

Did she? Dev was surprised to find that she did. And so, leaving out many of the classified details, Devlyn told Lauren the entire story. Ending with a ragged, "Geoff's… Oh, Jesus, Geoff's nephew was… was on board. I'm sorry. I'm…" the words trailed off into a mournful sigh.

Lauren's eyes shimmered with tears, and it took a moment to speak around the lump that had grown in her throat. "Was he there? Geoff, I mean." She felt Devlyn nod against her, moving her T-shirt, which was now damp with tears. "Oh, God," she whispered, tightening her hold on Dev. "I can't believe you had to do that. How horrible."

Dev shifted a little, her body stiff from lying in the same position for so long. "Don't feel sorry for me," she said flatly. "I wasn't blown to bits."

"Stop that," Lauren responded gently but firmly. "Of course I hurt for you, Devlyn," she murmured emotionally. "I hurt for you most of all." *God, she didn't just order it done. She did it herself.* Lauren shivered inwardly, horrified. Half of her was angry that Dev couldn't have delegated this soul-numbing task to a soldier whose job it was to kill. But the other half of Lauren was fully aware of how selfish that was. And that Devlyn would never expect someone to do something that was her responsibility. Problem was, sometimes it seemed like the entire world was her responsibility.

Dev's eyes began to burn again, and she sucked in a quick breath, fearing she was going to start crying all over again. "I-I'm not supposed to be doing this," she said helplessly, suddenly seeming very lost.

With the hand on her back, Lauren could feel Dev's heart rate pick up.

"I'm supposed to be strong."

"You don't have to be strong all the time, Devlyn," Lauren said with a sad smile. "Not like this, here with me." She sighed. "After what's happened, I'd be worried if you were doing anything else, honey. This is exactly right." She kissed Dev's head again. "Exactly."

Lauren's voice sounded so sure that Devlyn had no choice but to believe. She couldn't help herself. In a moment of crystalline clarity, Dev knew that this was something she'd needed for a long time. Some burdens couldn't be carried alone. Some secrets, she realized, needed to be shared if she was going to keep her sanity.

The blonde woman felt Devlyn begin to relax and her breathing slow and grow steady. "I love you" Dev burred, her voice the barest of whispers.

That's it, darlin'. Relax. Sleep. "I love you too." She stayed sitting up in bed, awake, thinking, with Dev pressed tightly against her chest sleeping, as the sun rose over the White House and another day began.

MAY 2022

Thursday, May 12th

Lauren pulled shut the door to her White House quarters and adjusted the strap to her laptop as she juggled her briefcase.

"Lauren," Ashley called from the other end of the hall, just as she began to dash toward her. "Wait."

Lauren glanced at her watch and schooled herself in patience. She was already late for an interview with the Secretary of Health and Human Services, who had known Devlyn since graduate school. "Hi, Ashley."

The girl came to a sliding stop in front of Lauren. "You can't go," she said a little desperately, a panicky look chasing its way across her face.

Lauren's eyebrows jumped. "I have an appointment. I—"

Ashley grabbed hold of Lauren's arm and dug her heels into the thick carpet. "Please!"

"Ashley, I don't understand. I—"

"Mom just called. Today's parent/teacher conference day."

"Uh huh." She gazed at Ashley expectantly.

"And she's stuck at some fund-raising speech in Chicago."

Lauren's eyes widened a touch. "Still? She was supposed to be back hours ago." Sometimes she just didn't know where the time went.

"She said I could ask you if you'd go in her place."

Lauren's gaze was soft and questioning. "Ashley, your mom should really be the one to go to that sort of thing, shouldn't she?"

"Please, Lauren?"

Pale brows drew together. Ashley looked especially desperate. Something wasn't right. "Are you sure, honey? I'm not—"

"Puhleeeeeeeeez!"

A deep sigh. "It's not that I don't think I should go." *Mostly.* "It's that I know your mom hates to miss this sort of thing. Can't you reschedule?"

Ashley shook her head wildly. "Nuh uh. The teacher gets mad when that happens. She's mean to kids whose parents make her wait and wait."

Lauren's eyes sparked. "Did she do that to you last semester?" She remembered Devlyn having to reschedule three times before she could attend the conference that took place just before Thanksgiving.

"Well, not exactly," Ashley admitted reluctantly, digging her toe into the navy blue carpet. "But Cathy Simpson told me when her dad missed his appointment that—"

Lauren held up her hand and let out a deep breath, then she looked down into those pleading brown eyes and began to melt. *Crap.* Any other arguments simply died on her lips. Her shoulders slumped in defeat. "What time?"

A relieved grin lit Ashley's face. "Fifteen minutes."

"Ashley!" Lauren's eyes widened in alarm, and she yanked open her bedroom door. "You could have given me a little time," she complained, tossing her computer and brief-case on her bed. She ran nervous hands through her hair. "What should I wear?"

Ashley blinked. "Huh?"

"Clothes, Ashley," she said as she dialed Beth's number. She quickly explained the situation and asked Beth to reschedule her appointment. She scowled when Beth chuckled and wished her luck. *What was that all about?* She tossed the phone alongside her briefcase and refocused on the eight-year-old. "Can I wear this or do I need to change?" Never mind that what she was wearing was good enough for her business meeting. This was something… well, parental and she wanted to be prepared.

Two sets of eyes fixed on Lauren's tailored, russet-colored pants suit. Lauren held open her unbuttoned trench coat to give Ashley a better look.

Ashley shrugged. "You look fine to me."

Lauren sighed. "What does your mom wear?"

"I dunno." Ashley sat down on the bed. "What did your parents wear?"

Lauren thought about that for a moment. "I doubt they ever went to one." *That would have required Mama getting out of bed and Daddy coming home before eight.* She felt an instant pang of guilt for the unkind thought and mentally chastised herself.

"Oh, I get it," Ashley explained in a very grown up way. "They didn't have teacher conferences in the olden days when you were a kid."

Lauren gaped. "Olden days? I'm not *that* old." She grabbed Ashley's hand. "C'mon. I don't want to be late. Your teacher gets me in a business suit."

"It's pretty," Ashley assured her as Lauren dragged her down the hall.

Lauren stopped dead in her tracks and pulled the girl into an unexpected, enthusiastic hug. "Thanks."

"Lauren?"

The writer continued to squeeze her. "Yeah?"

"Yo… you're squishing me," Ashley croaked, her words muffled against Lauren's chest.

Lauren released her instantly. "Sorry." She winced.

Ashley thought about how Lauren was acting. "Don't be nervous. It's just a conference."

"You're pretty smart, you know that?" Lauren patted her cheek.

Ashley beamed. "Thanks."

Two minutes later they, along with Amy, the Secret Service Agent assigned to Ashley, were in a car being driven to Brightwood Elementary. President Marlowe believed that public schools were the backbone of the U.S. education system and that they needed her support. So despite the logistical nightmare caused by security concerns, all her children attended public institutions. Dev also understood that private schools offered subjects and smaller class environments that public schools simply couldn't. Toward that end, for an hour everyday after school, a tutor came to the White House, alternately instructing Ashley in art history and French.

It was a compromise that let Devlyn do what she thought was best for her children, while still allowing her to put her money where her mouth was when it came to support of public education.

Lauren turned away from the window. It was starting to rain. "So, are you ready?" She smiled at the little girl, who was wearing her trench coat over her jeans and sweatshirt.

"Ready for what?"

"The conference, of course."

"This is a parent/teacher conference." There was a long pause until Ashley finally gave Lauren a significant look. "I'm the *kid*. There is no 'kid' in parent/teacher."

Lauren scowled. "I knew that." *Shit. Duh.* "So why are you here then?"

"Because you dragged me along." Ashley giggled. "I tried to tell you but you just kept saying we're gonna be late. We're gonna be late."

Lauren smiled guiltily. "I did, didn't I?" She reached over and tickled Ashley's midsection, causing the girl to gasp and squeal with delight. "You won't rat me out to your mom, will you?"

Ashley finally fended off Lauren's hands and raised a single dark eyebrow in a move so reminiscent of Devlyn that Lauren's heart actually clenched. "Depends on whether you rat me out," Ashley told her. "I think we can reach a compromise."

Lauren's eyebrows crawled up her forehead. "You do, do you?" She pinned Ashley with a look of her own. "What have you done, you little troublemaker?"

Ashley bit her lip, her bravado evaporating as quickly as it had appeared. "Nothing."

Lauren waited.

"Much."

The writer groaned as the sedan pulled up in front of the school. "Oh, boy."

"I'll wait here," Ashley offered innocently, her face coloring as she thought of what Lauren was going to find out.

Lauren took Ashley's hands and squeezed them gently. "It's nothing that's going to give me a heart attack, is it?" *God, she's only eight, how bad can it be?* She glanced hopefully at Amy when Ashley wouldn't meet her gaze.

Amy smiled encouragingly. "You're going to be late," she reminded.

Lauren sighed and exited the car, along with an agent from the front passenger seat. Together, they entered the school.

"When did they shrink everything, Brendan?" Lauren asked, increasing her pace and eyeing the numbered classrooms as she walked briskly down the hall.

The stout agent laughed. "I think you just grew, Ms. Strayer."

Lauren wrinkled her nose. "At least it smells the same."

Brendan's alert eyes scanned the hallway. "I went to Catholic school," he said absently.

"It didn't smell like dust, kid sweat, and stinky feet?"

They both laughed.

"Yes," he admitted, "it did. And sometimes incense."

Lauren stopped outside room thirty-six B and stepped aside as a young couple hurried out of the room. They looked stricken and were mumbling something about killing little Jimmy. The blonde swallowed hard, feeling a bit like she was about to face a firing squad herself. *Hey, I didn't do anything wrong.* But a million guilty memories of all the horrible things she'd done in school assailed her. *This must be one of those "I hope it happens to you someday" moments Daddy warned me about.*

Brendan stuck his head into the room, seeing no one but Ashley's teacher waiting impatiently at her desk. He also caught sight of another agent's head through one of the small windows. A voice from a tiny transmitter in his ear gave the all-clear signal. "I'll wait out here if you like, ma'am." He gave Lauren his best wishing look.

"Coward," she mumbled, but Lauren drew in a deep breath and marched into the classroom. *I've interviewed the Pope, for God's sake. I can do this.* She mentally whimpered. *I think.*

The walls were covered with construction paper collages, posters showing the alphabet in cursive, and brightly colored maps. Row after row of desks was neatly lined up facing a large, clean whiteboard. It was cheerful, though a little overcrowded.

The woman behind the desk, Mrs. Lynch, was nearly sixty, with hair dyed a bright reddish color that reminded Lauren of a rusty bucket. Her desk was painfully organized, with the papers on it placed in perfect piles and the pencil can containing pencils all the same length. Ashley's teacher was short and plump, and her face held a perpetually annoyed look.

"Weren't you every elementary teacher I ever had?" Lauren asked under her breath, extending her hand and smiling brightly at the woman, who didn't smile back. "I'm Lauren Strayer. I'm here to talk about Ashley Marlowe."

Mrs. Lynch studied Lauren for a few seconds before saying, "Hello, Ms. Strayer." She didn't take Lauren's hand.

The reception was so frosty Lauren fought the urge to shiver. Apparently, Mrs. Lynch found something lacking in her. *Been there, done that. The more things change, the more they stay the same,* Lauren thought wryly.

"Won't you sit down?" The woman gestured to a chair in front of her desk, before reclaiming her own seat.

Lauren nodded and then nearly fell when she sank down into the midget chair. "Whoa!" Her head was now a full foot lower than Mrs. Lynch's. "Ugh." Lauren tried to move, but her rear end was crammed between the arm rails of the child's seat. "Can you even see me down here?"

Mrs. Lynch was not amused. "I just received a phone call from President Marlowe, sending her regrets and saying that you would be attending in her place."

Lauren shook her head. God love her, Devlyn was not only a work-aholic, she was an anal-retentive one at that. Thank goodness. "The President takes her role in Ashley's education very seriously, Mrs. Lynch. I hope you know that."

"And what about you?"

"Me too. Of course," Lauren said quickly, feeling as though she'd already made a tactical blunder. "I may not be Ashley's mother, but I do care very much how she does in school."

Mrs. Lynch smiled briefly, showing off canines that were just a lit-tle too pointy.

God, I'll bet you scare the shit out of the kids. "I'll do my best to convey everything you say to the President."

This seemed to perk Mrs. Lynch up a bit. And for a few moments she diligently explained Ashley's progress in her studies. She showed Lauren several of Ashley's math papers and drawings from art class, giving Lauren a very good idea of where Ashley needed to work harder and where she was doing quite well.

Lauren quickly became absorbed in the discussion and began re-thinking her initial and mostly negative impression of Mrs. Lynch. The woman clearly took Ashley's education very seriously. She forgot to worry about whether she was doing this right as she focused on the task at hand, her nervousness fading with each passing second.

Finally, when it seemed there was no more to talk about, Mrs. Lynch said, "I suppose Ashley explained to you and President Marlowe the shocking disciplinary incident that happened yesterday?"

Lauren's stomach lurched. *Shocking?* "Of course," she lied, after all, maybe Ashley had told Devlyn. "But I'd like to hear things from your perspective, Mrs. Lynch."

"Of course you would."

Lauren's lips thinned.

"Ashley got caught passing notes. *Again.*" Mrs. Lynch opened her desk drawer and a rank smell wafted from it.

Lauren turned a little green around the gills. "God."

Mrs. Lynch slammed the drawer shut in irritation, a piece of tat-tered paper in her hand. "It's where I keep my tuna sandwiches. The refrigerator in the teacher's lounge broke last spring and there's no money in the budget to repair it." She raised her eyebrows at Lauren, who looked back at her blankly.

"That's too bad," Lauren finally offered, wondering what Mrs. Lynch expected her to do about it.

Disappointed, Mrs. Lynch thrust out her hand. "Here is the note."

"Okay…" Lauren said slowly, eyeing the evidence of Ashley's unknown, dastardly deed warily. "Is it really that bad?"

"Judge for yourself." Mrs. Lynch sniffed haughtily and shook the many-times-folded piece of paper.

Lauren took it and opened it with not a little trepidation. The scrawled letters were large and uneven, though she could see they'd been carefully penned.

Dear John. I desided you can kiss me like you asked. But only on the cheek. If you still want to circle yes or no.

—Ashley

The word yes was circled by a bold heart. Lauren smiled gently when she finished. *Oh, Ashley.* She refolded the paper and put it in her pocket, ignoring Mrs. Lynch's disapproving stare. This didn't need to go in that permanent record teachers were always talking about. Surely Devlyn would want to keep it. "What seems to be the problem, Mrs. Lynch? This doesn't seem so horrible. Did they sneak out of class and make out in the coat room or something?" Lauren knew from personal experience that that would get you six weeks' detention.

Mrs. Lynch's back went ramrod straight. "Of course not!"

Lauren's eyes narrowed, and she felt her pulse pick up as a horrible thought occurred to her. "Is there any reason to believe this is something other than two kids just being kids? John isn't another teacher or a janitor or something?"

"Good heavens, no!" Mrs. Lynch looked like she was about to swallow her own tongue. "John is in Ashley's class. He's a good boy and excellent student, though Ashley does seem to distract him from his work. It's not the content of the note that is the problem, Ms. Strayer. That, I assure you, is quite normal."

Lauren thought she noticed a slight inflection on the word normal, but let it pass, deciding that calling Ashley's teacher a bitch wouldn't make the little girl's school life any better. "Then what?"

"It's what Ashley did after I read it to the class that was highly problematic."

Lauren's face hardened, and her gray eyes glinted with sudden anger. "After you did *what*?"

The look on Lauren's face caused Mrs. Lynch to involuntarily flinch. "I know it seems harsh, but—"

"You read this in front of everyone?"

Mrs. Lynch lifted her chin defiantly. "It's my policy to share notes. It discourages children from passing them."

Lauren felt her temper rising fast. "So your policy is to embarrass children as a method of discipline? Do you make slow children wear dunce caps as well? Or do you just brand them with a big D?"

Mrs. Lynch's face turned brick red. "I have been teaching in this God forsaken city for forty years, Ms. Strayer. I have thirty-nine students in my class. I have to keep—"

"What you have to do is teach these kids and treat them with respect," Lauren snapped. "Mrs. Lynch," she ground out, "I'm not a member of the local school board. You can take your complaints about your refrigerator and class sizes to them. I'm here for Ashley. *She* is who I'm concerned with." Lauren forced herself to take a slow, deep breath. "What happened after you read the note?"

Mrs. Lynch licked her lips. "Well… She grew very upset while I was reading it and asked me to stop, which I couldn't do. If I did it for her I'd have to do it for the other children. Just because she's the President's daughter doesn't mean she gets special treatment." She looked away briefly before unflinchingly meeting Lauren's eyes. "Then she began to cry."

Lauren's hands shaped into twin fists. "And," she prodded in voice far calmer than she felt.

"And then she called me an inappropriate name."

"Was it bitch?"

Mrs. Lynch gasped. "No!"

Lauren gave her a false smile. "Go on."

"It was," Mrs. Lynch paused for effect, "'battle-axe.'"

Lauren rolled her eyes. "That's the big trauma?"

"She said it in front of the entire class!" Mrs. Lynch defended hotly. "What sort of showing of respect is that? She should be setting an example."

"You read her private note to the entire class," Lauren shot back. "Maybe she's learning to be respectful from you?" With a grunt, she pried her butt out of the tiny chair and leaned forward until she was nose to nose with the teacher. "I don't know if it makes you happy to make little girls cry, but I do know this. Lady, you *are* a battle-axe."

She pinned Mrs. Lynch with a fierce glare. "What Ashley did was wrong. What you did was worse."

She leaned even closer. "Our conversation today had better not have a negative effect on the way you treat Ashley. She's a good kid who doesn't deserve your contempt." Abruptly, Lauren picked up the folder that contained Ashley's school papers. "Are we finished?"

Mrs. Lynch was too stunned to speak.

"Looks like we are." Without another word, Lauren strode out of the room, giving the next two waiting parents a grim smile as she passed them. She could see Ashley and Amy waiting on a bench at the end of the hallway, and Brendan quietly fell in step behind her, communicating their location status to the other agents.

Lauren could see Ashley looked pale and frightened. She stopped in front of the little girl, who refused to meet her stare. "Ashley," she said quietly.

Ashley glanced up, her soft brown eyes brimming with tears. "She read it to everyone." Her voice cracked, and so did Lauren's heart.

The blonde woman crouched down and silently opened her arms to Ashley.

The girl flew into them and began mumbling her apologies between her sobs.

"Shh… It's okay."

"Every… everybody la… laughed."

"I know, sweetie. That wasn't very nice." Lauren kissed the top of Ashley's head and hugged her as tightly as she dared. She let Ashley cry for several moments before she gently pushed her away and wiped wet cheeks with tender fingers. "You know you shouldn't have been passing notes in school, right?" Intently, she studied Ashley's face.

Ashley nodded, relieved that Lauren hadn't mentioned the note's content.

"And that no matter how utterly and completely fitting the name battle-axe might be," she smiled and Ashley let out a surprised burst of laughter, smiling back, "you're not allowed to say things like that to anyone. Much less a teacher. Even if they deserve it." Her voice turned serious. "Got me, darlin'?"

Ashley sniffed and the tension drained from her body, leaving her as limp as a dish rag. "Got you. I apologized after I said it."

Lauren gazed at her in understanding. "I figured you did." She gave her a quick kiss on the cheek, then straightened and wrapped her arm around slender shoulders. Okay, so she hadn't handled the teacher as well as she could have. But she still felt a little proud of herself. Ashley seemed to feel better, and the girl knew she'd done something wrong. So the afternoon wasn't a complete bust. "Do you want me to talk to your mom about you going to a different class?"

"No!" The girl looked a little panicky. "I like my class."

Lauren wasn't surprised. Ashley didn't seem reluctant to attend classes, as she herself had been. "Is Mrs. Lynch a good teacher, Ashley?"

Ashley thought about that for a second before nodding. "Except when she reads notes out loud," she added sullenly.

An indulgent smile twitched at the corners of Lauren's lips. "That was pretty rotten." She sighed. "Honey, your teacher does a hard job under tough conditions. Maybe she was just having a bad day. I know it seems impossible, but teachers are people too and everyone can have a bad day and make bad choices." She lifted an eyebrow. "Like passing notes in class instead of paying attention." In truth, that was more charitable toward Mrs. Lynch than Lauren wanted to be. But Ashley was a child inclined to forgive easily, and she didn't want to influence that with her own opinion.

Ashley winced. "I understand. I guess."

Lauren ruffled the girl's dark hair. "Good."

"Lauren?"

"Hmm?"

"Are you going to tell Mom?"

Lauren cringed as she thought back to her own harsh words. "I don't want to."

"Yes!" Ashley pumped her fist in the air.

The cringe intensified. "But I think I have to."

Ashley's face fell, but she didn't seem surprised.

They all started for the car. As they stepped outside, they were greeted with a blast of cool air that smelled like wet grass. It was still raining and shallow puddles had formed on the sidewalk, snaking their way into the schoolyard. Two of the agents popped open umbrellas and held them over Lauren and Ashley.

"Don't worry, honey," Lauren said, "before I tell your mother anything I intend to bribe her." *Kisses. Backrubs. Oh, yeah, this could be good.*

Ashley's face wrinkled in confusion. "For me?"

Lauren snorted. "Nuh uh. For me. You've got that short, adorable kid thing going. I, on the other hand, need all the help I can get."

The agents rolled their eyes and sniggered.

"What?" Lauren complained, taking off her wet glasses and stuffing them in her blazer pocket. "I do."

Dev tossed the pen down on her desk and stood up to stretch. Rolling her neck, she decided to take a walk through the plane and see what the press was up to. The group was on its way back to Washington after spending two days touring Jefferson County, Kentucky, which had been hit by multiple tornadoes in the past week. The devastation was severe, and Dev had promised federal aid to help the people rebuild their homes and businesses.

Thinking of home and a hot bath, she wandered to the back of Air Force One and entered the area where the press always traveled. As soon as they realized she was in the room, several of the reporters stood to greet her. She smiled and waved them off. "Relax, everybody. I'm just stretching my legs." Devlyn was dressed in black slacks and a casual sweater, having discarded her blazer after entering the plane. Taking a seat on a table in the front of the room, she let her hands rest in her lap.

"That was a good trip, ladies and gentlemen."

A round of general murmurs of approval met her words, and she relaxed further into her seat, pleased that things had gone so smoothly.

"How are the wedding plans, Madam President?" The reporter from the *Post* continued to twirl the pen in his hand, but made no move to record Devlyn's words. The atmosphere with the press on Air Force One was decidedly casual, with a certain level of mutual trust and respect between all the parties.

Devlyn laughed and bit her lip. "I'm not sure my mother is speaking to me at the moment. I haven't been around much lately and I haven't given her or my social secretary as much input as they would like. Unfortunately, or fortunately depending on how you look at it," blue eyes twinkled, "most of my participation has been via telephone and email."

A woman in the back lifted her camera high over her head, and Dev gave her a quick nod. Permission granted to take photos.

"Actually, Michael Oaks and my mom are working very hard to make sure things go off without a hitch. I'm a little worried though, because Secretary Oaks came into my office the other day and asked Lauren and me, 'blue or white?' That was it, nothing else, and he didn't say what I was giving my opinion on."

"You could have asked," a press corps member reminded her wryly.

"I could have," Dev agreed, saying nothing more.

"So what color did you select?"

"I said blue."

"And Ms. Strayer?"

"She looked up from her laptop and grunted what I assumed to be her agreement. Sometimes she gets a little engrossed in her work. I can't imagine how that could happen."

This time Devlyn joined in the laughter. "I may have agreed to something totally hideous." She adjusted herself at the table and got more comfortable. "Keep your fingers crossed for me."

"Madam President, getting information about the wedding has been darn near impossible."

"You don't say?" Dev answered wryly.

"Is there anything you can tell us?"

"C'mon, Madam President," another reporter joined in. "Throw a wild pack of dogs a bone."

Dev thought for a moment, then nodded. "I can tell you that the wedding will be a small ceremony held in Ohio with our family and friends. A few members of the press will be invited to the reception, sans cameras…"

There was a chorus of groans.

"But the ceremony will be private." Dev nearly laughed at the devastated looks on their faces. "Don't worry, when Lauren and I get back from our honeymoon, we'll host a formal reception at the White House. It should be a grand event, and cameras, and all of you, will be welcome."

Dev's expression went serious. "As most of you know, Lauren is an extremely private woman, who is still adjusting to life in the public eye. But even if she were used to all the hounding, it wouldn't matter. Our wedding is something just for us that we want to share with the people we love. I hope you can all respect that."

"How do your children feel about this?"

A smile crossed Dev's face. "My children are ecstatic. They love

Lauren, as does my entire family. As a matter of fact, Lauren has already attended her first parent/teacher conference, while I was stuck in Chicago."

Devlyn remembered how nervous Lauren had been when she explained what happened at the parent/teacher conference. The blonde woman had waited until Dev was nearly asleep and had been buttered up to the max before spilling the beans. Dev hated having to punish Ashley, but the look on her daughter's face when told that her next month's allowance would be donated to the charity of her choice, assured Dev she was doing the right thing. Ashley would hold her tongue next time. Or, as Lauren pointed out, be really, really poor.

Devlyn still wasn't quite sure why Lauren used her last three weeks' poker winnings to buy a used refrigerator and have it sent to Ashley's school. She silently vowed to ask more about that later.

"Have you considered running for a second term?"

The question brought Dev out of her musings. "I've been considering it, but before I make a firm decision, there's a lot I need to discuss with my family and my advisors."

"Where are you going on your honeymoon?"

Dev was used to the ping-ponging of questions from topic to topic, and she easily rolled with the punches. "I have no idea. The honeymoon is Lauren's wedding gift to me, and it's a surprise."

"Is it hard to keep a surprise from you?"

Devlyn rolled her eyes. "You'd think it would be, wouldn't you? But I can assure you she and my chief of staff are managing quite nicely. As President, most of the surprises I get aren't that pleasant, so this will be a very nice change of pace. I'm just holding my breath and hoping that we'll get two weeks together that aren't interrupted by anything big." She blinked as she thought about what she'd said. Then she reached over to the table and knocked on it twice. "You don't need to print that last statement; let's not tempt fate and give the nuts any ideas."

"Will Ms. Strayer assume the typical duties associated with being First Lady?"

"That will be up to Lauren. I do know that she has hired Beth McMillian as her chief of staff. I think she and David McMillian will be the first husband and wife team in history acting as chiefs of staff."

"Madam President, just about everything associated with your presidency is a first."

Dev smiled. "True enough."

"Will Ms. Strayer be taking the name Marlowe?"

Devlyn was careful to keep her expression neutral when she answered this question. Samantha had eagerly taken her name. Dev knew she was being silly and that her ego was rearing its sometimes-inflated head, but the fact that Lauren wanted to keep her name had stung a little. It wasn't until Lauren teasingly suggested that they could solve the problem by Devlyn and the children taking the name Strayer that Devlyn realized how silly she was being. "No, she'll be keeping her name. As will I."

"Isn't it traditional for the wife—" The man stopped midsentence, clamping his jaw down hard as he felt his face heat

"The wife to take her husband's name?" Devlyn finished gently, feeling sorry for the man and hoping that the other reporters would have mercy on him and not quote him. "I believe it is. Though it's increasingly rare. However, since there will be no husband in this marriage, we'll be making our own traditions, don't you think?"

The man nodded, grateful Dev had taken his stupid comment in her stride.

"It's a brave new world, people. Let's not chicken out now." She clapped her hands together. "Enough business. Who wants to play cards?"

Friday, May 20th

Dev was looking forward to calling it a day and grabbing a shower before the party. It wasn't being called a bachelor or bachelorette party, it was just "The President's party" and Lauren's was just hers. The children had indignantly demanded their own when they found out they weren't invited to the others. And their mother had eagerly complied. By necessity and protocol, her children were excluded from ninety-nine percent of the social events at the White House. When an opportunity arose for them to have their own fun, she never begrudged it.

She couldn't help but grin as she recalled Ashley saying, in a slightly miffed voice, "Fine, be that way, but don't be surprised if I don't invite you to my party." When Dev inquired about what party that might be, she was told it would be held in the family room, involve *Sorry*, *Junior Monopoly*, cartoons, all the popcorn you could eat, and was "invitation only." Dev wondered if the children's party might not turn out better than the one David was planning for her.

Dev pushed away from her desk and slowly padded back to the residence. Liza trailed after her, quickly informing her of the next day's appointments, and a bevy of Secret Service and various other aides clustered around her. By the time she turned the corridor for the Presidential apartment, the Secret Service agents had taken their posts at the ends of the hallway, and she was allowed to walk the rest of the way alone. She sighed happily, already plotting the quick removal of her pantyhose and the heart-stopping kiss she wanted to give Lauren.

When she opened the door to her apartment, the smell of warm, fresh-baked cookies tickled her nose. She all but groaned.

Emma walked past holding a treat-laden tray. Dev snagged one before Emma could move it away. "Mmm... I'm still too quick for you, Emma," Dev teased as she chewed with extra relish. The only thing better than eating a cookie was eating a cookie that you weren't supposed to be eating.

"Humph." Emma glanced down at the tray. "Those are for the children's party. We managed to round up most of the children of the people attending your and Lauren's party. Besides, aren't you turning forty this year, Madam President?" Emma's eyes twinkled.

"Maybe," Dev answered warily.

"Then you should be slowing down enough for me to keep you away from the cookies soon enough."

Dev scowled at the good-natured barb, then winked at the matronly woman, reaching out to give her a fierce one-armed hug. "Have I told you lately that I love you?"

"Devil," Emma only used the Marlowe family nickname in the most private of times with the tall woman, "you know I hate that song."

Dev burst out laughing.

"But I love you too, and these children." Emma beamed at her employer and long-time friend. "I'm so happy for all of you. Lauren is a wonderful girl."

"Girl?" Dev gave Emma a look, and the older woman smiled unrepentantly. "She's not that much younger than I am!" Dev groaned. "Remind me not to tease you again, Emma."

Emma snorted, the action so enthusiastic her large bosom jiggled. "Like you ever listen."

Dev ignored that last comment, knowing it was completely true. "I did hit pay dirt with Lauren, didn't I?"

Emma nodded fondly, enjoying the gleam in Dev's eye that had been missing for so many years.

"How can one person get this lucky twice in a lifetime?" Dev marveled, looking skyward.

"Madam President," Emma said haughtily as she leaned against the sofa. "After all this time, haven't you realized that you make your own luck?"

Dev grinned broadly, loving that thought.

"Besides, I always had faith you'd find someone. You weren't meant to be alone."

Dev felt a lump developing in her throat, and she leaned over and kissed Emma's cheek as she wrestled her emotions under control. Then she stepped back. "So are you going to chaperone the kids' wild party?"

"Oh, yes, I'll be here until bedtime, then I'll take you and Lauren both up on your invitations and stop by each of your parties. But I'd better stay for the entire length of the children's party. I expect Security will have to be called in when Ashley's *Go Fish* tournament gets out of hand because Aaron has an ace up his sleeve."

Dev shook her head. "Don't give them any ideas; I can barely keep up with them as it is." She let out a slow breath as she bent and slipped off her shoes. Removing them brought her an inch closer to Emma's height. "Well, I'm off to take a shower and get dressed. Tell the kids I'll try to sneak back to tuck them in, and they get an extra hour tonight."

"Oh, goody," the older woman said dryly, rolling her eyes as she rearranged the cookies. "Have a good time until I get there. Just not too good. I don't want to miss anything. I don't get out much, you know."

Dev prudently didn't remind her about the exploits Emma and her sister had regaled her with after their Christmas cruise. When those two women got together, they were something else. "I intend to. If you need me..."

"You'll be the last to know. Later, Devil."

"See you later, Emma."

Emma waved at Devlyn as she made her way to the family room to set up her tray. Devlyn headed in the opposite direction. She blinked when she opened her bedroom door and heard the faint hum of her shower in the attached bathroom. "Her shower is still broken? I really should make sure somebody does something about that. Heh." Dark eyebrows waggled lecherously. "I wonder if she'd notice if it mysteriously broke again next week? And the week after that. And the week after that." Even though they saw each other and often slept in each other's beds, the separate quarters thing was wearing very thin for Devlyn. *Only another month,* she told herself with no little irritation.

She tossed her shoes into the corner, shucked her blazer, and began unbuttoning her green silk blouse. As it fell to the floor, she attacked her skirt, visions of Lauren's flushed, soapy body surrounded by steam spurring on her actions. "Stupid clothes," she growled, tugging furiously at her skirt's zipper.

Just as her skirt passed her hips, the water stopped. "No," Dev cried, closing her eyes. She opened the bathroom door, clad only in her bra and pantyhose. The steam poured out and it took a moment for her to spot her quarry.

"I'll give you a thousand dollars to get back in the shower," Dev begged, a puppy dog look on her face.

Lauren laughed lightly. Her blonde, wavy hair was slicked back, her skin flushed a bright pink from the hot water. She wrapped a large blue body sheet around herself, tucking the end between her breasts.

Dev whimpered.

"Sorry, can't do it, darlin'. I have to meet your mom and Beth in about twenty minutes."

"They'll understand," Dev promised. She took several steps forward and laid warm hands on the hot skin of Lauren's shoulders. "They remember what it's like to be young and in love."

"Oooo." Lauren squealed as she squirmed away. "I'm going to tell your mom you called her old."

"I never said that." Her hands reached out again. "You're misquoting me. You should go to work for the *Times*; they're always misquoting me."

"They hate you," Lauren said crossly as she picked up a wide-toothed comb from the bathroom sink and began tugging it through her hair.

"Here." Devlyn plucked the comb from her hands and gently set to work on Lauren's hair.

The smaller woman smiled, utterly charmed by the affectionate gesture.

"Tell me about it. They've done everything but print that I'm a card-carrying member of the Nazi party and out to destroy the American family with my evil lesbian ways. Ultra conservative doesn't even begin to describe that rag."

Lauren closed her eyes, enjoying the gentle attention. "Uh oh. They did another article, didn't they?"

"Oh, yeah." Regretfully, she passed the comb back to Lauren after getting out the worst of the tangles. She still needed a shower herself. *But it would have been so much more fun with you,* her mind grumpily supplied. "This time they attacked my DNA Registration Act."

Lauren just bit her lip and toweled off her face.

Dev's head tilted slightly to one side as she tried to catch a look at Lauren's face in the steam-covered mirror. Dev mimicked a slight Southern drawl. "That sucks, honey. I'm sorry."

"Okay." Lauren nodded reluctantly. "That's good. I could have said that."

"So why didn't you?"

Lauren set the comb down and turned around. Her voice was soft and warm, and she hoped it would take some of the sting from her words. "Devlyn, darlin', do we have to get into another debate over this? You know how I feel about it. I love you and I've never made my opinion public, and I never will," she reminded her firmly. "But you know there are a few issues where we differ politically. And that's one of them."

Dev made a face. "If I lose re-election by one vote you're in trouble."

Lauren just shook her head and walked out of the bathroom, leaving Devlyn to strip out of her bra and hose. She didn't miss the President's sigh of relief. She went over to the bed where she'd laid her garment bag. "Are you going to?"

"Am I going to what?" Dev called from the bathroom.

"Run again."

This brought the President back into the bedroom. They'd talked generally about this. But they'd never given it the attention it needed.

"I don't know." Dev's expression grew thoughtful. "There are days when I think yes, and then there are days when I wonder why in the hell I'm here in the first place." *And what living like this is doing to you.*

Lauren shed her towel and walked purposely back to Dev, wrapping her in a warm, skin-on-skin embrace. Reflexively, her eyes closed at the delicious sensation. "Listen to me good, Devlyn Marlowe, because I'm only gonna say this once. So don't forget it." She pressed her lips to Dev's ear, feeling warm hands splay across her back, holding her tight. She sank deeper into the embrace. "It's in your blood, Devlyn. This insanity that is the presidency. And more important, you're a good president." The hands on her back increased their pressure. "Even the people who don't agree with everything you do trust you. They are smart for doing so, Devlyn."

Lauren drew in a deep breath. "You need to do what's going to make you happy. And I'll support you no matter what that is."

Dev smiled and pulled away, reaching up to cup Lauren's cheek with one hand. "You have no idea how much that means to me."

Lauren kissed Dev's palm. "We'll talk about this more when we have time, all right?"

"Deal." Dev's brow rose as Lauren moved back to the bed and un-zipped her garment bag. "You wearing that to the party?" she squeaked loudly.

"I am." Lauren grinned. "It's a tropical-themed party, Devlyn."

Dev's mouth was still hanging open at the sight of Lauren's bright purple, flowered bikini top and the loosely fitted, wraparound skirt.

"You know, beach theme."

"Oh, yeah. Can I come?"

Lauren chuckled. "You know you can't. Besides, I know for a fact David has been planning you a really nice party." Lauren wriggled into her top, much to Devlyn's dismay. "Do you know anything about it?"

"All I know is that we're watching a boxing match. It's not tele-vised but David spoke to the promoters and we're getting a private sat-ellite feed."

Lauren grimaced. "Sounds bloody."

Dev shrugged. She'd always enjoyed that particular sport, but knew her weak-stomached partner wouldn't make it past the first bloody up-percut. "Could be. It's supposed to be a good fight. They're the two top-ranked heavyweights."

Shimmying into panties and the skirt, Lauren examined herself in the mirror. After a month of hard dieting she'd taken off twelve pounds and was nearly back to her normal weight. "Well," she kissed Dev on the cheek. "How do I look?"

"Fabulous. Let's stay in the room."

"Devlyn," Lauren scolded, but she eagerly absorbed the praise. "You won't miss me. You'll have fun watching two idiots pound each other silly."

"I always miss you," Devlyn said seriously.

Lauren just smiled. "Have fun."

Dev smiled back. "You too."

"We will."

"Don't do anything I wouldn't do."

Lauren let a thousand easy retorts ease their way from her mind before promising, "I won't." She stepped forward and laid warm palms on
Devlyn's cheeks, feeling the flesh beneath her hands ease into a genuine smile. On tiptoes, she brushed her lips against Devlyn's.

Dev turned her head and kissed Lauren's palm. "I love you." Then
she kissed her again, sinking into the moment.

Warm breath tickled Lauren's face and she relished their closeness
and the undercurrent of passion that crackled between them. "I love
you too."

The sensual rhythm of tropical drums and the smell of roasting pork
and fish floated down the hallway that led to the indoor White House
pool, causing Lauren to sniff appreciatively and her hips to pick up the
beat of the music as she walked. A relaxed smile eased across her face,
and she tried not to think about how badly she needed this. An evening
of fun and relaxation, where she could truly be herself and laugh and
drink rum punch to her heart's content. There would be no worries
about protocol or minding every word that she said. The only photographs would come from the small thirty-five-millimeter camera slung
around her neck, and they would end up in her personal scrapbook instead of the tabloids. The one missing ingredient was Devlyn, whom
she fully intended on coaxing into her bed after their respective parties
anyway.

She smiled as she walked across the thick carpeting in flip-flops she
hadn't worn since college. Beth hadn't told her much about her party
other than giving her specific instructions on what to wear and to come
hungry. The latter, Lauren admitted wryly, would not be a problem after her crash dieting. She only hoped Beth had ordered enough food.

Gremlin and his mate Princess trotted alongside her, apparently
finding the prospect of fifteen children under the age of ten too daunt-
ing to face without her, even with the prospect of eating up the moun-
tains of food that would be dropped on the floor. "Cowards."

Her pug lifted his head at her and snarled, baring his tiny crooked
teeth.

"Don't whine," Lauren chastised, giving her a pet a dismissive wave of the hand. "You know it's true."

She stopped in front of the door that led to the pool and bit her lip to keep from laughing at the agents who were standing guard. It was Jack and Brendan. Both men were wearing their suit coats, but Jack had on a pair of bright orange swimming trunks and Brendan was wearing a red bandana over his head and sporting a tie covered in gaudy palm trees.

"Ms. Strayer," both men greeted, barely able to keep a straight face.

"Agent Kieser. Agent Wochowski," Lauren replied just as formally, her gray eyes twinkling with mischievous delight. She'd been itching to see a great many of the men and women who worked for the Executive Branch in a more relaxed setting. Tonight, she would get her wish.

Lauren rocked back on her heels. "Are you going to let me in?" She could hear laughter and music behind the door, which was vibrating a little from the raucous sounds behind it. Apparently, the party had started without her. She tried to peek inside, but black construction paper had been taped over the glass windows in the door.

"I'm sorry, ma'am. We'll have to take that camera." Brendan gestured toward Lauren's chest.

Lauren blinked at them. "What are you talking about?"

"We have our orders, Ms. Strayer."

"Orders?" Lauren very nearly stamped her foot. "Christ, this is *my* party. Shouldn't I be allowed to take photographs?"

Jack and Brendan looked at each other and then back at Lauren as they both shook their heads.

Lauren's eyes narrowed.

Wordlessly, Jack opened the door, and a blast of wonderful-smelling food and pulse-pounding music nearly blew Lauren off her feet. She peered inside, her eyes growing wider with every second. "Oh, my God." Three dancers were bumping and grinding away alongside the pool, while onlookers hooted and howled their approval. *Is that Beth?* For a second Lauren was rendered mute, then a dark blush stained her cheeks and she quickly handed her camera to the smirking agents.

Smiling, she walked in. Jack shut the door behind her and turned to Brendan. "When is someone coming to relieve you so you can go to the party?" He lifted the camera.

An enormous grin split Brendan's cheeks. "Half hour. Same as you. Heh. It's gonna be great."

Click. The flash went off as Jack took the picture of his smiling fellow agent. Both men then faced forward, and their smiles disappeared as they projected their normal stoic demeanor, guarding some of the nation's most interesting people.

After her shower, Dev killed another hour checking on the kids' party and looking at some paperwork before she wandered into the multimedia room to find about two dozen of her friends and colleagues. A large table of food had been set up; it looked like it had all her favorites. Pure, unadulterated junk. She had sympathetically been staying away from fattening foods while Lauren was dieting; she figured that David knew she was near the breaking point.

David placed a cold beer in her hand and patted her on the back. "Hiya, boss." He waved a hand over the delectable spread that contained enough calories and grams of fat to end world hunger. "What's your pleasure?"

"She's having her own party by the pool."

"I meant food."

Dev lifted her chin. "I was speaking of dessert."

"Dev..." he growled playfully, glancing around to see who might have heard.

"David," she growled back with a grin, "cut me some slack and don't mother me tonight. Let me relax. These people are my friends or else they wouldn't be here." She stepped closer to David. "Except for Michael Oaks. What the hell is he doing here?"

"I had to invite him, Devlyn," he answered in a hushed voice. He chewed on his thick, red mustache unhappily. "It would have looked bad to the other staff members if I hadn't."

"I know." Devlyn sighed. Then she had a thought. "Has he seen the food?"

David thought about that for a minute. "I don't think so. He's been over in the corner sulking because I wouldn't let him plan this with me. He hasn't been over here at all."

"Hehehe. Good. This will give his Mr. Proper ass a heart attack."

"Great idea!" David gestured toward the young social secretary. "Oh, Michael," he called out. "Can you come here for a moment?"

Michael nodded and slowly got up from his seat. Everyone else was in casual clothes; he was still wearing a three-piece suit.

"I'll bet he's really hot."

They shared childish smiles. "I'll bet so too," David agreed.

Dev clasped David's shoulder and left the breaking of the news about their dining selection to her friend. Her mind drifted to Lauren's party for a moment when she glanced around the room and noticed that, while most of her friends were here, the number of male agents in attendance could be counted on a bird's foot. *This is what happens when there's a clothes-optional pool party.*

The atmosphere was relaxed and friendly and everyone was laughing as Dev regaled the group about how she had accidentally caught sight of a very naked David once during their years as college roommates.

From across the room, David gave a loud whistle to get everyone's attention. "The fight is ready to start."

"Sure it is!" someone called out.

"Very funny." He pointed to the large image that had materialized in the front of the room. "It is."

Dev happily marched up to the front of the theater and took her customary seat, placing her drink on a small table next to the chair. She chuckled when she saw that Attorney General Evelyn Sanchez had taken the seat right next to her. She liked Evelyn, and Dev was proud of the unexpectedly solid friendship and the level of trust that had grown between them since she'd appointed her.

"Why, Evelyn, I didn't know you were a fight fan."

"I'm not really. But I couldn't very well turn down an invitation to your party, now could I?" She gave Devlyn a wry grin and stole one of the M&Ms out of the large bowl on Devlyn's tray. "Besides, it'll be fun to see people other than my staff beating each other up."

Dev chuckled at the mention of last week's incident, where two deputy chiefs had gotten so frustrated with each other they had a fight inside a men's bathroom in the Department of Justice.

"That wasn't one of my stellar moments, Madam President."

Even in the darkened room, Dev could see the flush covering Evelyn's olive-toned skin. She leaned over and whispered, "I've had my share of those moments too."

The holographic image of the two boxers and a referee took center stage, making it look as if they were actually in the room. The announcer finished his spiel and a loud clang filled the theater, which was taut with anticipation. Dev turned and retrieved her beer.

"Holy Christ!" Evelyn exclaimed as she rose to her feet. "What a punch!"

Dev's head whipped around, and her eyes bugged out when she saw one of the boxers lying on the mat. The crowd was roaring, and the referee began to count to ten. "Oh, my God," Devlyn said slowly.

The bell rang.

She shot out of her seat and turned to David. "What the hell happened?" she cried in disbelief.

"It's over," he mumbled unhappily. "Didn't you see?"

Dev's hands flailed wildly. "It took two seconds!"

"It's not my fault that—"

"Whoa!" Frank Marlowe shook his head in appreciation of the perfect punch. "They just showed it again."

Dev spun back around, but the image was right where it was the last time she looked. With one boxer on the mat, unconscious, and the referee counting him out. "I missed it again!" She covered her face with her hands. "Nonononononononono."

"There it was again," David said. "Wow. What an amazing hit!"

Dev's hands flew from her face, but it was too late. She whirled around and pointed at the crowd of her friends, who were now laughing. "Is this some sort of a sick joke?"

They all pointed back at the screen, but when she turned around, she'd missed it a fourth time.

"Arghhhhhhh!" Dev wailed. The "Fight of the Century" had been a complete and total failure; no one had been expecting a K.O. in the first two seconds of the first round.

"It's over?" Dev repeated in disbelief, her eyes round. "I was robbed."

The room laughed again. The Secretary of the Army sipped his beer as a speculative looked overtook his rugged face. "That's what Jackson is gonna say when he wakes up and wonders how Maccio cleaned his clock."

Dev groaned. "Turn it off. I can't take it anymore." She moved over to David and put her arm around his shoulders. "Now what, mighty party planner?"

"Never fear, we've got digital replay. Hang on."

"Forget it, David. The entire point is seeing it happen *as* it happens."

David's mind raced for something else to do. "This is where I unveil my brilliant contingency plan for just such an occurrence, right?"

Dev smiled, relieved. "Yes."

"Damn."

Lauren leaned against the wall, an empty, still frosty, beer mug dangling loosely from her hand. She let out a deep, satisfied breath as her eyes slid closed and any remaining tension she felt eased its way out of her system. The rhythm of the music had long since seeped into her blood, and she felt a light buzz from the various margaritas, Mexican beers, and fruity island punches she'd sampled over the past several hours.

It felt sublime.

"Hello, love."

Lauren's lips twitched into a genuine smile at the sound of the deep, lilting voice.

"You didn't think you'd avoid me all night, didja?"

Lauren chuckled and opened her arms, feeling the solid warmth of Alex as he wrapped large arms around her and pulled her into a fierce hug. "I was thinking perhaps you were angry with me for appearing on that dreadful American television show?"

"Nah," Lauren answered good-naturedly, pulling back to examine her former lover with a fond eye. "I was just waiting for Beth and Janet Marlowe to finish dirty dancing with you."

Alex exploded into laughter. "Beth, that firecracker, headed off toward the bar, leaving me and Janet alone. I was havin' a high time of it too, until a man with a white beard threatened to cut off me privates if I didn't back away from his wife."

Lauren muffled her surprised snort. She glanced across the room to see Frank and Janet Marlowe slow-dancing, their bodies pressed tightly together despite the quick beat of the tropical music. "That would be Devlyn's daddy, Frank Marlowe." *Hmm... I thought he was going to the other party? Huh.*

Alex scratched his jaw as he eyed the happy couple. "Well, even though Janet laughed at his bold words, the man seemed serious enough to me. I haven't stayed alive this long by not knowing when to

quit. Besides, I'm afraid I'm not man enough for those two wild lass-
es."

Lauren backhanded him gently in the belly. "That's not true, and
you know it."

Alex just shook his head. "Lordy, if I'd known you were such a
wild bunch in Washington, I would have come years ago." He winked
at her, then his expression went a little serious. "By the way, love looks
grand on you, Lauren. I've never seen you smile so much."

Lauren beamed. "It feels as good at it looks."

"Ah," Alex sighed wistfully. "I'll just bet it does."

She patted his forearm. "It'll happen to you someday, Alex. But until then—"

"I'll continue to share myself among the ladies of the world," he interrupted, grinning from ear to ear.

Lauren nodded at the handsome, undeniably charming man. "Just to
be fair, of course."

"Of course."

They shared conspiratorial grins. Their love affair had been brief,
torrid, and sweet and had ended when Lauren had to take an extended
trip from Ireland to Italy while working on her last biography. Their
short time together was something they each recalled fondly, but both
were well aware, even then, that they were good friends and nothing
more. It was that sure knowledge that made things easy for them now.

"I must admit, I was surprised to hear who your president was marrying." He gave her a pointed look. "If I'd known you liked the ladies,
we could have double dated when you returned to Ireland. I've got a
cousin who's studying to be a nurse, with eyes the color of emeralds
and a shape that could bring a man... or woman... to her knees," he
said dreamily. "It's God's own joke that we're related and she's forbid-
den fruit for me, but you'd love her."

Lauren felt a surge of affection for her friend, and she hugged him
again. "That means a lot to me, Alex," she murmured against his broad,
dark chest. She suddenly felt as though she were going to cry. Why
couldn't her father's reaction to Devlyn have been half that accepting?
But Lauren pushed those thoughts aside for the time being; tonight was
a night for fun.

Alex opened his mouth to say something but was interrupted by a
shrill scream.

"Get him away from me," Liza cried, doing her best to slog through the pool water. In one hand was a pork-loaded sandwich, in the other a tall drink with a cheerful umbrella poking out the top. Gremlin's will power had finally snapped. His tiny teeth bared, he was doing a frantic doggy paddle, swimming after her, intent on stealing her sandwich.

Alex lifted an eyebrow. "Gremlin! I've missed him so." He stripped out of his bright Hawaiian shirt, leaving himself clad only in a pair of skimpy black Speedos. "Time to be a hero." Without another word, he bolted for the pool and executed a perfect dive into the deep end as he headed to rescue Liza's sandwich.

The noise in the room was suddenly cut in half, as nearly every woman and even a few men stopped in mid-conversation to gape at the specimen that was Alex. Multiple sighs and whistles sounded as he smoothly swam over to Liza, who nearly dropped her sandwich when his muscular torso emerged from the water.

Beth stalked over to Lauren and demanded, "What is wrong with you?"

Lauren tore her eyes off Alex long enough to say, "Huh?"

"Look at him." Beth pointed. "How can you not like men? How?"

Lauren lifted a pale eyebrow and lowered her voice so that it was for Beth's ears only. "I do like men, Beth. The damn press are the ones who, for some reason, insist I have to pick men *or* women just on principle. Well, I've got news for them, I'm—not—doing—it." Her eyes drifted to Alex again, and she smirked. "He was every bit as good as he looks too," she said, knowing full well it would torture her friend.

It did. Beth bit her lip and whimpered.

"I find both sexes attractive, but I'm in *love* with Devlyn and want to build a *life* with her. She's funny and gorgeous and sexy as hell and… and…" she put a hand on her hip, "why am I telling you all this?"

Beth laughed. "Because you've had too much to drink." She reached over and lifted Lauren's empty mug.

Lauren looked hard at the glass and grinned. "Oh, yeah."

"Let's go and get a refill."

Lauren's eyebrows drew together. She licked her lips. "I dunno, Beth," she said skeptically. "I've—"

"Stop being such a party pooper. C'mon." She grabbed Lauren's hand and began tugging her toward the bar."

"Beth," Lauren laughed.

"Excuse us. Excuse us. Coming through." Beth and Lauren side-stepped a wildly wriggling conga line led by Jane, Devlyn's private secretary.

"Hey, wasn't she at Devlyn's party?" Lauren asked, craning her head backwards to see as Beth continued to lead her across the room. "Hi, Wayne!" Lauren waved at her agent from Starlight Publishing, who was wearing a floppy straw hat, T-shirt, shorts and black knee high socks with his sandals, and trying his hand at playing the bongos. "You sound great!" Lauren gave him a thumbs up.

"Thanks!" he called back, returning the gesture.

When they reached the bar, it took a moment for Beth to get the attention of one of the bartenders. "Can I get the bags behind the bar now, please?"

He nodded and pulled out a large paper sack. When he handed it over, Lauren detected the clanking of metal.

Beth stood on a chair and motioned for the band to stop playing. The room suddenly went silent, and all eyes turned to Beth.

"Strip!" someone shouted, and Lauren turned to find a smiling David fixing himself a plate at the buffet.

"Later," Beth answered sassily, and the room erupted in cheers.

David heaped more food on his plate, figuring he'd need all the carbohydrates he could get for later.

What's he doing here? Lauren wondered.

"Okay, everyone," a wild grin split Beth's face, "pick a partner— it's time for the limbo contest!"

There were more cheers and several groans from a few of the less limber partygoers.

Beth held up the bag in her hand and shook it. It clanked loudly. "Limbo with a twist!"

Lauren's eyebrows shot skyward.

Dev walked down the hall, scowling as she looked up at a grandfather clock and realized how quickly her party had broken up after the pathetic fight. "Should have let Michael plan it," she grumbled to herself. Her guests had disappeared one by one until even David snuck out while she wasn't looking.

The reprieve, however, gave her a chance to check on the kids before deciding what she would do with the rest of her evening. She opened the door to Ashley's room and smiled at the moonlit lumps under her daughter's blankets. One belonged to the energetic child and the other belonged to the largest teddy bear that Devlyn had ever seen. Lauren had gifted Ashley with it after one of her business trips, and the little girl never slept without it.

She straightened the covers until she was sure that Ashley wouldn't smother herself, then kissed her eldest on the forehead. "I love ya, Moppet."

For a few minutes she just watched the even rise and fall of the girl's chest. A peaceful wave gently washed over her, and she was instantly glad she took the time to do this, every night that she was home. Only Lauren knew the long, calming moments she would spend simply watching her children sleep. It was here that an often crazy world could sometimes be seen with crystalline clarity. Satisfied that her daughter was romping through dreamland, she walked just down the hall to the room where the boys slept.

They had recently given up their race car beds for a set of bunk beds that they swore they needed more than anything else in the world. Dev and Lauren had put the beds together themselves after they'd accidentally been delivered unassembled, still in their original boxes. Several people in the maintenance department, of course, practically begged to be allowed to do it, but this was a parental moment she found herself very much wanting to share with Lauren.

Dev was proud of the good job they'd done. Good being measured by the fact that the beds hadn't collapsed under the rambunctious boys yet.

Christopher and Aaron were breathing deeply, and Dev picked up a baseball off the carpet and set it on their toy box before padding quietly to the bed. Aaron's pajama-covered legs were sticking out from beneath the covers, and Dev lifted her son into place and readjusted his blankets, all without waking him. She had to uncover Christopher's face and push aside a shock of messy, slightly sweaty blonde hair before placing a tender kiss on his forehead. "Love you both," she whispered fondly. "Sweet dreams."

Leaving the room, she lasted all of five seconds before heading back down the long hallway to Lauren's apartment. She knocked on the door. When there was no answer she tried the knob and stuck her head in. "Lauren, honey?"

The room was still and dark, and Dev could tell Lauren hadn't been back there since earlier this evening. She spun in a circle then dropped to her knees and lifted the comforter to look under the bed. No dogs. "How long can one party last?" she wondered out loud.

She decided it was time to find out.

Dev approached Lauren's party with increasing wonder. The sound of music and laughter could be heard at the far end of the corridor leading to the pool area. She nodded her greeting at the two agents guarding the doorway. One was a woman clad only in a sleek, maroon swimsuit. The other agent was a tall slim man who had tropical flowers in his hair and smelled of tequila. "Hello," Dev drawled as she took in their smiling, bleary-eyed appearance.

They both stood up a little taller, and the woman began to giggle despite herself, waiting for the man to speak. "Hello... ma... ma... ma... You," the male agent said, proud that he'd thought of the word.

Dev blinked. "You two aren't wearing your guns, are you?"

They both shook their heads wildly. "This is una... una... unaoffish unoffishel..."

"We're off duty," the woman finally finished for him, smacking him hard on the arm.

"Whew." Dev wiped mock sweat from her forehead. "I wouldn't want to get shot."

"You can get a shot inside," the woman said, and both agents burst out laughing. "Bacardi is my favorite."

Dev just stared at them incredulously. What kind of party did it take to loosen up this crew? *In* the White House, no less. She had to know. "Is Lauren in there?"

Suddenly, from behind the closed door, Dev heard the deafening chant, "Lau-ren. Lau-ren. Lau-ren."

The agents nodded obediently. "I think the answer is yes."

Dev lifted an eyebrow. "Ya think?" Dev gestured between them. "Step aside, please."

The man began to move away, but the woman grabbed his arm. "Don't you remember?" she ground out harshly, glaring at him.

"Oh, yeah!" he blurted, reclaiming his spot in front of the door. He lifted his chin. "Sorry. Nobody comes in."

Dev's jaw sagged. "What?"

The woman crossed her arms in front of her chest. "Nobody."

"I'm not nobody. I'm the President!"

The woman's eyes went wide, and for a moment Dev thought she was going to let her pass. Then the agent simply shrugged and said,

"Sorry. You're still somebody. And nobody gets in."

Dev scratched her chin and considered her options. She could just let Lauren have her fun, or she could go in there and have some fun too. She was, she decided, in the mood for fun. And tormenting these agents was just the place to start. "Tell me, do you two know anything about protecting penguins?"

The agents looked at each other and then blankly back at the President. "Uh... No."

"Well, I'm sure if I don't get in there, I could arrange a transfer to someplace nice and cold where there are lots of penguins."

"I grew up in Minnesota," the male agent wailed, a desperate look on his face. "I can't go back to that kind of cold!"

"Hold on, hold on," his companion soothed. "I'll get Ms. McMillian." She pointed a slender finger at Devlyn. "Watch her. I don't trust her."

Dev sneered as the younger woman disappeared behind the door.

"What's that smell?" Dev nearly swooned when the door opened and closed, sending the scent of roasting meat floating out over her.

"Food," the agent answered with a grin, as though he'd revealed a big secret.

"You're never going to make it on Jeopardy, are you agent?"

Just then Beth came to the door and poked out her head. It was dripping wet, dark curls hanging haphazardly in her face. "You can't come in," she snarled, making a shooing motion. "Go away!"

"Dammit, Beth," Dev complained bitterly. "Puhleez! I wanna see what's inside."

"I know you do."

"Bitch."

"A bitch at a rockin' party, you mean."

Dev frowned, and her long-time friend took pity on her.

"Okay, you can come in if you know the password and promise not to wreck the party."

"Wreck the party?" Dev gasped. "I would nev—"

"Ahem." She tapped her bare foot against the cool tile of the floor. "Aren't you forgetting something?"

Dev sighed. "I don't know the password."

"Sorry then." The door started to close.

"Wait!"

"Yessss…" Beth poked her head back out of the room. "Can I help you?"

Dev shot daggers at her. "Please?"

"Nope. Try again."

"Pretty please?"

Beth rolled her eyes. "As if."

Dev ground her teeth together while strongly considering busting her way in. But she thought about whom she was dealing with and tried one last time. "My party sucked and I want to come to yours."

Beth's eyes lit up. "And?" she prompted with undisguised glee.

The muscles around Dev's jaw tensed. "And I'm a big loser."

"That'll work," Beth said casually, reaching out and grabbing Dev by the wrist. "Keep up the good work," she told the agents as she and the President disappeared inside.

"I shouldn't have made you say the same thing in college, should I, Beth?"

"Paybacks are a bitch," the older woman sniggered.

The music was loud. The beat was throbbing and the scents coming off the buffet, intoxicating. Dev's eyes flitted from wall to wall—bright, fragrant flowers and decorations filled the room, transforming it into an island paradise. "Wow. This is great."

A loud chorus of cheers drew Dev's attention to the pool. At least fifty people were clustered around it. Most were standing in pairs. "What's happening? Swim races?"

"Not exactly." She looked Devlyn directly in the eye. "Now remember, Devil, you have to be a good sport. This is all in fun."

"Yeah. Yeah. I'm a good sport." She hurried over to the pool and peered over her mother's head at the same moment that Lauren burst up out of the water, followed immediately by Alex.

"The winners of our underwater limbo contest!" someone cried and the crowd applauded and hooted their admiration.

Lauren blinked the water from her eyes. "Devlyn?"

"That would be me." She looked over at Alex, stunned.

"Remember, you're a good sport, Dev," Beth whispered in the dark-haired woman's ear.

"Uhh..." A slightly panicky look chased its way across Lauren's face just as a long wooden bar and the two partygoers who'd been holding it popped up from out of the water behind her. "Let me introduce you to my friend."

Dev remembered the Irishman from the *Gary Kramer Show*. He hadn't said anything bad about Lauren so she couldn't exactly hate him. But did he *have* to have perfect abs? And was that swimsuit he had on even legal?

Dev thrust out her hand, trying not to think about the fact that this was someone who knew her fiancée intimately. *But she's mine now, sucker. And I'm never giving her back.* And with that thought, her mood suddenly brightened. "It's a pleasure to meet you."

"Likewise." When the man thrust out his hand, Lauren had to turn her body. His right hand had been handcuffed to her right hand, causing them to face opposite directions. He grinned. "Alex Doolen."

Dev ignored his hand and focused on Lauren. "You're handcuffed together?" she said incredulously, noting that Lauren suddenly looked very uncomfortable.

Lauren smiled weakly, then hiccupped. "All the teams were."

Frank and Janet raised their linked hands, as did several other couples.

"Don't worry. There's a lifeguard watching." Lauren pointed to a passed out Secret Service agent who was snoring at the end of the pool.

"Dev, it's not that bad. It's, well..." Beth gestured toward the very attentive agent who was watching the pool and was very much on duty.

"Handcuffs?" Dev repeated, pinning Beth with an evil glare. "And whose idea were those?" Then she looked around the room and recognized that it was half-filled with the guests from *her* party. Comprehension hit her like a two-by-four and her face turned a bright red. "Traitors!"

The room went silent. Even the band stopped playing. Dev let them all stew for several long seconds. "David," she finally yelled loudly. "Get over here."

David appeared at her side instantly. He knew his friend had a seldom-seen jealous streak and didn't want things to spiral out of control. "Alex is here legally on a visa, Devlyn," he whispered urgently. "I will not deport him for you."

Dev ignored his remark and kicked off her shoes as she grabbed his hand. She jumped into the pool wearing her jeans and cotton shirt and taking the tall man with her, causing an enormous splash. When she emerged, she held her hand and that of a sputtering, very startled David out to Beth. "Cuff us and lower the bar." She smirked at Lauren, who had a slow, relieved smile of comprehension spreading across her face. The blonde woman mouthed a silent "I love you" and Dev fought hard not to melt on the spot. "I refuse to be beaten in my own house."

The entire room relaxed, and the buzz of conversation began again as Beth scampered off to find another pair of cuffs. She only hoped she had remembered the keys.

Dev leaned close to David and whispered in his ear. "Do you know how to limbo?"

"Why do you think I don't have a partner?"

"Uh oh."

JUNE 2022

Wednesday, June 8th

Lauren sat in silence for a long moment before moving to exit the rented sedan. The Secret Service agent unbuckled his seatbelt to join her.

"You need to wait here."

"Ms. Stray—"

"This is a private matter." She reached over and patted his hand, doing her best to soothe his distress. "I know that David probably told you not to let me out of your sight, but I'm going to be fine. No one even knows I'm here." And it was true. They'd flown out of Baltimore and slipped through Nashville International Airport without anyone taking so much as a second look.

Lauren was dressed in a pair of worn jeans, comfortable sneakers, and a gray, soft cotton short-sleeved shirt that Devlyn always liked because she said it was the exact color of Lauren's eyes. She'd recently had an extra few inches shorn from her wavy locks and the new cut accentuated her slender neck, and, to her surprise, finally made her look her age instead of a handful of years younger. A pair of Ray-Ban Sidestreet sunglasses sat on her nose, and a bright orange University of Tennessee baseball hat covered her head, with tufts of thick blonde hair popping out from the back.

The agent looked nearly as casual, though he wore a vest to conceal his weapon.

They'd come directly from the airport to the Wyndham Nashville Airport Hotel, where Lauren had dropped off her overnight bag. She wanted this over.

"Actually, the President instructed me to give you all the privacy you required."

Lauren blinked. "She did?"

"Yes, ma'am." He gave her a gentle smile and a slight nod.

You get a kiss for that one, Devlyn.

"I'll be here if you need me."

Lauren smiled warmly. "Thank you. Wish me luck."

"Good luck."

She drew in a steadying breath and opened the car door, slowly walking up the narrow, cracked sidewalk that led to her childhood home. She was struck by the familiarity of the moment. How many times had she traveled this short path in the past? And were there ever times when her stomach was not churning with dread at being in this place?

Yes, her mind instantly supplied, *you know the ones*. She closed her eyes and relived those few precious moments, well-worn memories she held close to her heart. Her mother helping her stand on roller blades for the first time and both of them laughing as Lauren fell again and again, taking her mother with her each time she tumbled to the ground. The sweltering July day when her father stayed home an extra hour at lunchtime to run alongside a nervous rider as she pedaled a rickety bicycle for all she was worth. Carving a Jack-O-Lantern on the front porch and being told by both her parents that hers was the prettiest one on the block.

Lauren shook herself from her memories and glanced around. The sun was just starting to set, painting shadows across a small lawn that wanted cutting. She climbed the three steps to the porch, hearing the familiar creak of the last stair as it groaned slightly under her weight. She lifted her hand to knock and swallowed hard, regretting that she'd insisted that Devlyn stay in Washington rather than coming to baby-sit her here. At the moment, however, she felt very alone. *And it's my own damn fault.* Before she could change her mind, she rapped on the door.

It took a moment, but finally the door opened and Howard Strayer stood there, slack-jawed at finding his wayward daughter looking up at him with soft, worried eyes. There was a painfully long silence where each of them shifted uncomfortably, waiting for the other to speak.

Finally, Lauren cleared her throat and said, "Hello, Daddy."

He was standing in the shadows, but even there Lauren could see how much older he looked than the last time they were together. The creases in his face were deeper and he looked thinner and weary. Howard gently cleared his throat, his gaze drifting to the curb. "That your new boyfriend?" With a square chin, he gestured toward the Secret Service agent waiting in the car. "Get tired of being famous so you picked an ordinary man instead?"

Lauren sighed. "I'm still with Devlyn, Daddy. That's Jack, an agent assigned to try to keep me safe."

Howard's gray-eyed gaze flicked to Lauren and ignited with indignation. "Safe from me?"

Shit. "Of course not."

He grunted and dismissed the agent from his thoughts. "Why are you here? I told you before, if you—"

"If I left Tennessee to go back to Washington when my mama needed me that I wasn't welcome here again," Lauren interrupted, her voice steady, though her heart was pounding. "How could I forget?"

"Don't you sass me, girl." Howard's expression darkened. "Your mama taught you better than that."

They stood there staring at one another, searching for family, but seeing a stranger's eyes instead. Howard finally looked away and sighed. "Do… um… do you want to come in?"

"Yes," Lauren blurted. "Or… well, maybe we could go out back?" Nervously, she stuffed her hands into her pockets. "It's cooler outside."

It wasn't a particularly warm day, but he drawled a low, "All right," and headed around back with Lauren trailing behind him.

The back yard was small and surrounded by a white picket fence that was missing planks every so often. "Don't come out here much," he said, seeing Lauren's gaze travel to the fence. "No kids playin' back here anymore."

Several lawn chairs were clustered around a small table that held an ashtray and an empty soda can. Howard sat down first. When Lauren remained standing, he lifted grizzled eyebrows. "What?" His voice was gruff but held a resigned note that surprised Lauren. It was as though all the fight had gone out of him.

She looked at the ashtray. "I thought you quit."

"I thought you were *normal*." He shrugged one shoulder. "Guess neither one of us knows the other as well as we thought we did."

She wasn't surprised by his attitude, but the remark hit her in an unexpectedly deep place. It stung, but she refused to be baited. "That was cruel, Daddy."

His jaw worked, and he pushed the table away and stood, ready to bolt. "I know," he whispered. "Go back to Washington, D.C., Lauri. This place hasn't been home for you for a long, long time."

"No," Lauren agreed, reaching out and laying her hand on his forearm. "It hasn't. But you're still my father." She swallowed. "Please wait. I… um… I came here to talk, not to argue."

Howard let out a slow breath and nodded. He sat back down and steepled thick fingers on the tabletop. "Do we have anything to talk about?"

A lump grew in Lauren's throat, nearly cutting off her speech. "I really hope so, Daddy." She sat down across the table from him, her mind scrambling to come up with something to say. She'd truly expected him to slam the door in her face, and now that she was actually here, talking to him, she found herself uncharacteristically tongue-tied.

After a long flustered moment, he broke the silence by a whispered, "How could you do it?"

Lauren winced. That wasn't the beginning she'd been hoping for. "How could I do what? You'll have to be more specific. Seems like I'm disappointing a lot of people these days. Whether I mean to or not."

Howard leaned forward intently. "How could you leave when we needed you? And all to take up with… that… that woman?"

"Her name is Devlyn."

"I know her goddamned name!" he shouted, a shaking hand coming up and sweeping back a shock of pale hair mixed liberally with gray.

She tried not to flinch, lifting one hand, only to let it drop again. "Jesus, Daddy, what do you want me to say? That I'm sorry I left Tennessee for Washington? Well, I'm not! Devlyn needed me and I couldn't do anything to help Mama. I never could." Her temper flared when he opened his mouth to speak. "And don't dare you say different-ly!"

"No, no," he murmured, still heartsick. "She was in the hospital."

"So was Devlyn," she shot back.

Howard slammed his hand down hard on the white, plastic table, causing it to wobble furiously. "That woman is *not* your family. Whatever you feel for her, it's not the same thing as blood."

"No," she agreed slowly. "I guess it's not. But even then I was closer to Devlyn than I ever was to Mama. She needed me. And, Daddy," she paused and looked him directly in the eye, "she's my family now."

"Does that mean she'll get the same respect we did?" he challenged. "We needed you, Lauren."

Feeling slightly sick, Lauren dropped her gaze from his and spoke in a whisper. "I'm sorry I had to choose."

Howard grunted his acknowledgment of her words, though not his acceptance. "And if you had to choose all over again?"

She looked up from her hands, her expression as fierce as he'd ever seen it. "I'd choose exactly the same way."

He let out a low groan. His voice grew quiet and Lauren was shocked to see his eyes go misty. "What happened to make you want a woman that way?" he asked with all the bewilderment of a confused child. "Did someone touch you when you were a girl?" Desperately, he cast about for an explanation as Lauren stared at him, her mouth slightly open in shock. "Did—"

"No," she insisted. She glanced skyward, waiting for some divine intervention she knew wouldn't come. "God, it's nothing like that, Daddy. Nothing *happened* to me except that I fell in love. It's a wonderful thing, not a tragedy."

He looked at her as though she were crazy, and Lauren felt her heart sink.

"But Judd—"

"Was a nice guy who should have stayed my friend instead of becoming my husband."

Howard crossed thick arms across his chest. "You were happy."

Lauren shook her head. "I was happy with my *job* and my dog," she corrected firmly. These misconceptions had gone on for far too long. "I was never happy with my marriage." She bit her lip. "Daddy, how can I explain that we grew in opposite directions and didn't even care? We wanted different things from each other. Things that neither one of us could give. It was a mistake from the beginning."

"He's a good man."

"You're not hearing me! Didn't you ever wonder why I spent most of my marriage overseas?"

"That was none of my business," he answered gruffly, reaching to his shirt pocket for a cigarette.

Lauren nodded a little. "The details of how I live my life aren't your business. But my happiness is."

"And," he waved his hands in the air, "whatever sort of thing you have with *her* makes you happy?"

Without hesitation. "More than you could imagine."

He lit his cigarette and turned his head to blow out a stream of pungent smoke, his brow furrowing deeply as he thought. "It's wrong," he said quietly.

"What about it is so wrong? We're not hurting anyone."

"Christ, I'm too tired to answer stupid questions, Lauren." He stood. "Nothing has changed. Every night on the damned evening news I see pictures of you two together, and *every night* I'm reminded that you chose her and some life that makes no sense at all over your own mama. ”

“We’re getting married,” she said in a rush.

“I heard,” he commented dryly. “About a million times.”

She licked her lips. “I know you don’t approve. But maybe in time you’ll change your mind. And then we—”

“What you’re doing is *not* getting married,” he broke in harshly. “What your mother and I had was a marriage. Not some joke cooked up by liberals from San Francisco or some other screwed-up place full of perverts and druggies.”

The fine hairs on the back of Lauren’s neck bristled. “What you and Mama had? *That* is what I am supposed to aspire to? A life of denial and blame? No, thank you!”

Howard’s voice dropped to its lowest register. “You don’t know *anything* about what we had, little girl.” His entire body began to shake. “There was more to your mother than just her being sick.”

“And there’s more to my relationship with Devlyn than the fact that we’re both women. Please, Daddy. Please,” she whispered brokenly, her anger melting into pain. “We can at least try.”

“Try what?” His voice was flat.

She blinked several times, unsure of whether he was being sarcastic or serious. *C’mon, Daddy. Please.* “Things don’t have to be this hard. They don’t. We could try to be a real family,” she said, a hint of resignation in her voice. She could see that she wasn’t getting through to him. A wall had been put up between them, and every time she climbed to the top, he was there to knock her down.

For Lauren, it seemed a true relationship with even one of her parents would always be just out of reach. “We could try to at least know, if not understand, each other, couldn’t we?” She honestly wasn’t sure anymore.

The corner of Howard’s mouth quirked upward, and the reluctant smile showed off deep creases around his eyes. “But don’t you see, darlin’? That’s the trouble. Now that your mama is gone, there isn’t anything to hold us together. You’ve never thought much of me, and to be honest, I’ve never had a single clue as to what was going on inside that pretty head of yours.” He shrugged one shoulder and swallowed hard before admitting, “We’re strangers who once lived in the same house and happen to have the same color eyes.”

Lauren recoiled at the softly spoken words, feeling as though she’d been struck in the chest with a heavy board.

"I don't know you any more than you know me, and understanding you is way beyond what this man can handle," he muttered numbly, trying not to think about what the words were doing to his daughter. As surely as he stood there in the setting sun, he knew what he was saying was hurtful. But in his heart of hearts, he truly believed this was best for them both.

"Oh God, Daddy—"

"No," he said firmly. "You've said your piece. Now let me say mine."

Lauren's mouth snapped shut, a reflex to her father's command.

"I won't pretend that I approve of the sort of madness you're living now. I've tried, I swear, but it's wrong and I can't convince myself otherwise. You say you aren't hurting anyone, but that's not true." His eyes hardened a little. "It hurts me to know I've done such a pitiful job of teaching you right from wrong that you don't even understand why I'm upset now." The tears shimmering in his eyes for several moments finally spilled over. "Stop beating a dead horse, Lauri." He sighed loudly, tired to the bone. With a flick of his wrist, he tossed his cigarette to the ground and crushed it beneath his shoe.

Howard sniffed self-consciously, angry with himself for the display of emotion in front of this self-assured woman, who bore only a shadow of resemblance to the girl he'd raised. Or maybe this is who she was all along. And somehow he'd simply missed it. A watery smile pulled at his lips as he had a sudden flash of a headstrong little girl who demanded to be allowed to play baseball with the boys across the street, even after they'd chased her off more times than he could count. She'd pestered the boys for three summers before they gave in. "You were always too stubborn for your own good."

To Lauren's surprise he stepped forward and placed a tender kiss on her cheek. She felt the roughness of his stubbly cheek against hers and the warmth of strong hands grasping her forearms, before he took a step backwards and cocked his head to the side.

"For once in your life, listen to your daddy." He pinned her with a sad, defeated look that lanced through her, causing her stomach to twist painfully. There was no anger in his gaze, only resolution. "Leave this," he gestured with a hand stained from a lifetime of manual labor, "in the past. You won't find what you're looking for here. Go home."

Lauren's tongue was still frozen in her mouth as she watched her father step away and amble toward the backdoor. She took a step to follow him, but slowed then stopped as his words echoed in her head. *"You won't find what you're looking for here."* The screen door slammed shut behind him and Lauren's eyes slid closed. *God.*
Goodbye, Daddy.

Dev sat at the desk in the hotel room, doing her best to concentrate on the pile of work in front of her. She was supposed to be studying the effects of global warming and fossil fuel emissions and all she could think of was Lauren. Her lover had insisted on going to Tennessee alone, saying that her relationship, or current lack of relationship, with her father was something she needed to deal with herself and that Devlyn needed to stay right where she was and concentrate on her job.

After Lauren had left Washington, however, Devlyn realized she'd made a grave error. Offering her partner emotional support when she really needed it *was* part of Devlyn's job. In her mind, in fact, it was a big part of what being true partners meant. The reality of Dev's world was sometimes a big, old, cranky bitch. All too often, there were instances when she simply couldn't be every place she was needed. Today, however, after a lot of last-minute planning and a little yelling, she was going to be the woman who was there for her partner when or if she needed her. So here she was, spending her evening in an airport hotel, pretending she was doing something other than worrying.

Dev had ordered the Secret Service to be as unobtrusive as humanly possible. A full detail of agents currently occupied the rooms on both sides and across the hall from Lauren's. She'd sworn on her mother's life that she wouldn't set a foot outside of Lauren's room, allowing her to have a single agent at each end of the hallway, rather than directly outside her door. Upon arriving in the hotel, extra security cameras had been added and bulletproof glass had been suctioned on the inside of the hotel windows, making the room as safe as possible, given the extreme time constraints. No one knew she was in Tennessee, and she refused to have what she was offering Lauren tainted by having security around at every turn. There had to be *something* in their lives that could be remotely normal.

Getting up from the desk, Devlyn wandered around the room,

glancing at the clock on the nightstand. Impulsively, she reached up and banged on the wall. "C'mon, boys."

The door to the adjoining room opened, and two agents entered, their eyes flitting from surface to surface, their hands already reaching for their guns.

"Whoa." Devlyn held up her hands in a placating gesture. *Okay, Dev, that was stupid.* "I'm fine."

Both men visibly relaxed. "Is there something you needed, Madam President?" one of them asked.

Dev pursed her lips. "I need to do something that's probably going to get me in trouble."

"Ma'am?" The agent did his best not to scowl. "Are we going somewhere?"

"To a two-bedroom, brick home on Hancock Street." She began walking to the door, noting that the men's feet appeared rooted to the floor. "Coming?" she called over her shoulder. "Or will I need to call a cab?" Dev heard what she was sure was a softly muttered curse before the men scrambled in front of her, and they headed out into hall.

The dark sedan cruised down the street slowly, finally stopping when Devlyn tapped lightly on the window.

Jack had received a briefing explaining the turn of events and he was at Devlyn's door by the time the vehicle came to a complete stop.

In fading twilight, curious eyes surveyed Lauren's childhood home. Devlyn felt a pang deep within her chest at the plain, somewhat gloomy sight. But for once her timing was perfect and Lauren appeared from behind the house.

The biographer had her head down, clearly not paying attention to her surroundings. Her head came up when she heard the slamming of a car door. "Oh, God." Her breath left her in a quick rush when she caught sight of Devlyn. For a few seconds she stood motionless, watching Devlyn sheepishly stuff her hands into her pockets, then she bolted toward her.

Dev opened her arms, grunting a little at the impact of Lauren's compact body. "Hey," she whispered, "it's okay."

Several neighbors noticed what was happening in front of the house, which was now a famous landmark in Nashville, and they rudely clustered on their porches, openly gawking.

Instinctively, the agents clustered around their charges, turning their backs on the couple and leaving a few feet to afford the women as much privacy as possible.

Devlyn glanced up to see Howard Strayer standing in the shadows behind his screen door, glaring. She felt Lauren's breathing hitch against her and tightened her hold on the younger woman, throwing him the iciest look she could muster. *Rat-bastard coward.*

Lauren let her arms drop and gave Devlyn's stomach a quick pat before taking a small step backwards. She tilted her head up and looked at Devlyn with red, puffy eyes. "Hi," she said hoarsely.

Dev swallowed as her heart clenched. "Hi." *Shit. I should have come here with you to begin with. You won't talk me out of it next time, Lauren.*

"I didn't expect to see you here."

Dev's eyes went round and she winced inwardly, hoping that Lauren would forgive her meddling. "I'm... well, I thought maybe... err..."

Somewhere Lauren found a small, grateful smile. She reached for Devlyn again and buried her face against the warm skin of her neck. "I love you" she whispered simply. "And thank you. I'm so glad you didn't listen to me." She felt silent chuckles shake the lanky frame pressed tightly to hers, and she greedily absorbed the warmth and comfort she found there, clinging to Devlyn as though she were a lifeline. "Guess you never expected to hear me say that, huh?" She swallowed thickly. "I was going to see if I could get an earlier ticket home. The thought of being alone here tonight was making me sick."

Dev slowly stroked her back and placed tender kisses on the top of her head. "You're not alone, honey."

An agent discreetly gestured toward the vehicle, which was still running. It wasn't safe to be standing out in the open like this.

Over the top of Lauren's head, Devlyn nodded.

"I guess I don't have to tell you how things went," Lauren finally whispered after a few moments of comfortable silence. "He's never going to forgive me. I swear, after so much pain in our lives I don't understand how he can begrudge me honest happiness."

Dev sighed. "He just doesn't understand."

Lauren nodded against Dev's shoulder. "I... I know it's stupid. It's not like we were ever that close." She sniffed a few times. "This shouldn't feel worse than all those years where we hardly saw each other, but it does. It's not much different. But…" She shook her head in frustration. "But he's still my dad and I already missed my chance with Mama."

"Maybe," Dev paused, not wanting to offer useless platitudes. "Maybe things can be different someday." She slowly stroked her partner's back. "Time takes care of a lot of things, Lauren."

"Mmm…" Lauren let out a shuddering breath. "Maybe." She placed a kiss on Dev's jaw and resolutely told herself to look forward from this point on. As much as it hurt, her father was, at least to a certain extent, right. There was nothing left for her here now. "What are you doing here?" she murmured against Dev's neck.

Devlyn gave her a lopsided grin and let all the love she felt show in shimmering blue eyes. "I'm here because this is where I needed to be." *I can't do anything to fix this, honey. But… yeah, maybe. Just maybe I know someone who can.*

Devlyn walked into the bathroom of her Nashville hotel room, her cell phone in hand. The lights were low and her lover was snoring gently, an exhausted, unhappy expression marring her face even in sleep. "Please be there."

"Hello," a sleepy voice burred.

"Hi."

"Devlyn?" The words came quickly now. "Is something wrong? It's the middle of the night."

"No, well… sort of. But physically, at least, we're all okay."

"Why are you whispering then?"

Devlyn could hear the sound of creaking bedsprings in the ultra sensitive earpiece she was wearing. "I want to keep this private."

A long, silent pause.

"All right."

Dev sighed. "Thank you. I need a favor. I need someone to… well, it has to do with Howard Strayer."

A pair of pale eyes narrowed. "Go on…"

Wednesday, June 29th

Dev sipped from a glass of iced tea and from the front porch of her parents' home watched the sunset paint the world in ruddy colors. She pushed off with her feet, just enough to keep the old porch swing swaying in a gentle motion. A hundred yards away she could see the large, sturdy tent which had been set up to house the brief ceremony and what she hoped would be a hearty, memorable reception.

In the distance the kids were laughing and carrying on with Janet and Frank. Dev sighed and wiggled her toes, realizing this was about as relaxed as she could get. An unconscious smile swept across her face, stretching her cheek muscles, and for a single moment she was overcome with the feeling that her life simply couldn't get any better than this—her smile broadened—until tomorrow. "Hard to believe that tomorrow's the big day," Dev mumbled with a touch of marvel. "Wow."

Warm, firm hands began a massage of her shoulders.

"Are you nervous?" Lauren asked, leaning over and brushing her lips against Dev's cheek.

Dev, hearing the smile in Lauren's voice, reached back and took her hand, guiding her around to sit next to her on the swing. "Not yet. It won't hit me until tomorrow morning. Then I'll be a pile of nerves."

Lauren sat down next to Devlyn and snuggled close. The wood felt cool and slightly rough against the back of her pants as she wiggled into a comfortable position. They were both wearing jeans and soft cotton shirts, just warm enough to ward off the slight chill of the evening breeze. She took Dev's glass and helped herself to a sip before handing it back. "Mmm."

"How about you?" Dev winked.

"How about me what?"

"Nervous?"

Lauren cocked her head slightly to the side as she gave the question serious thought. "No."

Dev blinked. "Really?"

Lauren nodded and laughed. "I'm really not. I can't believe I'm saying that. But I think I'll be more relieved than anything to get the actual ceremony behind us." She smiled impishly. "Besides, then you're stuck with me forever."

"Promise?"

"Uh huh."

"But we still should have eloped."

Lauren fondly noted Dev's mischievous smile and the gentle creases just making inroads around vivid eyes. "And had your mother hunting us down for the rest of our natural lives? No thanks."

Dev laughed and put her arm around Lauren, remembering the first time she'd tried a similar move and Lauren had swatted at her, thinking the tentative touch was a bug. Dev pulled her close, deciding this level of comfort was much, much nicer. And much less terrifying. She sighed. "You and I have come a long way, Boris. Yeow!"

Lauren pinched Dev hard in the side for using her newest Secret Service code name. "Not nice," she groused, her eyes narrowing. "Why do *I* have to be Boris?"

Because it fits. "Beats me," Dev said innocently, glad Lauren wasn't looking at her face.

Last year they'd been Mighty Mouse and Wonder Woman. This year, it was Boris and Natasha. Dev wondered if the agent in charge of code names was going to torture her for the rest of her tenure in the White House. She suspected so. The tall woman laughed again and pulled Lauren closer, kissing her temple.

"You may laugh now, darlin', but if I don't get a better code name next time, I'm holding you personally responsible."

"Well, that's fair," Dev muttered sarcastically. But she was still smiling as she pushed her foot against the porch again, causing the swing to sway gently. "I love you."

Lauren turned and kissed Dev's throat. "Mmm... I love you too," she murmured dreamily. "But sweet talking me now won't save you later if I end up with another horrible name."

"What could be worse than Boris?"

Lauren snorted. "Don't even say that. I didn't think it could get worse than Mighty Mouse."

"I saw a list once," Dev paused as she deftly used her tongue to remove an ice cube from her tall glass. She began to chew. "It was of the names the Secret Service was considering for me. Trust me," an elegant eyebrow lifted, "it can get worse." She bit down on the cube and Lauren chuckled. "What?"

"You know what they say about crunching ice, don't you?"

"It's fun?"

"No." She sniggered and patted the denim-covered thigh next to hers. "Supposedly, it's a sign of sexual frustration."

Dev looked aghast. "Well, *they're* wrong, whoever *they* are. I am not sexually frustrated."

They hadn't heard Janet come up the steps, and both women nearly jumped out of their skins when she spoke.

"I can only hope that's true." She leaned against the rail of the porch and crossed her arms over her chest. "When was the last time you two..." Janet wriggled her eyebrows, then looked pointedly from Dev to Lauren. "You know."

"Mom!" Dev nearly knocked her glass over as she turned playfully to put her hands over Lauren's ears. "Don't go there."

"Good." Janet petted Lauren's bright red cheek. "I didn't really want to know anyway. But I am glad to hear that you're such a satisfied woman, Devil. That way you won't mind not spending the night together tonight."

"Bullshit, I won't!" Dev exploded.

"Yeah," Lauren chimed in forcefully. "I mind."

"All right, you two, don't make me get the spoon."

"Mom..."

Frank Marlowe stepped up onto the porch with Aaron perched on his shoulders, Christopher and Ashley bringing up the rear. "No, now Devil, you listen to your mother." Another few seconds and Gremlin and Princess were circling Lauren's feet, looking for a good place to sit down.

Gremlin decided that Dev's foot looked like a very good cushion. The chubby pug plopped down right there, earning a sub-vocal growl from Devlyn. Gremlin growled back.

Frank smiled. "You've always respected tradition, Devlyn. No use deviating from that plan now. Besides," he winked, "it's for luck."

Dev rolled her eyes and let loose an exaggerated sigh.

Lauren chuckled and rubbed her lover's back. "I don't think she sleeps very well alone."

"Very true." Dev nodded as she glanced over at her mother, hoping she would take pity on her. When her mother showed no signs of yielding, Dev's eyes narrowed. "You don't want me cranky from lack of sleep. I know where *the* button is."

"What button?" Ashley asked innocently.

"Never you mind," Janet answered quickly.

Frank chuckled at the poorly veiled look of outrage mixed with helplessness that colored his daughter's face. "Sorry, Stinky. You're out of luck tonight. Come on, the boys and I will walk you down to the cabin."

Ashley charged up the steps and took Lauren's hand. "Me and Grandma are going to take Lauren into the house."

"Grandma and I," Lauren and Janet corrected in unison, turning to each other and exchanging small, slightly embarrassed grins.

Bewildered, Ashley scrunched up her face. "No. *I* am."

Lauren smiled at the girl. "I'll explain later."

Dev reluctantly relented with a groan and stood up. "All right, I can see the whole family is in on this so I'll just surrender now and save you all some time." She held her hand out to Lauren. "Can I at least say goodnight to her?"

"Sure, go ahead," Aaron said from his grandfather's shoulders.

Lauren bit her lip to keep from laughing as she watched Devlyn stand there, waiting impatiently for everyone to leave so she could kiss her goodnight.

No one moved.

Dev glared at her parents. "Fine." She leaned down and kissed Lauren soundly before turning on her heel. She started descending the porch steps, then changed her mind halfway and stopped on the bottom one. She turned and pinned Lauren with loving, fiery blue eyes. The younger woman fought hard not to swoon on the spot. "I love you. I can't wait for tomorrow."

"Me too," Lauren heard herself say as she stepped closer to Devlyn.

Dev smiled and leaned forward, bracing her hand on the railing as she stretched to steal one last kiss before heading down the walk. She spoke without turning around. "Does *anyone* want to sleep with me tonight?"

Lauren was so close to shouting "Hell yes!" that she had to clamp her hand over her mouth, much to Janet's amusement.

The older woman couldn't help but chuckle indulgently.

Frank winced as his eardrums shook from the sound of childish squeals as Aaron began climbing down his back.

"Me! Me too! I wanna come," Aaron and Christopher screamed, beginning to scramble toward Devlyn.

Ashley looked torn, glancing between her mother and Lauren with slightly panicky eyes. The blonde woman smiled gently at the girl and mouthed a silent "thank you." Then she gestured toward Dev with her chin and winked. "Go on. There'll be lots of nights just for us, sugar." Affectionately, she petted Ashley's soft, dark hair. "I promise."

Ashley beamed and bolted for the stairs. "Me too, Mom!" she called out, quickly catching up to her brothers.

Frank wrapped his arm around Lauren's shoulder as the porch's remaining occupants watched Devlyn's children rush to her, eager for her time and undivided attention, two things which were all too rare in the President's life.

Gremlin sat down next to his mistress, content to let Princess scamper off after the children. It was hard to be truly lazy in the company of his sometimes-demanding mate.

"One last night of freedom for you then?" Frank said to Lauren, wondering if the young writer knew exactly what she was letting herself in for by marrying into the Marlowe clan.

The corner of Lauren's mouth twitched as her gaze followed her loved ones. She sighed. "I've already had freedom, Frank. It's not all it's cracked up to be. That over there…" She paused and joined Janet in a quiet round of laughter as Devlyn tried to pick up both Aaron and Christopher at the same time and ended up flat on her bottom in the middle of the path. Then Ashley threw herself on the pile, and Dev looked up and flashed Lauren a beaming smile… just before she yanked up Christopher's shirt and began mercilessly tickling his belly.

Lauren's heart skipped a beat at the happy sight. "That's the good stuff."

Thursday, June 30th

Dev paced back and forth, stopped, ran her fingers through her hair, and then paced some more. Moments before, she'd ordered all staff members, except for David, out of her parents' home, and sent the children downstairs. They were making her crazy. Normally composed and confident, she was nervous as hell and couldn't find it in herself to even try to hide it.

She hadn't seen Lauren all morning, her stomach was in knots, the weather had turned nasty, and she was quite sure—mostly because she had been pointedly told so by Michael Oaks—that no amount of cover-up was going to hide the dark circles around her eyes.

Last night had been filled with restless dreams, none of which, to her frustration, she could remember. "Bet you slept like a log, Lauren," she mumbled, admittedly jealous that her lover never appeared to mind their occasional nightly separations as much as she did. Devlyn had never liked sleeping alone, and she couldn't count the number of nights she'd sneaked into her parents' room and climbed in between them. A smile touched her lips at the comforting memory.

She hitched up her pantyhose, cursing the ever-sagging crotch, and plopped down in the chair by the window of her childhood bedroom, its soft, soothing blue tones doing little to calm her nerves. Devlyn realized, with a start, that after she began bringing Samantha home, she'd stopped coming into this room completely, having graduated to one containing a queen-sized bed.

But here she was, and it was just as she remembered it. An extra-long twin bed was tucked neatly in the corner. Maps of the world and pictures of far-off, exotic places she'd dreamed of visiting adorned the walls, and photos of her parents and cousins sat neatly on her windowsill. Her bookshelves were crammed with paperbacks and dotted with a few trophies she'd collected during her high school athletic career. It even smelled the same, like the strawberry candles she'd taken a liking to in her teenage years mixed with the faintest hint of Brasso, used to polish the eagle bust that sat proudly on her desk. She smiled faintly at the statue that her mother had lovingly maintained all these years.

Wistfully, Devlyn wondered why she hadn't taken the childhood treasure when she moved away from home. She reached out and touched the cool metal, letting her fingers warm it as she thought. The answer came to her with surprising speed. It belonged here, just as she did. She nodded a little to herself. She liked the fact that she knew it was here waiting for her if she ever needed it.

Dev stuck her head between the curtains and watched the caterers doing their best to avoid the fat, pelting raindrops and Secret Service agents filing in and out of the large tent, which appeared to sway a little in the gusting wind. She gulped, vowing to kill Michael Oaks if that tent, which was his idea, came down with her family inside. Hell, maybe she'd kill him anyway, just for fun.

Indulging herself, she smiled wickedly at the thought.

Thunder boomed overhead and Devlyn tilted her head skyward.

"Please don't let a tornado pick up our wedding tent." She was mostly joking, but when the thunder boomed again, even louder, her eyes widened. She began thinking of all the things that could go wrong, and her heart began to thump wildly. Hastily, she rattled off a long list of promises in exchange for smooth sailing on this day, including her eternal devotion to her family, the Constitution, and everything else she considered sacred, ending with a heartfelt, "And puhleeeez don't let me throw up in front of everyone. Again. Amen." Her father still teased her about her high school graduation commencement speech, despite the fact that she'd become an accomplished and charismatic public speaker over the years.

Growing too nervous to sit and do nothing while she waited for her dress to be brought in, she shrugged into a bathrobe that was a little too small and opened her bedroom door. Peering over the second floor railing, she spied David and her dad, dressed in their tuxedos, sitting in the breakfast nook by the big plate glass window, having coffee.

"Oooo…" she cooed appreciatively, taking a big whiff of the heady aroma. "Any of that left for me?" Dev tightened the sash of her robe and bounded down the stairs. Her hair was plaited in a neat, glossy braid that trailed down her back and a light coating of makeup was neatly in place. She could always redo her lipstick after she drank her coffee.

"Careful there, young lady," Frank chided gently, eyeing her intently as she bounded down the stairs, full of nervous energy despite her lack of restful sleep the night before. "The last time you did that you twisted an ankle." A white eyebrow arched. "Besides, shouldn't you be getting dressed?"

Several creases appeared on Dev's forehead as she frowned. "My dress isn't here yet. I assumed Mother was bringing it. She must still be with Lauren." She grabbed David's wrist and looked at his watch. "I'm starting to get a little nervous; the wedding is due to start in an hour." She glanced around. "Where are the kids?" Then she heard the sound of arguing, squealing, and running coming from the next room and rolled her eyes. "Never mind." She lasted all of two seconds before yelling, "Boarding school in Antarctica for the lot of you, if you don't quiet down!"

The children giggled at the familiar but meaningless threat, but did quiet down.

David picked up the coffeepot and poured Dev a cup. "Your dress will be here soon, Dev. Sit here for a few minutes and relax." He pushed the sugar and cream toward her. "I remember a time when you drank it black."

She lifted the sugar bowl. "Lauren didn't start drinking coffee until after she met me and this is the way she prefers it. I started using a little cream so now we can drink each other's coffee without gagging."

David smirked and made a quick motion with his wrist to simulate the snapping of a whip.

Dev's eyes narrowed. "Is there a problem?"

"Ugh. That is just *too* sickly sweet," David teased.

Ebony eyebrows lifted. "This from the man who doesn't mind sharing his wife's toothbrush."

"David," Frank gave him a squinting stare. "As a physician, I can safely say that that is truly disgusting."

David's jaw dropped. "One time! I used Beth's toothbrush once after I lost mine on a camping trip and no one will let me forget it."

Dev smiled at her chief of staff's indignant look. It was easier to focus on him rather than her own rattled nerves. She asked, "How long did Beth make you sleep on the couch for that? Hmm?"

David opened his mouth to answer. "Well—"

"Enough chit chat," Dev interrupted grumpily. "I am *not* getting married in my bathrobe." She looked at David, suddenly feeling a little unsure. Maybe she should have paid more attention to the planning of this event. "Right?"

David blinked. "Of course not!"

"Then where's my damn dress?"

Frank asked, "Haven't you seen it?"

Dev shook her head in short, jerky movements that made her agitation clear. "They only took my measurements," her gaze narrowed, "a dozen times. I've never seen it." She turned panicky eyes to David. "What if the designer forgot it and is too afraid to admit it?"

With an exaggerated sigh, David pulled out his cell phone and dialed. He spoke quietly into the tiny device then flipped it closed, placing it on the table. "It's on the way right now. Your mother is bringing it over after she takes care of some special guest." The tall man shrugged.

Dev chuckled. "Since when is Aunt Myrtle special? The last wedding the woman went to, someone told her to bring birdseed to shower the happy couple with—the crazy old bird threw the entire bag at the bride and knocked her unconscious. The whole wedding party ended up in the emergency room, waiting for my cousin to come to."

David just looked at Devlyn. "Is that a true story?" he asked incredulously.

Frank sighed. "I'm sorry to say it's true. Aunt Myrtle is one of my more interesting relatives."

"I guess that answers my question," David muttered, taking another sip. "I'll make sure security frisks her on the way in. Anyway, according to Agent Tucker your mother is due here in three minutes."

Dev let out a tiny grunt. She didn't want to be late for her own wedding.

"By the way," David said, "the no-fly zone is in place." A loud clap of thunder boomed. "Not that the tabloids would risk their helicopters in this weather anyway. Between that order and this weather, you're going to have a nearly normal wedding."

"Thank God." Dev slumped down in her chair. She looked at David's watch again, missing Liza and her ever-present alarms and electronic calendar. "Aren't the three minutes up yet? I want to see the dress that's costing me a small—"

"Ahem." Frank gave his daughter a look.

Dev blushed. "Sorry, Dad." She trained her eyes on her coffee cup. "That's costing *you* a fortune."

Frank gave her a small smile. "Devil, do you really think, with all the people working to make this day a success, not the least of which is your mother, that anything is going to go wrong?"

Dev's shoulders slumped. "I know, Dad, but I love Lauren so much. And I want this to be perfect for her. And you always expect something to go wrong on your wedding day. And—"

"Don't say another word," Frank warned, pressing his fingers against Dev's lips. "Let's not give the wedding gremlins any ideas, okay?"

"Good plan," Dev mumbled against his fingers.

The door opened and Janet entered with a huge garment bag. She was wearing a cream-colored suit, and low appreciative murmurs—that she was too preoccupied to hear—bubbled forth from Frank and David. She licked her lips and drew in a deep breath before addressing Dev.

"Now, honey…"

"Oh, my God. Oh, my God." Dev bolted from the chair. "That's bad. You never start a conversation with those words unless it's bad." She turned wide eyes on David, who did nothing to comfort her.

"Very bad…" he agreed readily.

"What is it?" Frank asked impatiently, getting up from the table and loosening his bow tie as he moved toward Janet.

Janet closed her eyes and laid the garment bag on the table. Then she took a step back as though the bag were filled with explosives. Instinctively, everyone in the room mirrored her actions.

Gaping at the black bag, Devlyn began to sweat. "Oh, God. Oh, God," she repeated numbly.

"You already said that."

"Shut up, David, or you'll be wearing whatever's in that bag."

Dev's voice was as menacing as he'd ever heard it, and the red-headed man turned to gauge his boss' sincerity. He gulped and looked back at the bag. "Oh, my God. Oh, my God."

"Come on, now," Frank said reasonably. "How bad can it be?"

Three sets of incredulous eyes swung his way.

"Really," he persisted. "Surely you've seen it before this morning, Janet. You—"

"No," Janet corrected quickly. "That damn designer got all sensitive when I wanted to see it. He pitched a fit and started to cry. To *cry*!"

"Real tears?" Frank asked, astonished.

"I swear to God," Janet answered, wringing her hands. "There was so much else to do and Michael assured me that Devil had approved everything. But—"

"Enough!" Dev groaned. "Mom, I take it you peeked in the bag?"

Janet nodded miserably, her lower lip trembling, though Dev couldn't tell if it was from laughter or tears. "May God have mercy on my miserable soul."

"Where's the liquor?" David asked loudly, on his way to the refrigerator to see what he could scrounge. "I need a drink."

Dev's arm shot out, and she grasped David by the lapel. "Oh, no you don't. You're going to open that bag and show me what I'll be wearing on the biggest day of my life."

"A smile?" David said, trying to salvage a bit of good humor.

"Only if I get to kill someone."

"Open the bag, Frank," David instructed, rapidly moving as far away from Devlyn as he could. Where was Beth when he needed her? She could tackle Dev if she had to, while he ran and hid bchind the Secret Service.

"For Pete's sake! What in the Sam Hill is *wrong* with you people? It's only a dress." Frank quickly unzipped the bag and, with some effort, pulled out the dress, not really taking the time to look at it as he tugged it free. "There." He held it up, and his voice faltered. "See?"

Collective gasps went around the room.

"Holy shit!" Frank exclaimed, dropping the dress as though it were on fire.

Janet's mind raced as she tried to think of something, anything, to make Devlyn feel better. "Well, it's… um… pink and… err…"

"Poofy," David supplied. "Really, amazingly, gravity-defyingly-poofy."

"Sweet Mother of God!" Dev's eyes were the size of saucers. She wasn't sure whether to burst into tears or laughter. Maybe she'd just do both. "No!" She scrambled away from the dress as though it were a plague shroud. "Wait." She suddenly stopped. "You don't really think I'm going to wear this, do you?" She looked hopefully at her mother, who couldn't meet her gaze." *I don't believe this!* "No way! No! I will not wear that to my wedding. I'll look like Cinderella's Fairy Godmother… on crack!"

"But I like the big floppy flowers glued onto the sleeves," David supplied, smiling wanly at Dev's murderous glare. "They remind me of those things you put on the bathtub floor to keep from slipping. Only the ones in my house are better looking."

"I won't do it," Dev announced, lifting her chin. "I won't." She waggled her finger at her mother. "And you can't make me. I don't care if you went through twenty-nine hours of brutal labor. No. No. No."

"Honey," Janet soothed. "The wedding is due to start in twenty minutes. You could wear the pants you came over in, I suppose. Or just go ahead and wear the dress; it is the style… umm… somewhere, I'm sure." But the doubtful note in her voice was clear. "Anyway, we just don't have time to find anything else. You're too tall to borrow anything of mine."

"Maybe it's not that I'm too tall," Dev said pointedly. "Maybe it's that you're too short. Ouch!" She wasn't quick enough to move away from her mother's pinching fingers.

Devlyn began ticking off examples on her fingers. "Jeans. Sweat pants. My underpants. *David's* underpants. Bare-assed, buck-naked. *All* of those options are better than that dress!"

"Devlyn," David began, taking a deep breath and hoping his life insurance policy was up-to-date, "Toby Yagasuki is Japan's most renowned designer and the emperor's cousin. The emperor himself called to say how honored he was that you selected him for this momentous occasion and what an honor it was for his family as well as his nation. Next month we begin trade negotiations in Tokyo. If you don't wear this dress—well, I hate to say it, but it could hinder everything we're trying to do there."

Just then Ashley, Christopher, and Aaron burst into the room. The boys were in tiny black tuxedos, their fair hair slicked back and their chubby cheeks pink from playing more rowdily than usual while all the grownups were preoccupied. Ashley wore a pale yellow dress that set off her dark hair, which was styled just like her mother's.

For a second, Devlyn forgot about the dress and smiled down at her children, her gaze full of maternal pride. "Don't you all look great," she said softly.

"Thanks, Mom," Ashley chirped.

"Is this your dress?" Christopher questioned with wide eyes.

Spell broken, Dev made a face. "Yes."

"Whoa," Aaron crooned loudly. "It's beautiful."

"It's the greatest, Mom," Ashley agreed heartily. "I can't wait to see you in it. Lauren will be so happy."

"You are going to wear it, right, Mom?" Christopher asked, touching the fabric with a tentative finger. He'd been told by several adults that the wedding was almost ready to begin. "It's just like you promised. I knew you'd keep your promise!"

Dev covered her face with her hands and whimpered her defeat, sending a silent wish to Lauren that she, at least, was having better luck with her specially designed wedding day creation.

"Stop cursing."

"I will not." Lauren's face was the very picture of disgust. She and Devlyn had traded locations earlier that morning and she was getting dressed in the cabin. "Beth, there is no way on God's green earth that I am going to wear this monstrosity. *None.*"

"It doesn't look as bad on as it did off." Beth winced, knowing her lie was pitiful.

"Bullshit. I'd rather go naked. And don't give me that Japan trade negotiation excuse again. That won't work on me. I prefer to buy American anyway. And I saw Mr. Yagasuki skulking around earlier. He was wearing Armani. And his clothing," she pointed at herself, "wasn't bright, blinding, and a hideous purple!"

Beth bit back a smirk. Mostly. "It might have been Armani, but he was still wearing lime green slippers."

"Shut up."

"You and Dev said no white," Beth reminded, perching against a tall oak dresser. She was dressed in a tasteful, silk, coffee-colored pant-suit and was, for the first time, glad she was a good forty pounds heavier than Lauren, who was eyeing her outfit enviously.

With difficulty, Lauren lifted her purple-encased arms and rubbed her throbbing temples. "We didn't want white because we've both been married before. Not because I wanted to look like a *whore* today."

"You do not look like a whore."

Lauren just stared.

"Much."

"Yankee bitch."

Beth couldn't help it; she burst out laughing. She loved the way Lauren's gentle Southern twang made "bitch" sound like "bee-ach." "Okay, enough lying. That is the most hideous thing I've ever seen."

"Of course it is," Lauren said reasonably. "Michael Oaks is out to get me, the bastard. I should have known he'd pull something like this. He won't have the nerve to do it to Devlyn though." Her voice turned wistful. "I'll bet she looks stunning."

Beth rolled her eyes. "Like always."

"Yeah." Lauren laughed throatily, feeling immensely appreciative of that fact. "Pretty much like always."

"I don't think Michael did this on purpose, Lauren." Beth didn't much like being in the position of defending the annoying man. But in this case it was only fair. "Did you see the Oscars this year? I saw a dress or two like this."

Lauren threw her hands in the air. "On whores!"

Beth's forehead wrinkled. "Jesus, Lauren. Duh. They weren't *really* whores. They only played them in the movie."

"Did you *see* the movie? Those were their costumes!"

A tiny snigger escaped Beth.

"God, I hate you."

"And who could blame you?"

Lauren put a hand on her hip, gestured down her body and looked at Beth with a beseeching expression. "Would you wear this?"

The dress was strapless and very low cut, with nothing but feathers covering both her breasts. The body of the dress fit her like a second skin, lizard skin to be exact, and the hem, which reached the floor, was slit up to mid-thigh and also covered in purple feathers.

Beth bit her lower lip. "Not on a dare."

Lauren nodded. "Help me out of this then. I think I have a skirt in my bag back at the main house. It's better than jeans. Devlyn will understand."

Beth pushed off the dresser only to pause mid-step when there was a knock on the door.

Lauren's gaze burned a hole through the door. "If that's Michael Oaks or that designer from Hell, tell him to come right in."

"Uh oh." Beth scrambled to the door before Lauren tried to open it herself. "Who is it?" she asked warily, her eyes darting from the door to Lauren.

"It's us!" the Marlowe children shouted happily. "And Grandma," Ashley added.

"Let us in, Beth," Christopher called through the wood. "We want to see Lauren's pretty dress and flowers."

The unbridled enthusiasm in his voice made Beth smile. There were times when both the boys, but most especially Christopher, reminded her very strongly of a boyish version of a certain handsome redhead with whom she fell in love in college.

"Yeah!" Aaron and Ashley joined in. They'd been briefed by their Secret Service agents, who had taken up positions just outside the cabin under large umbrellas, as to what to expect on this day. And the children were so excited they were nearly ready to pass out. They were going to get to walk down the aisle with Lauren, who would have no family of her own there to give her away.

Before Lauren could answer, Beth opened the door, and the Marlowe children and Janet filed in. They all stood before the blonde woman, staring.

Janet did her best not to explode into laughter, but she couldn't stop the tears that streamed down her cheeks from the effort. Beth took one look at Janet, who was nearly convulsing in her efforts not to laugh, and lost it. Together the two women dissolved into a puddle of hysteria.

Lauren stood ramrod straight, plotting both their deaths.

"Oh, Lauren!" Ashley exclaimed, running up to her and almost, but not quite, touching the feathers. She was too afraid to touch the most beautiful thing she'd ever seen. "You look like a movie star!"

"Yeah. A purple one!" Christopher said, his blue eyes shining with undisguised delight. "Wow! That dress is the best!"

"What about Mom's?" Aaron said, giving his brother a shove. "It's good too!"

"I know!" Chris scowled and only kept from socking Aaron because Janet stepped between them.

"It's really fabulous," Ashley told Lauren, her voice telegraphing genuine awe.

Lauren melted a little under the child's sincerity. "You don't think it looks a little... umm... wild?" she asked the little girl, mentally crossing her fingers.

Ashley shook her head. "Oh, yes, it's incredible." Soft brown eyes were wide with wonder. "You must *really* love Mom if you're going to wear something so beautiful to get married in."

Lauren closed her eyes and whimpered. *Damn. Damn. Damn.* "Not fair, Ashley," she muttered under her breath. "Not fair at all!" Lauren's shoulders slumped.

Beth wiped her face, hoping her tears of laughter hadn't smeared her makeup. "I take it you'll be wearing the 'creation' then?"

Lauren looked down at the three eager faces, looking so earnestly at her. She sighed. "Yes," she moaned through clenched teeth. "I'll wear it." *These children's opinions mean more than a bunch of strangers ever will. I only hope Devlyn forgives me. If she laughs...even once, no sex until... well, until I get horny. Damn, but that won't be very long! What kind of punishment will that be?* she privately lamented, cursing the fact that Devlyn had the most gorgeous thighs she'd ever laid eyes on.

"All right." Janet lifted her chin and tried to stay composed. She marched over to Lauren and kissed her warmly on the cheek. "That was just about the sweetest thing I've ever seen. You are the perfect second mother to my grandchildren, Lauren Strayer. And I love you dearly."

Tears leapt into Lauren's eyes. "I love you too, Mom." Her voice cracked a little on the last word, and even Beth felt her eyes sting.

Janet nodded and swallowed. "Time to get you and my daughter married," she whispered.

Lauren's stomach fluttered wonderfully at the words.

"Are you ready?" Beth asked, picking up a small bouquet and handing it to Ashley, who cooed over the fragrant white roses.

"No," Lauren blurted out, her eyes wide as she recalled what was about to happen. She was more than ready to be married to Devlyn. It was the actually getting married part that suddenly made her nervous.

Janet and Beth laughed again. "Then you're all set." Janet patted Lauren's bare arm.

"Devlyn won't say a word about the dress." Her eyes twinkled. "I guarantee it. Besides, with this rocky start, what else could go wrong?"

Thunder boomed.

Lauren clamped her hand over Janet's mouth. "Don't you dare even ask."

Fifteen minutes later Lauren was all ready to head to the tent. She opened the bedroom door, surprised to see that the cabin was nearly empty. "Am I late?" she worriedly asked Beth as they traversed the stairs.

"Nope. You're just on time."

Janet appeared at the bottom of stairs, trying not to look directly at Lauren's dress, lest she throw up. "There's a family member who wants to say hello before the wedding. Do you mind terribly?"

"Must be Dev's favorite, Aunt Myrtle. Myrtle James. She's as crazy as the day is long, but as interesting as hell," Beth whispered to Lauren. "And she loves Devlyn."

Lauren nodded. "Sure," she said to Janet. "So long as we have time, I'd love to meet someone close to Devlyn." She glanced at her wrist before she remembered she wasn't wearing any jewelry or a watch as per Mr. Yagasuki's instructions. She rolled her eyes.

"You have time. I made sure of it." Janet pointed toward the kitchen. "Right in there. We'll be waiting when you're finished."

Beth joined Janet at the bottom of the stairs.

Lauren gave them a strange look, but headed for the kitchen. She was supposed to meet the old woman alone, looking like she'd just escaped from an Old West brothel? "Okaaay," she said slowly, drawing out the word in her confusion.

The writer pushed open the swinging kitchen door, talking as she walked. "Hello, Mrs. James, I'm—"

Her feet froze and her jaw sagged.

"I should think I would know who you are."

Lauren had to swallow a few times before she could speak. "Daddy?"

He stood up from the small wooden table and smoothed his jacket. "Don't recognize me in a suit, I guess." Self-consciously, he dusted the lapel of his jacket. "Or with my new haircut."

Lauren took a step forward, not hearing her heels hit the wooden floor over her pounding heart. "What..." She cleared her throat around the sudden lump that had developed there. "What are you doing here?"

"Well..." Howard Strayer looked directly into her eyes and felt his courage fail him. "Shit."

Lauren blinked. "I... um... I think I need more information if I'm going to figure out that one, Daddy," she teased very gently, trying to feel her way around what was happening.

Howard nodded and lifted his chin. "I had a visitor the day after you left Nashville. Seems the President's mother wanted to give me a piece of her mind."

"What?" Lauren gasped. "I didn't tell her to do that. I mean—"

"I know that," Howard said quietly. "I don't think anyone ever told that mouthy woman a thing in her entire life." He could see Lauren's hackles rising, and he held up a hand in apology. "After I told her to go to hell and she told me the same thing, well, we ended up talking a little. I'm still not sure how it happened."

"You talked?" Lauren still couldn't believe it.

"All night," he confirmed. He drew in a deep breath. "Seems I was a little confused about things."

"You were?" She knew she wasn't being very articulate. But she was afraid if she said the wrong thing, he'd turn around and walk out.

The man nodded, and stuffed his hands into his trouser pockets. "Very."

Lauren shook her head, still stupefied. "You mean you're all right with this now?" She gestured broadly with one hand. "With me and Devlyn and—?"

"No." His deep voice was unequivocal. "I am certainly *not* all right with this. I don't believe two women or men should be getting married, much less... well, they don't need to be more than friends, is all. It's just not the way things were meant to be." He shifted a little, very aware that Lauren was hanging on his every word. The look was unfamiliar, and at that moment he realized how few times in his life he'd captured his daughter's genuine interest. "My opinion there hasn't changed one iota. Not that Janet Marlowe didn't try her damnedest."

Lauren's brow furrowed and she felt a sinking sensation deep in the pit of her stomach. "Then why—?"

"Janet reminded me that I don't need to approve of what you're doing. Or even understand you." He lifted a single fair eyebrow. "And I don't... understand you, that is." He shifted from one foot to the other. "Seems she wasn't too keen on her daughter's life taking the same direction you're going now."

Lauren blinked. *She wasn't?*

"But she got over it."

Lauren smiled a little. "She did."

Howard's gaze pinned his daughter. "I was reminded that the most important part about being your father is not trying to teach you to make the right decisions in life." He shrugged one shoulder. "It's loving you no matter what you decide." Never a man for words, he felt a little silly making this speech and his cheeks reddened. This had sounded much better in the car.

Lauren's chest contracted.

"And," he looked down, taking Lauren's silence as a bad sign, "that much I can do, Lauri. So after a lot of talking and..." his lips twitched, "a lot of yelling. I was persuaded to come to this over-publicized wedding in Ohio. I... um... I hope you don't mind." He lifted watery eyes and stepped forward, not stopping until he stood directly in front of his daughter. "It's what your mama would have wanted," he whispered emotionally. "It just took me a while to remember that."

"Oh, Daddy." Lauren flew the last step into her father's arms and buried her head against his chest. She was bombarded with the familiar scent of her father's cologne and sank into the warmth of strong arms as her tears spilled down onto his collar. Her heart threatened to pound out of her chest, and she felt his heart doing the same thing. She silently thanked Janet for a wedding gift whose worth had no measure. "I love you."

It took a second for Howard to return the embrace, but when he did, he put his whole heart into it. "I... I—" He had to clear his throat before he could continue. "I love you too, honey." Their differences hadn't disappeared and neither had the years of indifference that would always lie between them. His approval and even true acceptance might be a lifetime away, but on this day Howard Strayer reluctantly heeded the advice of a total stranger. He had allowed himself to be reminded that there wouldn't always be "a tomorrow" to make things right and that if he had a chance to be there for his daughter, it was not his duty, but his *privilege* to take it.

After a moment, he grasped Lauren by the biceps and gently pushed away from her. He surveyed her clothes, and two grizzled eyebrows disappeared behind bangs still slightly damp from the rain. "Nice dress."

Twin sets of gray eyes met, and Lauren and her father did something they hadn't done together for more years than Lauren could count…

They laughed.

David and Devlyn stepped into the cabin. David took the light cloak from Dev's shoulders and gave it a shake, sending a shower of raindrops in the opposite direction, speckling the floors and walls.

Devlyn looked at her mother and then toward the kitchen door. "Did it work?" she whispered.

Janet grinned smugly and nodded. "He's got a seat in the back row. He wouldn't agree to participate in the wedding or stay for the reception, but he's here now and that's a small miracle in and of itself." She sighed and shook her head. "He's a stubborn one, Devlyn. You've got your work cut out for you."

"I know," Dev said seriously. "But I've got time to work on him, and I wanted this for Lauren. She said it didn't matter. But—"

"But you knew differently," Janet finished, wiping an errant raindrop from her daughter's cheek. "I think you were right." She patted the cheek she'd just wiped. "Go on upstairs to your room. I've got a surprise for you up there too."

Dev blinked. "You do? Can't it wait till after the wedding, Mom?" Why wasn't anyone else in a hurry? Ever since she'd become President her life was always on fast forward, and now somehow everyone had decided to relax? What was wrong with these people? "I'm supposed to be walking down the aisle in ten minutes!"

"No, it certainly cannot wait." Janet's expression grew stern. "I went to a lot of trouble for this, Devlyn Odessa Marlowe. Don't you dare—"

"Okay, okay!" Dev raised her hands in surrender and padded toward the steps. "God knows I wouldn't want to upset you on *my* wedding day," she mumbled sarcastically.

"Exactly," Janet told her unrepentantly. "You'll get your chance to be Supreme Ruler of the Universe with your brood, Devil. Don't ruin mine. Now scoot. Lauren will be coming out of the kitchen any minute, and I don't want you to see her." She tried not to laugh. "You *really* don't want to see her."

"Stupid superstitions," Dev groaned as she slowly walked up the stairs. Her dress was so wide she could barely make it around the corner when the staircase shifted directions. "Stupid, damn, God-awful dress…Why couldn't it be the pantsuit from hell? Then I wouldn't need nylons."

Janet and David, who were watching from the bottom of the steps, smiled wickedly. This was simply too much fun. Frank and the children came in the front door, escorted by a bevy of Secret Service agents with umbrellas just as Howard Strayer exited the kitchen. He caught sight of the President as she ascended the stairs and his face wrinkled into a look of confusion and horror. "What is wrong with kids today?" he asked Janet.

"That's a very good question, Howard. I wish I had the answer." Janet turned to her right. "Say hello to my husband, Frank." Frank stepped forward and the two men shook hands. Then Howard was led out the front door by the agent who would take him directly to his seat, neatly avoiding the two security checkpoints that the rest of the guests would be forced to wade through.

Lauren stepped out into the living room, wiping her wet cheeks. When David and Frank got a good look at her, they paled.

"Don't say it," Lauren warned. She smoothed down a particularly unruly feather that seemed to sprout directly from her left nipple. "Not a word. Not a single word!"

David began to shake. "I can't stand it," he moaned pathetically, trying not to laugh. The veins in his neck were bulging, and he looked as though he were about to come apart at the seams.

At the sight of her husband, Beth began to howl.

Lauren took a step toward her chief of staff, intent on killing her on the spot, but Frank gently intercepted her. "I have a surprise for you," he whispered.

"Not another one," Lauren said seriously, peering around his slender frame to glare at David and Beth. "I don't think I'll live through another one."

Frank smiled. "Oh, but you'll like this one." He leaned down to whisper conspiratorially. "That big-haired designer, Mr. Yagasuki, is upstairs. He was hoping you could stop up and tell him what you thought of the dress before the wedding."

Lauren's eyes twinkled with evil glee.

"He said that?"

"Oh, yes." Frank nodded. "I told him you'd be right up."

Lauren licked her lips. The thought was so tantalizing she could nearly taste it. "But do I have time?" she mused, praying that she did.

"How long should bloody murder take?" Frank asked seriously.

Lauren pursed her lips, a little surprised that it would be the mild-mannered Frank Marlowe who would facilitate her would-be-dastardly crime. But she was too swept away by her emotions to ponder that thought for long. "It'll take two minutes, tops. I'll be right down." She began climbing the stairs, cursing under her breath when her tight dress wouldn't let her go as quickly as she wanted.

The room's occupants watched her go with varied levels of disbelief and good humor, not quite believing how well this day was turning out.

Lauren threw open the bedroom door. "All right, you. What the hell is this?" She gestured to her dress.

Dev jumped up off the bed. "Lauren?"

"Devlyn?"

Each woman blinked stupidly at the other.

"Oh, holy shit!" Lauren sputtered. "Your dress is as bad as mine!" Her face twisted in a mixture of disbelief and revulsion. "How is that possible?"

"I don't know," Devlyn sighed, covering her eyes to block out the view before her. "You are always beautiful, Lauren. But you look *ridiculous*," she said flatly. "Why are you dressed like a hussy?"

"How should I know!"

Reluctantly, Devlyn glanced again at her bride-to-be... and flinched.

"Right back at you, Madam President," Lauren said tartly.

"Fucking designer and Michael Oaks," Dev growled loudly, her hands clenching. "They die!"

Low and deep, Lauren chuckled. "Now there's a plan to get behind." She circled Devlyn, stepping forward to get a better look, then snorted a little. "How could you agree to wear that? You're... you're—!"

"An idiot?"

"I was going to say the President."

"Oh." Devlyn shook her head. "I am wearing this for my children..." Her voice had taken on a pious edge. "And I'm doing this for trade relations and for American autoworkers." She paused, her brows drawing together. "If I run again and lose Michigan after this, I'll go mad."

"That can't be a far trip from here."

Dev ignored Lauren's comment and ran her finger down the skintight material covering the blonde's belly, causing her partner to slap her hands away. "And how did *you* get talked into this?"

"Same reason as you," she admitted sheepishly. "Well, not the part about the auto workers; they're on their own. But when the kids said how beautiful my dress was... Jesus, Devlyn," she gave her eyes a dramatic roll, "I didn't have the heart to disappoint them."

"You're wearing this for *them*?" Dev croaked. *How can something so stupid make me feel like crying?* "Wow. That's amazing." She reached out and gently took Lauren's hand. She kissed it tenderly, before threading their fingers together and giving a gentle squeeze.

Lauren focused on Dev's proximity, her nearness more than enough to wreak havoc on her senses. "It is?" she asked absently, her cheeks turning pink as she easily lost herself in the bright blue eyes regarding her so fondly.

A smile tugged at Devlyn's lips. "You're wonderful, you know that?"

"My, my, aren't you full of compliments, today, Madam President." Lauren sighed dreamily. "I'm starting to get the impression that you're sweet on me."

A charmed smile worked its way across Dev's face. Truer words had never been spoken. "Imagine that." She was nearly overcome with the urge to taste the tempting coral lips that were curled into a beautiful smile.

Lauren drank in the look of unbridled desire in Dev's eyes and reacted without thought, rubbing the hand in hers with her thumb then lifting herself to her tiptoes to meet Devlyn in a searing kiss.

Dev moaned softly. "Do we have enough time?" she whispered against Lauren's mouth. Then she cupped Lauren's cheek and began dotting her face with tiny, feather-light kisses, forgetting her question completely.

Lauren sucked in a deep breath and let it out slowly, her eyes fluttering closed at the sweet, startlingly erotic contact. "God, Devlyn," she breathed thickly. "Who cares?"

"Think they're naked yet?" Beth asked David, in a voice for his ears only.

He looked at his watch. "Yup. It's been at least five minutes." He glanced at Frank, who was talking quietly to his wife as the children showed off their outfits to Mr. Yagasuki, who had just entered the room. "Is it time?"

Janet and Frank nodded. The white-haired man scratched his short, snowy beard. "Any longer and we run the risk of encountering a very embarrassing situation."

"And we wouldn't want that," Beth quipped, causing David to snigger. "Nothing embarrassing for the President and her First Lady."

"It wouldn't be proper," David said solemnly.

The adults and the children shared a round of devilish smiles and sniggers.

Toby Yagasuki knocked on the bedroom door, then nervously tugged at his suit coat and smoothed back his glossy black hair with a slightly shaky hand.

"Go away," Devlyn murmured between kisses, feeling Lauren's fingers dig deeply into her hair. "The President is gone."

He knocked again and this time it was Lauren who answered. "We are not coming out. Send the minister up in about... Mmm, Devlyn...

Err… a half, mmm… no, an hour."

The designer smiled. The women were just as he'd been told. Absolutely in love. The third time was a charm, and the small man straightened his back as he heard loud footsteps grow closer and closer to the door.

It was Devlyn who yanked the door open. Her hair was slightly mussed and her dress was seriously askew. "What?"

"May I come in, Madam President?"

Recognition flared and Devlyn took a step back to allow Mr. Yagasuki to enter. She wondered briefly if Lauren would kill him… before she got the chance. "Please," Devlyn took several more steps backwards, "come in." Then she moved aside so that Lauren could peek beyond her enormous dress and see their visitor. She heard a growl explode from behind her, and she almost felt sorry for the designer. Then she caught sight of her reflection in his rose-tinted glasses. Her pity evaporated.

"You!" Lauren accused, pointing an angry finger at the designer. "You're… you're…"

"In so much trouble," Devlyn finished.

His blood pressure skyrocketed. "Wait, please. Before you do… something." He was trying not to babble, knowing that his heavily accented English was nearly impossible to understand once he started down that path. But to his horror, he wasn't having much luck. "I have something for… for you. And something to say," he added hastily as he quickly stepped back out into the hallway. A few seconds later, he returned holding two heavy garment bags. "These are for you, Madam President and Ms. Strayer." He bowed again.

Devlyn and Lauren looked at each other. "More dresses?" Devlyn asked.

"Made by you?" Lauren gazed warily at the man.

He nodded proudly.

"No, thank you. Been there, done that."

Mr. Yagasuki's mouth trembled with alarm. "No, no, please. I assure you, that these will be more to your liking." He carefully draped the bags over the footboard of the bed, whose quilt was in disarray. He fought the urge to blush at the implication.

"If you have something to say for yourself, Yagasuki-San, you'd best do it now," Dev warned. She crossed her arms over her chest.

His eyes widened, and he tamped down an icy tendril of fear. "I was told Americans appreciate a well-executed practical joke." He paused, watching with interest as Dev and Lauren nearly fainted. Then he smiled. He would live to see tomorrow. "I can see now that I was told the truth." He bowed again. "It was my honor to work for you, Ms. Strayer, and your mother, Madam President. It is my sincere hope that you enjoy your *real* dresses." He glanced toward the bags. "You have plenty of time to dress and... Well, you have plenty of time. The time the wedding is scheduled to begin is, in actuality, one and one-half hours from now." He let out a shaky breath, relieved beyond measure that his part in this plan was finished. "If you will excuse me?"

Slack-jawed, Dev and Lauren just stared.

He didn't move. "If you will excuse me?" he repeated a little louder, growing worried once again. He'd thought he'd made it through the dangerous part. Now he wasn't so sure.

Dev was the first to come to her senses. "Yes. By all means, please feel free to go, Yagasuki-San," she said quickly. She shook her head, still stupefied. "Thank you. I think."

Yagasuki backed out the door, bowing as he went, not daring to turn his back on these women. His blood was still a little chilled from the looks they had given him when he first came to the door. Besides, he'd been told not to turn his back on the blonde woman. He wasn't taking any chances.

"Oh," he said as he reached the open door. "I was to tell you something else." His forehead creased and he scratched his chin, poking his fingers through a sparse tuft of longish black hair there. "But I am afraid I do not understand this part of your language."

"Yes?" Dev asked.

"Your parents, Madam President, and the Chiefs of Staff all wish me to say..." He smiled widely—just as David McMillian had asked him to do during this part—"Gotcha." And with that, he bolted out the door.

Lauren and Devlyn could hear the gales of laughter from downstairs. The younger woman blinked slowly and turned to face her partner. "Your *children* were in on this too? Those sweet little faces were *lying* to me?" Lauren's eyes were round with wonder. "Oh, my God," she said with exaggerated slowness. "What kind of family am I marrying into? I can't handle them, and they're not even teenagers! You're all pure evil!"

Dev flopped backwards onto the bed, causing her dress to puff up and nearly cover her head. "Pah!" She slapped at the springy material, knocking it away from her head. "I don't believe it." She stared at the ceiling, shifting slightly when she felt the bed next to her move with Lauren's weight. "They got us."

"Oh, they didn't just get us, Devlyn." Lauren let out a low chuckle that was half surprise and half awe. "This was the mother of all practical jokes." She grinned at her gullibility. "They got us *good*."

Dev had to smile too. "You know, this is odd, but I'm not really nervous about getting married anymore." She turned to face Lauren, fought with her dress for a moment, cursed, braced herself with her elbow, and then rested her head on her hand, letting out a massive sigh. "In fact, I can't wait to marry you," she said decisively.

Lauren's smile mirrored Devlyn's. "I feel the same way, darlin'. You know that." Her eyes took on a twinkling glow as they raked down her lover. "Would you like some help *out* of your dress, Madam President?" A slender eyebrow arched suggestively and Lauren snuggled a little closer. "We do have an entire hour and a half."

Dev's smile stretched farther across her face, deepening her laugh lines.

Lauren traced the tiny lines around her eyes and lips with tender fingertips, enjoying the quiet, strangely intimate moment.

The older woman turned her head and brushed her lips against Lauren's hand, taking her time to place a lingering kiss on a very sensitive palm.

Lauren shivered.

"I always wondered what it would be like to be with a lady of the evening," Devlyn commented saucily, attaching her lips to Lauren's throat.

"Hush up, Devlyn." Lauren laughed. "Or I'll suddenly grow allergic to those flowers on your arm and make you undress yourself."

"Perish the thought!" Devlyn glanced down at Lauren's breasts and began plucking feathers.

Lauren gasped as feathers were removed one by one, tickling her in very sensitive places.

"Oooo… Maybe this dress isn't so bad after all," Devlyn said with more than a hint of lechery in her voice.

"Oh, yeah," Lauren groaned out, sinking deeper into the bed and a sensual haze from which she wanted no reprieve.

"You know," Devlyn whispered between incendiary kisses, "it's bad luck to see the bride before the wedding."

It took a moment for Lauren to realize that Devlyn was actually talking to her. Devlyn did, she acknowledged fuzzily, have a tendency to ramble at the oddest moments. She sighed when persistent lips moved to her shoulder and began to nibble and her hips bucked forward of their own accord, seeking greater contact with the body astride her. "That may be true," she gasped when Dev's mouth trailed even lower. "But somehow I can't imagine myself... Oh, God. As anything but really, *really* lucky right now." She felt a short burst of warm air against her breast as Devlyn chuckled.

"Me too."

Lauren shifted from one foot to the other as she waited for her cue from Michael Oaks, who was impeccably dressed, lording it over the events like King Tut as he strutted back and forth in the rear of the tent. *He's gloating*, Lauren thought. *But rightly so.* The inside of the tent looked amazing, and despite the joke that nearly gave her and Devlyn twin heart attacks, it appeared that things were about to go off without a hitch. She was flanked by the Marlowe children, who were dancing around and chatting with guests seated near them. They were so excited that Lauren was sure that one or more of them would need to be rushed to the bathroom at any moment. Suddenly, she had a horrible thought and took stock of her own bladder, pleased that she'd followed an old piece of parental advice and gone before she'd left the cabin.

Much to Lauren and Devlyn's delight and relief, Mr. Yagasuki's one-of-a-kind creations had gone in a direction that no one had expected. Lauren's fingers drifted over the fine silver-colored embroidery that covered her fitted, pale green Celtic wedding gown that, everyone readily agreed, was to die for. Far from feeling like a costume, the simple but elegant dress had Lauren unconsciously correcting her posture and holding her chin a little bit higher.

Her shoulders were bare and her hair was swept up into a simple knot, showing off her slender neck and the plain silver chain that adorned it. The designer had allowed her to escape without a veil or even headpiece, instead insisting that a few simple flowers woven into her wavy hair would be perfect.

He had been right. Devlyn had stopped breathing altogether when she'd first seen Lauren completely dressed.

The tent was well-lit with dozens of tall, ribbon-wrapped, honey-scented candles, their sweet perfume mingling with that of hundreds of delicate white roses. It was also darker inside the tent than Lauren had expected, a testament to the storm that still shook the canvas sides of the tent with every great gust of wind.

She could see Devlyn across the tent, flanked by two very proud parents, her pale eyes flickering from person to person as Lauren awaited her cue to begin walking down the aisle. Somehow, at that exact moment, Devlyn's head slowly turned, and the women's eyes met and held for a long moment.

The President's gown wasn't in the least bit "poofy." It was similar in style to Lauren's, but was the color of warm desert sand. It had a fitted bodice, crepe skirt, and draping chiffon sleeves that hung gently over her slim wrists. Her train was longer than the younger woman's and the fine, amazingly detailed embroidery that covered the bodice was stitched in pale gold thread.

Lauren admired her lover. She was more than a little star-struck with Devlyn, who appeared nothing short of regal, and she had to laugh at herself for it. She actually lifted her hand to her mouth to make sure that it was closed and she wasn't drooling. How, she wondered gratefully, had she ever gotten so lucky as to end up here... on the verge of getting everything she'd ever dreamed of... even though she hadn't known it? *Amazing.*

Neither woman could keep from grinning wildly. Both their hearts were pounding, but more from anticipation than fear.

This was it.

Above the steady patter of rain on canvas came the gentle strains of a string quartet situated near the front of the tent, and suddenly Lauren was walking down the aisle without feeling her feet touch the ground. Then she was standing next to Devlyn, who grasped her hand with a sure, firm grip. She let out a slightly shaky breath, feeling much better in the company of her tall friend.

Dev smiled appreciatively at Lauren and whispered, "Fancy meeting you here."

Lauren squeezed Dev's hand, her lips curling upward. "Don't tell me you were expecting someone else?" she whispered back, as Devlyn's parents took their seats in the front row and the children found their places next to David, Beth, and the minister.

There were a few seconds of silence as the minister, a friendly look-ing young man who Devlyn suspected was barely old enough to drive, looked over his notes. *Or maybe I'm just getting really, really old*, she mused privately, making a mental note to ask her mother what Boy Scout pack the older woman had borrowed this boy from.

"Dearly beloved—"

"Wait!"

The band stopped playing.

A hundred pairs of eyes swung to the far right, rear side of the tent and landed on a short, chubby woman with a head of short, white hair.

Everyone on Devlyn's side of the family closed their eyes and moaned silently, and Michael Oaks collapsed into a chair, looking as though he might burst into tears.

"Devlyn?" Lauren questioned from the side of her mouth, her voice barely audible.

"Lord, help us. It's Aunt Myrtle," she explained, tempted to sic an agent on the old woman.

Myrtle stood up, clutching her enormous handbag. After the Secret Service forced her to allow them to search it, she refused to put it down for fear it would be stolen. "What's going on here?" the old woman asked, clearly confused.

"Hi, Aunt Myrtle," Aaron piped up cheerfully. "This is the wed-ding."

"Shhh!!" Christopher and Ashley scolded simultaneously, their voices managing to carry all the way to the back of the tent. "No talk-ing or we won't get cake later!"

Aaron's eyes widened and he clamped his mouth shut. Aunt Myrtle would have to figure things out for herself. Nobody was getting be-tween him and a four-foot cake. Nobody.

"Why are these women dressed as if Robin Hood is going to burst into this tent and save them?" Myrtle looked down at the guest in the seat next to her, who happened to be Howard Strayer.

"Don't ask me," he said a little defensively. "Like I understand. I'm a plumber."

Janet stood up and quickly scrambled toward Myrtle. "Carry on, carry on," she said, waving at the minister. "Don't mind us."

"How can you carry on without a groom?" Myrtle asked reasona-bly.

"You aren't the only one who's wondering that," Howard muttered under his breath.

"Myrtle," Janet warned, thinking that Frank really should have disclosed a list of all his insane relatives before she'd agreed to marry him.

"What the hell kind of messed-up wedding is this?" Myrtle continued, not worried one bit that she had interrupted the entire ceremony. "Why is that other woman standing so close to Devlyn? Did the groom stand poor Devlyn up?" She scanned the audience for the dastardly coward, ready to hit him with her purse.

"Aunt Myrtle," Devlyn suddenly said, trying to muster more patience than she knew she had. Myrtle never could figure out who Samantha was and why she kept appearing at Marlowe family functions. Then when she found out she had the name "Marlowe" she surmised that Janet and Frank had secretly adopted her, and no one could convince her otherwise. "There is *no* man, Aunt Myrtle. Remember how we've talked about this before?" She turned to Lauren and mouthed, "Sorry."

Lauren only smiled and shrugged. There was no need to explain crazy relatives to a Southerner. They were to be expected.

Myrtle made a sour face and addressed Devlyn as though she were an errant child. "I always told you that men couldn't stand tall, mouthy women." She waggled a gnarled finger at her great niece. "Now look what's happened! You've been stood up at the altar."

Lauren and Beth snorted loudly, unable to contain themselves any longer.

Dev tilted her head skyward and whimpered. Then she addressed God. "This is because I was secretly considering raising taxes, isn't it?"

"Don't you tell me to be quiet, Janet Marlowe," Myrtle complained, her voice drowning out Devlyn's conversation with the Divine. "Is this how you treat your guests? Why, not half an hour ago I was molested by that handsome young man in the black suit." She motioned at a Secret Service agent. "He made me open my purse!"

Janet fought hard not to roll her eyes. "I know, Myrtle. I know," she soothed.

"Do you suppose he's single?" Myrtle asked, sincerely. "Devlyn's gonna be an old maid soon, if you're not careful. People will talk."

Most of the guests were laughing now, and the minister was looking so flustered at the unexpected interruption that Devlyn wasn't sure he would be able to speak when the time came. She leaned down and pressed her lips to Lauren's ear. "You didn't think this would be a normal wedding, did you?"

A laugh bubbled up from Lauren.

"Would you still love me if we skipped over the singing, poetry, and praying and got right to the vows and the kissing?" There was a hint of pleading in Devlyn's voice.

The shorter woman lifted a sassy eyebrow, but smiled warmly, her eyes conveying her true feelings. "What do you think, Devlyn?" she whispered back.

Devlyn drew in a deep breath and turned slightly to address their guests. "Well, folks, it looks like despite the fact that I've been stood up at the altar..." she paused as everyone laughed, "my heart *will* mend."

Any remaining tension in the room fell away when everyone realized that neither Devlyn nor Lauren was going to have Myrtle shot for the interruption. Then their wedding guests leaned forward a little in their seats as they sensed that the wedding was about to begin. All except Myrtle, that is, who had been drafted by the two agents and taken outside under two large umbrellas to hunt for Devlyn's errant groom.

Devlyn wound her arm around Lauren's and pulled her closer. "Okay, Reverend." A genuine grin split her face. Despite everything, this was shaping up to be the best day of her life. "Make me the happiest woman on earth. And this time," her voice dropped a register, causing the young man to blink a few times and the audience to lean even further forward in their seats, "don't stop until she's mine in every sense of the word." She turned and looked deeply into Lauren's eyes, her own eyes filling with sparkling, unshed tears. "Forever."

There was a soft chorus of "awwwwws" from their friends and family that caused Devlyn's cheeks to flush pink, but there was no doubting the solid truth of her words.

The younger woman could only hoarsely repeat the sentiment, barely getting the words out around the lump that had grown in her throat.

Many years later, after a lifetime of conversation, Lauren Strayer would still recall Devlyn's words from this day as the single most romantic thing she'd ever heard. And they were all hers.

It wasn't a perfect wedding, but it was theirs... and they were keeping it.

JULY 2022

Friday, July 1ˢᵗ

Devlyn yawned and wrapped a protective arm around Lauren's waist. She was grateful for the relative seclusion of the cabin as she and Lauren wove their way between the deep puddles on the tree-lined path. The reception had gone on much longer than either she or Lauren would have liked. But its purpose was to honor their newly blessed marriage. It was so rare and wonderful to have all their friends and family in one place that they endured the endless toasts and raucous, familial chatter with a dose of good humor and several longing looks toward each other and the door.

Those same heavy-lidded looks, in fact, along with sweet, stolen kisses and hour after hour of casually intimate touches had left the women aching for some peaceful time alone together. David had assured her that, for what little remained of their wedding night, come hell or high water she and Lauren would be left alone. Devlyn knew that promise only went so far, but for the time being the world seemed to be letting them have their special day. She smiled as she put her hand on the front door's knob and felt Lauren's hand come to rest directly on her bottom. "Madam, I might remind you that we still have eyes upon us."

"Like I care about those agents and their night-vision goggles." She turned her head and stuck her tongue out just to be ornery, then tilted her head back and yawned, observing the now clear night sky. "They're lucky I don't throw you down on this porch and have my way with you."

Dev smirked, knowing full well that most of the Secret Service and a healthy number of FBI and CIA agents had crushes on her wife. "Somehow I doubt they consider you controlling yourself to be their good fortune." She turned to regard her companion. "Too much to drink, Boris?"

"Eh…" Lauren wiggled her hand back and forth. "Close, Natasha."

Devlyn sniggered as the hand on her rear began to slowly move up and down.

"Devlyn, just get the door open." Her voice was a low growl. "Ugh! If one more mosquito bites me, I'm going to get malaria!"

"I thought you liked it in the woods," Dev said.

Devlyn poked out her lower lip, and Lauren was tempted to grab it. The blonde sniggered loudly. "I like *it* everywhere. But I like to *sleep* in the cabin. *Big* difference."

"Mmm… True." Devlyn opened the door and took a step backward to stand behind Lauren. She gestured for Lauren to enter by placing her hand on the small of the shorter woman's back and pushing slightly. "Our honeymoon suite awaits."

"Tsk, you mean you're not going to carry me over the threshold?" Lauren teased, already moving forward.

"If you insist."

"Wh—!" Lauren's squeal rang out into the night.

Before Lauren could stop her, Devlyn swept her off her feet and carried her into the cabin, managing to muffle a groan when she turned and kicked the cabin door closed. She set a very surprised Lauren down and tried not to look too pleased with herself. Which was exceedingly difficult. She crossed her arms and waited for her reward.

"Wow." Lauren said, clearly impressed. "That was nuts, Dev. Did anyone ever tell you you're pretty strong for a middle-aged desk jockey?" She reached out to squeeze Devlyn's biceps, all the while emitting a low whistle.

Devlyn bared her teeth in a false smile and slapped away her hands. "I am *not* middle-aged," she said, straightening her back and throwing her chest out, much to Lauren's delight. "I plan on living to be at least one hundred and seven, which means—"

"Stop." The blonde woman held up her hand. "Don't do the math. I'm too tired to think about math."

They both laughed softly and leaned against the cabin door, the wood feeling cool against their hot skin. The rain had stopped sometime during the reception, ushering in a wave of thick, muggy air that the air-conditioner had to work hard to repel. Candles, already burning low, had been lit and placed along the banister leading to the loft and around the fireplace in the main room. They emitted a soft, golden glow and sweet, vanilla scent.

Devlyn turned to face her new bride, her expression serious. She slowly ran her knuckles over Lauren's cheek. "I love you."

Lauren smiled, a little amazed at the fluttering in the pit of her stomach that Devlyn could incite with one touch, or look, or sultry whisper. "You know," she said thoughtfully, as though she'd just had the revelation that very second, "I really love you too."

Dev's smile reached her eyes, and she kissed her partner on the cheek and then turned her toward the living room.

"This is beautiful." Lauren shook her head a little as she took it all in. "Your folks?"

"No, as I understand it," Dev paused to remove her shoes, tossing them next to the door, "Beth and David did this. I did the same thing when they used this place for their honeymoon." Dev's gaze bounced around the room, then her eyes narrowed. "Only I was thoughtful enough to provide cold beer."

"Oh no, you don't." Lauren groaned and moved to the sofa, settling down heavily as she struggled out of her own shoes. "One more toast after dinner and I would have ended up face-down in the punch bowl. I stopped just in time, though I'm still a little buzzed," she admitted. "Lord knows, I don't want to be drunk on my wedding night." She left off the word "again," surmising that was more information than Devlyn really wanted to know. She covered her face with her hands and spared a thought for her first wedding night, now seeing what she thought was ordinary wedding jitters with very different eyes. *What a moron I was.*

"Ahhh." Devlyn found an ice bucket loaded with bottled water. "I knew you weren't my best friend for nothing, David," she murmured as she grabbed two bottles.

Lauren wiggled her sore feet. "God, I'm tired."

"Even I feel tired after today, and I gave up sleep for Lent last year." Dev handed over a cold bottle of water. "Why don't you go take a nice hot shower and change into something more comfortable?" She eyed Lauren from top to bottom and her voice softened as she said, "Though I've never seen any woman look more beautiful than you did today, Lauren."

Gray eyes sparkled with appreciation as Lauren returned the favor, happily giving her mate the once over. "I think you know I feel the same way." The blonde drained her bottle and handed the empty back with a grin. "How about we go to bed now and do something that will require a shower later?"

Devlyn laughed low in her throat and extended her hand, suppressing another yawn with her other hand. She pulled Lauren into a long hug, allowing herself to revel in a moment of pure happiness.

Finally, Lauren gently pulled back enough to lay her palms against

Dev's upper chest, feeling the other woman draw in a slow, deep breath. "If you're too tired...?" she whispered.

Dev's eyes popped open. She could hear the smile in Lauren's voice, and she blinked hard, feeling disoriented. Then she recalled what Lauren had said. "No! Not on your life!" Devin cupped Lauren's warm cheek and spoke against soft lips as she kissed her. "But, honey, I'm inching toward middle age as we speak. Let's go."

Bathed in soft moonlight, they lay together on the bed, nude. Sheets and blankets lay crumpled on the floor as they traded slow, deep kisses. Two sets of smooth, damp legs were tangled tightly together, tingling skin being caressed with each shift of their bodies. They'd been kissing for so long that they'd lost track of the time, their bodies thrumming lightly with excitement.

Without warning, Devlyn rolled Lauren on top of her. The blonde's head swam, and she suddenly felt a little queasy. Even in the faint light, Devlyn detected the change in her coloring and pinned her with concerned eyes. "Lauren," she said quietly, sinking her hands deeply into Lauren's hair and tilting the younger woman's chin up just a fraction so that she could look into her eyes. "Are you okay?"

"Ugh." Lauren grimaced. "I drank at least a bottle of champagne tonight, sweetheart. Gymnastics are *so* out for the evening." Her body shook with Devlyn's soft laughter. "Can we do this without spinning, please?"

Dev smiled fondly and used the tip of her index finger to lovingly trace pale eyebrows. "We can. But we can just go to sleep." She leaned upward and softly bussed Lauren's chin. "If you're too tired."

"Are you?" Lauren asked, half-hoping Devlyn would say yes. She was exhausted and that, in combination with the alcohol and food, had her yearning to crawl underneath the covers and sleep for a week. Problem was she also wanted to kiss and lick every square inch of the beautiful body beneath her. She was well past the point of no return and this *was* their wedding night.

"No," Devlyn answered quickly, looking for any sign that Lauren might want to put this off. There was no doubting how aroused she was, but the bed was so soft and even the moonlight seemed too bright for tired eyes.

A genuine smile twitched at Lauren's lips for a split second before she captured Devlyn's mouth in a delicious, wet kiss.

Devlyn let out a soft, encouraging moan, forgetting all about being sleepy and reveling in the sensation of naked skin beneath her fingertips and Lauren's soft, warm tongue against her own.

Lauren's mouth moved to Devlyn's ear then neck. "Mmm... Devlyn, you smell so—Ack Phft!" She lifted her head and tried to dislodge the chunk of hair stuck to her damp lips and chin.

"What's wrong?" Devlyn moved her head, effectively cleaning Lauren's face.

"Your hair tastes like hairspray." She made a face and wiped at her tongue. "Yuck."

"You're not supposed to *eat* it."

"No talking," Lauren murmured playfully, attaching her lips to Devlyn's throat and lightly sucking just as she brought up one hand to cup Dev's breast.

The taller woman arched her back and groaned at the contact, her eyes fluttering shut of their own accord.

Lauren moved to begin kissing lower as Devlyn squirmed a little under her touch. Her elbow jabbed Dev's breast and the President nearly shot up off the bed.

"Ouch!" Her eyes flew open, and she grasped herself in a gesture that made it look as if she were having a heart attack. She sucked in a huge breath, then let it out explosively. "Christ!"

"Oh, shit!" Lauren began to panic, just knowing that her accidental jab, in combination with the ridiculous stress of the Presidency, had been too much for Devlyn. "Shit! You're having a coronary? Oh, my God! Is your arm numb?" She grabbed at Dev's arm and shook it.

Dev wrenched her arm out of Lauren's hands. "You... you're insane!"

"I can't remember which arm is supposed to be numb." She scrubbed her face with rough, jerky movements. "Shit. Shit. Shit!"

"Nothing is numb," Dev ground out, unable to keep from laughing. "Goddammit, Lauren, I told you I'm not even middle-aged! I am not dying! It's my *boob*!" Miserably, Dev pointed at her own nipple.

"Oh." Lauren blinked. "*Ohhhhhhhh.*" She let out a relieved breath, finally getting the message. "You nearly scared the life out of me," she said, her heart still pounding. She was tempted to smack Devlyn for nearly giving her a heart attack of her own. Then her eyes narrowed as she thought about what Devlyn said. Had she bumped her breast? "I can't even remember doing it. I couldn't have done more than barely touch you!"

Dev's jaw clenched, then she forced herself to relax. "I'm near to cycling and they're a little sensitive," she told her, a little embarrassed at what might be characterized as an overreaction to the accidental jab. She was more startled than anything. "And if you even *think* the word 'menopause,'" Dev said it as though it were a curse, "your next vacation spot will be adjacent to Jimmy Hoffa."

"Aww... I'm sorry, honey," Lauren said, trying her best not to laugh and utterly failing. She removed the hand that was clutching Devlyn's breast and replaced it with her own, letting her mate feel the warmth of her palm. She made a concerted effort to let all the love she felt for Dev show in her eyes as she kissed Dev's hand, paying special attention to each long finger. "It was an accident." Her eyebrows lifted in entreaty. "Forgive me?" she said softly. "I would never hurt you on purpose. Please?"

Dev placed her hand over the one on her breast and squeezed gently, melting a little under the loving attention. "Of course. I'm sorry I scared you."

"Kiss it and make it better?" Lauren gestured toward the breast in question with a tilt of her head. Her own arousal, which had been like a pendulum all night, had all but evaporated at the thought of Devlyn croaking. But the soft, desire-filled eyes gazing so intently into hers were more than she could ignore.

The dark-haired woman nearly said no, that they could just resume this in the morning, God knows it wasn't exactly going well, but Lauren looked so earnest she couldn't bear the thought of disappointing her new bride on their wedding night. "Sure."

Lauren smiled and kissed her way down to Devlyn's breast, peppering her soft skin with even softer kisses.

It only took seconds before Devlyn was drifting on a wave of emotion. It was, Dev decided, utterly divine. The warm feeling of Lauren's breath and lips and tongue gently caressing her nipple and the sides and undersides of her breast was so breathtaking that she relaxed under the tender ministrations, sinking deeper into the bed, mesmerized.

Lauren's mouth drifted lower and lower and she dipped her tongue in Dev's navel, knowing Dev was especially ticklish there. Instead of the chuckle she expected, she heard a... Lauren's ears perked and she suddenly lifted her head from her task and gazed up at her lover. "Was that a *yawn* I just heard?"

"Nooo…" Devlyn insisted, her mind snapping back into the moment with almost brutal force. "A moan." She was sure going to hell for such a blatant lie, but some things just couldn't be helped. There was no way she would hurt her lover's feelings tonight.

"Okay," Lauren answered a little skeptically, fighting the urge to yawn herself. "Because if you're too ti—"

"I am not too tired. I'm not!" Dev said sheepishly, knowing she sounded a little like a three-year-old who was fighting bedtime. Devlyn gently urged Lauren's head lower. "Carry on." She flopped her head back on the pillow and licked her lips in anticipation.

And Lauren did, settling herself between Devlyn's legs and tenderly kissing each thigh before making more intimate contact. Both women groaned languidly at the first touch of Lauren's tongue. But soon the contact wasn't quite enough for Devlyn, who was thrashing around like she was on fire. Rather than instruct Lauren verbally that she needed to move just a teensy, tiny, bit to the left, Dev kept shifting over in the bed, frustrating her partner no end. Dev, unfortunately, mistook Lauren's frequent, helpless chuckles and growls of frustration for those of pleasure.

Lauren was hanging onto Dev's hips, thinking her tongue might fall off soon, when Devlyn sat up, desperately grabbed her face, okay… her ears, and said, "Almost, baby. Right here!" Abruptly, she pulled Lauren's face forward and the younger woman's teeth collided with a very, *very* sensitive spot.

"UGH!" Dev yelled, her face turning beet-red. Then she let out a protracted wail that shook the rafters and sounded very much like a cross between Tarzan and a cat whose tail had just been caught under a rocking chair. Her legs slammed shut with stunning force, boxing Lauren's ears and causing her to howl.

"AHH!" Lauren rolled over and grabbed her ears… and took a nosedive off the side of the bed. She landed with a loud thump.

When Devlyn could think again, she looked up, trying to find Lauren. She couldn't see her, but she could hear pitiful whimpering and the occasional curse word coming from somewhere in the darkness.

Finally, Lauren weakly crawled up onto the bed and laid her head carefully on Devlyn's stomach, wrapping her arms around her waist and kissing the soft skin beneath her lips.

Devlyn slowly stroked Lauren's hair.

"Devlyn?"

"Yeah?"

"Is this supposed to be as dangerous as running with scissors?"

They both dissolved into laughter.

"I never thought so until now," Devlyn admitted. "I guess that 'for better or worse' stuff starts early with some couples, huh?" She could still feel Lauren's chuckles warming the skin of her belly. "C'mere." She scooted over a little so Lauren could share her pillow. Twin sighs escaped them as blonde and ebony hair mixed against the pale blue pillowcase.

"Can we just go to sleep?" Devlyn asked. "Please, oh please? There's always tomorrow."

"For the love of God, yes!" Grunting happily, she kissed Devlyn's cheek, then nuzzled her neck, drawing in a satisfying breath of Dev-scented air.

Dev sent up a silent prayer. "How are your ears?"

Her voice was filled with concern, and Lauren snuggled closer eager to reassure her. She was sure the ringing in her ears would stop. Someday. "I'll live, sweetheart. More importantly, how is your—"

"I'll live too," Dev said quickly. She sniggered at herself. "But just barely."

"Darlin'" Lauren whispered after a few silent minutes. "That was *still* better than my wedding night with Judd."

Two sets of giggles filled the cabin along with the morning sun.

The cameras couldn't be avoided as they made their way across the tarmac to Air Force One. Dev had given Lauren a questioning glance when they got out of the car, and she nodded, smiling bravely as she followed Dev toward the crowd of reporters. After only three and a half hours of sleep, their eyes were bloodshot and their backs stiff, but they consoled each other with promises of long naps on the plane and many hours of doing nothing more than being together on their honeymoon.

Once they were in range of the press corps, the questions started flying like bolts of lightning from the storm the day before.

"Where are you going on your honeymoon, Madam President?"

"I have no earthly idea." Dev grinned, tightening her hold on Lauren's hand. "Our honeymoon is classified and only the First Lady, whoever her co-conspirators were, and the pilot know where we're going."

"And I'm not telling," Lauren said enigmatically, deciding to give up the fight for now and make the best possible impression she could. She held her breath for a few seconds until the reporters began to laugh at her comment.

"Where are your children?" a reporter asked, his nose in his notepad.

Devlyn answered, "The children are safe and sound and enjoying a vacation of their own with Chiefs of Staff David and Beth McMillian."

"So you're going into hiding for a romantic getaway and escaping the kids?" a woman near the back of the pack asked.

Lauren's back stiffened. She didn't like the way the question was phrased; who took their children on their honeymoon? But she knew what the reporter was getting at. "I'm quite certain that where the children are going we won't be missed. And the President and I are very much looking forward to some downtime alone. I think we're due, don't you?" she couldn't help but add, feeling Dev squeeze her hand. "They'll be joining us later in the week."

"Will you be working on the President's biography, Mrs. Marlowe?"

"It's *still* Ms. Strayer." *Which I know you know because Devlyn was forced to issue a press release on the subject last week.* "And, no, I won't be working on the book." Her patience was thinning faster than she'd imagined. "I hope I'm going to spend most of my time totally nak—"

"Well!" Devlyn jumped in. She smiled broadly. "It's certainly a warm morning here in Ohio, isn't it? Any other questions?"

Just then, Liza, who had arrived in another car, caught Devlyn's attention by pointing at her watch.

"That's all for now, ladies and gentlemen. But somehow I'm certain we'll run into each other again soon." There were more chuckles as the Agent-In-Charge escorted Devlyn and Lauren to the gangway. The President returned the brisk salutes of the servicemen flanking the gangway as she and Lauren separated from all but a bare-bones staff and quickly disappeared inside the plane.

Once inside, Lauren sighed and leaned against the wall and closed her eyes. "I'll never get used to that."

"You will," Dev assured her, nodding her greeting at several crew members.

On his way to the galley, a scurrying steward offered both women a beverage, which they politely declined.

"Remember, Lauren," Dev fondly brushed a piece of windblown hair from Lauren's face. "I won't be President forever."

Lauren sighed. "Thank God." The sudden silence in the room caused her to open her eyes. "I'm sorry, honey." She stepped closer to Devlyn, her eyes conveying her regret. "I didn't mean that the way it sounded." She was very aware of the disapproving stares she was receiving from several junior staffers, and she felt the tips of her ears heat.

To Lauren's relief, Dev smiled. "I know how you meant it." Then she lowered her voice for Lauren's ears only. "I think the same thing about half the time."

"Madam President?" A young Air Force officer approached her hesitantly. "We have a secure call for you. It's urgent, ma'am."

Dev sighed. She closed her eyes and nodded slowly. *We're not even in the air yet!* "I'll take it in my office. Will you escort the First Lady to our quarters please?"

Dutifully, he nodded. "Of course, ma'am."

Devlyn leaned forward and gently kissed Lauren on the lips, ignoring the blush the serviceman was now sporting. "I'll be as quick as I can. I promise."

"I know you will." Lauren rested her palm on Dev's cheek and gave her a loving, if tired, smile. "Such is the life of the wife of a superhero. Go save the world, Devlyn. I'll see you in a few." She watched as two aides instantly appeared at the President's side and her partner's demeanor shifted into that of the no-nonsense Commander-in-Chief. One of the aides pressed two thick folders into Dev's hands and the other opened her office door and ushered her inside. A worried expression overtook Lauren's face.

"Ma'am? Excuse me, ma'am?"

She looked up to find the serviceman still waiting for her. "Sorry," she muttered absently, her fingers moving to her glasses.

He motioned toward the door that led to the private living areas on the plane.

"No, thank you." She paused and read the man's nametag and took note of his rank, something she'd learned to recognize in recent months. "No, thank you, Lieutenant Felznick. I think I'll go to my office instead." Lauren laid her hand on his forearm. "You don't need to bother showing me, I know the way. Thank you." She smiled warmly.

"Of course." He smiled, pleased she'd addressed him by name. He couldn't wait to send a letter back home to Iowa and tell his mother. He politely excused himself, feeling ten feet tall.

When Lauren opened the door to her office, she found a large stack of mail on her desk and a note from Beth that said:

Lauren,

*I know how boring these long flights can be while Dev is busy **not** working <smile>. In the future, I'll assign one of your new admins to sort through this kind of thing. For now, however, I thought it might be fun for you to get a taste of what type of mail you can expect. Aren't we "Miss Popular"? You'd think you were... oh, I dunno, The First Lady!*

Congrats, my friend. I can't tell you how I happy I am for you and Devil. The difference you've made in her life...well...I think you already know about that.

*Okay, back to business. If by some miracle, Dev is actually **not** busy and you have no time to look at these, don't worry. That's why you have a staff.*

I know how important it is to you that you be able to continue working on the biography, Lauren. Being First Lady doesn't mean you have to trash your own career or put it on hold. Well, it has in the past, but while this administration is making history, we might as well change that too.

Have a safe and wonderful honeymoon!

Beth

Taking a seat, Lauren pulled the chair closer to the desk and adjusted her glasses. The first ten letters were all invitations for her and Devlyn or her alone to attend charitable functions. Then came one asking for a private interview from a *New York Times* reporter who was interested in her personal opinion of the DNA Registration Act. "Yeah, right." Lauren snorted, recognizing a can of worms when she saw one.

That piece of legislation was a significant place where their political views diverged. "Like I'm that stupid."

The next three letters contained invitations to a birthday party for the Chief Justice of the Ohio Supreme Court, an anniversary party for the Emancipation Party leader, and a Labor Day fundraiser for the League of Women Voters (LWV) that was to be held in the nation's capital. "Oh, boy." Her eyes widened. How can I decide between these? Neither one of us has time for any of them!" she moaned, but after a few more moments of thought, she put every envelope but the LWV invitation into a large manila folder marked "Declined." The LWV invitation went into another folder marked TBD (To be Determined).

"No complaining, Lauri," she told herself as she grabbed the next stack of letters. "Soon you'll be feeling the warm sun on your face." She paused a moment to let out a wistful sigh for what she knew was coming. "And whatever Devlyn's dealing with is a lot worse than this." With that, she sent good thoughts to the office next door and got back to work.

Dev sat behind her desk, rubbing the bridge of her nose, trying to quell the headache that was creeping up on her. They'd been in the air for close to two hours. Her aides had been dismissed so this phone call could take place in private.

"Madam President?" Secretary of Defense Brendwell inquired somewhat curtly. "Your orders, ma'am?"

Devlyn asked, "Can I assume that the appropriate parties have been notified, including Vice President Vincent?"

"Absolutely, Madam President. We sent a complete intelligence report to everyone, as you were being contacted. Vice President Vincent is awaiting your decision."

"Okay." Devlyn nodded, satisfied, for now. "I want to continue to monitor the situation. If those missiles move an inch I want to know about it." She sucked in a quick breath, remembering where she was. "Scratch that. I am to be kept abreast only of any significant changes in the current situation. Geoff is there for a reason."

There was a long silence on the other end of the line before, "I'm not sure what you mean, ma'am."

"The hell you aren't, John," Dev shot back, irritated. "You can advise him all you want, but Vice President Vincent will determine what is and what is not significant. And if he decides that it's necessary, only *then* am I to be notified." It was killing her to let go of the reins, but she'd trusted Geoff enough to make him her running mate. At some point she had to have the man do more than go to State funerals and finagle votes out of Congress. It was time to put her money where her mouth was. She couldn't help but add, "However, I want a full written report summarizing the day's events ready if and when I have time to review it. Understood?"

"Yes, ma'am," came the grudging answer.

"Our presence hasn't been detected, correct?"

"Correct, ma'am. We have a contingent of operatives in the area to supplement our satellite surveillance. At last report, they were undetected."

"Those operatives are a top priority, Secretary Brendwell."

"Understood, Madam President. We have an evacuation plan in place, if the need arises."

"Anything else?"

"No, ma'am."

There was another uncomfortable pause before he said, "Enjoy your honeymoon, Madam President."

Detecting no sarcasm in his voice, Devlyn smiled. She knew the pugnacious man was still struggling to overcome his natural hostility to reporting to a woman. And to his credit, he had made some progress, his commitment to professionalism resolute. But that didn't mean he wasn't a complete asshole. "I intend to, John. Thank you."

She ended the call with a string of security codes and sat back in her chair, her gaze still lingering over printouts showing hostile troop movements and covert transportation routes being used for weapons of mass destruction that supposedly didn't exist. She carefully rolled up the blueprints and placed them in her desk using another series of codes and a retinal scan lock to secure the documents.

Devlyn pushed a button on the intercom. "Can you please tell the First Lady that I'm lonely?" She heard a muffled chuckle on the other end of the line.

"Right away, Madam President."

A few minutes later, there was a light knock on her door. She smiled reflectively. "Come in."

Lauren stuck her head in and said in a deep voice that sounded like

Lurch, "You raaaaaaang?"

Devlyn laughed. "That show was over before you were born."

"Tsk. Old television shows never die, Devlyn. They just go to Nick At Night." She made her way to Dev's desk, seeing the lines of tension on her face. "Finished working?"

Devlyn rubbed her temples. "For now."

Lauren almost didn't ask, but curiosity got the best of her as she perched on the corner of Devlyn's desk. "Something important?"

Dev chewed on her lower lip and unconsciously began stroking the soft cotton of Lauren's chinos. "Yes and no. The North Koreans are playing with their toys again. They don't know that we know they have them." She regretted once again that her predecessors hadn't been able to resolve a conflict that was far older than she was. "So we have to be careful," she said absently. "We don't like it when they move missiles around. Let's go sit down." With a groan, she rose from her desk and threw herself on the sofa. She closed her eyes.

Lauren eyed her suspiciously, then pressed the intercom. "Hi. Could we get a couple of bottles of water and some aspirin, please?" She still felt a little funny about having other people do things that she could easily do for herself. But she had long since learned that if she went in search of something as simple as aspirin she'd spend more time explaining herself and fending off the helpful staff than if she simply asked for it to begin with.

A single blue eyeball rolled sideways and regarded Lauren as she moved to the door. "How did—?"

"You have another headache," Lauren said. It wasn't a question. She frowned as she stepped around the sofa and laid her hands on Dev's shoulders, feeling the tension there. "You're getting those too often, darlin'." She stopped talking long enough to allow a steward into the room with Dev's aspirin. When they were alone again, she popped the top on the bottle of pills. "Is it a bad one?"

Devlyn smiled weakly. "Nah. Besides, I see them as a good sign. It means I'm still getting blood flow to the gray matter. Did you rest at all?" she asked, wanting desperately to change the subject. "I'm sorry about that call. I didn't plan on being pulled away as soon as we were on board."

Lauren shook her head as Dev sat up and took the pills, and then made a spot for her on the sofa. "No. I was waiting for you." She spoke over Devlyn, who had just drawn in a deep breath. "No arguments,

Devlyn. You might be able to function on a few hours sleep. I, however, cannot. And I sleep best if you're with me."

Devlyn smiled, charmed by the admission. "You do?"

"Mmm... hmm." She found herself pulled into a surprisingly fierce hug. "What was that for?" Lauren laughed.

"I thought it was just me who slept better when we were together."

Lauren cocked her head to the side. "Is that something you've wondered about?"

Devlyn nodded. "I thought maybe I bothered you or something... at night. It's hard for some people to get used to sleeping together after going it alone for a while," she quickly added.

"I... I don't... If you were worried about that why didn't you just ask?" She reached up and softly petted Devlyn's dark hair, smiling at the few silver strands she saw at the very top of Dev's head.

Dev shrugged. "Ask me something easier."

Lauren let out a heavy breath. They were both tired. The last thing they needed was a serious talk... at least about them. She eyed the phone. "Think that thing will leave you alone long enough for me to ravish you repeatedly this week?"

Her words were met with a brilliant smile. "It had better. I left pretty explicit instructions."

"You're trusting Geoff to handle things?" Lauren was a little surprised. Devlyn was the most professionally driven person she'd ever known. Delegating responsibility and learning to let go were basically foreign concepts to her.

"I'm trying. Really." Dev shifted just a little, placing a particularly sore muscle right under Lauren's hands. "And leave my gray hairs alone. I've earned all of them in the last year," she teased even as she rolled her neck. "That feels really good. I luuuvv you."

Lauren smiled, her gray eyes twinkling. "I don't know if you'll luuuvv me," she touched Devlyn's nose with the tip of her finger, "when you see what I have in the back pocket of my pants."

Dev's eyebrows shot skyward. "The back pocket of your pants, huh?" She gave herself a few seconds to allow her imagination to run wild, and a slow, but slightly wary, smile spread across her face. "Dare I ask?"

Lauren grinned back. "Dare."

"Okay."

Dev waited for moment, but Lauren didn't move. "Lauren," she said in her lowest voice, "you know how I feel about being kept in suspense. Tell me what's in your back pocket."

Lauren smiled innocently. "But you didn't say please. Yeow!"

In a flurry of motion, Devlyn reached around and grabbed Lauren, flipping her over on the sofa, causing them to end up in a tangle of arms and legs. A quick shift and Lauren was lying across Devlyn's lap in the spanking position.

Lauren blew a strand of pale hair from her face. "You wouldn't dare!" she squawked.

Dev chuckled, the sound starting low in her chest and evolving into a full laugh. "We've already determined that I would dare, haven't we? Now, show me or I'll look myself."

Lauren squirmed. "You big—"

"Too late." Dev reached into the pocket in question and snagged two very small pieces of material. Her face scrunched up as she examined the bright red spandex from all directions. "Dental floss, how considerate of you, darling."

"If you recall, you did ask me to pack for you." Lauren craned her head backwards and smiled sexily at her partner. "So I did," she said simply. "Surprise."

Devlyn held up the items in hand. "You want me to wear *this*?"

Lauren's smile shifted into an outright leer. "Oh yeah."

"But it's, it's… it's… umm… there's nothing to it!" She examined it again. "I assume we won't be going out to dinner."

Lauren smirked. "Well, *I* won't be going hungry. That's for damn sure."

Dev laughed to herself before delivering a quick smack to the backside across her lap. "You're evil. This bikini, if you could call it that, would get me arrested in half the states in the country. Have you been taking lessons from my mother?"

"Ouch!" Lauren began to wriggle when another sharp smack was delivered. She laughed. "Do you know what's really sick, Devlyn? That feels sort of good." That little comment got her two more for good measure. "Wait! Wait!" she screamed, laughing so hard that she was feeling a little dizzy. "I changed my mind."

"Uh huh."

"And I'll have you know I was evil long before I met Janet, she just solidified my belief in that way of life... Yah! Devlyn! No more."

Smack!

"You'll be sorry when I start asking for this."

Dev was quick to grab her squirming partner and flip her around.

"You know," she paused to bend and kiss Lauren's ear. "I have a lovely bed onboard. Are you now, or have you ever been, a member of the Mile High Club?"

"If I answer that question honestly, will I ever see you on a sleazy talk show telling the world about it?"

"You could buy my silence." Dev wiggled her brows.

"Ooo." Lauren nuzzled Dev's neck. "My little tramp." She let out an explosive breath when tickling fingers found her sides. "Yikes! What's gotten into you today?" She glanced at Devlyn's face and found her beaming. Lauren's heart skipped a beat at the sight.

"I'm happy." Her touch gentled and she pressed her lips to Lauren's forehead. "My life is better than I ever thought it could be. I've heard it's okay to be happy under those circumstances." Dev finally allowed Lauren to sit up all the way, using her lap as her chair.

"It's *way* okay, Devlyn." She leaned forward and kissed her softly, taking the time to explore Devlyn's mouth and reveling in the intensity of emotions she could feel flowing between them. "I feel exactly the same way," she said, her lips barely touching Dev's. Then she pulled back and smiled impishly. "Do you have any idea how fantastic you're going to look in this bikini... with those legs that go on for miles?" Playfully, she fanned herself with one hand. "I can't wait."

"I take it we're going someplace warm?"

"You'd look great if you were wearing that," she snatched the bikini bottoms out of Dev's hand and twirled them on one finger, "even in Siberia." Fondly, she cupped Dev's chin. "But I wouldn't want you to catch a cold." Those lips were just too close, and she was way past trying to restrain herself so she kissed them again.

After a few minutes of intense kissing, Lauren drew in a deep, contented breath. "Mmmm..." She smacked her lips happily, not bothering to open her eyes. "Did you just ask me a question?" She'd thought she heard Dev talking. But that couldn't be right—Devlyn's mouth was busy!

"I was gulping for air."

Lauren clamped her hand over her mouth to keep from laughing.

Dev's grin took on a sexy edge that caused all the moisture in Lauren's mouth to instantly dry up and fly southward toward a happier home. "Come on, Lauren. Let me show you the new bed I had put in and what a great massage I can give."

"Like I could ever say no to that."

And she didn't.

Dev looked out over the balcony to their private beach and smiled. She drew in a deep breath of salty air. "This is a wonderful surprise. Thank you."

"Wow," Lauren murmured appreciatively as she leaned over the balcony railing. "I do rock! Look at this place."

A light sea-scented breeze stirred their hair as they gazed out at the Hawaiian sunset that illuminated the sky with stripes of deep purple and vibrant pink.

Dev let her arm drape over Lauren's shoulder. "It's perfect. Absolutely perfect." She pulled Lauren into her arms and kissed her on the temple. "I feel more relaxed already."

Lauren bumped her hip against Dev's. "Do you snorkel? I'm itching to get you into that warm water and very teensy bikini."

Dev shook her head. Lauren was nothing if not persistent. "Wasn't my modeling on Air Force One enough?"

"Nope."

"Well, that answers that question, and no, Ohio isn't known for its snorkeling. You're a lot better traveled than I am, Lauren."

"Maybe," Lauren conceded. Most of her reputation for writing biographies had been gained through her work overseas. "Let's go snorkeling tomorrow morning then." Her voice dropped a register. "I'd love to teach you."

"Why does everything you say suddenly sound like a proposition?"

"Because it is?"

"Now *that's* the answer I was hoping to hear!" Dev's eyes gleamed with excitement. "I've always wanted to learn to snorkel, so you're on."

"Excellent!" She grasped Devlyn's hand. "There's some equipment in the storage shed. An early bedtime for us then?" She gave Devlyn an entreating look that she knew wouldn't be denied. Sleeping on a plane is not the same as sleeping on land. No matter how nice the mattress is.

"Early bedtime," Devlyn agreed, tugging Lauren off of the patio and padding in her bare feet through the condo. It was decorated in shades of beige and white, with low, comfortable-looking overstuffed furniture. It had a light, airy feeling that Devlyn found Washington,

D.C., almost completely devoid of. She loved it. "How did you find this place?"

Lauren clicked off the lights as they passed through the living room and small kitchen. "It belongs to Starlight Publishing. Wayne talked them into letting us use it." She decided not to mention that a bevy of Secret Service agents was guarding the perimeter, or the state-of-the-art alarm system that had been installed, or the fact that the ship sailing a mile or so off the beach was manned by a security team. She knew she wasn't fooling Devlyn by remaining silent, but she told herself there was no reason to go out of her way to mention what was already ever-present in their lives.

"That was nice of Wayne. He's a good friend to you, isn't he?" Devlyn remembered him sniffling his way through their wedding and wondered whether it was because his hopes of dating Lauren had finally been dashed or if he was simply happy for a dear friend.

Once in the bedroom, Lauren stripped out of her pants and began working on the buttons of her cotton blouse. "He is. And he's good at what he does too. I don't think my writing career would have taken off the way it did without him fighting for me."

"Maybe, many, many years from now, I'll see if he'd like to handle me working on my memoirs. It's almost a presidential must."

Lauren gave Devlyn a pointed look. "He'd sell his first-born, hell, he'd sell *my* first-born, if either of us had first borns, for that opportunity."

"Well, the man is a total maniac when it comes to business. Why I..." Devlyn's tongue froze when Lauren's blouse hit the floor. Dev swallowed. "No bra?"

"I'm on vacation, Devlyn." Lauren grinned. "No bra."

Dev looked up toward God. "Have I said thank you in the last five minutes?"

Saturday, July 2nd

The weather was crystal clear and in the low eighties with just a hint of a breeze. The surface of the water was calm, and both women felt remarkably refreshed when they hit the beach.

Lauren patiently instructed Dev how to clear her mask and her snorkel and fit her fins tight enough that they wouldn't slip off when she kicked, and then they ventured into deeper water.

"Maybe we'll see a shark," Dev said excitedly, before glancing down at her feet. "Fins are hard to walk in." She lifted her foot in an almost comical motion and scowled.

Lauren couldn't help but smile. "I know, but you'll get used to it. Do you remember what I told you about blowing out your snorkel?"

Dev's eyes narrowed with faux anger as she glanced over her shoulder at Lauren. "Contrary to popular belief, I can retain instructions for more than thirty seconds." She made a face before spitting into her mask. "Are you sure you're not joking me about this part?"

Lauren laughed and crossed her heart. "Honest."

Once Devlyn was wearing her mask, she placed the snorkel in her mouth and followed Lauren's lead by watching her swim a few meters.

The surface of the water shone like diamonds, reflecting the bright sun. But she managed to keep an eye on Lauren as she swam. After a few seconds she began to follow Lauren to a shallow reef, taking care to keep the inside of her mask and snorkel free of water. *Wow!* She watched as a small school of neon-yellow fish swam beneath her as though they didn't have a care in the world. *They're fish, Dev, they don't.* She nearly remembered too late that smiling could lead to drowning, but she was hard-pressed to contain her emotions at seeing the beauty that surrounded her.

She turned her head when Lauren tugged on her hand and gestured to a small green turtle, paddling along under the water, but the movement was too quick and water flooded into her snorkel and an instant later, into her lungs. Choking, she thrust her head up above the surface of the water, with Lauren right behind her.

Lauren pulled off Dev's mask, knowing that sometimes it made people's panic even worse, and grabbed Dev's arm to help her keep afloat. "Are you okay?"

Coughing, Dev nodded and sputtered, "Yeah, I... I—"

"Got a big mouthful of water." Lauren finished the sentence for her partner as she gave her a contrite look. "I'm sorry. I shouldn't have startled you. I was just excited about the turtle."

Dev nodded again, still coughing. "S... s'okay." She sucked in a deep breath when her lungs finally stopped spasming and pushed her hair out of her face. "Whew."

"I'm sorry." Lauren handed back her mask.

"It's not your fault." Dev took Lauren in her arms, able to easily tread water because of the long fins she wore. "Thank you for teaching me. I'll get the hang of it eventually."

Lauren's smile returned. "I'm sure you will and I'm glad it's something you enjoy. It'll be something we can do together when we can sneak away. Okay?"

Devlyn's expression brightened. "It's a deal."

Tuesday, July 5ᵗʰ

This was, Lauren decided, nearly perfect.

Dressed in a one-piece bright teal swimsuit, she sat on the private beach beneath a brilliant blue sky dotted with just a scattering of white, puffy clouds. Her bare toes were snuggled into the warm sand, and her hair was just beginning to dry from her last dip in the salty, tropical water.

She drew in a deep breath and let it out slowly, adjusting her sunglasses as she gazed across the sea to the horizon. She let a feeling of utter contentment wash over her. "Nice," she murmured, already deciding she was going to badger Wayne into begging Starlight Publishing to allow them to use this place as much as possible.

"Well, don't you look ready for a life of leisure?"

Lauren's lips pulled into a smile and she turned her head. She could hear the Marlowe children's squeals of excitement down the beach and shaded her eyes as she looked up at her tall lover. Lauren sighed. "*Now* everything is perfect. I thought you'd never get here." She reached out and tugged gently on Devlyn's hand, urging her partner to join her on her large, soft beach blanket.

"Why can't I get that sort of greeting whenever I address Congress?" Dev huffed playfully, dropping down onto the blanket with a groan and kicking off her sandals.

A pale brow lifted slightly. "I guarantee that if you do to the members of Congress even a fraction of what you do to me, you'd get a standing ovation every time you took the floor."

Dev made a face. "No thanks. I don't want tax reform *that* badly." Her eyes suddenly glinted. "Although the representative from Wyoming is sort of cute."

Now Lauren's other eyebrow lifted. "I heard she has to shave off her mustache every morning."

Dev snorted so hard she began to choke.

"Heh." Lauren patted Dev's Hawaiian-shirt-covered back. "Careful, Devil. You choking on your tongue on your honeymoon would be really hard for me to explain."

"She does not shave her face!" Dev paused. "I hope." She gave a little shiver. "What a horrible mental image."

"I do my best," Lauren answered smugly, waving at the boys as they raced up to greet her. "How was Disney World?"

"Great!" Aaron flopped down on the blanket next to Lauren and threw his arms around her in an enthusiastic hug. "We went on a roller coaster! And we ate ice cream at the airport!"

Lauren smiled indulgently at the boy. "I'll bet you had chocolate."

Aaron's blue eyes widened. "Wow, how did you know?"

Lauren bit back a smile

"You're magic?"

She shook her head and pointed to a chocolate stain the size of an egg that was plastered squarely in the center of his chest. His eyes tracked hers and he blushed. "Oh." He glanced up, cringing. "I spilled."

"Imagine that," she said fondly, knowing full well that Aaron wore nearly as much as he ate.

"Hi, Lauren!" Christopher bent down for a kiss on the cheek, making room for himself by giving his brother a playful shove.

"Hi, sweetie." Then she turned to Ashley, who had come up from behind her, and wrapped her arm around the girl's legs, giving them a solid squeeze in silent greeting. "I missed you all." And that was, she admitted to herself, startlingly true. While the peace and quiet had been a glorious, bordering on orgasmic, experience, she found herself wondering what the kids were doing and looking forward to seeing how much they were going to love the beach.

"I'm so excited!" Christopher sputtered. "I've been thinking about this forever!"

Lauren's ego purred a little under the attention. "Well, I'm happy to see you too—"

"Have you seen any sharks yet?" Aaron broke in, his face a cross between anticipation and stark fear.

"Yeah! Have you? Have you?" Christopher leaned closer to Lauren as he awaited her answer with bated breath.

"Have you?" Aaron questioned again, looking incredibly anxious.

Dev muffled a laugh and Lauren sent a low-watt sneer in her direction.

"They do have an uncanny way of bringing you back to earth, don't they?" the President commented seriously, making a space for Ashley to sit next to her.

"Oh yeah." Lauren reached out and ruffled Dev's bangs. "But I recall a certain six-foot-tall woman who was excited about the very same thing."

"Well?" Aaron asked impatiently, his gaze darting around the sand. "Where are they?" His chubby body was slightly shaking.

Lauren laid a comforting hand on his leg. "They're not on the beach, honey. You don't have to be afraid."

"I don't?" he questioned, his voice skeptical. "But Christopher and Ash said—"

"Whatever they said, you don't need to worry. All the sharks are in the water."

Fearfully, the boys looked out to the rhythmically crashing waves.

A wicked smile transformed Ashley's deceptively innocent-looking face, and she tugged at Aaron's swimming trunks. "Ready for a *swim,* Aaron?"

The boy gulped.

"In the *water,*" she continued, her expression the very picture of evil glee.

Christopher's gulp matched his brother's.

Ashley finished on a high note. "Where the *sharks* live."

Both boys screamed, and Lauren dropped her face into her hands. She moaned a little, hearing Devlyn's unsympathetic chuckles. "I walked right into that one, didn't I?"

Dev chewed on her bottom lip and nodded. "Pretty much." Then she glared at her daughter. "I think you should be the *first* one in the water, Ashley. The boys are a lot smaller than you. And bloodthirsty sharks are the hungriest in the late afternoon."

Ashley's eyes went round as saucers. "They are?" she asked, her voice ending in a squeak.

"Oh God," Lauren moaned. "Bloodthirsty?" She gave Dev a swat. "You're as rotten as the kids!"

"Of course," Devlyn said proudly, brushing a little sand off her leg. "They're all quick learners and I *am* their role model."

"Lord help them," Lauren teased. She decided a change of subject was in order or none of the kids would be going into the water today. "Tell me about your trip."

For a moment Lauren listened as they all chattered about Disney World and their favorite rides and treats. Then she reached out and touched a new necklace Ashley was wearing, but her attention was drawn to the sour look that had transformed Dev's face. "What is it?"

Dev motioned down the beach, groaning a little. One of the Secret Service agents who had been watching them, but remaining discreetly out of view, was walking toward them with a phone in his hand.

"Christ," Dev mumbled. She turned pathetically sorry eyes on Lauren.

"Go, go," Lauren made a shooing motion with one hand. "It's not like you have a choice."

Devlyn winced inwardly. "Laur—"

"S'okay." Lauren leaned forward and kissed Dev lightly on the mouth. "Just hurry back, okay?" she said softly, smiling a little to show Devlyn she wasn't angry. Annoyed—yes. But not angry.

Dev let out an explosive breath, her relief so clear that Lauren felt a little guilty for being annoyed at all. There had been regular, if short, interruptions in their time together, and she'd been an exceptionally good sport about the whole thing. But she was only human, and her patience only stretched so far.

"As soon as I can. I promise." She jumped to her feet and began jogging down the beach.

"Here." Christopher pulled a giant bottle of sunscreen from the back pocket of his lime green, Bugs Bunny swimming trunks and thrust it in Lauren's face.

She blinked a few times, moving her head a little so her eyes could focus on the bottle.

Christopher said, "Emma told me to tell you or Mom to dip us in this."

"Dip?" Lauren questioned, looking at the bottle. "Like a dog with fleas?"

Christopher shrugged. "I dunno. She just said to do it." Then, unaccountably, all the children began to giggle.

Lauren's forehead creased. "What? What's so funny?"

Aaron began to jump up and down a little and excitedly said, "Emma said if any of us come home with a sunburn she'll spank your and Mom's bottoms!"

All three children dissolved into helpless giggles as Lauren's eyebrows jumped. "Well, get down here then." She poured a large dollop of thick, coconut-smelling lotion in her palm. "Lord knows I don't want a spanking." *At least not from Emma*, she thought wryly.

Ten minutes and a half bottle of sunscreen later, the boys were coaxed into making a sandcastle at the edge of the water with Ashley and Lauren occupying comfortable spots on the beach blanket. Lauren picked up her camera and trained it on the boys. Then she quickly changed lenses and snapped off several pictures of them playing. It had been months since she'd been able to indulge her passion for photography, and she was grateful that Devlyn had reminded her to pack her equipment.

"You're awfully quiet today," Lauren ventured after a few moments of unexpected silence. Like her mother, Ashley was at times introspective, at times a chatterbox, but after she had just come back from three days in the "Happiest Place on Earth" Lauren hadn't expected her mood to be so serious.

"I guess."

Lauren trained her eyes on the boys and the sea. "Wanna talk about it?"

Ashley hesitated, taking a moment to examine a small white shell near her foot. "Me and Chris and Aaron asked Mom what we should call you. She said to ask you and that we should do whatever you wanted."

Lauren exhaled. Even though she knew this talk would be coming soon, she was still a little startled that the time had finally arrived. She also knew how important this was to Devlyn and figured that rapid-paced acceptance of co-parents must be some part of lesbian culture that no one had clued her in about. The older woman had wanted the children to address Lauren as "Mom" or "Mama" the moment they became engaged, which was well before Lauren, herself, felt she was ready. Luckily, the matter came up at a staff meeting, and Michael

Oaks had interceded with a mini-protocol lesson, explaining that a parental title wasn't appropriate until after the wedding. When Lauren had agreed, Devlyn begrudgingly let the matter drop.

Now, however... Now. A slow, easy smile worked its way across Lauren's face as she thought about the difference the past six months had made. "What is it that you want to call me, Ashley? Forget about your mother for a minute."

Surprised, Ashley's gaze darted sideways. "I... I guess I'm not sure."

Lauren nodded slowly. "So why don't you take some time to think about it? There's no hurry." *Despite what a certain president might think.*

Ashley frowned. "I have thought about it. A lot."

Pale brows lifted. "Oh."

"I don't remember my other mom." The girl sighed and continued to examine the shell in her hands. "I mean, I thought I did. I thought I remembered her taking me to the park when I was Aaron's age. But the other day I was looking at some old pictures and what I remembered was right there." She sniffed a few times. "I think I was remembering the picture and not really her. Does that make sense?"

She turned heartsick eyes on Lauren, who could only nod. "That makes perfect sense, honey. But it's not necessarily bad. I know your mom and Emma have kept Samantha alive for you through stories about her and lots of pictures and recordings."

"She wasn't really my mom," Ashley said, abruptly changing the direction of the conversation. "Not by blood, I mean. We're not related."

Lauren felt like she was on a roller coaster and her stomach did a flip-flop. *Yikes.*

"We learned about reproduction in school. You need a man and a woman for a baby, and that doesn't change just because you call two people Mom."

Lauren's eyebrows inched a little higher. "Err..." She cast about for whatever it was she was supposed to say in this instance. "Have you talked to your mom about this, Ashley?"

"I can't." Ashley's lips turned downward. "I don't think she'll understand."

Lauren opened her mouth to disagree, but the words wouldn't come. Ashley did have a point. This was one subject where Devlyn was too close to the situation to really see anyone's viewpoint but her own.

She had loved Samantha dearly, and their decision to raise a family together was the final word on parenting as far as Devlyn was concerned. And while Lauren tended to agree that love, support, and deeds were more important than biology ever would be, she also understood those were mature concepts that any child would have trouble dealing with.

"You wanna talk to me about it, then?" Lauren asked gently, her gaze darting down the beach in the direction that Devlyn had gone.

Ashley made a face. "I thought I was."

Lauren smiled a little. "Oh, right." She edged a little closer to Ashley and perched her sunglasses on the top of her head so they wouldn't be between her and Dev's much-loved daughter. "Go on."

Ashley shrugged one slim shoulder. "That's it, I guess. I still love my other mom. I just wanted to say that. Nobody ever does." Her expression turned thoughtful. "People act like my family is just like everyone else's."

Lauren reached out and softly petted Ashley's hair. "I suppose they do. But I don't think it's because they're keeping secrets from you, Ashley."

"You don't?"

"No way." Lauren shook her head. "Everyone knows what a bright girl you are. And that most *especially* includes your mama."

Ashley looked even more confused and something inside her seemed to snap. "Then why—" Her hands flailed around as she searched for the right words. "Why… ugh!"

Luckily, Lauren had a pretty good idea of what she was asking. "I think that sometimes when two women or two men want to have a baby, they're not too happy about the fact that they can't just… Umm… reproduce the way you learned about in school. It would be easier if they could have a baby the way most people do. But they have to put a lot more effort and thought into it."

Ashley nodded. "I guess."

"And so when they do finally have a baby, and they're so happy, the way your mom and Samantha were when you were born, they don't want to focus on what it took to get you. They want to think about how wonderful it is to *have* you." She stopped and searched Ashley's face. "Does you understand?"

Dark eyebrows drew together. "Sort of."

Sympathy shining brightly in soft gray eyes, Lauren gave her an encouraging pat. "It's hard, I know. But I do agree with your mom on one thing, Ashley." Lauren's voice grew more resolute. She wanted to emphasize this part. "Samantha *was* your mom. She earned that right by the time she spent loving and taking care of you, even if you two aren't related by blood."

"I know," Ashley said quickly. "I know she loved me and took care of me. It's just that I really don't remember much. And I... I..." She groaned and threw her shell into the gently rolling waves. "I don't know!" She turned so that she was fully facing Lauren. "I don't know what I think or what's wrong. I just wanted to tell someone what I was thinking, I guess. I do love Mom *and* Mom. But if I call you that, then it's like you're the same as them to me and you're not. You're different!"

"Hey." With infinite tenderness, Lauren wiped the tears from Ashley's face, her own heart clenching. "It's okay. We *are* all different to you."

Ashley's voice took on a sudden, panicky edge. "You won't tell Mom I said this, will you?" Her eyes widened with alarm, the thought of her mother's disapproval stinging her to the core. "She'll be mad and—"

"Wait a second, Ashley. Hey," she grabbed the girl's arms and held on tight, just as Ashley was going to bolt. "Hold on. You haven't done or said anything wrong. Your mom has strong feelings about this, but she's not some ogre. It's good to talk about things that are bothering you." *When there is someone around to listen. Shit.*

Lauren waited a few awkward moments, allowing the sounds of the beach and the boys' laughter to slowly fade back in and Ashley to relax a little. Slowly, she released Ashley's arms. "You can call me 'Lauren' forever. It won't change how I feel about you if that's what you decide to do. I only recently started to call your grandma 'Mom,' because it felt right to do it now when it didn't before. But even then I loved her just the same."

"But I don't love you all the same! I love you more!" Ashley shouted miserably, her face crumbling.

Lauren sucked in a shocked breath, then after several heartbeats while they stared at each other, she let it out shakily. She blinked several times as the words penetrated her brain. "I—I—"

"Not more than Mom..." Ashley's tear-stained cheeks flushed red as she struggled to get the words out. "The same there, I guess, but... bu... but different too. I can't help it. I... I... do love you more than my other mom." She started to cry again. "I know I shouldn't and Mom will probably be mad…" she began to hiccup and had to stop speaking.

"Oh, Ashley." Strong arms pulled the sobbing child into a firm embrace. "I love you too," Lauren whispered fiercely, her lips pressed near Ashley's ear. She felt her own eyes begin to fill. "You don't have to love us all the same. I swear that's not something you have to feel bad about." She hugged her tighter, her heart going out to the trembling girl in her arms.

Ashley shook her head, unwilling to release the guilt she felt she so rightly deserved. "I think I… I'm supposed to love her more. That's why Mom told us all about my dead mom, so I would." She sniffed loudly. "We used to go to the graveyard and bring flowers and—"

"Listen, okay? Listen." Lauren pulled away from Ashley and cupped her quivering, wet cheeks with warm hands. "Your mom wanted you to know about your other mother because *she* loved her. And because of how much Samantha loved you. And it's because of that love that you were even born. And, you're right. Your moms had a donor to help them with the biology part of things. That's something someone should have talked with you about a long time ago. I'm sorry for that, Ash. I should have been paying better attention. I didn't know you felt this way."

The girl drew in a breath to say something, but Lauren pressed ahead, not giving her the chance to jump in. This needed saying. "The only reason you're here at all is because your mom and Samantha wanted you." She looked deeply into Ashley's eyes, finding fear, but also comprehension. "Got it?"

Mutely, Ashley nodded.

"Just because your mom doesn't want you to forget your other mom doesn't mean you can't love me too. There are no rules for how much you have to love people or who ranks above who. *None.* If there were, I would know it."

Ashley shook her head wildly, dislodging a tear that hung precariously from her quivering chin. "That can't be—"

"It *is* true," Lauren insisted. "I swear it." She gave Ashley a watery smile. "I sort of know how you feel, Ashley. I love your grandma in a way I never did my own mama."

"Do you love her more?" Ashley questioned, her voice barely above a whisper.

Lauren closed her eyes, feeling hot tears spill over and streak her cheeks. "I... I—" *No. The truth. She doesn't need your bullshit!* She gathered her courage and swallowed hard. "I think I do care for her a little more, because she's more a part of my life than my mama ever was. Your grandma is a good parent and took me into her heart when I needed her. She was there for me, Ashley. And my mama wasn't a bad person, but she was never there."

"Did you feel... ba... bad about it?" Impatiently, she wiped at her face, hoping her brothers wouldn't see her tears. "About loving Grandma more?"

Lauren nodded. "I did." She sniffed a few times. "Until I realized that Mama would *want* me to love someone that much. Your other mom would want that too, Ashley. Love is a wonderful thing." The corner of her mouth quirked. "You don't have to be stingy with it. The more you want to give, the more you'll find you have."

Ashley licked her lips as some of the anxiety that had been bubbling up in her belly faded. "So it's okay to call you whatever I want? And it's okay to feel this way? I'm not being horrible to my mom who is dead?"

Lauren let out a soundless sigh. "Yes to the first questions and no to the last one, Ashley."

"And Mom won't be mad at me?"

Lauren sat back on her heels, the boys' laughter interrupting her thoughts for a second. She turned her head to find them dipping their toes in the surf and chasing each other. Then she refocused on Ashley. "I don't think she'll be mad. But you know this is sort of complicated stuff, right?"

Despite herself, Ashley snorted, drawing a smile from Lauren. "Yeah."

"Well, it's hard for grownups too. But I think you should give your mom a chance to talk to you about this, don't you?" Lauren squeezed Ashley's hand. "She hasn't killed you yet, and she is a *really* good mom."

Reluctantly, Ashley nodded. "She is." She pinned Lauren with a pleading look. "But will you be there too? Please?"

"Of course." They hugged again and this time, Lauren couldn't feel the girl's heart pounding out of her chest. After a moment, Ashley and Lauren let go and both of them fell back on the blanket, looking up into a gorgeous bright sky.

"Could I call you Mama?" Ashley asked shyly, not turning to face

Lauren.

A small smile twitched at Lauren's lips. "I would love that, darlin'." She swallowed thickly. "But only if it's something you're ready for."

Ashley chewed her lip for a moment, giving the matter her most serious consideration. "It is," she pronounced finally. "It's different than what I call Mom. And it still shows that you love and take care of me and that I love you right?"

Lauren nodded. "Absolutely." She hoped her voice didn't sound as hoarse to Ashley as it did to her own ears.

Quickly warming to the idea, Ashley said, "Plus, it's what you called your mom, right."

This time she couldn't answer at all. So she just nodded and reached out for Ashley's hand.

"Good," Ashley said brightly, her mood lifting almost immediately. She stood up just as her brothers ran up to the blanket.

"What's wrong, Ashley?" Christopher asked, clearly concerned. He began to fiddle with the stems of his small, wire-rimmed glasses, something he always did when he was anxious.

Aaron instantly wrapped his chubby arms around his sister, offering comfort the best way he knew how, short of offering pie—with ice cream.

Lauren's heart ached at the sight. One minute the Marlowe children could be at each other's throats, and the very next they would band together so tightly Lauren was sure that no outside force, no matter how strong, could come between them

"It's my turn for a hug," Christopher insisted. "Don't be a greedy pig, Aaron! She's my sister too."

And like most beautiful moments, Lauren thought wanly, this one was short-lived.

Ashley solved the problem by wiping her cheeks, then giving both brothers a quick one-armed hug. "Nothing's wrong," she told them. "We were just having girl talk." She smiled at Lauren, who grinned back knowingly.

"Did you ask her?" Christopher whispered, loud enough for everyone to hear.

"Yup," Ashley informed her brother. "We can call her whatever we want. *I* am going to call her Mama. Grandma told me that's what Lauren, I mean *Mama*, called her mama."

Lauren sat up and both the boys turned toward her and regarded her curiously.

The blonde woman felt the blood drain from her face. *Oh, no*, she mentally dithered. *I don't think I can go through all that again soon. I haven't recovered from the first kid conversation yet!*

"Can we call you that too?" Christopher finally asked.

Lauren blinked. "Umm... of course." Her words lilted upward in question. "If that's what you want?"

"Sure!" Aaron shouted.

"Cool!" Christopher agreed. "Thanks, Mama!"

"Can we have a Coke?" Aaron asked. When Lauren didn't answer right away, he added, "Please? We ate all of our lunch," thinking that was the problem.

"Uhh...sure. There are some cold drinks in the house."

"Thanks, La... errr, Mama," he said.

Christopher yelled, "Race you to the house, Aaron." Before his brother could answer, Christopher took off running.

"No fair!" the younger boy complained, breaking into as fast a run as he could manage, his small feet kicking clouds of sand as he went.

Shell-shocked, Lauren could only blink.

"Beth says boys are easier," Ashley said wisely.

Lauren shook her head and smiled. "I think that, even if that's true, I couldn't love you more." She caught sight of Dev walking past Chris and Aaron on her way toward them. "Would you like a Coke too? We can save talking to your mom for once we're back home in Washington. I don't think she'd mind."

Ashley grinned and nodded. She bolted off the blanket to join her brothers, stopping to kiss Devlyn along the way.

When Devlyn's bare feet reached the blanket, she worriedly glanced down at Lauren. "Are you okay?"

"I've just been through the emotional wringer. More than once." She nodded a little, taking stock of herself. "But I actually feel pretty good."

Devlyn looked over her shoulder at the retreating forms of her children. She smiled and offered Lauren her hand. "Welcome to motherhood, Ms. Strayer."

"Is it always like this?" she asked weakly, wrapping her arm around Devlyn's waist as they headed back to the house and toward most of her birthday cake, which she'd saved from the day before. She could feel a low, rumbling laugh work its way from deep inside her partner.

"Far be it from me to spoil the surprise."

At the same moment, they turned their heads, and their eyes met. Lauren couldn't help but smile. The next fifty years were going to be nothing if not interesting.

AUGUST 2022

Thursday, August 4th

Dev reached into her desk and pulled out a small inhaler. Placing it in her nostril, she compressed it and drew in a deep breath at the same time. This was faster than migraine tablets and didn't come with the bitter taste that made her gag.

She glanced back at the stack of papers in front of her, willing her eyes to refocus so she could get through them before calling it a day.

She'd been up since four a.m., so she could make a seven-thirty a.m. meeting in Chicago, which had quickly turned into three meetings that droned on until mid-afternoon. Her schedule had been shot to hell, and Liza was nearly fit to be tied.

The entire flight home she'd been stuck in conference calls with various members of her cabinet. Somehow, she managed to make up most of the meetings she'd missed. But to her disgust, she'd been forced into taking desperate measures by personally contacting two recalcitrant Democratic senators from New Jersey in order to explain how a piece of environmental legislation they were expected to oppose was worth a second look. To top it off, on her way back to Washington, she'd stopped in Pittsburgh for a quick speech at the annual meeting of the Health Insurance Association of America.

The day had been a raging political success, with things falling into place in a way that exceeded most of her staff's expectations, if not Devlyn's. But she wondered if the price was destined to be her sanity or her health. She'd barely eaten all day, had drunk no less than three gallons of coffee, and had lost track of how many people she'd yelled at. Despite her migraine medication, her head was pounding so fiercely she felt nauseous. And her vision had been blurring on and off all day. The next person who said something stupid or rearranged her schedule to fit in just one more meeting was slated for a slow, painful death.

When the door to her office opened, she snapped the pencil she held in half. She looked up to see Liza, who was at least as frazzled as she was, and took a deep breath to calm her ragged nerves.

"Madam President." Devlyn could see Liza's grip on her electronic calendar tighten and by the tone of her voice knew the other woman was walking on eggshells. "I wanted to let you know that I managed to reschedule the meetings we had to cancel this morning for tomorrow. I can also arrange to have all your morning correspondence sent to the residence if you like. You wouldn't have to be in the office until at least nine-thirty that way."

"Have I been that bad today?"

Liza groaned inwardly. "It's been a difficult day for all of us, ma'am. I let your schedule get out of hand." She looked away and gently blew at a piece of curly brown hair that bobbed down into her eyes. Shame colored her voice. "I'm sorry, ma'am."

Dev was very aware that Liza hadn't directly answered her question. Still, the message was loud and clear. "I approved all the changes in my calendar, Liza. It wasn't your fault."

"Yes, ma'am." But she didn't appear to be convinced.

Dev sighed and willed the pounding in her head to stop. "I would like to deal with my correspondence in the residence tomorrow. Thank you, Liza. Is there anything else?"

Liza hesitated.

"Spit it out, " Dev snapped, her exasperation clear. With effort, she lowered her voice. "Whatever it is it's not your fault and I won't kill you for it." *I hope.*

"There is just one thing, ma'am." Reluctantly, she handed Devlyn a folder containing a recent study of the world's remaining oil reserves and the geopolitical ramifications of the United States' increased usage over the past two decades. "You don't need to deal with that right away. But it's earmarked as information you should be aware of for tomorrow's ten fifteen a.m. meeting, ma'am."

"I see." Devlyn reached for the folder that was at least a half-inch thick. "This is a summary, I assume?" She gave the heavy folder an openly distasteful glance.

"The original findings were over ten thousand pages, ma'am. I have those completely covering my desk at the moment. I can have those sent to your residence if you'd like to review them as well."

Devlyn stood up and snorted softly. "No, thank you, Liza. I think I'm going back to have a late dinner with my family." She peered at Liza's watch, unable to distinguish the time. "If they haven't eaten, that is."

"Emma called an hour ago, ma'am. The children ate late lunches and Ms. Strayer left for the residence about two hours ago."

Devlyn looked a little startled. It couldn't have been more than ten minutes since she'd last seen Lauren, could it?

"They're waiting for you to have dinner, so long as you're not past eight," Liza went on. "It's seven-fifty now."

Dev gave the younger woman a sympathetic glance. "I'll see you tomorrow and I promise to be in a better mood."

"Yes, ma'am. Good night."

"Liza?"

Wary eyes tracked Devlyn as the President stuffed the file into a dark-brown leather briefcase and reclaimed her navy blazer from a cedar coat rack. "Yes, Madam President?"

"Go home."

The slender woman nodded, and for the first time all day, a small smile touched her lips. She slipped out of the Oval Office, closing the door behind her.

Few people spoke to Dev and fewer people made eye contact with her as she padded down the hallways. Even the agents who flanked her every move maintained an unusually respectful distance behind her. *You've been a real bitch today, Marlowe. Even the people with the guns are afraid of you.*

She didn't go right into the dining room. Instead, she dropped her blazer and briefcase off in her private office, dropped down into her office chair and quietly rested her head in her hands, thankful for the room's dim light.

After a few moments, the already ajar door was slowly pushed open and Aaron came into the room. "Mom?"

Sighing she lifted her head and looked to him. "Yeah?"

He ran around the side of her desk. "Mama wants to know if you'll be coming in to dinner?"

Devlyn smiled at Lauren's new title. She leaned forward and gave her son a gentle hug. "Yeah, buddy, I'll be there in just a minute."

The boy's pale eyes shone with concern. "Are you okay?"

"I'm fine." She patted him on the shoulder. "Just tired. Go tell everyone I'll be there in a few minutes."

"Yes, ma'am." He gave her a bright grin before bolting from the room. "We're having chili!" he called to her on the way out.

Devlyn quickly changed into a pair of soft cotton slacks and a polo shirt. The children and Lauren were already seated by the time she made it to the table.

Lauren looked a little harried herself, having followed Devlyn around for most of the day. But for security reasons, she wasn't permitted to be present during Devlyn's last meetings.

"Hi, Mom," the kids chorused as Dev took her place at the table.

"Hi, guys."

"Hi, Mom," Lauren repeated with a tired smile.

Dev chuckled weakly, then motioned the kids to dig in. She wasn't surprised to see that Emma wasn't joining them. They had recently instituted a standing rule that after seven-thirty p.m., Emma's time was her own, unless neither Dev nor Lauren had made it home yet.

"Are you working tonight, Devlyn?" Lauren tried to make the question sound casual by starting to pick at her food.

"I have some things to deal with after dinner, yes." Dev didn't even look up as she began putting food on her plate.

"But, Mom," Ashley moaned, suddenly looking very upset. "You promised we'd work on my Brownie project. I've been waiting all week and it's due tomorrow."

"Nuh uh, Ashley," Aaron broke in sharply. "It's not your turn to do something with her. It's mine. You were last week."

"Aaron, Ashley," Lauren warned quietly, seeing the darkening of Dev's features from across the table.

"Shut up, Aaron." Christopher nudged his brother's foot from underneath the table. "You're going to get us all in trouble. You're being too loud."

"Am not!"

"Are too!" Ashley said tartly. "And besides, you're wrong."

"Am not! Mom said—"

"All right!" Dev slammed her hand down against the shiny wooden table, sending her fork clattering across it. "That's enough!" Her face was beet-red, and she was breathing hard. "Just stop! I need five damn minutes of peace and quiet. Can you manage to give that to me, please?"

The children instantly went deadly silent, and all Devlyn could hear was the pounding of her own pulse in her ears.

After a moment, Lauren gently cleared her throat. "Will you kids excuse us?"

All three nodded quickly, and Dev's eyes closed in self-disgust.

"I'd like to talk to your mother in private," Lauren continued. "Carefully take your bowls and eat on the table in the game room, okay?"

Ashley bolted from the table in tears, leaving her dinner behind, while Christopher and Aaron slowly retrieved theirs, neither one daring to glance at their mother and risk incurring her wrath.

Even Gremlin and Princess scurried out from under the table, where they were hiding in hopes of a major food spill, and scampered down the hall. Though not without twin growls in Devlyn's direction.

"Well," Lauren said, once she and Devlyn were alone. "That was different."

Dev was shaking, but instantly contrite. "I'm… Shit, I'm sorry." She ran a trembling hand through her hair. "I don't know what just happened, I umm… I'll apologize to them. Today was just—" She didn't finish, knowing that her bad day was no reason to yell at her children.

Moving from her seat to take the one Ashley had vacated, Lauren reached out and covered Devlyn's hand with her own. "S'okay, darlin'. We all have bad days. The kids will live. You can explain things to them later." She paused, debating whether or not now was the right time to bring this up. *No,* she mentally corrected herself. *Now is the perfect time. This is when she needs to hear it.* "You shouldn't work tonight, Devlyn. You haven't had a day off all month. I know you're making amazing progress in your Middle East negotiations and with the legislation you want to propose this fall, but that doesn't change the fact that you're tired and too edgy and you need to go to bed before two a.m." She held her breath and waited. *This is where she explodes and tells me to mind my own damn business.*

Looking very introspective, Dev remained quiet for a moment, feeling the tears born of exhaustion and frustration that wanted to come, but forcing them back before she spoke. Finally, she nodded. "I know I should do that, but I don't have a choice. I have things that have to be done." Her voice had taken a resolute quality that meant her mind was made up.

Lauren sighed. "You *do* have a choice. Devlyn ″

"I'll try to be in bed before midnight." Dev dared a glance at Lauren and was relieved to see nothing but concern shining in her partner's eyes. "Could you do your chicken-shit spouse a favor and deal with the kids tonight? I'll make it up to them at breakfast tomorrow. And see that Ashley gets her dinner and works on her project. I'll call her troop leader if I have to."

"Of course, honey, but—" Before she could finish her thought, Devlyn stood up, her dinner untouched, and stalked from the room, leaving Lauren alone at the table. She blinked, and then let out a long breath. Her stomach was in knots. "Well…." Another breath as she tossed her napkin on the table. "That went well."

Friday, August 5th

The women were talking across their chessboard, a fire in the fireplace lighting their play and sending long, dancing shadows against the paneled walls. A good night's sleep had restored Devlyn's good mood and cured her headache. A few kisses and promises to spend some extra time with the children had gone a long way toward mending hurt feelings.

Lauren leaned forward, placing her elbows on her knees. They hadn't talked like this in a while, she realized. The conversation was easy and honest and reminded her very much of her first few months in the White House, when Devlyn had made such an effort to answer questions for the biography and special time had been set aside for them alone to discuss all manner of subjects. It was those private glimpses of the woman behind the office that had captured Lauren's heart so completely. *And when I fell in love.*

"It's your move."

That low, familiar voice washed over her and Lauren looked up from the board and smiled. "I know. I was just thinking." Gray eyes sparkled with happiness.

"Mmm… But not about the game."

Lauren's grin turned sheepish. "No."

"I'm not really into it either." Dev gently set down the pawn she'd been twirling between her fingers. "Let's save you beating the snot out of me for another day."

"How did it feel being sworn in?" Lauren asked suddenly, giving Devlyn some idea as to where her thoughts had been. "I can't really imagine what it must have been like, standing there, the entire country watching while your political dreams became a reality."

"On the record?"

"Hmm… Please." Lauren leaned forward a little in anticipation.

"Professionally, it was nirvana." Dev smiled and her eyes went unfocused as she thought and sipped her herbal tea. It was a concoction given to her by the Chinese ambassador, along with the assurance it would ease the stresses of even her job. "I knew from the age of twelve that I wanted to be President. The part that seems so odd, but normal to me, is that even then, I was certain I could do it. So I set out to make it happen. That day, on the steps of Congress," she sighed wistfully, "was the culmination of a lifetime of work." She glanced over at Lauren. "It was the first moment when I could really feel what I had accomplished and how far I'd come, you know?"

Lauren just smiled. She didn't know. Not really. But Devlyn's enthusiasm was nothing if not infectious.

"Being sworn in was probably the greatest moment of my professional career. I felt like I was going to float away." Then Dev's expression grew more contemplative as her thoughts shifted to the present. "I'm at the top of my game, Lauren. I have the chance to do so much. To really make a difference."

A chill ran down Lauren's spine at the fiery tone in Devlyn's voice.

"Politically, nothing else I do will ever be as important as what I'm doing right here, right now."

Lauren's smile grew. It was commonly accepted, even among her critics, that Devlyn's accomplishments in her first year and half in office were immense, already ranking her among the most influential presidents of the last one hundred years. But that success exacted a hefty price that Devlyn and those around her paid every single day and, at times, Lauren was hard-pressed not to resent the job completely.

"But," Dev shifted a little in her chair, setting down her mug, "while that was the best day professionally, it still pales in comparison to some of my private ones. When the kids were born, for instance." Her eyes took on a happy twinkle. "I have never felt so wonderful as I did the first time I held my children." A thousand-watt smile lit her face. "Those tiny little people, depending on me to take care of them and make everything all right."

Lauren took another sip of her tea, careful not to drink the steaming hot liquid too quickly. Her brows knitted as she carefully regarded Devlyn, whose expression had changed dramatically. "What is it?" Her voice was soft and low.

Dev licked her lips and fidgeted a little in her seat. "What's what?"

"That face." Lauren reached out and tenderly drew her finger across

Devlyn's lower lip. "You only do that thing with your lip when you're upset." She carefully set her drink down on the table next to the chessboard. "What's the matter?"

"I'm not upset." Clearing her throat, Devlyn anxiously met her partner's eyes. "Talking about the children just got me to thinking, that's all." Her fidgeting became more pronounced. "We've never really talked about having more kids."

"True. I mean, there's not really anything—" Then Lauren stopped as the seriousness of Devlyn's expression hit home. She felt her heart rate pick up a little. "Wh—? I don't... Oh," she said finally, as all the air in her lungs exited in a giant explosion. She couldn't have been more surprised if Devlyn had just announced she'd decided to quit politics and join the circus. "Is that something you'd like to talk about now?"

"Yes."

"Jesus!"

"That's not exactly the reaction I'd been hoping for." Dev tried not to think about how much Lauren's answer mattered to her. "Are you okay?"

"I'm sorry." Lauren shook her head as if to clear it. "I just... Is that something you'd ever want? *More* children?"

Slowly, Dev nodded, as she studied Lauren's reactions with growing fear. "Actually, I had hoped to have a couple more. But I'm not really sure how you feel about it."

"How could I not know this?" Feeling deeply adrift, Lauren began to gesture wildly with her hands and asked, "Why haven't you ever mentioned this before?"

Devlyn scratched her jaw. "That's a good question that I don't have a good answer for," she admitted honestly. Her posture grew more rigid even as she tried to relax. "I guess it's because, deep down, I already know how you feel about it. I mean, the kids we have are a handful for someone who doesn't have a lot of parenting under their belt."

Lauren tried not to let that last part sting. She didn't really see this as having much to do with whether the kids were a handful or not or how much parenting experience she had. "I love the kids. You know that. And I'm doing my best."

"I know that." Dev winced internally as she realized how Lauren had interpreted her words. "I didn't mean I thought it was something you couldn't handle."

"I can see that."

"Lauren... I didn't mean it that way. Really." Feeling even worse, Dev tried to lighten the mood by chuckling weakly. "But let's face it, the kids do have their moments. I know they're a lot to deal with. For anyone."

Lauren leaned back in her chair, blinking dazedly, as her mind raced. Part of her was angry and hurt that Devlyn's desire to have a bigger family was something she hadn't imagined. Another part of her was sickened by the thought that she could be the one to dash Dev's hopes for the future. Her stomach lurched a little. "I... I hadn't really thought about having more children," she finally said. "I just assumed that Ashley, Chris, and Aaron were all the kids you wanted."

"I had hoped for a big family." Gingerly, she leaned forward and stroked Lauren's arm, not sure whether they were having an argument or not. "I promised my dad I would talk to you about this, Lauren, because he said that you deserved the opportunity to tell me how you felt so that we could work it out. Rather than my assuming I knew what you wanted. I think he was right."

Lauren pulled away. "I can't believe you were discussing this with your father when you hadn't even spoken to me about it. God, I feel like you intentionally waited until after the wedding to spring this on me, Devlyn. We've been together for months, and you never said a single word." Some frustration spilled over and her voice rose a notch. "Not even a hint!"

Dev's lips thinned. "That's not it at all. My dad brought it up when we were in Scotland. I told him how I thought you felt and that I was just going to leave it alone. He's the one who said I should..." Without warning, Devlyn withdrew. "Lauren, honey, I know you don't want more children and that's fine. Yes, I'm a little disappointed. But I'll live. What you want is just as important as what I want and we already have three great kids. I can be happy with three."

"Scotland was months ago. And long before the wedding."

"I know." Devlyn threw her hands in the air. "*Why* are you focusing on the when and not the what of what I'm saying? I'm talking about this with you *now*. The only reason I didn't do it before was because I thought I already knew how you'd feel. Lately you've been so great with the kids and you seem really happy. But I know—"

"Don't. Don't say that." Lauren's temper began to get the better of her and this time she didn't try to censor herself. "You don't *know* what I want because until now you haven't bothered to ask me! Where did this master plan for a huge family come from?" Her gaze suddenly cooled as her own jealousies and insecurities flared. "This was something you had planned with Samantha, wasn't it?"

Dev sat back and closed her eyes, feeling her own ire rise. If it were anyone other than Lauren bringing Sam into this conversation she would have taken his or her head off. "No, this is something I've always wanted. Me. Not Sam. Not my parents. Me."

Lauren bit her lip hard to keep from interrupting. In her heart she knew it was foolish, but she couldn't stand feeling like the "replacement wife" for Samantha.

Dev shifted into full persuasion mode. "I love children. I want a house full of them. I'm sorry that I didn't ask you before now, but considering that for the first six months of this year I've been in the air more than I've been home, I never thought the time was right for a conversation that I knew was going to be difficult."

Lauren looked at Devlyn as though she were seeing a stranger. "That's an excuse you wouldn't put up with from anyone else, Devlyn, including me. And you know it."

"Shit! I don't understand why you're getting angry with me." Devlyn's breathing was coming faster now. "I want to have a bigger family with you because I love kids and I love you! What in the hell is so wrong with that?"

"You're not getting it. Devlyn, I'm not upset because you want more children. I feel like you're keeping things from me and making decisions on my behalf without me even knowing it. I thought I knew you better than that. I *should* know you better than that," she admitted softly.

"I shouldn't have assumed I knew what you'd say. This is something I want us to talk about and decide on together. I apologize for not bringing it up sooner."

What else do you want her to say? She's apologized. Let it go. Lauren sighed. "Look, Devlyn, you've just thrown me. C'mon." She stood up and retrieved her cooling mug of tea. "Let's go sit on the sofa together." She offered her hand to Devlyn, who took it with an audible sigh of relief, and the women made their way to a small, comfortable leather sofa that sat facing the fireplace. "I've never thought about having a big family, much less being a stepparent to three." She lifted an eyebrow and forced a tiny smile. "And we really need to talk about what the word 'big' means, okay?"

Grateful for the effort, Devlyn tried for a smile of her own. "You already think we have big?"

Lauren nodded and sat down, feeling the sofa shift as Devlyn dropped down next to her. "Huge."

Devlyn chuckled. "Oh, boy."

"I accept your apology, okay?" Lauren looked a little heartsick. "But I need to say some things to you that I don't think you're going to want to hear."

Devlyn's heart started to hammer in her chest. "You don't want—?"

"Please, honey." Lauren pressed her fingers against Devlyn's mouth. "Let me talk?"

Mutely, Dev nodded.

Satisfied, Lauren said, "I love your children more than I thought possible. And that makes me consider things that I never had the guts to really think of before." She licked her lips nervously. "Judd and I talked about having a family. We decided not to." Seeing that Devlyn wasn't going to try to interrupt, Lauren removed her fingers from Dev's mouth.

"There were lots of reasons we didn't have children. But one of the big ones was that we were both so busy with our careers."

She could hear Devlyn's dry swallow, and so she spoke a little faster. "With the way we lived our lives, there was never enough time. I was never home. I never wanted to *be* home. Devlyn, we both had other commitments that we weren't ready to give up." Lauren's gaze strayed from Devlyn's face for a split second as she gathered her courage. Then she glanced back. "I don't see that our situation is any different right now."

The words hit Devlyn like a ton of bricks, and she sucked in a painful breath.

"I'm sorry," Lauren said, her voice catching. "I don't know how I'll feel in the future. But that's how I feel right this second."

Dev's jaw worked for a moment before she spoke. And when she did, Lauren knew that she was profoundly hurt. "I'm too busy, I know." She swallowed hard, feeling her throat closing. "But I'm not a bad mother," she defended quietly. "I'm not."

"Of course you're not!" Lauren grasped Devlyn's hand and held it against her own chest. "But, honey," her eyes conveyed her regret, "you're a wonderful mother who doesn't have enough time to give her children as it is. There are only so many hours in the day. It's past midnight now, because this was the only quiet time we could find. Emma is a wonderful help, but that's just not enough."

Devlyn gave a quick nod. She couldn't dispute what was so plainly the truth. "I know."

Lauren scrubbed her face. "Then... I... I'm confused. I know that nobody understands how busy you are more than you do." Her forehead creased. "You just couldn't think you could be pregnant while you were president, Devlyn?" Lauren began to panic a little, knowing that Devlyn was stubborn enough to try just that. "That would be impossible! You barely sleep and if Emma didn't hound you like a demon with a spatula, you'd eat Oreos for half your meals and skip the other half. What baby could survive that? God, I'd worry about you both every single second!"

"There is the possibility of you actually having the child, you know." Dev couldn't help her wistful smile. The mental image of a very pregnant Lauren was one that lived happily in the corner of her mind. She knew her partner would be beautiful, as would the child. "You would be enchanting."

Lauren snorted softly. "Nice try, but I can't imagine going to bed with some stranger. Sure, he'd have to be handsome and all, but—" She smiled when Devlyn nearly shot off the sofa, glad for a teensy bit of humor during a painful conversation.

"What the—?"

"I'm just kidding, Devil. Jeeze, stop scowling like that, it's not like it would ever happen." She dragged Devlyn back down onto the couch next to her and waited until she was settled in and her horrified look had dissolved before speaking. Then Lauren's tone grew very serious. "Loving a child and physically having one are two very different things. And I can tell you with one hundred percent certainty that I don't want to give birth, Devlyn."

The older woman's posture immediately deflated.

"I'm sorry, honey. That's just not something I want for myself." Worriedly, she searched Devlyn's face, which for once was utterly unreadable. Feeling her chest start to constrict she fought to explain herself. "Mama's depression is genetic. What if I passed that on? I couldn't live with myself after that. And you know how I feel about doctors and needles, and the thought of some stranger's sperm being inserted into me with some probe or something..." She shivered, her face turning a pasty white as she envisioned a doctor, his face covered with a mask, leaning over her to... "I—"

Dev's own face suddenly paled, and she shot up from the sofa, drawing a startled yelp from Lauren. She began to pace, and Lauren felt herself growing more and more frightened with every step.

"Why do I have a feeling this conversation is about to take a surprising turn?"

Devlyn cringed and stuffed her hands into her pockets. "Because it is?"

"Oh, Lord." Lauren's eyes widened.

Devlyn dropped down on her knees in front of Lauren and took her hands. "It's not that bad, truly." She chose her next words very carefully, already knowing that she was on thin ice. Despite her care, however, she braced herself for what she figured would be Round Two with her spouse. "I understand that you might not want to have children yourself, sweetheart."

Lauren let out a shaky breath. "I'm sorry," she whispered. "I just don't. A baby would take even more constant care than the kids do now. I wouldn't want someone else to do it, and I wouldn't be a good stay-at-home mom, Devlyn. That's just not me."

"You don't have to be," Devlyn replied, her voice equally low. "I guess I was just hoping." She paused. "Errr... But while we're discussing sperm donors I think there's something else you should know. If we had more children, it wouldn't have to be from an anonymous donor."

Lauren's brows knitted. How could Devlyn already have someone in mind when they hadn't even talked about it yet? It sounded like she had this all mapped out. Hoping she was wrong, Lauren said, "I don't know exactly what you mean."

"I already have someone's frozen sperm," Dev corrected, trying to minimize the surprise this announcement was sure to cause. "The kids' donor isn't a stranger. It's..." She steadied her nerves. "It's David." Not letting go of Lauren's hands, she rocked back a little on her heels and waited for the explosion.

Lauren blinked very slowly as her brain fought to process what she'd just been told. She opened her mouth and then closed it, swallowing hard before hoarsely saying, "W... What? *What?*"

"I said David is the donor." Her voice was a little stronger now, but still tremulous. Dev took a deep breath and let it out slowly, her pulse pounding so loudly she was surprised Lauren couldn't hear it.

Lauren looked away for a moment, her eyes unfocused. "David?"

"Yes."

Her jaw worked for a moment, and she was surprised to hear how calm she sounded when she heard herself say, "David, who is your best friend?"

Devlyn's entire body went taut with anticipation. "Yes."

"David, who I see nearly every single day of my life and who eats at our dinner table at least once a week?"

Lauren's voice was eerily steady, almost serene. And Dev took that as a very, very bad sign. "Yes, honey, David McMillian. Tall, redhead, mustache, you know, my chief of staff."

Lauren's gaze suddenly snapped back and landed on Devlyn face with palpable force. "Well, holy shit, Devlyn. *Ho-lee shit!*" She pulled her hands from Dev's and sank her fingers deep into her own hair, gripping the sides of her head as though she were afraid it might blow off.

Dev looked almost relieved. *That* was the reaction she'd been expecting.

"All of them?" Lauren asked incredulously. "He fathered them all?" *And no one bothered to tell me? What in the hell is going on?*

Dev wasn't exactly comfortable with the word "father" but something told her that splitting hairs at that very moment might end her up in the emergency room. So she just said, "Yes. All of them. He and Beth agreed to help Samantha and me when we wanted to start a family." She moved back onto the sofa alongside Lauren. "He's my best friend, and we wanted the children to have the same father. We did it for lots of reasons, including medical ones. Based on how the kids turned out, I think we made the right choice. He was willing to keep quiet about his contribution, but still be a positive force in their lives."

"And you didn't trust me to keep quiet about it?" Hurt colored her words. "Is that—?"

"No," Dev interrupted harshly. "Of course not, Lauren." Devlyn took Lauren's hand again, determined not to let go. "I trust you with my life. My family. My heart. *Everything.* I hadn't thought about David being the donor in years. We agreed never to talk about it, and we never have. Not once, Lauren, in all these years. It was actually sort of easy to imagine it never happened at all. But a few months ago, David came to me and asked me about some legalities having to do with the children's custody should something happen to me."

Lauren's eyes widened in alarm. "But—"

"Shh…." Devlyn easily read Lauren's fear. "I'm fine, honestly. It's just that the assassination attempt and our engagement brought up some things that needed to be addressed."

Lauren looked down at their joined hands and schooled herself in patience. "Then why didn't you tell me?" She was finding it harder and harder not to lash out or burst into tears. "I don't understand!"

"I know. Please let me explain," Dev said in a rush. "Please." There was a rare note of urgency and fear in Devlyn's voice that captured every ounce of Lauren's attention. Then something else flashed across Devlyn's face, something even rarer than fear. Shame. "After I spoke with David, I knew I needed to tell you, but I put it off because I was worried that you'd be upset that I didn't tell you earlier. And then I kept putting it off because the longer I waited, the more upset I figured you'd be."

Still dumbfounded, Lauren felt queasy. Tears welled up, stinging her eyes, and she found that she couldn't blink them back. "And you were afraid to tell me this, why? I love David."

"I was afraid that you would think I had been intentionally keeping it from you, which I hadn't." Dev stomach began to churn. "But everyday I didn't say something just made it worse. It was the wrong choice and I am so, *so* sorry."

Lauren sat in silence for a long time, trying to absorb what she'd just been told. Part of her felt irrationally betrayed by Devlyn's lack of disclosure. She was angry and hurt and suddenly afraid for her new marriage. "And—" Lauren had to stop and swallow. "And just what did you think I would do that made you afraid to talk to me? I know I have a temper, but... Christ, Devlyn," she hissed.

Devlyn squeezed her eyes shut. "I was afraid that you'd leave!" Tears slipped from between the closed lids, and Dev cursed softly, disgusted at herself for appearing weak and needy. "You did before, when Sarah kissed me and you were so angry you just left! I can't lose you because I did something stupid. I just can't!"

"I went to the park for a few hours to calm down. It's not like I shaved my head, changed my name, and moved to Brazil!"

"You still left, Lauren," Devlyn pointed out raggedly. "I tried to explain and you wouldn't hear it. I was afraid this time would be worse. What if I couldn't find you? I…" Blue eyes darted sideways and away from that penetrating gray gaze. "I'm not used to being afraid. I didn't know what to do."

For a moment, an internal battle raged. Lauren was well aware that her emotions were running so close to the surface that they would very likely get the better of her. She was equally close to saying something she'd probably regret later. She wiped at her face with an irritated hand and took a calming breath. "Devlyn, honey, look at me." She cupped Devlyn's chin and turned her face so that they were eye to eye. "I think the most important thing isn't that I left, but that I came back and that we worked it out."

Thickly, Lauren whispered, "I'm never leaving you. *Never*. I might need time and space to think about things." She threaded their fingers together. "But that's only so I don't go crazy and murder you in your sleep for keeping things from me." She offered Dev a weak smile, but it was clear that she was only half joking.

A little of the fear in Dev's eyes receded. "I meant what I said. I wasn't intentionally keeping this from you. I think of the kids as mine. *All* mine," her lips curled slightly, "and now ours, of course. At first, after Ashley was born, it was sort of like if I didn't think about it, it would be true. By the time Samantha had the boys, their biological parentage wasn't even something Samantha and I discussed anymore. I've grown used to not thinking about it, and the kids, all of them, they *are* mine, you know?"

They exchanged watery smiles and Lauren said, "I know." She ducked her head and picked a little at the sofa's fabric. "I'm sorry if I've made you afraid. I know I've wanted to run this year instead of face things sometimes. I'm trying to get past that." She suddenly looked up, confidence radiating from shiny gray eyes. "I *am* getting past that."

Devlyn felt her heart rate begin to slow. Things weren't spinning out of control as they had in the past. "You're doing great," she said emotionally. "Really great, Lauren."

"Then say that you believe that I won't leave you and I'll stick with you to work through things," Lauren ordered, her heart aching for her part in Devlyn's fears. "You're stuck with me." Her voice was hoarse and cracked as she spoke. "Say it."

Devlyn sniffed a few times, willing it to be completely true, even as she then drew in a deep breath and murmured, "I'm stuck with you."

Lauren drew their joined hands to her mouth and placed a tender kiss on the ring she'd given Dev at their wedding.

Devlyn allowed herself a few deep, calming breaths before she gave Lauren a lopsided, self-deprecating grin. "I really feel like shit for being such a coward. I didn't mean for it to get this out of hand. You're the one thing I count on. The most important thing. I know it's stupid, but I didn't want to risk that."

The golden light from the fire reflected off Lauren's damp cheeks and her eyes fluttered closed when Devlyn leaned forward and gently brushed away her remaining tears with slightly trembling lips. "I'm sorry too. For doing anything that made you think you couldn't talk to me." Her throat began to close, and she started to get upset all over again. "I don't want things to be like that between us," she said miserably.

"Please, don't cry. I hate it when you cry," Dev admitted in a hushed voice. "It's not your fault."

"Nuh uh, Devlyn." Lauren clutched Dev's hand tightly and held it to her heart. "It's both our faults."

"No—"

"Yes," Lauren corrected, her voice as gentle as she could make it. "We've got some stuff to work on." She lifted her eyebrows in appeal. "Okay?"

Dev's answer was immediate. "Anything." She licked her lips, feeling as though she'd just run a marathon. "Is… um… is there anything else you want to know? About David?"

Lauren drew in a shaky breath and let it out. "Everything, I guess. Does Beth know?"

Dev nodded. "Yes. We had to clear it with her first. There are only four people in this world who know. The kids don't know, even my parents don't know." She shifted her position on the sofa, neatly fitting herself into one corner. Then, with a quick pat on her lap, she invited Lauren to lay her head down. When Lauren didn't accept immediately, Devlyn felt the beginning stings of rejection and was on the edge of withdrawing her offer when Lauren let out a breathy sigh and moved to place her head in Dev's lap.

Lauren's eyes fluttered closed as Devlyn drew long, slender fingers through her wavy hair. Things were already becoming more manageable in her mind. They would work through this; her heart wouldn't accept anything less.

"What if the kids want to know when they're older?" Lauren asked. "That day is coming, Devlyn." Her mind was unerringly drawn to the teary conversation she and Ashley had in Hawaii.

"Mmm… we agreed to tell them if they ever asked, and I felt they could handle it."

"And David is okay with them not knowing? Forever?" Lauren found that a little hard to believe, especially considering how close David and Beth were to all the children.

"David doesn't want to interfere with our family, honey. He wants to be a part of it, and he and Beth are a big part of the kids' lives. Maybe deep down inside he wishes they knew, but I don't think he'd ever try to go against our agreement or my wishes on this. He's their Uncle David and they love him. He only wanted to know what would happen to the kids if I died. If that *had* happened, he and Beth would have raised them. That all changed when you came along. I'd want you to have them."

Thoughtfully, Lauren nodded, "I'd want that too. Just don't let something happen to yourself. I mean it."

Devlyn smiled grimly. "I'm being careful."

"Be more careful."

"Yes, ma'am." She bent down and kissed Lauren on the forehead.

"And when you said you wanted more children, you meant with David as the donor?"

Now Dev felt like squirming. "Not necessarily. We could look at other options, but I'm pretty sure there's still a few decent little swimmers on ice."

Lauren held up her hand. "Ugh. Never mind that last question, Devlyn. I don't want to think of David's swimmers. Besides, that's getting way too far ahead of ourselves. I need some time to digest all this. I guess I'm not really sure what to think. My head is still spinning."

"I don't blame you. And it's my stomach that's spinning." She gave Lauren an awkward hug. "I hate it when we fight."

"Same here." Lauren squeezed her back as tightly as she could, not knowing how much she had really needed that until right this second. Finally, they separated and she turned pleading eyes on Devlyn. "I'm going to need beer if I'm going to hear any more revelations tonight, sugar."

Devlyn touched the tip of Lauren's nose with her finger. "You're safe. There's nothing else. I promise."

They were quiet for long moments, their attention lost to the fire's flickering flames and their thoughts.

Breaking the silence Lauren finally muttered, "Ashley has his eyes." The slight slurred quality of her voice told Devlyn that she was nearly asleep.

Dev nodded, not quite sure how she felt about that. Her eyes moved from Lauren's shadow-dappled face then back to the flames, as her lover's breathing grew deeper and evened out. "I know."

Tuesday, August 16th

Dev smiled and shook hands with as many people as she could as she walked the rope line in Atlanta. She was covered in a light sheen of sweat, not only from the heat, but also from the thought that some unknown gunman might be in the crowd… waiting, wanting more than anything to steal the happiness she cherished.

Fucking shooting, her mind seethed. *Nothing will ever be the same. I used to thrive on meeting my constituents and feeling their energy. It actually made me high. Now all I can think of is that this bulletproof vest itches and won't help me if I take a bullet in the head.*

"I understand, ma'am," she told an elderly woman who was pumping her hand like there was no tomorrow. "Having an interstate highway built right through your living room would be a very bad thing. My friend, Congressman Preston," Dev motioned to the lucky candidate who was standing annoyingly close to her as she campaigned on his behalf, "will be happy to hear more of your story and see what we can do to help." Dev gave him meaningful look. "Won't you, Rick?"

The man tried not to wince. "It would be my pleasure, Madam President," he boomed with all the enthusiasm he could muster.

Devlyn leaned a little closer to the woman's ear so the words would be for her alone. "He really will find out what can be done. I promise."

The woman beamed, her false teeth shining in the hot sun. "Thank you, Ms. President. I knew you'd understand. Why I told my granddaughter, Thelma, she's the one who is going to college…"

Prudently, Congressmen Preston intervened so that Devlyn continued to move down the line of people. She offered a wave to the people who couldn't fight their way to the front of the crowd and hadn't been waiting there since dawn and gotten a spot along the rope, making eye contact with as many as possible. A suited man bumped into her from the back and her neck hairs bristled in reaction. For some reason the close proximity of the Secret Service agents made her feel itchy and claustrophobic. *Guess I'm not as used to their hovering as I thought.* Since the assassination attempt, public appearances like this one had been rare and the security intense.

But gamely, she kept her smile permanently affixed and listened as best she could to comments that ranged from mindless praise to her choice of foreign policy, hairstyles, clothes, and children—not necessarily in that order—to outright hostility. When the end of the line finally came into view, she fought hard not to scream, "Thank God!"

She'd been on the road for the past four days, stumping for various Emancipation Party congressmen who were up for re-election in the fall. Lauren had accompanied Devlyn to all but the last four states in her eleven-state whirlwind tour, but had decided to head back to Washington early in order to have some time to actually write up some of the things she'd observed. She'd taken the children back home with her, and even though it had been less than two days, Devlyn missed them terribly. They'd been playing some kind of sadistic game of phone tag, leaving non-urgent messages for each other.

The Senior-Agent-In-Charge discreetly touched Devlyn's arm and inserted himself between Devlyn and the crowd. "Madam President, we need to go."

She nodded and, taking a deep breath, stepped around the large man and shook hands with the last people in line. Seconds later, she was inside a fast moving limousine.

The air inside the luxury car was cool and dry, and she nearly whimpered as she pressed her overheated skin against the soft leather. Most of her aides had left before her in an attempt to use every single extra second to organize things before she arrived at her next destination. In the limo a silent agent sat in each corner of the seat across from her, alertly looking out at the dispersing crowd through the one-way, bulletproof glass. Thankful for the quiet, her eyes closed without her permission.

"Madam President?"

Devlyn whimpered when she heard Liza's soft, hesitant voice. She hadn't seen her in the car. "Yes?"

"I'm sorry to interrupt your rest, ma'am, but here are the notes for your next appearance. You'll be speaking to the UDC. The speech is nearly the same as it was for Charleston City Hall, with the exception of the last page. The changes are highlighted."

Dev's head came up and one eyebrow rose as she glanced across the wide seat. "Are any of them still alive?"

Liza blinked. "In Charleston, ma'am? Your speech wasn't that bad."

"No, not in Charleston," Dev said with a tiny snarl, but couldn't help but laugh. "I was *trying* to make a joke about the United Daughters of the Confederacy."

"Nice try, ma'am."

"Thank you so much, Liza," Devlyn shot back dryly. "Why the UDC?" Devlyn opened the folder that slid in her direction and scanned the coversheet.

"Same as usual, ma'am."

Dev scanned the information with a grunt. Big supporters, sizeable donation expected for her party, etc., etc.

"The UDC are very pleased with your performance in the White House, Madam President."

"I'm happy for them. Speaking of which, do you have this week's numbers?"

"Yes, ma'am." Liza removed yet another folder from the pile next to her. "Chief of Staff McMillian and Press Secretary Allen both commented that your numbers are up again this week. Having the First Lady with you for part of this tour was a boon to the numbers. The voters love her."

"They are wise people." Dev took a bottle from the holder next to her and took a long drink of the chilled water, which helped to ease her scratchy throat.

Dev held the folder, but didn't open it. Rubbing between her eyes she felt another headache coming on. "Please remind Michael Oaks and Press Secretary Allen that I want to have my blood drawn and be the first to register under the DNA Registration Act. Its effective date is coming up."

"Yes, ma'am."

As she began to skim the contents of the second folder, Dev patted her jacket, searching for a phone. Liza, as a staff member, carried a secure phone and handed hers over. The President nodded her thanks and dialed a number she had memorized.

"Hello, Ethan?" She sat up a little straighter as she addressed one of her aides who dealt exclusively with pending legislation. "What's the status on those six votes for the Well Family Act?" After a moment, her face darkened. "If I never get another piece of legislation passed, Ethan, I want that one." After a long moment of silence she said, "Fine. Do it and let me know." Looking pensive, she hung up the tiny phone and passed it back to her administrative assistant, watching as Liza dutifully followed protocol and wiped out the phone's memory in front of her boss.

"You know what he told me, don't you?" Dev gave Liza's foot a playful shove with her own. She had come to value Liza's mind and that the woman wasn't afraid to offer an opinion when appropriate.

"Yes, ma'am."

"I figured." Dev decided then and there that, no matter how much she depended on Jane as her secretary, she needed to keep her personal assistant permanently on the payroll, even after her tenure as president.

Dev's thoughts drifted back to her phone conversation. Cutting deals was part of the job, and she'd just traded an increase in medical benefits for pregnant women, small children, and heads of household in exchange for dropping her proposal to increase the import tax on foreign grains. She'd suspected that was what it would take to get the votes she needed. But no matter how many political deals she cut she always felt as though she were robbing Peter to pay Paul.

She *always* lost a little, even when she won.

Devlyn stepped out of her hotel bathroom, a cloud of steam escaping as she padded into the suite's bedroom while drying her hair with a fluffy white towel. The sun was setting over the city, and from the top floor of the hotel the view was spectacular. Glancing at the clock on the bedside table, she tried to remember what day it was. Then she smiled. Lauren and the kids wouldn't be at home for another hour. Tonight they were going to a production of "Beauty and the Beast" at the Kennedy Center. God, what she wouldn't give for a seat next to them.

Still dripping, she donned her robe, then felt something tickle her nose, then upper lip. She lifted her fingers and looked at them, smearing the warm red substance between her fingers. "Terrific." She retrieved a towel from the bathroom. After she cleaned her face, she sat down on the bed and pressed her nostrils shut with the cloth, allowing her eyes to close.

The phone ringing nearly caused her to jump off the bed. Her calls were being screened and since she'd made it clear not to disturb her unless the world was ending or her family was on the phone, she had a pretty good guess as to who was calling.

"Hello, sweetheart," Devlyn said into the receiver. "I miss you and I love you."

Lauren could hear the smile in Dev's voice, and it caused her to react in kind, her own voice unconsciously warming even further. "Same here, Devil. Why aren't you using the video phone?"

"Eh," Dev shrugged, even though Lauren couldn't see. "The scrambler is on the fritz and it's not secure. We're leaving for home tomorrow so I told them not to bother fixing it."

"Mmm. Gotcha. Do you think you'll make it home on schedule?"

"So far so good." Dev sniffed and removed the cloth that was pressed to her nose, only to feel a fresh trickle of blood slide down her face. "Shit." She quickly wiped it away and pressed her nose closed again.

"Are you okay? You sound sort of funny."

Dev winced at the red-stained towel. "I'm fine. Dry sinuses I think. I've got a little nosebleed." Her words were met with a long silence on the other end of the line.

After a moment of debate, over whether to bother to ask now or when Devlyn came home, Lauren sighed. "Please get that looked at. In fact, an entire checkup would be good. You know you're due for your annual anyhow."

"A checkup for dry sinuses?" Devlyn shook her head and said, "There's no way I have time for that."

"Make time."

Devlyn rubbed her temple with one hand and told herself not to lose her temper. It wasn't Lauren's fault she was dragging at the end of this trip. "I have that physical coming up in a month or two where the entire world gets to know everything from my blood pressure and weight to my cholesterol count. A little nosebleed can wait until then." Her voice softened. "It's really nothing."

"Don't make me call your mother." Lauren was only half teasing.

"You wouldn't dare!" Dev squawked, sitting up straighter against the padded headboard.

"Wouldn't I?" There was another long silence and Lauren could tell she wasn't going to make any progress over the phone. There would be time to talk about this when Devlyn came home. "Would you like to talk to your monsters?"

"You know it." Dev smiled eagerly as she waited for Lauren, who called for Ashley first.

"Hi, Mom!"

"Hi, Moppet, did you have a good time at the play tonight?"

"It was great! Emma and Jane came along too! They both said they could use a prince of their own. And Mama said she once went out on a date with a man with worse back hair than the Beast. They all laughed really loud at that. Can you come next time?"

A wistful expression chased its way across Devlyn's face. "I hope so, baby. But you know how it goes. I'm awfully busy right now."

"I know. It's okay."

But a little of Ashley's enthusiasm had faded and Devlyn knew it. "It won't be this way forever. I promise."

"Okay." Ashley sighed before adding, "I love you Mom."

"I love you too." Her heart ached for all these moments that she was missing with her children, and she swore to herself that she would quiz Lauren on every minute of the evening.

"Chris wants to talk to you."

Devlyn barely had time to say "okay" before she heard from her eldest son.

"Mom?"

"Yeah?"

"Next time can we go to a play for boys?" He was on the verge of outright whining.

Devlyn burst out laughing.

"It was all singing and dancing and kissing. Yuck!"

"Didn't the villagers go after the Beast?"

"Yeah, but it was so short! Two minutes and it was over. I liked the Beast better when he had fangs and fur, and—"

"All right, Chris, I get the picture. We'll see if we can find something you'll like better for next time. Maybe something with pirates or spacemen?"

"Or dinosaurs or bugs?" Christopher prodded.

"Well, I mean, we can try. But how many plays are there—"

"Thanks, Mom," Chris chirped. "Here's Aaron."

Dev wondered briefly how much sugar Christopher had consumed that night.

"Hi, Mom."

"Hi, Aaron. How was the play?"

"It was totally awesome!"

Dev blinked. "Really?"

"Oh, yeah. A girl threw up again and again in front of the food stand. It was really, really gross. It happened when Agent Tucker was taking Chris to the bathroom and he missed it all! It was great!"

Dev opened and closed her mouth a few times as she tried to think of an appropriate response. "Uhhh… That sounds… errr…" *Disgusting. Vile. Nasty.* "Interesting."

"Oh, it was. When you coming home?"

"Tomorrow, okay?"

"In time to read us a story or play Candy Land? Ashley's been teaching me how to cheat. Oops, I wasn't supposed to tell. It was gonna be a surprise."

"Oh, I'm surprised," Dev told him flatly. She shook her head, hearing Christopher and Ashley telling off Aaron. Then there was a set of muffled squeals before Lauren came back on the line. "Having fun yet, Lauren?"

Lauren laughed. "You could say that. Tell me honestly, Devlyn, how are you? I saw you on television this afternoon. You looked beautiful and the press is loving you, but you sound so tired."

"I am tired, but I've cleared this weekend entirely. How about a couple of days at Camp David?"

"I think that's the best thing I've heard all day. I'd love to have some time alone with you."

"Can we work on the next Adrian Nash novel? I've been coming up with lots of ideas. I have an entire notebook of them. It's what I do to relax between speeches and overcooked chicken luncheons."

Lauren winced in empathy. Since coming to Washington she'd endured a few million of those herself. "Sure. As long as we don't kill her off we can pretty much go crazy."

Dev clamped her hand over her mouth. It almost stifled her yawn.

"Devlyn, honey?" Lauren drawled. "I miss you and God knows I love talking to you, but go to bed."

For once, Devlyn didn't bother to argue. "Yeah," she sighed sleepily and took the towel from her nose. The bleeding had stopped and she tossed the soiled cloth into the wastepaper basket that sat next to the bed. "I am. I think I've finally reached my limit. I don't care if it is early. Campaigning for myself is one thing. But doing it for everyone else is about ready to kill me."

Lauren wasn't sure whether that answer made her feel better or worse. Devlyn's schedule had been so ridiculous that for the first time she'd talked to Liza and David without talking to Devlyn first, in an appeal for sanity. But they'd both thrown up their hands, saying that Devlyn herself had insisted on all the cities and the pace of this tour, determined to capitalize on her surge in popularity. "Tomorrow then. I love you."

"I love you too. Night."

Lauren hung up the phone, but continued to stare at it for a long time, her eyes unfocused. *You can't be all things to all people, Devlyn. No matter how hard you try.* Before she knew it, all three kids were back in the den, wearing their pajamas, their breath smelling of toothpaste. She gave them each a kiss and a hug, and they headed for their bedrooms for the night.

Lauren looked at her watch and debated heading back to her office. She stood, but paused when a photograph of Devlyn trying to catch her tenacious pug, Gremlin, who was running around the Rose Garden with one of Devlyn's shoes in her mouth, caught her eye. A tiny smile quirked the corner of her mouth, and she brought the photo to her lips and gently kissed Devlyn's head. "Sleep tight." She sighed, worry marring her youthful features. "And for God's sake, take care of yourself."

SEPTEMBER 2022

Friday, September 9th

Lauren looked at her dinner dress in the full-length mirror and smoothed the blue silk where it continued to roll at her midsection. "Damn thing."

Dev exited the bathroom, placing eye drops in each eye, blinking and dabbing at the corners with a tissue. "What's wrong?"

"This dress won't lie right."

"Mmm… You've lost a little weight lately." Dev crossed the room and placed her hands on Lauren's hips from behind, smiling a little as she gave the material a little tug to the right, settling it into place. She glanced up at the mirror to find Lauren smiling too. "There." She kissed her partner on the cheek. "You don't have to be nervous, you know."

"Yes, I do. This is my first formal State function as your wife. I know I've been to others, but this feels different."

Devlyn shrugged one shoulder. "There's nothing to it. Just smile, be charming, and try not to say something incredibly stupid that will come back to haunt you for years and years and years."

Lauren's mouth dropped open. "Gee, I feel so much better." Devlyn rested her chin on Lauren's shoulder and met the other woman's gaze in the mirror. "And to think I almost went to dinner tonight without hearing that sage advice first," she deadpanned.

Devlyn gave her a puppy-dog look, which was promptly ignored.

"Besides, that's easy for you to say. You've done this a hundred times." Lauren turned her head and kissed Dev's cheek before stepping forward to dig a pair of earrings from her jewelry box. After selecting a beautiful pair of diamond studs that Janet and Frank had given her for Christmas, she held them up and waited until Devlyn nodded her approval at her choice.

"Actually, I've only done it forty times," Dev said, applying a light coat of lipstick. She tossed the tube onto the vanity when she was finished. "Ms. Strayer, don't you pretend you were working at Wal-Mart before you accepted your position as my biographer. Your job with

Starlight Publishing had you attending plenty of nerve-wracking events. I happen to know you've had an audience with the Pope." Under her breath, Dev said, "Something I haven't done, if you must know."

The corner of Lauren's mouth curled upward as she worked on her second earring. "I was more excited than nervous then. First, no one was paying any attention to me. I was there with Cardinal O'Roarke, observing him for his biography, not participating. Second, I'm not Catholic. And third, the Pope is older than dirt! I could be standing buck-naked in front of him and I doubt he'd even notice."

Dev leaned forward and placed her lips right against Lauren's ear. "Honey," she breathed in a husky voice, "that would be *dead*, not old."

Lauren wrinkled her nose at the lame humor, but laughed anyway. "Do you have to make jokes when I'm nervous?"

"Does it take your mind off being nervous?"

"Mostly," Lauren admitted reluctantly. More than anything she didn't want to do something that would put more pressure on her already over-stressed spouse. "A watch, do you think?" She held up her naked wrist.

Dev's grin was smug. "Then my work here is finished. And no watch. You have to stay for the whole thing, no matter what time it is."

"Ugh." Lauren rolled her eyes and moved from her jewelry box to Devlyn's. "What did you say you wanted earlier?"

"The square-cut emerald necklace."

"Mmm." After digging for a few seconds, Lauren came up with the booty. She held it under the vanity light, which had been turned to its lowest setting, bathing the room in warm light, which wasn't conducive to putting on makeup, but was easy on the eyes. "Wow."

Dutifully, Dev presented Lauren with her back. She bent slightly at the knees and lifted her hair off her neck, feeling the cool weight of the stone come to rest between her breasts and the warmth of Lauren's body as the blonde leaned close, partially to work the clasp, but mostly just because she enjoyed the intimate contact.

Lauren finally gave Devlyn's rear end a little pat. "All done."

Dev turned around and lifted her eyebrow in question. If there were any pug hairs on her suit, Gremlin was done. "Well, how do I look?"

Lauren let out a low appreciative whistle as she circled Devlyn like a new car buyer about to kick the tires. The whistle ended with a little moan that actually made Devlyn blush. "Gorgeous."

Devlyn shivered from the sexy timbre that had suddenly invaded Lauren's voice. "Let's stay home and make out."

The look of frank desire on Lauren's face was more than enough to kick her libido into high gear, and Devlyn couldn't help but think that sometimes her endless responsibilities plainly sucked. "Don't tempt me. You know how I love it when you wear your hair swept up like that." To prove her point, she grabbed Lauren's wrist and pulled the smaller woman against her with a firm tug. When their bodies collided, she attached her lips to the silky-skinned, lithe neck before her and began to gently suck. "Mmm…"

Lauren gasped, then felt her knees begin to melt.

Dev sucked harder.

"No hickeys!" Lauren squealed half-heartedly. One red mark on her neck, and she'd have her excuse to stay in tonight, and she was fairly certain that with a few kisses and well-placed caresses her lovely partner could be persuaded to join her.

Regretfully, and after a tender kiss to skin only lightly tinted with Devlyn's lipstick, the President lifted her head. She sighed dramatically, making it very clear that she was more interested in feasting on Lauren's throat than a bland State dinner. "You were sent here by the Republican Party to ruin me, weren't you?" She lifted an accusing eyebrow.

Lauren arched one right back. "How did you know?"

Haughtily, Dev sniffed. "I'm not a woman to be trifled with. I'm—"

"Yeah, yeah, you're the President. Somehow I hadn't forgotten since the last time you told me." The banter was familiar and easy, and Lauren felt a good part of her unease begin to disappear.

Devlyn smiled and went to the bed to retrieve their small black purses. She was never sure why she brought one, knowing that she would hand it to an aide for safekeeping as soon as she arrived at the dinner. And that she'd never be able to locate that particular aide again, until it was time to go. It was always the same.

"If you need me," Dev held up her hands to give Lauren a good look at her, "look for the suit." It was a narrowly fitted, perfectly cut, bright malachite-green pantsuit that would certainly stand out in a crowd.

Just like its beautiful owner, Lauren thought fondly. "I'll keep that in mind and aim for Armani."

"May I escort you to dinner?" Devlyn bowed gallantly, causing Lauren to chuckle.

She was about to say "of course" when she stopped. Lauren really didn't want to go this very second. She wanted to play and she wanted something else, and both of those things, she decided, were worth pushing herself a tiny bit beyond her normal comfort zone. Besides, it was something she suspected her spouse would enjoy even more than she would. She gave Devlyn a sexy smile, and instead of answering Dev's question, she posed one of her own.

"Do you know how badly my fingers are itching to get to the beautiful body beneath that suit you're wearing?" Her hand drifted down her own abdomen, her fingers suggestively dancing across cool silk.

Devlyn's mouth went as dry as the desert in less than a millisecond, and Lauren fought hard not to laugh out loud at the stunned but totally interested expression. "Ummm—" Dev swallowed and tried again, her eyes riveted to Lauren's hand. "Ummm—"

Luckily, Lauren wasn't really looking for a verbal response. "Devlyn?"

Electric-blue eyes snapped up to meet Lauren's, their pupils already dilated.

"Do you know how much I love and want you, Devlyn?" She let out a breathy sigh, and her hand reached up to cup her own breast. "It makes me crazy sometimes."

Dev's hands went limp, and with twin thumps, the purses hit the floor.

A low groan bubbled up from Lauren's chest and she slowly licked her lips, giving her own breast a firm squeeze. "I can't think of anything more divine than slowly undressing you, then kissing," another squeeze, "and licking," this time she pinched her nipple and wasn't sure whether it was her or Devlyn who whimpered, "and wrapping my lips around—"

Lauren's words were cut off by the impact of a flying body. Their mouths crushed together in a fiery display of passion and raw want as loud, lusty moans filled the room. Long moments later, as a hot tongue caressed her throbbing jugular, Devlyn fuzzily, but finally, figured out the allure of being fashionably late.

Lauren took her place at the top of the executive grand staircase, which led into the State Dining Room, and was greeted by two hundred pairs of expectant eyes. She smiled weakly at the crowd below, saying a mental "thank you" when Devlyn moved away from her security team to join her.

The President blinked a few times, moistening dry eyes.

"How late are we?" Lauren managed to ask, without moving her lips.

Dev smiled down at the Secretary of Veterans' Affairs and his wife. The man raised his glass in silent tribute to Devlyn, and for a second the President just *knew* she had to be wearing a big old, lovesick, "I just had fabulous sex with my equally fabulous wife" smile on her face. She lifted her chin a little higher, deciding that was about the best reason to smile she could think of. "I don't care how late we are," she murmured back. While it wasn't quite the truth—Devlyn was, and always would be, compulsive about her responsibilities—just this once she was willing to cut herself a little slack. "Extra time and a few stolen kisses with you is worth giving all the apologies in the world, Lauren. It was time well spent."

Dev turned her head and smiled at Lauren with so much heartfelt happiness and love that, for a moment, Lauren's vision was blurred with unshed tears.

"Ready?" Dev whispered.

"No."

"Perfect." But Devlyn stood her ground, allowing the dozens of photographs of them to be taken, all as she surveyed the landscape of the room.

Lauren marveled at Devlyn's calm, powerful presence. The eyes that had been trained on her only a few seconds before were *all* now firmly resting on one very presidential spot. Guts were sucked in, shoulders thrown back, and conversations hushed all around the room the instant Devlyn took her place by Lauren's side. It was more than protocol or manners; Devlyn was the kind of leader whose presence alone commanded everyone's undivided attention.

The guests' expressions ranged from envy to awe when they took in the sight of Devlyn and Lauren standing together. Lauren felt a surge of pride for her partner, and a smile bloomed on her lips, despite her own niggling apprehension.

The music that had been playing stopped, and arm in arm they started walking, the Marine Honor Guard leading the way. She felt Dev's hold on her hand tighten as they descended the stairs.

"Ladies and gentleman, and honored guests," a deep, disembodied voice announced. "The President of the United States and Ms. Lauren

Strayer."

While many women kept their maiden name after they married, never had Lauren felt so conspicuous about doing so. Several nasty looks from some of the older guests below told her they would have much rather heard "Mrs. Marlowe" announced. She wondered briefly if they would have had collective aneurysms had Devlyn taken the name Strayer upon their marriage. *Heh.*

The reception line loomed large and long before them and Lauren plastered on what she hoped would be a permanent smile. Devlyn's, she noted, was wholly genuine, almost to the point of beaming. *No wonder she continuously works herself to the point of exhaustion. She loves this.*

It took nearly twenty minutes to traverse the reception line, and when they reached the end Lauren let out a long, relieved breath. She heard her spouse's chuckles from a few feet away. "Tell me you're not glad," she said discreetly, her voice playful.

"Oh, I'm glad." Devlyn steered her toward the large, formally set banquet table, knowing they would need to stop and mingle for at least a half an hour along the way. "I just hide it better."

Dev caught sight of David and Beth across the room and watched as David approached her with a grin on his face while Beth appeared far less pleased.

"Hello, Madam President, Ms. Strayer," David greeted formally, looking dapper in his tuxedo, his thick, red hair slicked straight back.

Dev could tell by the expectant look on her chief of staff's face that he had something to discuss with her, and she sucked in an excited breath in anticipation.

David clasped his hands behind his back and rocked back on his heels as he turned his head to address Beth and Lauren. "Will you ladies excuse us, please?"

"Yes," Beth said tartly. "Go. I don't want to look at either one of you."

David's shoulders slumped just a tiny bit, and his gaze softened as he looked at his wife. "Beth—?"

"Go on," she interrupted, but managed to give her husband a resigned bump with her hip. "Go so Lauren and I can say terrible things about you both while you're gone."

"Am I not going to like what you're going to say?" Dev wondered out loud. That was not what the piratical gleam in David's eyes had told her. She cocked her head in question.

"You're going to *love* it," David gushed, his enthusiasm instantly restored despite his wife's sour face. The tall man led Devlyn over to a quiet corner where they stood, heads tilted toward one another in conspiracy as they talked.

"What are they in trouble for?" Lauren asked, accepting a drink from a server. "Thank you."

Gesturing with her chin, Beth indicated the area next to an enormous vase of flowers that sat on a white marble stand. It was a relatively quiet area and would allow them a moment of modest privacy without Lauren appearing antisocial. Beth leaned forward to smell the flowers as she spoke. "You didn't have plans for your Sunday, did you?"

Lauren's eyes slammed shut.

"You're cursing in your head, aren't you?"

"Yes!" Lauren groaned. "What now?" She found herself wanting to wail and barely resisted the impulse. "She needs a day off!"

"Take it easy." Beth moved a little closer to her friend and lowered her voice to a whisper. "I know she does. And you probably do too. But I can guarantee that Devlyn won't be relaxing by the pool this weekend."

Lauren pulled an orchid from the bouquet and examined its delicate petals with unseeing eyes. "*I* know when to say I've had enough. She doesn't." Her jaw tensed as she replaced the flower, its delicate heady scent going completely unnoticed. "I seem to recall her taking off at least most of every Sunday. Now even getting her to do that is like pulling teeth. She's burning the candle at both ends."

"You're telling me? David's only a little better, and that's only because I outright threatened to divorce him if he didn't spend a little time at home. God help us if he actually lived where he worked too." Beth turned to see Devlyn, who was smiling broadly and patting David on the back. "But emergencies do come up."

"There's *always* an emergency." Lauren's face darkened. "And I won't do that to her, Beth. I'm not above playing dirty, but she's already worried that she'll do something that will make me leave her. I won't threaten her with that and add to her stress."

If Beth was surprised, she didn't show it. "I'm glad." She finished the last of her champagne and looked around for a place to deposit her glass. She decided to keep it in her hand when she realized she'd have to move to set it down. "Devlyn needs to be reassured that you're not going to disappear on her, Lauren." Her eyebrows knitted when her mind was drawn back to a very dark time in their lives. "I don't think she'd live through it if you did."

"That's not something Devlyn has to worry about," Lauren informed her. The resolute quality of her voice left no room for doubt. "But her health, family, and well-being *are*."

"I'm not disagreeing with you." Beth ran a hand through her dark curls. "But I don't know what to say about this weekend. David just got word that Sheik Haroun Yousif has finally agreed to come to the negotiating table. And he wants to do it tomorrow, with Dev and Secretary of State Jared Ortiz as mediators. Nothing is going to stop her from being there."

"Jesus. He said he'd never negotiate!" Lauren finished the contents of her glass in one long swallow, irrationally angry with a man she'd never met.

"I know. But it looks like if it's going to happen at all, it's this Sunday at Camp David."

Lauren studied the bottom of her glass for a moment. "I can't ask her not to take part in that. It's what she and so many others have been working on for months." She glanced up at Beth with a lost expression on her face. "But it's always something important, isn't it? She can never give enough."

Beth sighed. "She's a strong leader who hasn't accepted her own limitations because she doesn't believe she's reached them."

"She's not just a leader, Beth. She's a friend and a mother and a million other things that don't stop demanding her time just because some land-grabbing bastard has finally decided he'd like to spend the weekend at Camp David."

"Lauren!" Beth glanced around again, but Lauren's voice was so low she'd barely heard her herself. "You'd better hope nobody around here can read lips."

"She can't keep this pace up."

"Then you'd better prepare for a fight."

Lauren nodded grimly. "I can't bear the thought of her hurting herself."

Beth's smile was as gentle and reassuring as she could make it. "Neither can I. I'll help all I can."

Lauren gave her friend a quick hug. "I know you will. And I think I'm going to need all the help I can get." She pulled away and surveyed the milling crowd that was, in small groups, starting to work its way near the dinner table. "Time to make nice with the guests?"

"If we want to eat before midnight."

"What I wouldn't give for an icy cold beer and fat cheeseburger."

Beth's eyes rolled back in ecstasy at the mere thought. "With pickles, onion rings, and gobs and gobs of drippy ketchup."

"God, yes."

Both women moaned, then laughed. Their conversation wouldn't be forgotten. But for now, there was other business at hand.

Lauren set her sights on the Federal Reserve Board Chairman. Looking terribly uncomfortable, he was standing all alone and stuffing his mouth with meatballs and other hors d'oeuvres. She gave her dress a discreet tug and prepared herself for what she assumed would be the most boring conversation of her entire life. With a quick nod to herself, she was ready. "Let's go."

Dinner, which Lauren had to admit had been delicious, had come and gone, and now was the time for coffee and socializing and working the beautifully decorated room, before the band would strike up a waltz and couples would take to the dance floor.

Devlyn had just bent her head to whisper something in Lauren's ear when she saw Kenyan President Johibhi and his wife, smiling and heading their way. Devlyn guided her over to yet another spot in the room and Lauren smiled when she realized they were moving toward the President and his wife.

"President Johibhi." Dev took the man's hand. "I trust you're enjoying your stay?"

"Ah, Madam President, very much so." His voice had a pleasant lilt and cadence that made Lauren smile. When she offered her hand in greeting, the slender man promptly brought it his lips and kissed it. "It is my pleasure to finally meet you, Ms. Strayer."

"I'm very pleased to meet you as well," Lauren said.

The man gave her a radiant smile in return. "May I present my wife Ngini?" he announced, stepping slightly away from the brightly dressed woman so that both the President and Lauren could greet her.

"How are your daughters Akinyi, Wairimu, Muthoni, Sikudhani, and Eucabeth? I trust they are enjoying their time at the University of Nairobi?" Devlyn asked.

Lauren, for the umpteenth time that night, tried not to let her jaw hit the floor as Ngini, Devlyn and President Johibhi chatted happily about college life and the girls' majors. *I've married Rain Woman. How in the hell does she remember all this? She forgot Aaron's name last week when he went streaking through the living room after his bath!*

When their conversation was through and while they were on their way back to the dance floor, Lauren whispered, "You quoted everything from three different countries' gross national product to the name of Prime Minister Foster's cat! You're amazing, but you're not *that* amazing. What's up?"

They stopped on the dance floor and faced each other. Devlyn took Lauren's hand, grateful for the opportunity to pull her close. When the music began, they moved around the room with the practiced ease of two women who knew each other's bodies well... and had had lots and lots of lessons. "Ask me later," Devlyn murmured. "But... um, do you really think I'm amazing?"

Lauren rolled her eyes. "You know I do. You just want me to say it again." They laughed, and Lauren closed her eyes and let herself be carried away by the mesmerizing strains of a familiar waltz.

Dev crashed into their bed face first. The long night was finally over, and her voice was nearly gone from talking with so many people. Sleeping on this very spot, clothes and all, was a very good idea, she decided. "Tell everyone I died," she groaned when she heard the door close.

"Don't joke about that, Devlyn. It's not even close to funny."

Dev rolled over and gazed up at Lauren, who was standing at the foot of the bed with her arms crossed over her chest. "Sorry, I'm just tired." Dev looked away. "Are you mad at me about this weekend?"

Lauren sighed as she sat on the edge of the bed. "I'm not mad, Devlyn. But I won't lie and say I'm not disappointed." She glanced over her shoulder. "Unzip me?"

Devlyn sat up and set to work on Lauren's dress. "I'll make it up to you and the kids."

"And who's going to make it up to you?" the smaller woman asked quietly.

Dev's hands paused as she took in the suddenly rigid posture of Lauren's back. She didn't say a word, fully aware that she didn't have a good answer for that. When she finished with Lauren's zipper, she lay back down and changed the subject.

"Hey, would you be horribly upset if I got this cut?" She tugged on her own, dark locks.

Lauren allowed the subject change without protest, deciding she wouldn't make any progress at three-thirty a.m. and admitting to herself that Devlyn wouldn't put up with "handling." She needed a plan of action. "Why would you want to do that?" She pulled Devlyn's shoes off and then slipped out of her own dress, letting it pool at her feet.

"I dunno. I've always heard that when a woman reaches a certain age she's too old for long hair."

Lauren stepped out of her dress and tossed it over a nearby chair, deciding there was no use in hanging up what the White House laundry would dry-clean the next day anyway. "Mmm… And do you agree with that?"

"I guess so. I mean, I'm not sure. Maybe." She scooted over as Lauren climbed onto the bed wearing only a skimpy black slip. "Oooo… that's nice." Devlyn drew her fingertip across the smooth material as Lauren snuggled up to her.

"It's your hair, darlin'," Lauren said on a yawn, her breath warming Dev's neck. She turned and nuzzled the strands in question and drew in a happy breath. "You don't need my permission to cut it. But if you're asking my opinion, I happen to think it's beautiful the way it is."

"And if I get it cut?"

"I'm sure it will still look beautiful." She kissed Devlyn's cheek and laid her head on a warm shoulder. "There'll just be less of it." Her fingers sneaked over and began undoing Dev's buttons. "You're not going to sleep in this, right?" She gave the green material a little tug.

Dev yawned. "Depends on how fast your fingers are."

"Devlyn?"

"Yeah?"

Dev's eyes slid closed and she grimaced; they felt dry and itchy.

"How did you know everyone's hometown and spouse's name and a million other things tonight? God, you didn't slip once."

"Ahhh, yes," Dev grinned, "my secret." She crooked her finger. "C'mon here."

Pale brows jumped. "If I were anymore 'here' we'd be sharing the same skin."

"That does sound sort of nice, though, doesn't it?" Dev turned her head and brushed her lips against the tip of Lauren's nose.

"Focus, Devil."

Dev laughed. "I hate to ruin your impression of my performance tonight. But if you insist." She opened her eyes and looked into Lauren's from very close range, not even blinking.

There were a few seconds of silence before Lauren said, "Are you trying to say that you hypnotized them and me? If you are, then I'm truly impressed."

Dev rolled her eyes. "No, silly. Look at my eyes."

Lauren smiled. "If I do then I'm going to be forced to start kissing you." Then her expression changed as she took a slightly harder look. The light could be better for doing an up-close examination but she was almost sure... "Are you wearing contact lenses?" While they were no longer used to correct vision, they were still common for those who wanted to change their natural eye color. "Your baby blues are not fake!" She gave Dev a horrified look. "I know it!"

"Nope, they're very real. But these contacts are special. They each contain a micro-processor."

"What?" Lauren gasped, prying Dev's eyes open with inquisitive fingers and staring at them from very close range. "You're kidding. I don't see a thing."

Dev chuckled softly, doing her best not to let the organs in question cross. "Well, that is the point. These babies are still experimental and will have many... err... classified uses." When Lauren backed off, she blinked a few times as she tried to refocus on the pretty face so close to her own. "But one of their many uses I got to test out tonight. When I look someone in the eye, a retinal identification scan is performed and a mini-biography that includes relevant political and personal information appears next to their head in red letters. That only I can see, of course."

For a moment Lauren was speechless. Then, "Oh my God. Those were in a *James Bond* movie from a couple of years ago. I didn't know they were real!"

"They weren't." Dev grinned. "Then."

"I want a pair!"

"Too bad they cost about three million bucks apiece, eh?" With a pitiful groan, Devlyn climbed out of bed and headed toward the bathroom to remove the contacts, glad that Lauren's question had reminded her she was wearing them.

"Christmas is coming in a mere four months!" Lauren called after Dev as she wiggled her way under the covers.

Dev poked her head out of the bathroom and stuck her tongue out at her mate. "Sorry, honey, but unless Santa joins the CIA, these babies will not be in your stocking."

Thursday, September 29ᵗʰ

Lauren sat back in the seat and pinched the bridge of her nose, rubbing the spots that became slightly irritated by her glasses if she wore them for too long. She considered what Devlyn had been telling her for months, that the minor surgery that would correct her vision would be worth it in the long run. But as always, Lauren couldn't bear the thought. Glasses were fine. The problem was, she'd been wearing hers nonstop since six that morning, when she generally wore them only to read or write.

She'd just finished an excellent meeting with a long time associate of Devlyn's. The man used to be the head of Ohio's Department of Agriculture. Today, however, he was happily employed as a lobbyist for corn and corn products interests. The easygoing man had shared story after story about a very young and earnest former Governor of Ohio, whom Lauren happened to love very much. The material would be wonderful for Devlyn's biography, and so far, Lauren counted this day as a raging success.

From the back seat of a silver-colored sedan, Lauren watched the scenery slowly pass. The driver and front passenger were both Secret Service Agents. Sitting alongside Lauren was her new administrative assistant, Carol Becker, a fresh-faced Stanford graduate whose salary was paid fifty percent by the White House and fifty percent by Starlight Publishing.

"Lauren?"

Lauren turned and smiled at Carol. It had taken nearly two weeks for the woman to start using her first name as Lauren had requested many, many times. "Can we switch to some White House business, ma'am."

Lauren rolled her eyes at the word "ma'am," vowing to work on that later. "Sure, *Ms. Becker*," she said dramatically, laughing a little when Carol's eyebrows jumped perceptibly. *Heh.* "But only if we must."

Carol looked at her watch and nodded. "We must." She indicated a large file folder on the floor. "Mrs. McMillian indicated you would be releasing your guidelines on academic achievement next week. But she wanted to make sure you saw these papers first."

Lauren's eyes turned to slits. "She did, huh?" *Dammit, Beth. You already know how I feel about this.*

Carol looked a little unsure of herself. "Ummm… yes."

"I see." Lauren took off her glasses and tossed them on the soft leather seat next to her. "You can tell Beth I don't need to see those papers, because as I indicated before, I won't be releasing anything to the public. Especially when I don't know anything about the subject matter."

"If you read what is in the folder, you would know something about it," Carol offered reasonably, biting her lip at her own playful impertinence.

Lauren snorted. "No wonder Beth likes you so much." She let out a soft sigh, then Carol watched in surprise as the blonde's expression turned serious in a flash of an eye. "Rest assured, Carol, I won't be releasing any recommendations. I speak only for myself, or," she corrected herself, "occasionally for Devlyn, but not the Emancipation Party. Just because I share a bed with the President doesn't mean a few minutes of reading will give me the sort of background necessary to make serious recommendations to strangers. I don't care *what* prior First Ladies have done." Lauren pointed to the folders near Carol's feet with an irritated finger. "Those contain the Emancipation Party's recommendations. Not mine." She cocked her head to the side, her eyes sparking just a little. "Are we clear?"

"Yes, ma'am." Carol swallowed. "We're clear."

Lauren consciously softened her gaze. "Don't worry." Her voice took on added warmth. "I'll talk to Beth so you won't be caught in the middle of things, okay?"

Carol relaxed, her shoulders slumping with pure relief. "Thanks." She smiled and pulled her ringing cell phone out of her jacket pocket. "Excuse me, ma'am."

Lauren nodded and closed her eyes to block out the late afternoon glare of the sun. She leaned her head against the air-conditioning-cooled window and after only a moment, felt that familiar, slightly dislocated sensation of being almost asleep.

Without warning, there was a deafening explosion. Before she could even open her eyes, a searing hot pain tore through Lauren's head. Her body was violently thrown sideways, held to the seat only by the car's restraint system. A second later she was jolted forward with such force it knocked the wind from her lungs. She vaguely registered the sounds of squealing tires and a piercing scream before her world went mercifully black.

Dev laughed along with the rest of the room as the Secretary of the Interior related a story about his vacation. It was a welcome moment that eased the tension in the day's cabinet meeting. Even among this handpicked group, the meetings were usually anxiety-filled for reasons that Dev could never quite grasp.

She glanced at David's watch and realized they were just about to adjourn, when an aide rushed into the room with a slightly desperate look on his face. He looked torn between going to David or Dev. David ended the aide's mental debate by motioning the husky man in his direction. He leaned over and whispered something in David's ear.

Dev watched as the blood drained from her friend's face and she felt the bottom of her stomach drop out in response.

David whispered something back to the aide, but Devlyn could only barely make out Geoff's name.

Very slowly, David cleared his throat and rose to his feet. "If you'll excuse us, ladies and gentlemen. There's something that requires the President's immediate attention. Thank you for your cooperation; this meeting is adjourned." He circled the table as cabinet members filed out of the room and gently took Dev by the arm, whispering to her, "Come with me and stay calm."

Dev's chest tightened to a painful degree. "David?"

"Not here, Dev." He led her out of the room, turning in the opposite direction from which the still-milling cabinet members were walking. The crowd parted, and a distraught looking Jane met David in the hall and murmured something about television to him. She couldn't look at Devlyn, lest she burst into tears.

"What is going on?" Dev practically shouted, half-angry, half-terrified, feeling her heart begin to race when David told Jane to clear the rest of the day.

David pulled Dev into an empty conference room. He ignored Devlyn's question long enough to give the voice commands for the television and winced as a horrible picture, shot from a local traffic helicopter, flared to life in the corner of the room. He muted the sound but left on the closed-captioning as he quickly explained to Devlyn what she was seeing.

His voice shook slightly as he spoke. "That's Lauren's sedan, Dev. Our satellite has got the location too, and agents are on the way."

What had happened was fairly clear from viewing the accident scene. Another sedan, a white Toyota, had entered an intersection and had hit the side of the car Lauren was traveling in, crushing the driver's and rear passenger's side doors. The police escort that was following Lauren had run into them both.

Dev didn't say a word. Not even when the camera zoomed in and showed a lurid smear of crimson staining the driver's side rear window. It was clear the press didn't know who was in the car by the casual, almost understated way they were reporting the accident. The news crew had literally stumbled across the accident only seconds after it happened while on their way to filming rush hour traffic. The three cars, one of them a police car, were now sitting idle on a relatively quiet back street and there was no ambulance on the scene yet. The man from the Toyota exited his car quickly and stumbled to the curb, where he sat down with his head in his hands.

David could tell by the whiteness of Devlyn's skin and the panic in her eyes that she had heard what he'd told her, even though she remained completely silent, her eyes riveted to the television.

"David…" she finally managed to choke out.

He was there to catch her when her legs buckled, and he guided her to a chair.

She gulped down a few huge lungfuls of air and gripped the armrests of her chair with devastating force, her knuckles turning as white as her face. She forced words out between ragged breaths. "What do… what do we know?"

"Not much. The call came in maybe sixty seconds ago. The patrol car following called it in directly to the White House. The officer didn't say much—less than you can see from the TV, in fact."

David and Devlyn watched as two policemen and several Secret Service agents swarmed over the two cars, guns drawn. One agent instantly approached the Toyota driver and appeared to order the shaking man to lie down, face first, which the driver did. The other agents ran over to Lauren's car.

A low moan escaped Devlyn's chest. "I need to get there."

"Dev, an ambulance is on the way. ETA two more minutes, tops. She'd be gone by the time we got there."

Devlyn closed her eyes, her entire body shaking. "Where is she?" she asked in a remarkably calm voice, her mind's eye still focusing on the television image. *This can't be happening again*, her mind screamed. *It can't!*

"On the corner of 6th and A Street North East. That's about three miles from here."

Dev shot to her feet and bolted for the door.

Lauren opened her eyes to the sound of sirens in the distance. Dazed, she blinked a few times, realizing that she was lying sideways, nearly on top of Carol, who was moaning.

"What—?" She shook her head, wondering what was wrong with her vision and what was stinging her eyes. She instantly regretted the motion and cried out softly, her head throbbing.

"Lauren? You okay?" Carol's shaky voice asked.

"I think so," Lauren whispered, her hands moving to unhook the car's safety restraint system. Her fingers fumbled for a few seconds until she was able to release herself.

"Is everyone all right back there?" one of the agents asked, his attention quickly turning to his fellow agent, who was slumped forward in the driver's seat, apparently unconscious.

"Yes," Carol whimpered.

"Ms. Strayer? Talk to me, ma'am."

"Oh, God," Carol gasped. "She's bleeding."

Lauren wiped at her eyes, the metallic scent of warm blood filling her nostrils. Suddenly the sedan began to close in on her and she started to panic. Her entire body ached and things kept going in and out of focus. She felt as though she were swimming through thick pea soup.

"Stay in the car, ma'am," the agent ordered, as he drew his gun with one hand and, with the other, tried to rouse the driver. Alert eyes scanned the interior and exterior of the car.

"I can't," Lauren whimpered, her heart beating so fast she was sure it would burst in her chest. She tasted blood and her stomach roiled as she reached for the far door. "I—"

"Stay!"

But Carol had had enough as well; she pushed past Lauren's hand and opened the door. She scrambled out and fell onto the asphalt with Lauren right behind her.

The street felt hot against Lauren's palms, but she didn't feel the gravel digging into her skin. Bracing herself with her hands against her knees, she stood and started to realize what had happened. When she was upright and swaying precariously, she reached for her face and eyes again, this time looking at her fingers, which came away stained liberally with the sticky blood that was flowing from a gash on her forehead.

She saw stars and her knees gave way just as several Secret Service agents came running and screamed at her to get down.

"Devlyn!" David ran after her, having trouble keeping up with her even though she was wearing a skirt and low heels. "Wait, Dev!" he tried again.

She ran up to Jane's desk and jerked the phone from her secretary's hand. "Give me your car keys!"

Compassion shone in Jane's eyes. "Dev, honey—"

Dev's face contorted in rage. Never had she been so furious that she had no personal means of transportation. "Goddammit, I said give them to me!"

With wide eyes, Liza cleared the area around Jane's desk, ushering away anyone who could hear or see Devlyn in this all-out panic.

Panting, David put himself between Dev and Jane. "You can't go to her."

"Bullshit, I can't!" Dev barely kept herself from striking him.

"He's right, Dev."

The President turned to see Vice President Vincent shouldering his way past a very harried Liza. "We don't know if this was a true accident or an attempt to get you out of the White House with less than normal security."

Dev's hands shaped into quivering fists. "I don't care."

Geoff's tone softened. "I know you don't." He put a comforting hand on her shaking shoulder. "But I have to."

"Geoff," she whispered, tears blinding her. "I *have* to get to her. I—
"

David's phone rang and everyone held their breath as he answered it. With a curt reply, he snapped the phone shut. "Lauren and the agent who was driving are on their way to George Washington University Hospital. There's no in-depth medical assessment yet, but we do know that she's unconscious, her vitals are stable, and they're treating her for a head wound."

Dev nodded weakly and commanded her legs to move. All she could think of was going to the hospital after Samantha's crash; the look of hopelessness on the doctors' faces; their words of apology and pity that barely registered as the unthinkable actually happened. She closed her eyes and willed herself not to fall apart at the seams.

Not yet.

"Let's go," she ordered, making it crystal clear that no one on earth could stop her.

Word had leaked out about the facility's famous patient. Devlyn, David, and a bevy of Secret Service agents bypassed the writhing hoard of reporters camped around the hospital and filling its hallways to the brim by using a staff-only entrance in the private, underground parking lot.

The hallway was poorly lit with lurid fluorescent lights and the walls were slightly dingy, despite this being a state-of-the-art facility. They were forced to ascend the narrow staircase two at a time, and Devlyn could hear the Senior-Agent-In-Charge in front of her cursing under his breath. No one had told them about this, and it clearly wasn't to her security's liking.

She drew in a deep breath as she bounded up the steps, literally pushing on the backs of the men in front of her so that they would move faster. Dev winced when she caught a whiff of the bleach and the standard medicinal odors found in all hospitals. The air was muggy, giving the impression that a large swimming pool was nearby. She stopped and grasped the metal railing tightly, feeling lightheaded. She tightened her grip. "Shit."

"Dev?" David said worriedly, stopping one of the many phone conversations he'd been having since they left the White House.

She just shook her head. "I'm fine." She started up the stairs again. "You know where we're going?"

David nodded. "A right turn at the top of the stairs. Jesus, if I'd known we were going to go up seven flights…"

But Devlyn wasn't listening anymore. She just gritted her teeth and continued to climb, telling herself not to think of anything at all. *One step. Two steps. Another. Turn the corner. Breathe.*

Finally, a door in front of Devlyn opened, and she moved forward into better light and a fresher smell. Two doctors in crisp white lab coats were there to meet her.

"Madam President, my name is Doctor Emilio Castel. Let me assure you your wife is receiving the best care possible. I am Ms. Strayer's primary care physician. We have cleared her rooms of physicians and staff so you may have a moment alone with her." He indicated the woman on his right with a tilt of his head. "This is Doctor Yajra Chandra, our most senior plastic surgeon. She will be working on Ms. Strayer's face."

Dev swallowed hard, not sure whether to be horrified that Lauren needed a plastic surgeon or grateful enough to fall on her knees and thank God that she was alive, no matter what her condition. Just to be sure she asked, "She's alive then?" Saying the words aloud made her physically sick, and she could taste the bile rising in her throat.

"Oh, yes, Madam President," Dr. Castel answered respectfully, seeming surprised Devlyn didn't already know that. Then again, Lauren had only just been brought in. He glanced down at the chart in his hand and prepared to recite the most important patient status update of his career. "She—"

"Where is she?"

The man's eyes went round, and his dark eyebrows rose at the sharp, desperate sound to the President's voice. "I—"

"Where?" Dev shouted, not caring who heard her. Then, out of the corner of her eye and behind Dr. Castel, she caught sight of a room being guarded by three men in suits, all sporting crew cuts. She took off running, stiff-arming the doctor out of her way and sending the people around her into chaos.

The men guarding the door straightened at the sight of the President and barely had time to step aside as Devlyn whirled past them like a mini-tornado, opening the hospital door so violently that it slammed shut behind her.

David, who was only two seconds behind her, remained outside the room. He ordered everyone to stay clear except in the event of an emergency and began quietly conferring with Lauren's doctors.

Startled, Lauren looked up to find Devlyn bursting in. She hadn't expected Devlyn to be here this soon or looking this distraught. She was in bed, but still wearing her slacks under her mint green hospital gown, having only been brought to this room a few seconds ago.

Devlyn ran up to the foot of the bed and stopped dead in her tracks to stare at her partner, her breath coming in quick bursts. A white bandage stood out starkly against the summer-tanned skin of Lauren's forehead, and she was sporting the beginnings of a nasty black eye. Blood still stained the side of her face and chunks of her hair were sticky with it.

Sheepishly, Lauren smiled at her, embarrassed at the tremendous fuss the hospital was making. She'd skipped the emergency room altogether, going right to a private room where an entire team of doctors had been waiting. They had ordered about a million tests that were due to start at any moment. And all she wanted to do was go home and wash the remnants of blood from her hair, neck, and face and collapse into bed. "You look worse than I do," she said, not unkindly.

"Are—?" Dev rubbed her eyes, making very sure that what she was seeing was real. *She's breathing. She's talking.* Devlyn reached out and grabbed a nylon-covered foot, squeezing gently, feeling chilled but living skin beneath her fingers. "Are you all right?"

Lauren frowned. Devlyn looked as though she might pass out. "I'm okay, honey, really." Her gaze softened with sympathy. Thinking of Devlyn in the hospital last year still filled her with a helpless, panicky feeling that made her throat close and her eyes sting. "You wouldn't believe the headache I have. They'll know for sure if I have a concussion after some more tests." She reached out for Devlyn's hand. "Darlin'?"

"What else?" Dev asked, her voice grim and tight. She remained at the foot of the bed, her entire body tensed as though readying herself for a punch to the gut.

Lauren blinked and lowered her hand, stung and confused by Devlyn's implied rejection. "Okay. They said I still need a few stitches and something called a live-skin cell patch for scarring, and a CAT scan to rule out anything else." She sighed, wishing they'd been able to give her something for her throbbing head. "Other than that—" She paused as her partner's skin went from ashen to pale green. "Devlyn, honey?"

Dev bent at the waist and let out a low groan as the stress and heart-wrenching worry caught up with her all at once. Her knees turned to water and hit the floor with a loud thump.

"Devlyn!" Lauren's eyes went round as saucers and she scrambled to the end of the bed, reaching for Devlyn but not quite making it in time. She jumped out of bed, fighting the temporary vertigo the action caused and ignoring the sharp sting as her IV was torn from her hand. Lauren was at Devlyn's side just in time to steady the taller woman's shoulders as she turned her head and vomited all over the hospital floor.

Lauren hugged Devlyn from behind and murmured words of support and comfort as the President heaved out her stomach's contents. "It's okay, baby. I'm so sorry to have worried you like this."

"It—it's not your fault," Devlyn said fiercely, between retchings.

"Madam President?" David's disembodied voice sounded through the door.

"We're fine, David," Lauren called back, closing her eyes against the pain she caused herself by raising her voice. The words were still echoing in her head. "We just need a minute."

Dev began to dry heave.

"You're sure?" David questioned with renewed urgency.

"I'm sure," Lauren answered. "No one comes in until I say so, David."

The relief in his voice was palpable. "Yes, ma'am." David nodded to himself, pathetically grateful that Lauren wasn't seriously hurt, but also that she was able to reassure and comfort Devlyn now. It was, he knew, his friend's nightmare come to life, and finding out Lauren was relatively unharmed couldn't erase the damage that had already been done.

When Devlyn was finished, Lauren pressed her lips against the back of Devlyn's head and whispered a tender "I love you." She tried to get up and go for a towel, but Devlyn reached blindly for her, holding her in place.

Dev turned in Lauren's arms, hugging her with all her might. She began to cry. "Thank God, you're okay. Thank you, thank you," she repeated over and over, bringing tears to Lauren's eyes.

Dev cried for a long time as they sat there together on the cold hospital floor until she felt as though she'd purged a good portion of the misery from her system.

Lauren yelped a little when Devlyn gave her another good squeeze.

"God." Devlyn instantly pulled back and cupped Lauren's cheeks. She explored her face with her fingertips, and worried eyes took in every square inch of her Lauren that they could. "I'm hurting you. You should be in bed!" She didn't think it was possible, but when she saw Lauren's hand, which was bleeding from the violent removal of her IV, she felt even worse.

"I'm not badly hurt, honey," Lauren explained, carefully scratching around the bandage on her forehead. "Are you okay?"

Dev didn't even try to lie. She shook her head "no" and grabbed a tissue from a stand near the foot of Lauren's bed. With careful hands, she wiped away the slender trail of blood that had trickled down Lauren's ring finger and painted her wedding ring.

"Don't worry," Lauren said kindly, tugging gently on a strand of silky, dark hair. "You will be."

Wordlessly, Devlyn scrubbed a little harder, trying to remove the blood.

Finally Lauren had to pull her hand away. "Honey," she drawled quietly, "it's okay. I can clean it at home."

Dev tucked her hands under her armpits, unsure of what she should do with them. Then her gaze strayed to the stinky pool on the floor next to her. "Damn, I'm sorry about your room."

Lauren wrinkled her nose. "At least it wasn't on me this time, right?"

Dev smiled weakly, recalling a very embarrassing incident involving food poisoning and Lauren being in the wrong place at the wrong moment. "True. Are you *really* okay?"

"I could be brave and lie."

"I didn't," Devlyn reminded her, reaching back and pulling the blanket off Lauren's bed, intending to cover the vomit.

"I know." Lauren sighed and closed her eyes. She didn't want Devlyn to worry, but she wasn't sure how much longer she could stay standing. "Everything hurts. I feel like warmed-over shit."

"Ugh." Dev wiped her mouth with the edge of the blanket, then dropped it over the mess on the floor. "Don't make me barf again."

They both laughed weakly, but more from relief than humor.

"You know how I feel about doctors, Devlyn." Her eyes flicked around the room and the horrors of childhood filled with melancholy visits to the hospital to watch over her dangerously depressed mother rushed to the forefront of her mind. "I don't want to be here." For the first time today, she sounded very much like a scared little girl.

"I know. C'mon." Devlyn helped her back into bed, taking time to tuck the sheet around her partner's legs. She pulled a chair over to the bedside and stared down at Lauren with loving eyes, struggling to remember anything she'd ever heard about head injuries. She traced the edges of Lauren's bandage with a touch so light, Lauren wasn't sure she felt it at all. "Were you unconscious?"

Lauren sank deeper into the bed and closed her eyes as she thought. She realized very quickly she didn't have much idea of what had happened at all. "Outside the car, I think I fainted at the sight of my own blood. I can't tell for sure what happened inside the car. I... I was confused. I got my bell rung, Devlyn."

"Mmm..." Devlyn's brow creased. "You need to have more tests." Dev took her hand and gently stroked Lauren's palm.

"I just need you."

"You have me *and* you get more tests. It's like winning the lottery only with breasts and needles."

Lauren opened one eye and rotated it in her partner's direction. "Are you sure *you* didn't get hit on the head?"

"I'm not sure of anything. I—" Dev's face crumpled and she began to cry again, sobs wracking her entire body. "I w—would rather it happened to me tha—than you. I love y—you."

"Oh, Devlyn..." Lauren didn't know what to say. It had all happened so fast she hadn't really had more than a moment or two to think about how Dev would react to her accident. Yes, intellectually she understood this would be hard for the older woman. But nothing could have prepared her for the low keening sound that filled the room and tore through her heart like hot blades. Or for the outpouring of raw, unreasoning fear painted across her lover's face in scalding tears. "I'm okay. I promise," she said, feeling as helpless as she ever had.

Dev shook her head violently, and she wiped clumsily at her wet cheeks. "No. No. No! You don't know that yet."

"Yes, I do, darlin'. I can tell."

"No!"

"Yes, Devlyn. Believe it."

Dev shook her head again, crying even harder. "I can't!" Miserably, she hugged herself in mute despair, giving up any pretense of restraint or control. She couldn't bring herself to even try to hold it together.

Lauren's heart was breaking, but all she could think to do was to tell Dev that she loved her and reassure her that things truly would be all right. There were several stops and starts before Devlyn's tears tapered off.

"Better?" Lauren asked, knowing that a good cry could sometimes go a long way.

"I'm not sure," Dev answered, still seeming very emotionally adrift.

"How are Carol and the agents?" Both men were relatively new to the White House beat, and she hadn't had a chance to get to know either one of them.

Devlyn didn't answer for a moment as she tried to remember what David had relayed from the short phone update on the even shorter car ride from the White House to the hospital. She hadn't paid much attention past hearing that Lauren was stable and being examined. "I think I- I don't know about the driver, he's being attended to now. Carol and the other agent were unharmed."

Lauren let out a relieved sigh. "Thank goodness."

"Shit!"

Lauren jumped at the unexpected outburst.

"I haven't given them a second's thought." Dev swallowed thickly. "What in the hell is wrong with me?"

Lauren proceeded very carefully, but her voice didn't waver. "This is about more than the accident, darlin'." She held Dev's hand tightly.

"I…" Dev felt like she could cry forever and she had trouble speaking, but she tried her best. "Maybe. I shouldn't be falling apart. I shouldn't be but…" She sucked in a quick breath, afraid she might start to cry again.

"Shh… Okay, okay," Lauren soothed. "We'll deal with it all. Just one thing at a time, okay?"

Dev sniffed a few times. "I'm sorry—"

"Please, stop saying that." Lauren cupped Dev's chin.

"You need to get your stitches." Angrily, Dev wiped at her own eyes again. "Not me being a baby. I'm sorry. The only reason the doctors aren't swarming all over you is because I'm in here and they're afraid to come in."

"They're not swarming all over me because I have a tiny cut and a bump on the head and nothing more. And I told them not to come in, remember?"

"You need your doctors," Devlyn insisted stubbornly. She was still shaking.

To Lauren's eyes, Devlyn had never looked more lost. She suspected the unrelenting pressure and stress Devlyn had placed on herself lately had already left her emotionally tapped out. A white Toyota sedan had turned out to be the straw that sent the camel sprawling. "There is something I need," Lauren insisted, pointedly not letting go of Devlyn's hand. "It's what we both need... some time to heal. The shooting, the pressure, the press, they're still eating away at us both."

Devlyn's lip twisted into a sneer, but the gesture was directed inward and Lauren knew it. "At *me*, you mean."

"That's not what I mean," Lauren corrected, determined to make this happen if she had to get down on her knees and beg. "Please give us the time we need to heal. *Please.* We both need it desperately."

Devlyn looked away, her mind still spinning. She needed to talk to David and Liza and Emma and Jane. She needed to tell the kids what had happened, and her parents and Lauren's father. She needed to bring in the doctors. She needed to get someone to clean up the stinking mess she'd made. And with all that to do, she still wasn't sure she could tear herself from this very spot if her life depended on it. She wondered with a slightly hysterical, humorless inner laugh if they could do a CAT scan with her still attached to Lauren.

Dev's entire world still felt all wrong, as if everything were burning around her and she couldn't see through the blinding, acrid smoke. She cleared her throat gently and clung to Lauren's hand, trusting her, somehow, to guide her home. "Yeah." She sighed. "I-I think you're right."

OCTOBER 2022

Monday, October 3rd

Lauren awoke slowly, pale eyes fluttering against the stripe of early morning sunlight that was managing to sneak through the curtains while the rest of the room was still bathed in the blue, ethereal light of pre-dawn. If the sun was up at all, it was later than Lauren usually woke up. Something was different this morning. And it took her still-hazy brain a long moment to solidly register what that was. *No headache for the first time in four days. Thank you, God.* In sleepy satisfaction, she grunted and burrowed deeper into a soft feather pillow, allowing her eyes to slide closed.

"You can't fool me." Dev snuggled close to Lauren's back and wrapped an arm tightly around her partner, needing to feel the solid presence of her lover's compact body to reassure herself that she was safe, and here, and whole. "I know you're awake."

Lauren moved away from the warm breath tickling her neck and moaned into her pillow. "Shh," she murmured softly. "Lauren is still asleep and it's not morning yet. No matter what the sun says. Go back to sleep." *Wait a minute. Devlyn?* Lauren turned her head just a little so that she could take in a breath of cool air. "Aren't you supposed to be running circles around your agents and the White House track this morning? Don't tell me you're missing torture time."

The hoarse quality of Lauren's morning voice made Dev smile. "It's not torture. And I would have been finished running by now anyway. I just didn't feel like running this morning. I already told Jack to take the agents running without me." Devlyn swept a strand of Lauren's hair out of her way and brushed her lips across the warm skin she found there. "You don't have to get up. You get to laze around in bed all you want. President's orders," she said in a no-nonsense voice.

Careful to stay within Devlyn's embrace, Lauren rolled over and gently kissed a pair of waiting lips as her mind slowly processed what Devlyn was saying. "Morning," she whispered.

A fond smile curled Dev's lips and made it all the way to her eyes.

"Morning."

When they parted, Lauren gave Dev a curious look. "When did you call Jack?" *I didn't hear a thing.*

A guilty expression swept across Dev's face. "Umm… I've been up for a while," she admitted reluctantly.

"How long is a while?"

Dev looked away. "I dunno. I just couldn't sleep. No big deal."

Lauren bit her tongue. *She's not getting a single night's peace with those damn nightmares. Those muscle relaxants put me out like a light last night. I didn't hear a thing.* "Rough night, darlin'?"

Dev visibly flinched. "I'm fine. You can go back to sleep."

Lauren's gaze gentled as she saw the panic lurking behind Dev's eyes. She gave the warm body next to hers a gentle poke. "As much as I'd love to lounge around in bed all day, the doctor said after a couple of days of rest I could go back to work so long as I take it easy, remember?"

"Oh." Dev looked a little disappointed as she smoothed back a tuft of wild blonde hair. She tried to sound nonchalant, but the words sounded stilted, even to her own ears. "I was thinking of spending the day here at home with you. I… um… I called Jane and had her clear my schedule." The word "again" was left unspoken, but hung between them as vibrantly as the sunlight now splashing across the bed.

Lauren did her best not to frown. Devlyn hadn't strayed from her side for more than two minutes at a time since the accident. At first she was more than happy to have any excuse for Devlyn to have a little downtime. Now, however, she was starting to believe that Dev watching over her like a hawk had done nothing more than trade one stress for another. "Okay," she said slowly, not wanting to hurt Devlyn's feelings but resolving not to let this issue go another day without discussing it.

Dev brushed her knuckles against the downy-fine hairs on Lauren's cheek. "How's your head?"

Lauren's medical test had revealed a concussion, albeit a mild one. "Mmm." She stretched a little, tugging the sheet up over her pajama-clad hips. "Sore like the rest of me." A yawn. "Better though. How about you?"

The smile slid from Dev's face. "I'm fine, Lauren." Her voice cooled a little. "Just like I said."

"I can see that." Lauren noted the faint but clear lines of exhaustion that still ringed her partner's eyes. She girded her mental loins. "I won't ignore what's staring me in the face forever, honey. We need to talk," she said, but admitted privately that she didn't have a clue where to start. "Do you want to tell me about the dreams?" As soon as the words left her mouth, she felt Devlyn stiffen.

Without warning, Devlyn threw off her covers and jumped out of bed, her feet slapping loudly against the floor. She stalked toward the bathroom, her anger clear from the set of her shoulders. "Nothing to tell," she said flatly, not bothering to turn around. "I can't remember them. I'm sorry if I disturbed you."

Lauren opened her mouth to say something just as the bathroom door shut. "Dammit," she grumbled, tossing off the remainder of her own blankets. "Not this time, Devlyn," she said loud enough so that she was sure her partner could hear her, even over the running water.

But before Lauren could make it to the bathroom, there was a gentle knock on her door. She stopped and stared back to the nightstand, trying to make out the fuzzy numbers on the clock across the room. She cursed again, spying her glasses on the table next to the clock, and rubbed her eyes with irritated fingers.

"It's me," a quiet voice said from behind the door.

"And us," came two more chorusing voices, both a little louder than their sister's.

Lauren opened the door and looked down at the children. "What are you guys doing up?" she asked softly. The kids were still in their pajamas, though Aaron, for some unknown reason, was only wearing his bottoms, and they were all sporting various stages of bed head. Lauren's hand went to her own head, knowing she looked the same, but doubting it was as cute on her. "You don't have to get up today. Your teachers are at a convention. Remember?" She yawned and stepped aside when all three kids plowed past her and crawled into her and Devlyn's still-warm bed.

"We know," Ashley said happily. "But we wanted to get an early start on today." Despite trying not to, she mirrored Lauren's yawn.

"You do know what today is?" Aaron asked, giggling as he pulled his mother's pillow from Christopher's hands and wrapped himself around it. "Hmm?" Expectantly, twinkling blue eyes fastened on Lauren.

"Gee, I don't know," she drew out the words playfully, waiting until all three children were moaning and whining before she gave in. "Ahh… yes," she finally said. "I seem to remember…" She tapped her chin with one finger. "Something."

"Mama!" Ashley cried, very aware she was being teased, but unable to withstand it for another second.

Lauren grinned broadly, as much at the endearment that still sounded new and exciting as the teasing. "I remember, evil ones. We're off to the shopping center." The rare trip to such a public place with the children had been planned for weeks, and Lauren hadn't seen them as excited about anything since Disney World.

Ashley licked her lips nervously, her eyes trained on the stark white bandage that still covered Lauren's forehead. Her voice took on a fearful edge. "Can you still go?"

Christopher, who was propped up with Lauren's pillow and was lying with his head on the foot of the bed, sat up a little as he anxiously awaited Lauren's answer.

Most of her mind still on Devlyn, Lauren walked over to the bed and sloppily crawled over Ashley to plop down between her and Aaron. "I don't see why not. But um… I'm still a little sore, so we might have to take a rest at… oh, McDonalds or someplace after a couple of hours." Another excursion that was rare in the extreme for the children and had required more planning than Lauren had dreamed possible for such a mundane task. "Sound good?" She prepared herself for the explosion she knew would come.

"Yeah!" they all cheered and Lauren closed her eyes and covered her ears in a vain attempt to keep their joint cry from rattling her brains.

The bathroom door opened and Devlyn reentered the room, her face glowing and pink from being freshly scrubbed, her toothbrush still dangling loosely from one hand. "What's all the noise about?" She looked at the clock, then arched an eyebrow at her offspring. "And why aren't you getting ready for school?"

"No school today, Mom," Chris said.

"Today's the day I get my ears pierced," Ashley informed her. The girl was bubbling with excitement.

"And Toys 'R' Us and McDonald's," Aaron added, laughing as Lauren reached down and tickled his exposed belly.

"Ahh… Right. The teachers' convention." Dev trained her eyes on her daughter. "Are you still sure about the ear thing, Ash? It's gonna hurt."

Warily, Ashley glanced at Lauren, who nodded her agreement. "You know how I feel about needles, kiddo. I was too chicken to get mine done until college." She shot Devlyn a warning look when she heard the taller woman snicker. Ashley had been spared the version of the story that included Lauren having the procedure done in her friend's bathroom after consuming more than her share of liquid courage and passing out in the tub after the first prick.

Ashley swallowed hard, and both women could see the wheels in her mind turning. But the girl's voice didn't waver when she spoke. "I'm sure I'm ready, Mom. I'll be brave."

Dev nodded. "All right then." In truth she thought Ashley should wait a few years, but the little girl had been working them both over hard to get her way on this and her persistence had actually paid off. Ashley had even successfully talked the biographer into calling her teacher to confirm that all the other girls were doing it. The argument was still weak at best, but during a late night conversation between just the two of them, Lauren had mentioned that she thought Ashley was already struggling to fit in and that keeping her from doing the typical things other girls her age were doing only served to make her stand out even more.

It was the first time Lauren had ventured into parental decision-making and she had been so hesitant and unsure of herself that it made Dev's heart clench just remembering. It had been a big step for the younger woman, and so, hesitantly, Devlyn had allowed herself to be persuaded. Now, as she watched her daughter's dark eyes dancing with happiness, she couldn't help but feel better about her choice. "I think I'll come with you guys today," she announced, surprising everyone in the room.

Ashley and her brothers exchanged confused, then worried glances.

"It's not Sunday," Ashley reminded her mom.

Dev scowled. "I know. But I'm going to stay home today in case Lauren needs me."

"That's okay," Aaron said quickly. "You don't need to go, Mom."

"Yeah," Ashley agreed, both she and Christopher nodding. "You have to work."

Stunned, Devlyn could only stare at her children, blinking slowly. "What's going on?"

Lauren could hardly believe her ears.

"Well, we know how busy you are, Mom," Ashley tried again.

"You don't want me to come?" Dev finally asked, feeling stupid that the answer suddenly mattered more than she could say.

Sensing impending disaster, Lauren sat up. "Devlyn—"

Dev held up a forestalling hand. "I want them to answer." She turned intent eyes on her children, who instantly began to squirm under her stare. "Well?"

"You have to work," Christopher answered bravely. "That's okay. We want Lauren to take us. We can count on her."

"Chris!" Lauren turned disbelieving eyes on the middle child.

"Don't worry, Mom, we won't be gone forever. We'll make it up to you," Ashley soothed, the familiar words reaching out and slapping Devlyn harder than any blow she could imagine.

Dev's jaw worked for a few painfully silent seconds.

Lauren could see Dev's white-knuckled grip on her toothbrush and swallowed hard. "I don't think they meant it the way it sounded, Devlyn."

"I think they meant it just like it sounded," Dev finally murmured, reaching up and rubbing the bridge of her nose with one hand. Then, without a word, she turned on her heels and marched back into the bathroom, shutting the door behind her.

The children shared uncomfortable looks as Lauren ran an agitated hand through her hair.

"What was *that*?" Lauren demanded, knowing how badly Devlyn's feelings had just been hurt. "You beg her to spend time with you every single day and then when she offers you tell her no thanks?"

"We do want to spend time with Mom," Ashley explained reasonably, her face and voice so earnest that Lauren believed her at once. "But we want to go to the mall *today*. We've been waiting for weeks." She began gesturing with her hands, fearing that their trip would now be cancelled because they'd done something wrong. "We don't want to wait anymore."

"Yeah," Christopher said. "And if Mom says she'll come with us then we'll *never* go today."

"She's *busy*," Aaron said simply, moving out of his brother's reach as the older boy tried to steal the pillow back. He didn't understand why Lauren looked so upset. "Mom has to work," he repeated as though it was totally obvious.

Lauren covered her eyes with one hand and let out an explosive sigh. *Shit.*

"Is Mom mad?" Ashley asked.

"No, honey," Lauren advised her. "But I think you guys hurt her feelings pretty badly."

Chris gulped, his blue eyes round. "We did?"

Lauren nodded. "I'm afraid so, sugar. It's not often she offers to do something with you. And I don't think it felt very good when you all shot her down."

Ashley sucked her bottom lip into her mouth as her guilt-filled gaze drifted toward the bathroom door. "Will you tell her she can come if she wants?" She frowned unable to muster much enthusiasm for this last part. "It's okay if she has to cancel."

Christopher nodded quickly. "Yeah, it's okay. Will you fix it? We don't want Mom to feel bad."

Aaron, feeding off his brother's worried tone of voice, whimpered. "We didn't mean to be bad, but I don't want her to cancel!"

"Shhh... It's okay," she assured them kindly. "You guys weren't bad." She tried to kick her brain into mom mode, which was a little difficult considering she couldn't blame them for their reaction. "But... um... just try to think of other people's feelings before you speak, okay?" She looked at them expectantly, hoping that bit of advice sounded reasonable.

Her words were met with three instant, eager nods.

Lauren smiled, a little proud of herself. "Okay then." She gently patted Christopher's leg, his flannel pants feeling soft against her palm. "We can tell your mom—"

There was another knock at the bedroom door and Emma's voice interrupted them. "Does anyone want breakfast?"

"Me!" the kids answered, scrambling off the bed and heading for the door, more than happy to have an excuse to hide out in the other room. When they opened it and darted out, their nanny, Emma, who was clad in her bathrobe and pink fuzzy slippers, reluctantly poked her head into the bedroom. "I'm sorry they disturbed you." She grimaced a little. "Last night, I told them to wait until you were awake before barging in on you and Dev."

Lauren wrapped her arms around her up-drawn knees, and then made a dismissive gesture. "That's okay. We were already awake." She heard the shower and bathroom flare to life. "The kids are just excited."

Emma laughed, the movement causing her large bosom to jiggle merrily. "That's an understatement. Will you and Dev be joining the children for breakfast?"

Lauren tore her eyes away from the bathroom door. "Hmm?"

The older woman's heavy eyebrows drew together with just a touch of worry. Lauren seemed a little out of sorts. And after the trials of the past few days, that was saying something. "Breakfast?"

Lauren shook her head. "No, thank you, Emma."

Emma nodded and began to withdraw.

"Wait, Emma." Lauren got out of bed and went to the door. "Could we get a pot of coffee?" She chewed her bottom lip for a moment. "And could you keep the kids out of here until it's time for us to go? Our agents should be here by nine." She paused. "I... umm... I need some time alone with Devlyn first."

"Of course." Normally, Emma would tease the newlyweds over a request like that, but something told her that wouldn't be a good idea this morning.

"No phone calls or interruptions unless it's an emergency, Emma."

The matronly woman didn't know what was going on, but doing what came naturally rarely failed her. She walked over to the bed and leaned over to pull Lauren into a gentle hug, feeling the other woman relax into the calming embrace and then, after a few seconds, return it fully. "Whatever it is you're going to do, good luck."

Lauren closed her eyes, soaking in the rare moment of maternal or, more precisely, grandmotherly comfort. Anna Strayer, Lauren's mother, rarely had had an appetite. And the infrequent hugs she and her daughter shared invariably made Lauren think of what it must be like to wrap your arms around a walking skeleton. Despite being short in stature, Emma had a bulky, dependable presence that was so much easier to sink into. It surrounded Lauren, making her feel safe and boosting her confidence. "Thanks, Emma. This is something I can't afford to screw up."

Still towel-drying her dark hair, Devlyn emerged from the bathroom wearing a thick white robe with the Presidential Seal emblazoned across her right breast.

Lauren was dressed in a well-worn pair of jeans and a soft, red denim shirt. Her socked feet dangled off the end of the tall bed, as she sat waiting and fiddling nervously with the glasses in her hand.

Dev took in Lauren's outfit. "That's cute," she commented neutrally as she headed toward her dresser.

Lauren smiled, but she was too worried for the gesture to reach her eyes. "Thanks."

Dev let the robe fall to the floor and tugged out a pair of socks, panties, and gray sweat pants. She turned slightly as she began to dress and Lauren's eyes swept over her nude body, lingering on the scars that marred the pale skin of Devlyn's hip and shoulder.

The blonde drew in a deep breath and padded the few steps to the dresser and her wife. She moved behind Dev and laid her cheek between broad shoulders, and she reached out and traced the scar with sensitive fingertips, only to have her hand pushed away as Dev pulled up her underwear, then sweats. "It took a long time, but they're all healed," Lauren began, hoping that pushing Devlyn wasn't the wrong move altogether.

Devlyn's body stiffened, but after a few seconds she reached down and squeezed Lauren's hand. She already knew where this conversation was going, and she steeled herself. "We're going to have the talk I kept putting off while you were in the hospital, aren't we?" Dev pulled away a little to pick up her robe and drape it over a nearby chair.

Lauren nodded. "I think we should." She reached out, silently asking for Devlyn's hand.

Troubled blue eyes glanced at her for reassurance.

"Please," Lauren said, knowing that Devlyn wouldn't refuse her.

Dev's eyes darted down to her own naked chest. "I need—?"

"No, you don't, honey."

"But—"

"I know you feel vulnerable right now. But it'll be okay."

Dev's eyes widened a little as the remark hit home.

Lauren stepped closer, her hand still outstretched, her head cocked invitingly. "Maybe vulnerable is good. I need every advantage when it comes to you."

Dev reluctantly took Lauren's hand and felt an instant squeeze as her reward. "I already feel like I'm walking around without my skin. Trust me, you don't need any more advantage."

"Do you really think you need to be perfect with me? You've seen me at my lowest and my worst and you love me anyway."

"Damn straight I do."

Lauren smiled fondly. "Why should it be any different for me?"

"I umm…" Dev looked away, the image of how she'd handled the stresses of late at odds with the image she had of herself. "I just thought you might be getting a little sick of seeing me so… God, I don't know." She rolled her eyes at herself. "Weak. Indecisive."

The younger woman's forehead puckered. "I know I didn't have a good marriage with Judd, but that doesn't mean I don't know what one is. If I had wanted to go it alone, I wouldn't have proposed in the first place. We're a team and when one member gets a little tired, the other just works a little harder to pick up the slack, right?"

Charmed, regardless of the sick, niggling feeling in the pit of her stomach, Devlyn managed a smile. "Yeah," she said softly.

"So c'mere." Lauren gave Dev's hand a gentle tug and their arms wrapped around each other in a heartfelt hug.

Devlyn buried her face in Lauren's hair. "Why do I get the feeling I'm going to be hearing the word workaholic?"

Lauren tightened her hold on her partner. "We're going to talk about everything, okay?"

Dev's throat tightened. "That's good, because I got a call from the doctor after you went to bed early last night."

"My doctor?"

Dev shook her head. "No, mine. He called to discuss the results of my checkup last week... since... well, since I didn't want to leave you to go into his office or have the appointment here."

Lauren's heart rate picked up and she looked Dev directly in the eye. "Is there something wrong?" She was surprised to hear how calm her voice felt, considering her insides were now churning.

"Nothing serious."

Lauren's pupils dilated as the sliver of fear that had been jabbing her dug in with greater force.

"My mammogram, EKG, blood work," her face twisted in revulsion, "and *colonoscopy* were all fine."

"But?" Lauren held her breath, feeling a little lightheaded as the blood drained from her face.

"Are you all right?" Dev's concern was evident by her tone of voice. She gently untangled Lauren's glasses from the younger woman's iron grip and tossed them on the bed. "You're going to break them."

"Just tell me."

Dev's eyebrows jumped. "All right. I have high blood pressure." She sighed, part irritated but a bigger part uneasy. "The numbers have spiked since last year."

"Nothing else?" Lauren asked tightly

Dev's hands came to rest on her hips. "Isn't that enough?"

"Thank God. I-I thought you were going to tell me you had a brain tumor or something equally horrible." She let out a shaky breath, the relief coursing through her veins enough to make her weak in the knees.

Dev shook her head a little as if to clear it. "Buh—" She lifted one hand, then let it drop. "A brain tumor?"

"The headaches, nose bleeds, and irritability were signs of something, Devlyn." She felt a little foolish as she admitted, "I um… I looked those symptoms up on the Internet."

"And came up with the worst possible scenario?" Devlyn scowled. "I'm rubbing off on you far too much. Those are all symptoms of high blood pressure too." She quirked a half grin, unable to mask the fact that she was a little unnerved by the diagnosis. "But to be honest, my irritability is because I'm not feeling like my old self and I'm still pissed off there are truly only twenty-four hours in a day. I still think I was robbed."

Reaching out to stroke Devlyn's arm, Lauren regarded her seriously. "What can we do to make this better?"

"My doctor wants me to start on some medication." Dev's scowl deepened, the thought of having to swallow a bunch of pills irking her to the core.

"Will the medicine cure it?"

She glanced away and rocked back on her heels, wishing her sweats had pockets where she could stuff her hands. "It should help…some."

"Some?" Pale brows disappeared beneath tousled bangs. "What else?"

Dev lifted an eyebrow of her own and sighed. "I think you and my doctor conspired against me. He wants me to eat better, sleep more, and reduce the amount of stress in my life. By a lot. Which is the same thing I've been told at every checkup since I was nineteen, by the way."

Lauren said a mental "thank you" to Dev's doctor. "He's clearly a very, *very* sensible man. In fact, I think I love him."

Dev crossed her arms over her chest. "Too bad you're taken."

"Not bad." Lauren shook her head and leaned forward, letting her forehead drop lightly against the freshly-scrubbed skin of Dev's upper chest and smelling the clean fragrance of peppermint-scented soap. "I like that I'm taken."

Dev wrapped her arms loosely around her partner. "Me too."

"Your body is talking to you, honey. I think you should listen."

Devlyn pressed her lips to the top of Lauren's head, then moved to the bed and flopped down dejectedly, throwing one arm over her face. She sighed, surprised to find that she felt like crying. "I don't know what to do." She swallowed hard and admitted to herself for the first time just how many things she'd allowed to wander out of her grasp and how she had no earthly idea how to rein them all back in. "I fucked up." It was a faintly hoarse admission.

Lauren closed her eyes, glad to hear the words, but sad at the toll it had taken to get to here. She climbed into bed, shoving aside her glasses and lying close to Dev, her head propped up by her hand. "Devlyn," her voiced dropped to an intimate, easy tone that always captured Devlyn's attention. "You haven't done anything you can't fix." She cupped a warm cheek, her fingers sneaking under Dev's arm to wipe away the few tears that had managed to escape. "Nothing's too late."

"What about the kids?" Unconsciously, Dev's hands began to clench and unclench. "Jesus, I can hear Ashley in thirty years from now telling her own kids that she can't be with them, but that she'll make it up to them later!" She looked up at Lauren with a lost expression. "When did things get so out of hand? When did *I* lose control!" She closed her eyes in self-disgust.

"You haven't lost control." Lauren wiped away a few more tears, this time with her lips. "You're a spectacular president, a better friend and partner than I could have hoped for, and though I know you don't believe it this minute, you're a good mother." She exhaled. "But you can't control everything. You can't *do* everything yourself. You just can't. Something has got to give. And that something has been your health and your well-being, and *that* is affecting all of us."

Dev opened her eyes and glared at Lauren. "How can you say I'm a wonderful mother? I put my career and country above my own children! They're going to hate me for it, and I can't even find it in myself to blame them."

"You made your decisions, Devlyn, and what's done is done."

Dev's body jerked a little at the blunt truth.

Gray eyes softened. "But, darlin', it's how you live with that decision and the choices you make from now on that will make all the difference. The kids are *not* going to hate you."

"Even if I hate myself for not being there when they need me?" she rasped, feeling ill.

Lauren swallowed hard as her eyes misted over. "Even then." Tenderly, she drew her knuckles across Dev's cheek, wanting nothing more than to be able to kiss away the pain in her lover's eyes. "I know what it's like to question a parent's love. To want support for your hopes and dreams and be greeted with anger or ambivalence instead."

Devlyn's heart contracted painfully. "Oh, Lauren—"

"I can say that you're a good mother because you love and support your children and despite your ridiculous schedule, they do know that. They *believe* that, and they won't ever forget it." She licked her lips a little and drew in a big breath as she gathered her courage. "But I'm not going to bullshit you. In their eyes, you working to make the world a better place for them will never make up for the time you're losing with them now. Even with your love, Devlyn, the kids are going to resent the hell out of you, and they're going to feel the loss of you not being a part of their everyday lives. Sometimes they need to be at the top of your list, no matter what else is on it."

Dev's cheeks flushed red, and her voice shook a little as she spoke. "Don't you think I know that? Don't you think I know that's at least part of what keeps me awake at night?" She ground her teeth together, wanting to scream because Lauren didn't see her reality. "Everyone is counting on me. People who have nothing and no one to help them are counting on me. One more meeting, one hour less sleep, skip lunch today, and I'm just this much closer. And I don't know what to do when I don't have any more to give!"

Lauren groaned, fighting the urge to grab Devlyn by the shoulders and shake her and make her understand. "Don't you see? You don't need to give *more*. You need to give less before you run yourself into the ground. Rearrange your time priorities so that the children, and you yourself, get a bigger share of the time you do have."

Devlyn sat up and leaned against the headboard. "I don't know how to do that."

"Then we'll figure out how together. You don't have to do it alone. You have an entire staff to help you. And family and friends who love you. You driving yourself nonstop might not be hurting your work right now, but it is hurting you." She paused and then admitted the truth. "And that hurts the people who love you."

A wave of guilt crashed over Dev and a heavy feeling settled in her chest. "Damn," she said. "I never meant for that to happen."

Lauren's eyes begged Devlyn to listen to reason, and she drew in a shaky breath as she hugged her pillow tighter. "You can't keep going on the way you have been. I don't care about the President and her political successes. I don't care about global warming and the space program and the price of butter in Portugal and what you can do about it! I care about *you* and you've set an impossible pace that's tearing you apart." She threw a hand in the air, her frustration boiling over. "High blood pressure is serious! Does it really have to kill you and destroy our family before you believe what your doctor and I are saying? Is that what you *want*?"

A stunned, drawn-out silence hung between them.

Dev blinked slowly, feeling her heart jerk in her chest and having no response to Lauren's vehemently spoken, truthful words.

"Shit," Lauren uttered quietly, scrubbing her face with her hands and feeling the tears prick her eyes. "I shouldn't have said that. I know you don't want that." She glanced at her. "But I'm scared," she admitted miserably, sitting up and and hugging her pillow in mute comfort. "I feel like I'm watching a train wreck and I don't know how to stop it."

Dev's chin quivered. "I'm afraid too."

Their eyes met and held, a surge of stark emotion passing between them.

"Last week… It's like everything came crashing down on me. I'm scared that I'll let down an entire world full of little girls and women who are looking to me to pave the way for them. I'm scared I won't be strong enough to carry the banner for gays and working mothers and members of my party and a million other causes and people."

Dev gave Lauren a beseeching look, truly hoping her partner might know the answer. "Who am I supposed to turn away?"

"I can't answer that," Lauren admitted honestly, feeling the impossible weight of what Devlyn had committed herself to. "I just know it has to be someone."

"Over and over, I've managed to make that 'someone' you and the kids, haven't I? I'm scared I won't know my own children and they won't know me and I'll get so self-involved that I won't care. I'm scared that the Secret Service won't be able to stop the next lunatic with a gun and that everything I've left undone will be left that way forever. I'm afraid I'll fail and disappoint the people who've helped me and supported me along the way. They don't deserve that." Dev swallowed thickly, and her voice grew even softer. "But most of all, I'm so scared that something will happen to you and I'll lose you."

Lauren was certain her heart would break in two. "Oh, God, Devlyn, you can't tie yourself in knots over something that is pure chance."

"How can I not?" she demanded.

"I know what happened to Samantha broke your heart. But because something can happen doesn't mean that it will," Lauren reasoned, trying not to be utterly overwhelmed.

"And it doesn't mean that it won't." Her eyes went a little unfocused as she let herself think about what had been making her physically ill for the past four days. "Only I won't get through it this time." She opened her mouth to speak but had to swallow before the words would come. "I don't think I could deal with it if something happened to you," she whispered desperately. "I don't think I could get up in the morning and breathe and pretend like I was alive when I wouldn't be. I don't think I'd want to even try. I—"

Lauren couldn't stand it another second. She tossed aside her pillow and wrapped as much of herself around her partner as she could. The body against hers jerked as Devlyn fought off her impending sobs. "It's okay to cry," Lauren said into Devlyn's hair, needing the physical contact as much as her partner.

"I... I don't want to cr-cry." Dev's chest heaved with effort, but even then, her words were mixed with the tears she detested. "I want things to be back the way they were be-before I felt like the entire world had climbed on my shoulders and I was too tired and afraid to throw them off."

Lauren held onto her, gulping back her own tears long enough to get out the words she needed to say. "I want you to listen to me for a minute, okay?"

Devlyn nodded, her throat closed tight.

"I love you more than I can say. And I'll always be here for us to talk." She gave Dev another squeeze, wanting to reassure her with every ounce of her being. "And if crying makes you feel better then I'll hold you all day if I have to, okay?"

Dev nodded again, the words nearly undoing her.

"But I'm in over my head and I know it. You need more than I have to give to get through this. And there are professionals whose job it is to get people past things like this."

Devlyn drew in a breath and Lauren silenced her by plowing forward. "Just wait. A doctor could help put this relentless stress you're under into perspective and teach you to manage it. He could help you work past your fears and get you over this impossible notion that you have to be all things to all people."

"I... I know I can't do everything," Dev protested feebly, closing her eyes at what she knew was a loser of an argument.

Lauren shook her head. "You might know it, but you don't really believe it. Not in your heart, which is the part that needs convincing." Trembling lips grazed the side of her face and the blonde leaned into the touch, melting. "Please, baby, I wouldn't suggest it if I didn't believe it was important. I know how hard this week has been for you. Let someone who knows what they're doing help."

Devlyn forced herself to look past her first reaction, which was that she and Lauren could work anything out themselves if they tried hard enough. That she didn't need to invite some stranger to poke around in her head to do that. "I'm not sure I can talk about this with anyone but you," Dev admitted, not wanting to disappoint Lauren, but needing to be honest. She bit her lower lip and added, "Or maybe David."

Lauren had been expecting that, and she nodded, understanding completely, "I know it'll be hard. You're going to have to find someone you can learn to trust. But I have a list of names, and that's at least a place to start."

Devlyn's posture instantly went rigid, and Lauren backed away enough to look into wary blue eyes. She eased her fingers through dark, damp locks as she spoke. "Relax. I didn't put an ad in the paper for someone who could keep a secret and shrink the President's head."

A reluctant smile tugged at Dev's mouth. She was already feeling better. A plan was forming. It was tentative and raw, but comforting nonetheless. First and foremost, Devlyn was a woman of action. She could make a plan work.

Lauren tried not to look guilty. "I had a little help from some people who love you very much and whose first concern is your welfare and not the country's. We put this list together before the accident. That was just the last straw."

Dev's eyes went round as realization struck. "You spoke to my parents?" Her voice rose to a squeak at the end.

Lauren rolled her eyes. "They're concerned for you. I had to swear not to put off this conversation just to keep them off the next plane to Washington."

Dev's cheeks tinted and she rolled over to lie flat on her back. "I called them and told them about your accident while you were getting your CAT scan." She let out a low whistle. "I was…"

Lauren smiled gently. "In pieces. Just like I was after…" She couldn't bring herself to even say it, but she reached down and patted the scar on Dev's hip, letting Dev know just what she meant. "After seeing you in the hospital."

Dev sighed. "I know."

"So you'll do it?"

The hopeful note in Lauren's voice was more than Devlyn could ignore. "I love you and I'll do anything I have to to keep us happy and whole. I know it hasn't seemed like that lately, but I swear with everything I am that it's true."

Lauren nearly burst into happy tears. "I know it's true. I never doubted that."

"Never?"

"Never," Lauren confirmed. "Thank you."

Dev cupped Lauren's cheeks. "Okay, talking to a doctor is the first part of the plan. Part two—"

Lauren smiled fondly at her lover's analytical mind.

"I'll make sure that I'm in bed every night by one—"

"Ahem."

Dev blinked. "All right, by mid—"

Lauren cleared her throat again, this time a little louder.

"By eleven-thirty?"

Lauren was silent this time and Dev looked at the smaller woman as though she were crazy. "I had a later curfew in high school!"

Lauren cocked her head to the side in question. "Did you have high blood pressure in high school?"

"Touché." But Devlyn was smiling now, albeit a watery one. "And I'll talk to my staff about my schedule and try my best to make Sunday a family day again."

"Yes!" Lauren's face lit up like the Fourth of July. With even one day a week off Lauren was certain her driven partner could get the down time she needed for her mental and physical health. She would make sure of it.

Dev conveyed her apology in the form of a soft kiss. "I swear I never meant to stop having Sundays be for us. It just happened without my realizing it."

Lauren kissed Dev back, this time soundly. "Thank you," she said against soft lips. "This means more to me than you know."

"Good. Then you'll do something for me in return?"

"Anything," Lauren vowed.

"Call your father and invite him to Thanksgiving. "

Lauren's jaw dropped. "But…Ugh." She made a face. "You suck."

Dev smiled unrepentantly. "Only when asked nicely. And only

when the body parts are attached to you."

Lauren whimpered, knowing she was well and truly caught.

"I was in the room when you called your dad last month."

Lauren nodded slowly. "Yes, you were. And I'm sure you heard a conversation that was strained, stilted, uncomfortable, and mostly superficial."

"Yes."

Lauren offered a chagrined smile. "That's real progress. We're finally back to normal."

Dev's voice dropped an octave and she pursed her lips. "Lauren."

Lauren narrowed her eyes, but readily admitted defeat. So what if she hadn't spent a Thanksgiving with her father since before she was in college? The bigger issue was that he would be painfully uncomfortable, like a fish out water, at the White House. She wondered privately if the sometimes-abrasive man could keep from being arrested by the Secret Service while here. Still, a promise was a promise. "I'll call him on Sunday."

This time Dev's smile was more relaxed. They hadn't discussed it yet, but she desperately wanted to go to Ohio for the holiday. Not only could she use the time to regroup among the people who loved her most, but she had a feeling that both Lauren and Howard Strayer would be more comfortable there anyway. "Great."

"Will you kill me if I ask you to do one more thing?" Lauren gave Dev a beseeching look. "It's something good, I promise."

Dev's eyes widened. "One *more* thing? Do you want me to stand and give a press conference that starts with the words, 'My name is Devlyn Marlowe and I'm a workaholic'? Because I will. I've been worn into submission." She was mostly teasing, but Lauren caught a kernel of truth in her words.

"No." Lauren chuckled lightly. "I want you to come to the mall today with me and your children."

Dev's face fell.

Lauren sighed. "It's not what you think, Devlyn."

"What I think is they don't want me to come. They told me themselves!"

Lauren gave her a sympathetic look. "No, honey, they don't want you to say you'll come and then cancel and cause them to postpone their trip. That's all. They'd give their little collective ornery souls for you to come. In fact, they wanted me to ask you to come, even if it meant you might back out and delay the trip."

Dev looked at Lauren from behind dark lashes. "They really want me to come?"

"Jesus, Devlyn," she gave the older woman a firm poke. "Of course!"

Dev shrugged one shoulder, looking incredibly sheepish. "It sounded like fun and... well... I didn't want you to go without me."

"So come and give everyone what they want." Lauren patted Dev's arm, then pushed herself off the bed, on her way to the bathroom. Her appetite was back, her head didn't hurt, and she had a feeling today was going to turn out to be a great day. "You can't stay with me every second. But we can nag each other about that tomorrow, okay? For today we can both stand a little, no *a lot*, of togetherness." Her gaze softened. "I know I could."

A surprise burst of laughter escaped Dev. "Okay." Blue eyes sparked with added mischief. "Have you ever thought of getting something else pierced? You could do it with Ashley today."

Lauren gave her a droll look over her shoulder as she padded toward the shower. One look in the mirror on her way to brush her teeth had made it clear that her hair wouldn't be tamed with anything less. "Never."

"I think navel rings are sexy as hell," Dev tried again, nearly jumping out of bed to follow Lauren and feeling more positive and hopeful than she had in weeks.

"Then you should definitely get one," Lauren shot back, feeling her face stretch into a genuine smile.

Dev pouted. "But it would look sexy on *you*."

Lauren laughed softly and disappeared into the bathroom, but left the door open so her voice would carry. "I guess that's possible, darlin', but the answer is still no."

Devlyn's pout shifted into a questioning look as she stopped outside the bathroom and stripped off her sweats and underwear. She still wanted to be close to Lauren. When she was naked again, she said, "Hey, Lauren?"

A naked arm appeared from behind the door and a single finger curled to beckon Devlyn inside.

Sunday, October 16th

Pillows and light blankets littered the family room floor at the President's private residence. The same could be said for most of the First Family. Dev was lazing on the floor, with Ashley curled up against her, sound asleep. Aaron had his head pillowed on Dev's belly, and she was just beginning to feel the cool moisture of the drool that trailed from his mouth to her T-shirt. Christopher was sprawled asleep on the sofa behind them, next to Lauren, who was taking this moment of rare household peace and quiet to give her fat pug a good scratching behind his ears. Though she had to continually shush Gremlin as he growled out his pleasure, his back legs twitching rhythmically with every good scratch.

With a contented smile, Lauren watched as Devlyn shut off the movie they'd decided would be perfect for a family birthday celebration. Michael Oaks and Press Secretary Allen had pushed hard for a well-publicized and elaborate fortieth birthday bash, but after the events of the past few weeks, simple and quiet was more the order of the day. And for that, Lauren was truly grateful.

She pushed the pug over to his own cushion and slid from the couch to crawl next to her partner. She ran the tip of her finger over the ridge of Dev's ear. "You think we should haul the kids to bed? They're toast."

Dev glanced at the bodies covering her own. "Yeah, I think they're done."

"It was that pizza and the swimming. That gets them every time. I think Beth had to wake David to get him out of one of the lounge chairs."

"It was nice, though, right?" She gave Lauren a questioning look and was gratified to see her instant nod.

"It was great. *So* much better than a fancy party."

"Mmm…" She smiled. "It was my best birthday ever." Her smile grew. "Thanks."

Charmed by the rare look of comfortable, nearly blissful happiness on her partner's face, Lauren smiled back. "I had fun too." With a slight groan, she hefted Aaron. "Jesus, Devlyn. He's getting big." She fought to get to her feet, realizing that the days of being able to move the children around like sacks of flour were fast disappearing.

Dev sighed. "I know. I can't believe Ashley is nine today."

"Nine going on twenty-one," Lauren murmured affectionately.

"Bite your tongue," Dev shot back.

Lauren began walking toward Aaron's room, the boy's arms and legs swaying limply as she carried him to bed.

Carefully, Dev rolled to one side and disentangled herself from Ashley, giving her a little shake. "Hey, Moppet. It's bedtime." Dev moved over to the sofa and picked up Chris, smiling when he immediately snuggled into her arms and laid his head against her shoulder, his glasses going slightly askew.

On wobbly legs and with one eye still closed, Ashley stood up and grabbed onto the back of her mother's T-shirt as Devlyn guided her back toward the children's rooms.

"I'll never understand how you sleep through this," Lauren whispered to an oblivious Aaron, as she pulled a blanket up over him and tucked it around his chest.

Once the children were safely in their beds, Dev began making her way back to the family room, turning off lights as she went and settling heavily on the sofa. She paid close attention to Gremlin's location, in case the pooch decided that her defenses were low at this time of evening and she was ripe for a sneak attack. But the dog, along with his Pomeranian mate, was curled up in front of the fireplace, snoring louder than Dev would have believed possible.

Lauren returned and settled on the couch, laughing softly when Dev patted her own lap invitingly. Like she would say no to that. She spun sideways and reclined, letting loose a happy sigh when long fingers sank into her hair and began rubbing her scalp. "Ugh. Feel free to continue doing that for the next five years or so."

Dev chuckled, keeping up her ministrations with one hand as she grabbed the television remote with the other. She'd learned long ago that using the TV's voice control features was asking for trouble with a house full of kids. When she turned to the cartoon channel, Lauren looked up at her in surprise.

Seeing the confusion, Dev said, "I know I usually watch about twenty different news channels, but my doctor recommends I don't watch anything that remotely resembles the news after ten p.m. That way local and world events won't be the last thing on my mind at night before I go to bed."

"Sounds like a good idea to me." Lauren smiled gently and turned her head to kiss Devlyn's belly. She hadn't missed the small changes her partner had instituted since starting therapy and she wasn't about to make a fuss over this. But Dev was trying, and she felt good about that.

Though Lauren wasn't really a believer in unshakable faith, what she felt for Devlyn, her belief in her best friend, came darn close. "Bugs Bunny is good."

"A classic," Dev agreed. "I like my new doctor," she continued un-prompted, surprising Lauren again.

Lauren's eyes closed as she relaxed under Dev's touch. "I'm glad."

"At first I thought three times a week was a little much, but I'm finding more than enough to talk about, so I guess it wasn't too much after all." She glanced up as Bugs Bunny began trying to escape Elmer Fudd's hunting rifle. "You wouldn't believe what I heard myself say the other day."

"Mmm?"

"That the only people I really need to be a hero for are you and the kids."

Lauren opened her eyes, blinking slowly. "Do you really believe that, Natasha?"

Dev blushed. "Not yet, Boris. But with a little help, I think I can."

"I know you can, darlin'," Lauren drawled softly, unable to remember a moment where she was prouder of her spouse.

Dev's eyes took on a seductive gleam. "You know," she paused to give Lauren a sexy grin. "I've been very good all year and I think I deserve a reward."

"That's Christmas, Devlyn. Not your birthday."

"Oh." She frowned momentarily, but wouldn't be deterred. "Well, how about if I say that *you've* been good and deserve a reward?"

Lauren chuckled wickedly. "I am good." She sat up and placed a lingering kiss on Dev's throat, her words tickling sensitive skin. "And if you'd like to accompany me to our bedroom, I'll show you just how good."

A smile stretched Dev's lips as she sang a happy tune. "Happy birthday to me. Happy birthday to meeeeeeeee."

NOVEMBER 2022

Friday, November 11th

Lauren joined the rest of the audience in a hearty round of applause as Wayne Evenocheck, her agent, stepped away from the podium. It was Starlight's Twentieth Annual Writers' Convention, something Lauren had managed to attend several times during her time with the publishing house. This year, she'd been invited as a speaker and not just another writer, and to everyone's surprise, but most especially Wayne's, she'd accepted the invitation and made the short trip to Baltimore's Pier Five Hotel for this year's convention.

She was one of Starlight's best-selling writers, though her fiction titles written under a well-guarded pen name had always outsold her biographies by a margin of six to one. Lauren Strayer, however, was not the writer the paparazzi were interested in on this trip. To her utter delight, her presence had been almost entirely eclipsed by a swarthy writer whose mystery novel had been turned into a play and whose private life had been streaking across tabloid headlines since he began a love affair with the play's blonde and very buxom leading lady—who also happened to be a soap opera diva. Though it was clear she would never again be treated as *just* another writer, Lauren had to admit it felt good to let her guard down a bit, and talk freely with her colleagues about subjects that sparked her interest and fed her passion, all while the press hounded some other poor slob.

The atmosphere was one in which she could completely immerse herself: dozens of buzzing conversations, the crunch of snack foods, and the quiet hum of the laptops of those who couldn't stop work, even for a moment.

Wayne stepped off the stage and took a seat next to Lauren in the second row of the large conference room, wiggling his fingers at several Secret Service agents who were doing their best to look unobtrusive as they stood along the wall. "Hiya, sweetheart," he said in his nasal New York accent. "I'm sorry I didn't catch you before you spoke this morning. But umm…" He preened a little. "How'd I do?"

Lauren smiled broadly. "You did great." She leaned to the side and bumped shoulders with her longtime friend and her gray eyes danced with mischief. "Didn't you hear that applause?"

He sniffed and brushed an imaginary piece of lint from his shoulder. "Oh, I uh, I didn't notice."

A slender, pale eyebrow arched. "I can see that." She glanced around at the milling crowd, recognizing most of the faces. "So how'd you get so popular all of a sudden, and wasn't your goatee mostly gray at my wedding?"

Wayne clutched his chest in mock distress. "I've *always* been popular. Hell, I out-right discovered a third of these writers myself or rescued them from rotten agents and brought them to Starlight. And that includes you."

This, Lauren knew, was the absolute truth. Despite being a little old-fashioned in the way he did business, Wayne was an outstanding agent and had gone the extra mile for her more than once.

"And my new girlfriend thought a brighter color beard would look dashing on me."

"I'm crushed," she said dryly. "And here I thought you were saving yourself for me."

The heavyset man sighed and pulled a piece of peppermint candy from the coat pocket of his slightly too-tight suit. "That was before you married the hottie with an army and legs that go on for days." He unwrapped the mint and began crunching loudly, wishing he was sucking on a lovely nicotine-loaded cigarette instead. "Now I'm too afraid to do anything other than bury my timeless, unrequited love."

Lauren chuckled low in her throat, a deep gravelly sound. "She does have fantastic legs, doesn't she?"

Wayne snorted. "Hell, yes."

She narrowed her eyes at Wayne. "Do you really have a girl-friend?"

"Hell, no."

Lauren burst out laughing.

"I'm just vain and couldn't come up with a better excuse. The truth is, I wanted to look good today. I've never been to a convention that had press coverage."

"Well." Lauren leaned a little closer to Wayne, wrinkling her nose as she poked her fingertips into the wiry bristles covering his chin. "It looks good," she pronounced with a nod of her head.

His eyes filled with hope. "Really?"

"Hell, no." She gave him a sympathetic smile to soften the blow.

Now it was Wayne's turn to laugh.

Lauren focused her gaze a little harder. "It doesn't look like a color that occurs in nature at all. You look like a deranged," she winked, "but lovable Viking."

"Hey," he covered the flaming red hair with his hand. "The color was on sale! Besides," he let his hand drop. "I'm washing it out tonight. You should have heard the whopper my secretary told me this morning when she saw it."

His heavy brow creased unhappily as he looked at the pink mark that still marred Lauren's forehead. "I was worried about you, kiddo. I called the White House when I saw the accident on the news, but they just gave me the runaround. That must have smarted."

Lauren smiled gently at him, appreciating his kind heart more than he knew. "It happened so fast... I... well, it wasn't so bad."

Wayne shrugged good-naturedly. "Whatever you say. I would have cried like a little girl."

"I think I was in too much of a stupor to cry."

"I'm just glad you're all right."

"Me too." Not wanting to continue with this depressing topic, Lauren gestured to the stage where several tables had been set up for the next panel of speakers. "You said you wanted me to autograph a boxful of books. How about we do it there? I'm on the next panel anyway."

Wayne scratched his jaw. "Oh, um... did I say *one* box?"

Lauren voice dropped an octave in warning. "Wayne—"

"What's six tiny boxes?"

Lauren crossed her arms, ready to do battle on very familiar turf. "Two boxes," she offered.

"Five boxes."

"Three, and that's my final offer. You'd have me sign until my hand fell off."

"Four."

"Three."

"Four."

"Three!"

"Calm down." He patted Lauren's hand. "Three boxes, just like I said all along." He turned toward the stage. "Mike!" he barked to a young man, wearing a large nametag, who was performing a sound check on the microphone that Wayne had recently used. "Bring up four boxes of the First Lady's books and put them on that table, would you? They're in Room B and marked 'Strayer.'"

Lauren rolled her eyes. "Why do I pay you again, Wayne? You never listen to me."

"But I'm lovable." He grinned unrepentantly, his chubby cheeks creasing deeply. "Don't forget lovable." He groaned a little as she leaned forward, and he rose to his feet himself. "C'mon, let's get you signing."

Lauren motioned to two Secret Service agents, who, with curt nods, ventured onstage to give it a final security check. A third agent was dispatched with a metal-chemical-and-biological-agent-detecting wand to run it over the boxes and books. It wasn't long before Lauren and Wayne were waved forward to one of the long banquet-style tables.

"So how are things going with your new hot prospect?" Lauren asked as she took a seat and cracked open a bottle of water from an ice bucket in the center of the table.

"You mean Bobby?" Robert Rivera was Starlight's new golden boy and his novel-turned-play was set to open in less than a week.

Lauren dug around in her laptop case until her hand emerged with her wire-rimmed glasses and she carefully put them on. "Who else?"

Wayne grabbed a handful of Lauren's last biography out of their box and passed them over to her along with a pen. "I'll tell you, it's been wild. And here I thought things were crazy with you."

Lauren snorted as she penned her name on the cover page. "It's hard to imagine anyone surpassing my media circus." She signed a second book, set it on the first, starting a pile of signed books, then reached for another.

"Can you stay for tonight's dinner? I'd love a beautiful escort." Wayne's eyebrows bounced as he scooted his chair a little closer to Lauren's so Mike could pass behind them.

The neatly dressed intern and general gopher from Starlight Publishing began distributing note pads and pencils at the tables.

"Sorry." Affectionately, Lauren again bumped shoulders with the bulky man. "I'm due back in Washington by six to be present when Devlyn becomes the first person ever to have her blood taken for the DNA Registration Act." She kept her voice light and soft, not wanting to let on how uncomfortable events like that made her.

Wayne didn't miss the hesitancy in Lauren's normally vibrant voice. He raised his eyebrows and leaned close, covertly glancing around to make sure they were alone. And except for a few strategically placed agents who had taken up places around the stage, they were. "What about you, kid? Are they going to poke you?" He knew how his young client felt about needles.

"No," Lauren said quietly, her relief palpable. "I'll just be there for the show."

"So why the long face?"

Lauren finished writing her name and she glanced around to make certain Mike was long gone before she spoke. She grabbed another book. "Because I disagree with the entire thing."

Wayne blinked. "And the President knows this?"

"Sure." Lauren shrugged a sweater-clad shoulder. "I'm allowed my own opinion, Wayne." She hesitated over a book whose cover was creased. With a wrinkled nose, she handed it back to Wayne, who nodded his agreement and put it aside.

"So why participate in a publicity stunt at all then?" he questioned curiously, well aware of Lauren's headstrong tendencies and, frankly, surprised she would be present to promote something she didn't believe in. "Getting you to do any promotion at all has been hell. And God knows I tried."

Lauren sighed. Wayne's question was a very valid one. Fortunately, however, she had a couple of good answers. "First, I'm not married to you."

"My loss."

"True." She winked. "Second, the bill is already law. Nothing short of repealing it can undo it now, and my kicking up a fuss would only undermine the people whose job it is to enforce and implement it." She gave him a half smile, trying not to cringe at the hollow sound of her words. "How did that sound?"

"Pretty good," Wayne allowed, moving his head from side to side. "A few more days' practice and I'll actually begin to believe you believe it. No confusing who the politician in your family is."

Lauren chuckled. "I *do* believe that. I just don't like it. But here's the bottom line: I support my wife, even when we disagree. And this legislation is important to her. I respect that, and her, and if that means I have to make nice for the cameras every once in a while, then so be it. Ugh!" She held up Wayne's pen and shook it. "Couldn't you have stolen a pen from your bank that actually worked?"

Wayne grumbled as he fished another pen out of his pocket. "Here." He passed it over. "I can't believe the government not only wants to ban my precious smokes, but now it wants my blood, even if it is just a drop." He whimpered at the mere thought of having to quit smoking. "Next they'll outlaw coffee, sex, and good books, and then we all might as well be dead."

Lauren rolled her eyes at her agent's flair for drama. "Wayne, the DNA registration is voluntary unless you get arrested."

"It's voluntary *now*," he clarified. "The next logical step is registering everyone at birth, and then everyone period. Besides, do you have any idea how many unpaid parking tickets I have? Arrest is a serious possibility in my future."

"You could pay the tickets," Lauren said reasonably, more preoccupied by trying to make her signature legible with a second cheap pen than by their conversation.

Wayne visibly scoffed at the ridiculous idea. "I dunno. There's just something that makes me uncomfortable about the entire thing. I mean, I trust our current president, but what about the next bozo who gets her job?"

For testing purposes, and via a gallery in the back of the room, Mike switched on the microphones that had been placed in front of the panelists' seats.

Lauren nodded, agreeing completely. Devlyn was far more moderate than many members of her own party and certainly most Republicans. Who knew what some future administration might use the samples for? Cloning? Behavior modification through gene therapy? It was, she readily admitted, startlingly easy for her creative mind to spin out of control when it came to manufacturing chilling scenarios. Still, the possibilities for abuse were no joke. "The DNA Registration Act is unreasonable and invasive, and I admit that the thought of Big Brother wanting my blood makes me shiver."

Wayne's eyes suddenly formed twin moons as Lauren's words rang out around the large room and all eyes, including the cameras of several news crews that were interviewing Bobby Rivera, were trained on the stage.

Lauren's mouth sagged as a thunderous silence roared in her ears and the blood drained from her face.

Wayne quickly reached down and yanked the cord from the microphone. "I'll kill Mike , I swear it," he muttered.

Lauren lifted one of her books and held it in front of her face as though she were reading it, but with her peripheral vision she could still see several Secret Service agents doing their best not to blanch. "Oh, my fucking God," she muttered under her breath, her eyes closing. "Please tell me what I think just happened did *not* happen. Please, Wayne."

Wayne let out a slow, speculative breath. "That depends on whether you think you let the entire room, including that news crew who was taping live, know that you think the President's pet project is crap."

Lauren lowered the book in her hands, to see the news crew falling over themselves to scramble out of the room. Every other member of the press was now on his or her cell phone, sharing the joy. "I uh…" She swallowed hard. "I think I need to call the White House."

"And then escape the country?"

Lauren cringed, her mind reeling over what she'd just done. "Oh, yeah."

Dev sat at her desk in the Oval Office with her chin resting on steepled fingers. Her eyes closed momentarily. "She said what?"

The words were uttered so softly, David wasn't quite sure what Dev had asked. He loosened his tie and crossed the room to take a seat in front of the desk. "What was that, Dev?"

Her jaw worked and this time she spoke with a slightly louder voice. "I want you to repeat exactly what she said."

David felt a twinge in his stomach. Dev was being eerily quiet and it was nothing short of unnerving. He repeated Lauren's quoted statement that had already hit the television, radio, and wire services.

Dev let out a shaky breath and made her way to the window. She stood alongside Old Glory, her dark gray pantsuit looking grim next to the flag's bold colors, and presented David with her back. Her shoulders were rigid as she took a silent sip of coffee.

It didn't take long for David to be unable to stand the stillness in the room or the thick, cloying tension that hung in the air. "You need to issue a statement to the press. We've already got data from an unscientific poll showing support for DNA registrations has dropped from seventy-six to thirty-eight percent."

Devlyn could feel frustration laced with hurt welling up within her. Her nostrils flared and her grip on the mug increased until her knuckles stood out in vivid relief against the hot, bright red ceramic.

Outside Dev's office, Lauren arrived at the same time as Press Secretary Allen, Beth, and her new assistant Carol. They were all panting from their dashes inside the building, and Lauren could feel a bead of perspiration at the nape of her neck as it began slowly trickling down her back.

Liza and Jane were quietly conferring with each other at the head secretary's desk.

Beth glanced around, expecting to see David waiting for them. "Okay," she gave up looking. "We're here." In a gesture of silent support, she squeezed Lauren's shoulder.

Lauren reached up and patted Beth's hand affectionately. Message received.

"Where's the meeting?" Beth asked, still slightly breathless. She passed Jane her briefcase and the older woman locked it in a cabinet behind her desk. Then she slipped out of her coat and gathered the other women's coats to hang up.

Everyone looked at Liza, who merely threw her hands in the air. "I don't know yet. Chief of Staff McMillian is briefing the President on the situation now."

Lauren licked her lips nervously. "*Just* now?" She'd called the White House over an hour ago to give them as much notice as possible on what was sure to be a firestorm in the press.

"The President was in a meeting with the Secretary of Commerce until five minutes ago, ma'am. She'd asked not to be disturbed."

"That's not good," Lauren mumbled, cursing her indiscretion for the thousandth time and knowing she'd get down on her knees and beg if she could only turn back the hands of time.

She saw Beth's sympathetic nod. They both knew Dev usually needed some time to process bad news before being at her most effective. At first, the President was likely to be quiet and broody, followed quickly by anger.

Everyone jumped at the sound of a loud crash and the raised but indistinguishable voices coming from inside the Oval Office. But no one made a move toward the door.

"Son of a bitch!" In disgust, Dev turned away from her coffee-stained wall and the now decapitated bust of George W. Bush.

"Dev—"

"I can't believe she did that, David," she seethed. "You know how much time, planning, and money has gone into the DNA Registration campaign so that people will feel comfortable volunteering a sample. In one single sentence she's set us back months!"

David ran a hand through his hair. "It's not that bad."

"The hell it's not!" Dev stalked over to her seat and sat down, eyeing her pencil holder with evil intent.

David's eyes widened and he debated whether it was safe to sit this close to his friend.

Dev caught the look and despite the throbbing vein that was very visible in the center of her forehead quirked a weak grin at her friend. "Don't worry. You're safe. This is just me trying not to repress my feelings by expressing them freely."

David recognized therapist-speak when he heard it, and his eyes widened further. "My God. Were you *ever* repressed when it came to expressing your anger?"

Dev glared at him. "Not as far as I'm concerned. Either way, it doesn't appear that I'm repressed anymore, does it!"

"Does breaking things help?" David asked carefully, willing to see that Devlyn had plenty of mugs at her disposal if smashing really helped her deal with stress.

A scowl firmly planted itself on Dev's face. "I don't think so." To test her theory she snatched a pencil from the holder and viciously snapped it in half. She sighed. "Nope, not helping."

David got up and circled the desk.

Dev stood up and gratefully allowed her dear friend to pull her into a heartfelt hug. It was a rare moment of tactile comfort between them, despite the close-knit nature of their friendship. The dark-haired woman pulled away just enough to rest her forehead on David's broad shoulder. She soaked in the understanding given so freely that it oftentimes was under-appreciated.

"Lauren was really upset when she called," David said. "She apologized over and over again and she swore she'd explain."

"I'm sure it wasn't intentional, David. But, Christ, how could she be so careless?"

Dev was calming down quickly, and David let out a relieved breath, well aware that that throbbing vein in her forehead could not bode well for her high blood pressure.

Soothingly, he rubbed his hand in small circles on Devlyn's back, feeling the cool silk of her blouse. "Let me tell you, pal, if this is the worst thing she says in public while you're in office, you can consider yourself lucky."

Dev snorted. This, she was forced to acknowledge, was very true.

David smiled. "Besides, don't you remember when—?"

Dev's head jerked up. "Don't you dare say it," she threatened. But there was little heat behind the words. "I was a twenty-three-year-old Ohio State representative who didn't know my head from my arse! Lauren is a mature woman who has been living in the White House for the past two years. I hold her to a higher standard."

"Okay, okay," David conceded, lifting his hands in supplication. "Be that as it may, we still have to deal with things."

Dev nodded and took a deep breath, releasing it slowly. "You're right. But I need to talk to my wife before we decide what to do." Dev surprised David by dropping a quick kiss on his cheek before pressing the intercom button and waiting for Jane to answer. "Who's out there waiting for David to finish breaking the news, Jane?"

Jane rattled off a list of people, and Dev's eyebrows disappeared behind her bangs. She turned to David. "The gang's all here."

David straightened his tie and buttoned his jacket as Dev grabbed her jacket off the rack near her desk and shrugged into it with her friend's help. Then she eased back into her leather chair. "Jane, could you please send the First Lady in alone? And have someone bring Michael Oaks over to join the party. I'll be speaking to the group shortly."

"Yes, Madam President."

The Oval Office door opened, and a shamefaced Lauren padded into the room. She moved with all the enthusiasm and speed of a participant in the Bataan Death March.

David slipped out of the room behind her, whispering a wan "Good luck" as he went.

After he closed the heavy wooden door, Lauren took her place in the hotseat in front of Dev's desk. With an audible gulp, she folded her hands in her lap and waited.

They stared at each other in silence for a solid minute before Devlyn arched an eyebrow and asked, "Aren't you going to say hello to Big Brother?"

Lauren cringed, and her apology exploded from within her. "Oh, God, I am so, so sorry!"

The smaller woman was nearly in tears, and Dev felt a good part of her anger deflate in the face of her partner's obvious, heartfelt regret.

Lauren lay her head on Devlyn's desk and turned it sideways, exposing her neck. Half joking she said, "Here, cut if off. Just make it quick."

"Sit up, you nut." Dev crossed her arms in front of her. "I'm not going to chop off your head... though it was touch and go about ten minutes ago."

Lauren's gaze strayed to George W. sans his head. "Thank goodness I was hiding in the outer office ten minutes ago."

Dev followed Lauren's eyes and shrugged. "I actually think it's much improved now," she said seriously, drawing a hesitant smile from Lauren.

The President uncrossed her arms and leaned forward, pinning Lauren with an intense but not unkind stare. "What the hell happened? I thought you were in Baltimore to attend a writers' conference, not toss a grenade into my campaign to encourage voluntary registration." She leaned forward a little further, reaching out and caressing Lauren's cheek to take the sting from her words. "Hmm?"

Lauren's eyes closed at the gentle touch. "I can't think of anything to say but how sorry I am. The microphones were off and Wayne and I were alone on stage. We were just talking. DNA registration came up in our conversation, and without my knowing it, someone switched on my microphone just in time to blast my poorly articulated opinion to the entire room." She sighed, her hands shaping fists. "I-I felt comfortable with Wayne. The room was filled with other writers and people I know. I didn't feel like I had to be on guard every single damn second!" Lauren's expression hardened. "I was wrong."

"I don't want you to be paranoid, honey. But some bastard is *always* going to be lurking, waiting for you to slip up so they can crush you like a roach in their next article or newscast."

Lauren blinked. "No paranoia there."

"Tell me it's not true," Dev challenged.

Lauren opened her mouth, then closed it quickly, gracefully accepting defeat.

"You've got to make it harder for them to do that to you than you did today, Lauren!"

Her cheeks colored. "I know."

The older woman reached out for Lauren's hand and her eyebrows furrowed at the unpleasant sensation of cool clammy skin. Despite her own anger, Dev found it virtually impossible to let her beloved friend continue to twist in the wind. Her gaze softened. "I'm angry, yes. But I accept your apology, sweetheart. I know you wouldn't have done something like that on purpose."

Lauren looked as though she might pass out from relief. "Thank God you know that. I would never intentionally torpedo something you're involved in just because we disagree."

"I know you wouldn't, and you haven't torpedoed anything." Dev relaxed back in her chair. "But you've got to be more careful than you were today, Lauren. What you said made me look bad in a lot of peoples' eyes. If I can't convince you of something I feel so strongly about, then you must know some big bad government secret that they don't, right?"

"Damn." Lauren let out a breath that ended in a moan. "I've made a royal mess of things." She rubbed her temple with irritated fingers. "This has been the worst afternoon in forever."

Dev nodded. "I've had better."

"Have we made up yet?" Lauren asked hopefully, willing to apologize for as long as it took, but desperately in need of something else in the meantime.

Dev smiled a little. "I'd say so."

"Then can I have a hug? I could really use it."

"Me too. C'mere."

It took Lauren only a few heartbeats to get around the long desk and find safe haven in strong arms. She'd been sick to her stomach the entire way back from Baltimore and that sinking sensation was only now beginning to ease. "I love you," she whispered.

Dev tightened her hold on the younger woman. "I love you too." She kissed the top of Lauren's head. "It's time to call in the troops."

"Should I prepare to grovel? Press Secretary Allen looked as though she wanted to strangle me, and David barely looked at me at all as he flew out of here."

"They'll live," Dev said flatly. "Part of their job is dealing with things like this. I take it everyone is up to speed on exactly what happened in Baltimore?" Upon Lauren's nod, Dev pushed the intercom button on her desk. "Send everyone in, Jane. And you come too, please."

"Yes, Madam President," Jane answered dutifully, her voice still hanging in the air when the office door opened.

Wordlessly, the staffers trooped in and circled Dev and Lauren.

"Okay," Dev began. "The First Lady has explained what happened to my satisfaction." Her voice dropped an octave. "It's over now, people. She knows she made a mistake and I don't want to hear anything more about how she could have done it or why she was careless."

Unseen by Devlyn, Michael Oaks rolled his dark eyes.

"Dev—" Lauren began to protest, willing to take her medicine, even if it meant eating a serious portion of crow. After all, Dev was right about her lack of care. And now it would cost everyone.

"Assigning blame when you've already taken responsibility for your error only wastes time," Dev said for everyone else's benefit as much as Lauren's. "And that's the last thing we need. Besides," she paused, then met David's gaze with her own, blue eyes not revealing a hidden twinkle, "as my good friend David reminded me, I've, well… there's been a time or two where I said something I wished I hadn't."

David and Beth looked at each other, both recalling what was easily Devlyn's most embarrassing political moment. As a freshman Ohio State representative, she had angrily shot off her mouth within range of a taping film crew, and the results remained in the papers for weeks, giving Devlyn her very first national exposure. The McMillians drew in a deep breath and chorused Dev's near historic quote about a rival politician, "I'm not going to be bullied by an illiterate hilljack with the morals of a pimp!"

Dev narrowed her eyes. "You just had to say it, didn't you?"

"Yes, Madam President," they both answered soberly, having done exactly what Devlyn had wanted. And they knew it. Dev mentioning the much-hated 'hilljack incident,' as the press had dubbed it, was tacit permission for David and Beth to use the tale for good purpose. Lauren had made great strides in the past year, but she would misstep many times on her journey as First Lady. The support she received now would go a long way in making her more confident but more savvy in public in the future.

Lauren, however, wasn't the least bit shocked at the story. Sometimes, she mused, everyone seemed to forget that she was trailing around after Devlyn and conducting endless research and interviews for a reason. Other than enjoying the company. Lauren probably knew more about the President than all but a handful of people on the planet. And she loved that quote. "I hate to tell you, Devlyn, but your biography wouldn't be complete without a mention of the infamous "hilljack incident."" She chanced a tenuous grin at her partner. "Sorry."

"That's all right," Dev replied calmly. "Your quote from today will surely be in the biography that someone is undoubtedly writing about you."

Lauren's face shifted into a scowl.

Dev chuckled evilly. "Welcome to my world." Then she slapped her hands on her thighs and focused on her press secretary. It was time to get back to business. She grabbed David's wrist and lifted it so she could look at his watch, nodding a little to herself. "We need a press conference before our lovely friends in the press put their nightly news stories to bed. You've got thirty minutes. Here's my statement, and Sharon, quote me on this—"

Sharon's eyes widened and she fumbled with the pad of paper in her hands until Liza magically produced a micro-recorder and handed it to the woman. A beaming smile was Dev's ever-ready assistant's reward.

Dev leaned against her desk as she spoke. "Quote. The First Lady is a bright, talented woman who has a right to her own opinions just like the rest of us. On occasion, those opinions differ from mine, which is fine by me. She is my *partner*, not a yes-man, and I value the different perspective she might bring to any issue. However, the First Lady's comments about DNA registration do not signal a lack of support for the legislation," she paused and looked directly at Lauren, "but rather a genuine concern about the nature and amount of government intrusion into the lives of its citizenry. This is a concern this administration is not only sensitive to but shares. End quote." Dev winked at the impressed look on her wife's face.

Sharon stopped the recording.

"Wow," Lauren told Dev seriously.

"That works, Madam President," David commented thoughtfully.

"How do we demonstrate that we're serious about concerns like Lauren's?" Sharon followed up, making a few notations on her notepad.

"After you read my quote, release some of the crime statistics that show how helpful DNA records will be and follow them up by showing our projected successes in reduction of violent crime and in funding for state and local law enforcement. Show the public that they'll be getting something valuable in return for giving up those two drops of blood. Also outline the privacy safeguards that will be in place."

"Yes, ma'am." Sharon smiled and stuck her pencil behind her ear, her short natural-cut Afro holding it in place.

"Liza," Dev trained her eyes on her tall assistant. "Tonight's press event was going to be held at George Washington University Hospital and we were expecting minimal press coverage, correct?"

Liza flew through the screens of her electronic organizer at the speed of light, the flashing lights reflecting in her eyes. "The room capacity is fifty and no additional electrical hookups were requested. That puts expected attendance at no more than eight camera crews."

Dev made a face. "That won't work. Everyone will want to be there to see if Lauren bothers to show up." She shot a quick questioning glance at Lauren, who nodded vigorously.

"I'll be there," the blonde assured.

"Good." Dev's eyes suddenly widened as she had a thought. "You won't pass out will you?"

Beth chuckled.

"One chair for the First Lady." Liza added it to her list.

"Okay," David jumped in, "let's move the press event here. There's more room and everything is set up. We might as well milk the publicity."

Sharon batted her eyelashes at David. "A man after my own heart."

Dev considered David's suggestion. "That works. And get on the phone to Party Chairman Jordan. If we're going to get some good exposure I want some willing volunteers from both Houses over here and ready to show their support." She pinned David with a serious glare. "Stress the word "volunteers." I don't want anyone here who is the least bit uncomfortable or ambivalent. I won't have this blowing up in our faces later."

"Consider it done. In fact, I've had a hankering to get my finger pricked all day."

Dev gave his shoulder a hearty pat. "Good man. Sharon?"

"Yes, Madam President?"

"The usual spin doctors?"

"Will be there with bells on, armed with all the stats."

Dev exhaled. "Mr. Oaks?"

Michael lifted his jaw. "Ready, Madam President."

"When are Lauren and I scheduled for our next social appearance in public?"

"Eight days from now," he answered easily. "An Emancipation Party fundraiser in Georgetown. Semi-formal."

Dev made a face. "Not soon enough." She turned to Lauren. "Would you like to go on a date with me so the world can rest assured that you really like me?"

Lauren bit her lip and nodded. "Anywhere."

"Someplace romantic," Dev added, still looking at Lauren. "We might as well kill two birds with one stone."

Michael was too busy mentally sorting through possibilities to roll his eyes again. But Dev's words filled the room with faces wreathed in indulgent grins.

"That leaves one more thing for the First Lady," Dev said.

Lauren felt her stomach jump into her throat. "Yes?"

Dev pointed to the evidence of her mini temper tantrum. "You owe the administration reimbursement for one very large coffee mug."

"I'll buy a half dozen," Lauren promised.

Michael sniffed. "What about the bust of George W. Bush?" he pointed out, visibly angry at the defilement of one of his political heroes.

"You're absolutely right, Mr. Oaks," Dev said seriously. "Lauren?"

Lauren blanched. God only knew how expensive that statue was. "Yes, Devlyn?"

"We'll call it even for the coffee mug." Dev grinned as Michael's face flushed with anger. "That's it, people," she finished. "Go to it."

With a round of murmured goodbyes the room quickly cleared, leaving Lauren and Dev alone.

Lauren blinked a few times, shaking her head as if to clear it. "All that after one sentence from me?" She blew her bangs out of her face and joined Dev on the corner of the desk. "Wow. I don't think I'll ever speak again."

Dev chuckled. "Why don't I believe that statement?"

Lauren backhanded her spouse lightly on the shoulder. "Because you aren't that lucky?"

Dev's chuckle turned into a full laugh that was music to Lauren's ears.

Friday, November 18ᵗʰ

Aaron sat down on his brother's bed, his eyes raking over the open backpack that was half full of heavyweight, autumn clothes. He was clutching his own full canvas bag to his chest. He hugged it a little closer as he gave Lauren a sheepish look. "Mama…Um…I wanna bring my snake." The item in question was tucked beneath Aaron's arm.

Lauren held up a sweatshirt for Emma's approval and the older woman nodded. She spoke to Aaron as she rolled up the sweatshirt and stuffed it in his bag. "So then bring your snake, sugar." She reached out and ruffled Aaron's fair hair. "He'll fit in your bag if we shove things around a little."

Christopher's face went very serious as he joined Aaron on the bunkbed. Unlike his younger brother, who was wearing his blue uniform and gold kerchief, Chris was in jeans. "He can't bring a doll camping!" He ignored Aaron's look of outrage, then disappointment. "The other scouts will laugh and call him a baby."

This was the boys' first away from home outing with their Cub Scout troop and they'd been looking forward to the grand adventure for weeks. It was thrilling and a little scary. David had volunteered to accompany them, eager to spend quality time with the boys he adored. It was, both Dev and Lauren acknowledged, one of those rare situations where David was a better-suited candidate than either of them. And they considered themselves lucky to have him. The boys' Secret Service agents would accompany them, of course, but they wouldn't participate in the scouting events and had been instructed to be as inconspicuous as possible. This was a time for fun and relaxation.

Lauren stopped what she was doing and plucked the four-foot neon green beast from Aaron's armpit. The snake was made of soft felt and had definitely seen better days. She smiled fondly at Phillip, the very unsnakelike name Aaron had chosen for his bedmate. Lauren turned to Emma to seek the nanny's advice on the subject, but a firm knock at the front door of the Presidential apartment sent the matronly woman scurrying out of the room, grumbling under her breath.

Lauren chewed on her lower lip as she joined the boys on the bed, trying to recall what it was like to be their age. It was surprisingly easy. "Well, Aaron," she sighed, "I'm afraid Chris is right. Some kids might tease you if you bring him." She tugged on the snake's slender, forked tongue. "On the other hand, he is sort of cool."

Aaron looked crestfallen.

"Sorry, Aaron," Chris said, genuinely distressed for his little brother.

Lauren's brow furrowed. "How about if we make him a little fiercer looking? Less like a doll and more like a mean snake?" She stared into the snake's beady eyes and did her best to think about a day in the life of a neon green snake. "I know. We could paint blood dripping out of his mouth with red nail polish."

"Yeah!" the boys crowed in unison.

An enormous grin split Aaron's chubby cheeks. "That would be so cool!"

Lauren smiled and nodded. "I think so too. Let me finish getting these last few things packed and we can work on it together. Your Uncle David is coming by to get you soon and your Mom is going to stop by after her dinner meetings and say goodbye." She hoped Devlyn would be home in time.

Christopher turned pleading eyes Lauren's way. "I want something dripping blood too, Mama? Please?"

Lauren chuckled. "Sure, darlin'. Go pick out something we can make look disgusting." Inwardly, she swore that she wouldn't shame herself by passing out at the sight of fake blood.

Chris looked around the room, but he wasn't nearly as fond of stuffed toys as his brother and he had little to choose from.

"How about my lizard, Chris?" Aaron suggested, his eyes sparkling with enthusiasm. "The one with the big claws and white teeth. You could borrow him and we could put blood all around his jaws."

Christopher jumped in place, his excitement bubbling over. "And down his chin!"

The boys ran for the door, only to be stopped by Emma, whose body filled the doorway. She shot them a scolding look that reminded them they weren't allowed to run inside the apartment. "Lauren, Michael Oaks is here to see you. I asked him to wait in the—"

"He's right there." Aaron pointed over Emma's shoulder.

The man straightened his suit coat and sniffed. He didn't want to be kept waiting and he decided the best way to keep that from happening was to take the bull by the horns. "Ms. Strayer," he greeted stiffly. His gaze strayed downward to the boys and he tried to think of what to say to them. Coming up empty, he nodded in their direction.

"Hi, Mr. Oaks," Chris said brightly. "We're gonna paint pretend blood on my snake and lizard and bring them to Cub Scout camping. Isn't that cool?"

Michael blanched, and mumbled a quiet "Hardly." But the boys didn't seem to notice. They moved quickly past him, on their way to Aaron's lizard.

With a look of distaste at the man, Emma excused herself to hunt for some red nail polish.

It was silent for a few seconds as Michael curiously glanced around the room he'd never seen before.

Lauren remained seated on the bed, angry not only that he'd shown himself into her home, but at his attitude toward the children generally. She had the impression he was annoyed that they existed at all.

Michael opened his mouth to discuss the reason he was here, but try as he might, he couldn't let the fake blood thing go. Someone had to ensure propriety. And it didn't appear that Lauren Strayer could be trusted with that task. He cleared his throat. "Blood on toys is not a good idea," he informed her bluntly.

"I'm not really interested in your opinion on the subject," Lauren said evenly. "It will make the boys happy and it's not hurting anyone." She winced inwardly, angry at herself for bothering to justify their plans.

"It's inappropriate."

"You say that as though that's a bad thing."

Michael ground his teeth together. "It's unsuitable for the First Family in addition to being revolting."

All traces of humor vanished from Lauren's voice. "It's none of your business."

Michael smiled a little, not above acknowledging how pleasurable it was to annoy someone he regarded as little more than a thorn in his side. "It *is* my business."

"Your delusions of grandeur are getting out of hand, Michael. You have nothing to do with the children." Her voice hardened a little. "And you never will." She set aside Aaron's snake. "The President is still in her dinner meeting with Party Chairman Jordan. Wait for her some-place else."

Gremlin padded into the room. He stopped when he got a look at whom Lauren was talking to and paused his journey long enough to wrinkle his flat nose at the supremely irritating human who never failed to aggravate his mistress and always smelled of too much cologne. Then he joined Lauren on the bed, grunting a little at the effort.

"I'm not here for the President."

Lauren's eyebrows lifted and she reached down to stroke Gremlin's coarse fur, waiting for Michael to elaborate. She didn't feel like playing twenty questions this afternoon and she mentally gave him three seconds to answer before she kicked him out.

"I'm here to check on the *President's* sons."

Lauren's eyes turned to slits.

"Christopher isn't wearing his uniform. That simply won't do. I can see now it was a good thing I took the initiative to stop by the residence."

Lauren pushed off the bed and crossed the room until she was standing toe-to-toe with the immaculately dressed black man. She spoke slowly so there would be no mistaking her message. "What the children wear is none of your concern. What the children do is none of your concern. And most especially, my relationship with the children is *none* of your goddamn concern! I don't know what you think you're doing, but because I'm not the jackass you are, I'll extend you the courtesy of informing you that uniforms aren't required at all on this trip. Aaron was just excited and wanted to wear his on the drive."

Michael was a little unnerved by Lauren's vehemently spoken words, but was determined not to let it show. "Christopher will look much better for the photographers if he's wearing his uniform. If you would please inform his nanny, he needs to change quickly." The chance at a successful photography shoot involving Chris and Aaron would be feather in his cap that he wasn't about to give up. It would all be worth it in the end.

Lauren looked at Michael as though he'd lost his mind. "What photographers? The press wasn't invited to this campout and the boys are leaving from the private entrance out back. They can wear nothing but their Batman underpants and a coat if they like."

Michael bit his tongue, not liking that he was now the one being tweaked. "The plans have changed. We've decided to make the most of the chance to show that the boys have a positive male influence in their lives. A real father would be better, of course, but this is the best we've got to work with."

Lauren's lips thinned and she could feel her skin flush with anger. "I resent that."

"I imagine you do," he said simply, not bothering to sugarcoat his words or tone.

This was the first time they'd been alone in a room together for months and they both seemed to recognize that fact as the tension that had been present since their very first meeting ratcheted up a notch and threatened to explode.

Michael took a calming breath against the palpable waves of anger rolling off Lauren. "But be that as it may, we have to hurry. There's no need for you to attend." He girded his mental loins. "In fact, it would be better if you didn't. You're not part of the image we're trying to convey to the public in this particular shoot. I'll take the boys." Lauren was as silent as the grave, and he took that as a good sign. He relaxed a little, feeling more in control of the situation. "We need to be outside in less than fifteen minutes."

"The boys aren't going anywhere with you, Michael."

Gremlin jumped off the bed and moved to stand by Lauren's feet, perhaps sensing the tightness in his mistress' voice.

She ran a hand through her hair as she shook her head. "Devlyn would never allow—"

"The photography session has already been approved and everyone is in place," he said stiffly, his eyes daring her to continue her challenge. His heart sped up. He hadn't meant to go that far, but there was no backing down now.

Lauren blinked. "Devlyn wouldn't do that."

"Some people actually understand that their *personal* needs must sometimes give way to the greater plan." Michael could feel perspiration gathering around his collar. "This is one of those times."

"You don't seem to understand me," Lauren ground out. "I don't care what's been approved and what hasn't. I don't care if Jesus Christ himself is standing out back with a camera. There will not be one single picture taken of those boys or you'll have me to answer to!" Her lips twisted into a snarl and her expression darkened to a degree he'd never seen. "*I* don't approve!"

Coal black eyes widened.

"And I don't believe for one minute that Devlyn would either."

"I told you—"

A low growl erupted from Gremlin's throat, causing Michael to stop what he was saying. He took a large step backwards...and bumped right into the President.

He shivered a little as a low voice tickled his eardrums, the breath so close it lifted the fine hairs on his ear.

"Hello, Michael," Dev rumbled dangerously. In one hand she was holding a large felt snake and lizard, in the other, a bottle of blood-red nail polish.

Lauren watched in satisfaction as the color drained from Michael's face. She smiled at her partner. "Hi, darlin'."

Dev's eyes were flashing, but when her gaze swung from Michael to Lauren, it softened instantly. "Honey, I'm home," she teased dryly, using her foot to kick closed the bedroom door.

Michael jumped a little as it slammed shut, rattling the pictures on Christopher's wall.

Lauren reached out for Dev's hand, savoring its warmth and strength as her wife moved alongside her. She backed up a couple of paces, putting a little needed distance between them and Michael. "Devlyn, Mr. Oaks was just explaining how you approved of a photography session for the boys."

Dev cocked her head to the side, her eyebrows at their zenith and hidden behind a scattering of dark bangs. "So I heard."

"I said no such thing," Michael defended hotly, his mind casting for a way out of this dilemma. He hadn't counted on any resistance to the photos at all, especially when they were so clearly the right move to make. And he'd assumed Lauren would be with Devlyn at the President's meeting. "I merely said it was approv—"

"I heard what you *merely* said, you lying son of a bitch." Dev let go of Lauren's hand and stalked toward him. "No one can approve anything having to do with *our* children except for Lauren or myself. No one."

Michael's stomach flip-flopped. She'd heard every word.

"So who *exactly* approved the photography session, Michael?" Dev asked, her nostrils flaring.

Michael swallowed hard and lifted his jaw. "I did, Madam President. As your social secretary it's imperative—"

"Get. Out." Dev closed her eyes, fighting the urge to throttle him. "Get out of my house. I've had enough of your snobbery, pettiness, and insubordination to last a lifetime. You don't work here anymore."

His mouth worked ineffectually for several long seconds. Then he began to sputter, "I—I—"

"Did you really think you'd get away with intentionally misleading the First Lady?" Dev seethed. "Wait." She waved a hand dismissively. "Never mind. I don't want any more of your excuses. I've done my best to overlook your personality conflicts with my entire staff and, worst of all, with my wife. But this time you've crossed the line. I'll expect your resignation on my desk by morning. Now leave."

But Michael didn't move. His feet were frozen in place and all he could do was stare at the President and Lauren Strayer and listen to the terrible sound of his career crashing down around him. How had he misjudged things so badly?

Lauren smiled coldly, her eyes never leaving his as she spoke. "Do I need to call an agent in to have him removed, Devlyn?"

Dev lowered her voice to a reasonable volume and leveled a glare at Michael. "Does she, Michael?"

"No," he said finally, his voice flat. "I'm leaving." He moved for the door on wobbly legs, and then suddenly he turned back, his eyes boring a hole into Lauren. "Bitch," he spat, deciding he had nothing to lose by getting in the last word now.

Lauren saw Dev throw down the items in her hands as they balled into fists. In a lightning quick move, she grabbed hold of her partner's sleeve and inserted herself between the President and Michael, before Dev could lunge forward and put him into the emergency room.

To everyone's surprise, Gremlin sprang into action, teeth bared, stopping almost midair when Lauren commanded, "Down!"

For several heartbeats only four sets of labored breathing could be heard.

When Lauren finally spoke, her voice was low and controlled. "I might very well be a bitch." Behind her, she felt Devlyn bristle at her words. "But I'm also *your* First Lady. And at least this bitch still has a job." She waited a few seconds, watching as he absorbed her words. "Now get out."

--*--

Thursday, November 24ᵗʰ

Thanksgiving

Howard Strayer stood outside Frank and Janet Marlowe's front door, the large box that had traveled with him from Tennessee resting near his feet. Unhappily, he glanced down at it, wondering now if his rather impulsive gesture had been a foolish idea. Then he turned so his gaze could travel down the long, tree-lined driveway. He caught sight of two Secret Service agents drinking steaming cups of coffee, their eyes alert and scanning the property as they walked the perimeter. Maybe this entire trip was a mistake.

He lifted his hand to knock, but before his knuckles struck wood, the door swung open. Howard blinked a couple of times, a little overwhelmed by Devlyn's sudden and unexpected presence.

The President's hair hung loose over her shoulders, and she was wearing a pair of comfortable-looking Levis, an oversized navy-colored cable-knit sweater and nothing on her feet but a pair of thick, white sweat socks. It was the most casual Howard had ever seen the woman, and it took a moment for his brain to reconcile the image before him with the buttoned-up professional he'd seen on television so many times.

Just before he switched the channel.

Dev smiled what she hoped was a warm greeting. "Won't you come in?"

Howard merely grunted and grabbed the box at his feet before entering a well-lit foyer. He glanced around at the expensive furnishings and polished brass scattered throughout the large entry. "I... um... expected a servant to open the door."

Dev arched an eyebrow as she reached out and took his coat. She opened a small closet and pulled out a hanger. "My parents have a housekeeper, Mr. Strayer. But she's busy working on dinner, so I'm on door duty." Not quite true. A set of gates secured her parents' property, and when Howard had passed through the security check at the main gate, she'd been notified by cell phone of his arrival. She'd insisted that an agent merely escort him up the walk, rather than inside. She could tell by the way his eyes followed the agents that they made him uncomfortable.

Howard rocked back on his heels, his eyes flickering from surface to surface. "Nice place."

"Thanks."

"And, I suppose…" He drew in a deep breath and grudgingly pushed ahead. "I suppose you should call me Howard."

This time Dev's smile was warmer. She'd win over this curmudgeon of a southern plumber if it took twenty years. She just hoped that, for Lauren's sake, she could manage it a little sooner. "Thank you. And you could call me Dev?" She lifted her eyebrows in question, very well aware that he tended not to address her at all. After her and Lauren's wedding ceremony, he'd given his daughter a quick goodbye hug and disappeared before the reception could begin.

"All right," he said slowly.

"Good." Curious, Dev glanced down. "What's in the box?"

Howard was tempted to say "none of your business," but he bit back his natural impulse and shrugged. "Nothing much. Some old stuff for Lauri."

Janet entered the foyer, carrying a mug of spiced cider. "Hello, Howard."

The man visibly relaxed.

Janet smiled. "We're so pleased you could come."

"Thank you for having me," Howard answered politely, causing Dev to blink.

Then Frank Marlowe strode into the room. "Howard." He extended his hand and the men exchanged firm handshakes. "I hope you're hungry. There's enough food here for an army."

Dev watched in amazement as Howard's demeanor relaxed even further, the look on his face becoming almost placid.

"I'm starved. I'd always heard you got food on planes." He'd driven up for the wedding, but his truck was acting up and he decided to splurge on a plane ticket this time out. "There wasn't even a measly bag of peanuts on my flight, that's for dam—" His gaze shot to Janet, and to Dev's amazement, he blushed. "Excuse me, ma'am, I meant to say for *darn* sure."

Frank chuckled and clasped Howard's shoulder. "No harm done. Janet's been known to make sailors blush herself."

"Frank!" Janet gasped, but her eyes were merry and everyone, even Howard, seemed to know that was as far as she'd take her token protest.

"Traveling always makes me hungry," Frank continued. "And the day I'll pay thirteen dollars and fifty cents for a cheese sandwich in the airport is the day I bare my butt on Main Street!"

Howard snorted his agreement, finding it very easy to like Frank, despite the fact that he was very aware of their different social classes. "I'd starve first." He stuffed his hands in the pockets of his trousers, feeling a lot better about being here. When the silence in the room lengthened, he cast about for something to say. "So... um... Frank. I hear you have horses here?"

Frank's ears perked up. "I have a half dozen beauties," he said proudly, rocking back on his booted heels and suddenly reminding Howard strongly of Frank's daughter. "Would you like to see them?"

He nodded. "I've bet on them plenty, but never touched one in person." He half smiled. "Too much of a city rat, I guess."

"You'll need a coat," Frank advised. "And you might as well take off that necktie." He gestured to the sedate blue tie circling Howard's thick throat. "We don't stand on ceremony as you can see." He gestured at his neatly pressed but casual shirt. "C'mon, my jacket's on the back porch."

Everyone looked at Dev, who belatedly sprang into action and retrieved Howard's heavy jacket from the closet.

"Much obliged," Howard told her absently, already following Frank out of the foyer and unbuttoning the top button of his shirt. He suddenly stopped and looked a little unsure of himself. He addressed Dev. "You'll tell Lauren—"

"I'll tell her you're here," Devlyn assured. When the men were gone, she gazed at her mother in wonder. "What the hell just happened?"

"What do you mean?" Janet moved Howard's box away from the front door and toward the wall so no one would trip over it.

"You all are friends?"

Janet nibbled her lower lip. "'Friends' may be a little strong, Dev. But we're in-laws and we're friendly. We've spoken by phone a few times since the wedding. As a matter of fact, Frank and I called him after Lauren's accident." She shook her head sadly. "He saw the reports on television before anyone knew whether she was all right. I think that took five years off the man's life."

"Buh..." Dev let out a frustrated breath. "He didn't even call her afterwards! He only sent flowers and a card."

Janet's brows contracted. "Surely you don't think that's because he doesn't care about her welfare?"

A guilty look swept across Dev's face. "Well—"

"Devlyn!" Janet's voice took on a scolding edge. "You should know better than that. Lauren does. Was she upset by the card instead of a call?"

Dev frowned. "No. I guess not." She plucked the mug of cider from her mother's hands and stole a deep drink. "Though I was plenty pissed," she murmured against the cup, wincing as her thievery resulted in a burnt tongue.

"Mmm." Janet took a step closer to her daughter. "I know Howard Strayer wasn't the father you had, and Lord knows Lauren didn't deserve any less. But the man has his own ways, just like you and I do. And he's truly trying, or he wouldn't be here at all."

Dev pursed her lips. "True."

Janet's gaze softened. "Don't be so hard on the man, dear, and stop trying so hard yourself. He's not going to meet your expectations for a long time, if ever. But I do believe, eventually, he'll come around where you're concerned."

A slender dark brow lifted. "After he gets over the fact that I've lured his daughter into an unnatural, immoral lifestyle in addition to subjecting her to the vile, twisted world of politics?"

Janet's blue eyes sparked with good humor. "I don't recall him using the word 'vile.'"

Dev whimpered as she wrapped her arm around the smaller woman's narrow but sturdy shoulders. "I just want her to be happy, Mom."

Janet eased her own arm around Dev's waist and began guiding her back into the family room, where Lauren, the McMillians, and the kids were all draped across various pieces of furniture, either asleep or watching football. "Who have you been living with, dear? That girl curled up on the sofa in there *is* happy."

Dev groaned inwardly. "I know. But—"

"But you want the best for her and you want it all yesterday?" Janet quipped, laughing slightly as Devlyn's mouth clicked shut.

Dev scowled as they moved through the hallway and descended a set of stairs. "You make me sound so unreasonable. I'm a *very* reasonable person, I'll have you know. I've been known to be patient and reasonable for entire minutes at a time!"

Janet rolled her eyes at her daughter, before a knowing smile overtook her face. She stopped their progress and looked up into her daughter's eyes. "I make you sound like a woman in love," she said softly, her heart near bursting. "And love has nothing to do with reason." She had to stand on her tiptoes to kiss Dev's cheek. "I couldn't be happier for you, Devil."

Dev wrapped long arms around her mother and closed her eyes, careful not to spill the cider. "Thanks, Mom," she said, surprised by the sudden rush of emotion. There was nothing like the holidays to bring out the mushball in the Marlowe clan. "Me too." She sighed happily. *Me too.*

The food was long gone and everyone sat around in the family room with bloated bellies too full to even think about moving. Everyone except the children, that is, who were still buzzing around the room on what appeared to be an electric high.

David groaned, too stuffed to do more than point weakly at the boys, who were rolling around in the corner, tickling each other. "Ever wonder what's wrong with them?" The adults in the room, except for Howard, all laughed.

"It is amazing," Beth agreed. "I know for a fact that Aaron consumed an entire turkey leg." She paused to yawn, wishing she'd worn pants with an elastic waist. "And Christopher had a slice from each of the three pies. Shouldn't they be passed out somewhere?" She sighed, sure that if she opened her mouth, her last bite of mashed potatoes would still be visible in the back of her throat. She'd regretted that final forkful the instant it hit her tongue, when she realized it had no place to go.

Dev chuckled. "The little fiends are immune to being too full. Food jazzes them up and it takes them an hour to come down off the energy high."

"It's just not fair," Frank said, thinking fondly of his own youth and those thirty-three-inch-waist jeans he used to buy and actually be able to button.

"Well," Howard slapped his hands down on both of his knees and stood up. "I need to walk this off." His gaze swung to Lauren, who was sitting in a turkey-induced catatonic state in front of the fireplace. "Would you like to join me, Lauren?"

Lauren's head jerked up at the mention of her name. She had to think for a second to recall what he'd said. "You want me to walk with you?"

Howard shrugged one shoulder, not liking that all eyes in the room were now on him. "I don't know my way around and don't relish taking a bullet between the eyes from one of those agents."

"They won't shoot us," Aaron piped up, moving alongside his stepmother. "We're the good guys."

Howard's face colored. "Of course not, boy. I didn't..." He lifted one hand and then helplessly let it fall.

"He was only teasing," Lauren explained to Aaron, ruffling his corn-yellow hair.

Howard looked relieved. "That's right."

David lifted his cell phone. "I'll let them know you'll be on the path to the cabin, yes?"

Lauren nodded, a little nervous at the prospect of being alone with her father. She and Dev exchanged curious looks. "That's a pretty walk," she agreed slowly, then turned back to her father. "Daddy?"

He shrugged again. "Fine by me."

"Can I come?" Ashley asked, and the boys quickly followed suit.

Lauren gave Devlyn a questioning look and the President tossed the ball back in her court with a gentle tilt of her head. "Sure, kids. But get your coats."

A wry smile twitched at Howard's lips as he thought about his independent, often quiet daughter living with these tiny whirlwinds.

Christopher and Ashley were in a dead heat for the stairs, only breaking their stride when they heard a firm "Walk, please," from their mother.

Aaron had lingered behind. "I wanna walk with Grandpa," he stated as he pinned Howard with hopeful pale eyes. "Can... I mean, may I?"

Confused, Howard looked over his shoulder at Frank. "I don't mind if—"

"Daddy," Lauren interrupted gently. "I think he means you." When she saw the panicky, stunned look on her father's face, her heart leapt into her throat and she decided then and there if he said something to hurt that little boy's feelings she wouldn't be responsible for her actions.

Dev's grip on her cup of cider tightened to almost a painful degree.

Everyone held their breath as Howard blinked stupidly. "I... um..."

Aaron looked around at all the expectant adult faces. "What's wrong? I'll hold his hand and won't get lost," he added, sure that was the problem. "Please?"

Howard found his head bobbing, and before he had time to even think about what he was doing he heard himself say, "Sure, son. You can walk with me if you like. I'll..." Self-consciously, he cleared his throat. "I'll hold your hand."

Devlyn looked up from her son to find two sets of glassy gray eyes locked on each other, something indefinable and profound passing between them. *This,* she thought happily, *is turning into such a damn wonderful day.*

"Great!" Aaron enthused. On the way out of the room he threw his arms around Howard's thighs and gave him an impressively strong hug. "Be right back!" Then he bolted.

When the kids were out of the room, Lauren wordlessly approached her father. On tiptoes she bussed his cheek, feeling the short stubble that was always present by early evening. "Thank you, Daddy."

A smile flickered on Howard's face for just a few seconds, then his normal gruff expression slid firmly back into place. Unseen by Lauren, he lifted his arm a few inches, as though he might slip it around her shoulders.

Dev sucked in a hopeful breath, but then watched in disappointment as Howard lowered his arm. Something had stopped him. Perhaps he had felt the weight of her stare or maybe the realization that he had a place in this family if he wanted one was suddenly too much. Instead, and a little awkwardly, he patted Lauren's arm.

Dev's forehead puckered in response. *You've got to walk before you can run,* she reminded herself. *Baby steps.*

Lauren had just seen her father off and made her way back to the comfortable guest bedroom she and Devlyn shared while visiting the Marlowes. It had been a long day. Howard Strayer had booked his return flight on that night's red-eye, and he insisted on getting there the full three hours before that was required for domestic flights.

Thanksgiving with her father had gone both better and worse than she'd expected. Her father seemed to be nearly comfortable around Frank and Janet, something she made a mental note to ask Devlyn about later. And she could tell the children had made sizeable headway into wiggling their way into his heart.

Lauren sighed. Then there was Devlyn. As the evening wore on, it became clear that though her father would remain polite, he would also do his level best to steer clear of her spouse. She could tell that bothered Dev, and she made another mental note to add a few extra kisses of reassurance to make it clear that the problem lay not in Dev but in her and her father's relationship as a whole. Still, when all was said and done, it hadn't been unpleasant, and nobody had ended up being shot by the Secret Service or in a fistfight. Norman Rockwell it wasn't, but it could have gone worse.

Their walk had been uneventful but nice. They shared remembrances of the few close moments they'd had as a family, and for the first time Lauren had been able to look beyond the gruff exterior of her mostly-absentee father and see a still-grieving husband. And it made her think.

She pulled over the box her father had left for her and undid the top, wondering what was inside. Lauren didn't have to wonder for long, and a wistful smile touched her lips when she saw the first item.

"You sure you don't want the cabin for the night?"

"Nah," Dev said, passing over Beth's coat. "The kids are watching a movie with Dad in the family room. They'll fall asleep in no time and I promised that we'd spend the holiday together. So it's easier to keep them here than carry their little carcasses to the cabin."

Beth laughed and shrugged into her coat, looking forward to a short walk in the cold night air. Now all she needed was David, and she spotted him approaching over Dev's shoulder. "Shit." Beth closed her eyes. He was carrying his cell phone and was scowling.

Dev looked behind her and then caught sight of the phone and groaned.

"I'm sorry, Dev," David said. "There's been a development in the Middle East negotiations." He gave his wife a contrite look.

"Let me guess. Hmm..." Dev tapped her temple like an oracle ready to announce her prediction. "Secretary of State Ortiz's presence this weekend at Camp David is not enough. Monday isn't near soon enough for my presence there either. You want me there now," Dev accused bluntly.

David fought the urge to sink into the floor. "It's not just me, Dev." He steeled himself as he turned to face Beth. "Can you excuse us for a minute?"

For a few seconds, Beth didn't say a word. She was on the verge of taking David to task when she reminded herself about the realities of a life she went into with her eyes wide open. Her gaze fell to the floor and she drew in a deep breath, letting it out slowly and ending with a sigh. "Sure. I'll take out the dogs."

Beth and David's pugly was currently wreaking havoc in a DC kennel. But the Marlowe children couldn't bear to be separated from their pets when they traveled, and so the First Dogs were lying along one of the foyer walls, taking in the human activity with uninterested, coal-black eyes. "Outside?" Beth asked in a deceptively perky voice, considering her sullen mood.

Princess jumped to her feet and scurried to the door, bouncing at least three feet high with every excited leap like a deranged yo-yo. Her mate rose slowly, leaning forward, first on his front legs to stretch his back, then yawning and showing his crooked teeth and leaning backwards in another long stretch.

Beth lifted an eyebrow. "If you're through?" she teased and smiled a little when the pug lifted his flat nose into the air as he passed Devlyn, refusing to give her the time of day.

Dev's lips curled into a sneer and she bared her teeth and glared at her twenty-pound nemesis.

Beth rolled her eyes at the President as she opened the door and headed out into the night. Over her shoulder she chuckled and said, "If the press ever catch you making that face, Devil, it'll be the picture of you that makes the cover of *Time Magazine*."

"Very funny," Dev shot back, unable to keep from smiling. When the door shut again, she was all business. She squared her shoulders and took a step closer to David so they could lower their voices to just above a whisper. "You've got about thirty seconds until that portly demon dog decides it's too cold to be outside and they come back. So you'd better talk fast and make it good." She crossed her arms over her chest.

David swallowed hard, then launched into a rundown of the briefing he'd been given only moments earlier.

Lauren was sitting cross-legged on the floor, with several items spread out on the floor around her, when Devlyn poked her head inside the bedroom door. She smiled. "Where have you been? I thought you were coming up as soon as you got the kids settled with your dad and said goodnight to Beth and David?" She glanced at the clock. "That was over an hour and a half ago."

"What's all this?" Dev gestured to the items surrounding her wife.

"Just a few things my dad brought me. I can show you in a minute. But first," she paused and gave Dev a direct look, easily sensing that something had happened. "You didn't answer my question. Where were you?"

Without looking at Lauren, Dev shut the door and padded slowly to the bed. "Something's come up."

Two fair eyebrows rose. "Okay," she drew the word out slowly. "Something serious?"

Dev sighed and rubbed her eyes. "Yes."

Lauren bit her tongue for a moment, her heart sinking. She sighed resignedly, already wondering what they would tell the children. "When are we leaving?"

The corner of Dev's mouth twitched. "Sunday."

Lauren blinked. "But weren't we already leaving then?"

A full smile eased across Dev's face. "Yes and no. We were all flying out Sunday evening. Now I'll be leaving at an obscene hour that morning and going directly to Abu Dhabi without the Sunday night stop in Camp David I had planned. Sheik Yousif and King Qasem had a major falling out today. At the moment, negotiations are up in the air."

Lauren took a moment to digest this. She knew how important these intense and usually untimely negotiations were to Devlyn. They were requiring more and more of the President's time, though to her credit, Dev was on the verge of several preliminary, but substantial, breakthroughs. "Jared's in over his head?" She joined Devlyn on the foot of the bed, sitting so close their thighs were touching.

Dev shook her head. "Secretary of State Ortiz is smart as hell, but sometimes these things can't be avoided. I think he's doing pretty damn good, especially when you remember the man has spent the last few days in hell-negotiations and hundred and five degree heat to boot, instead of eating turkey with his wife and son at home in Nebraska." She leaned back on the bed and braced herself on her palms. "Ortiz talked the men into tabling their argument overnight, hoping to give things a chance to cool down a little. But when seven a.m. Abu Dhabi time rolled around, neither Yousif nor Qasem bothered to show up for the early session."

"Things sound like they're in a mess! How did you avoid having to go right now?"

Dev shrugged. "I told David no."

Lauren was at a loss. "God, Devlyn." She shook her head a little, not believing she was about to say this. "Are you sure you shouldn't go? I mean, if the negotiations are really on the line. Or—"

"It's okay." Dev smiled gently and leaned forward to brush her lips against Lauren's. "Thank you for understanding; that means a lot to me. But we're doing something else instead."

"So you're not going to ride in on a white horse and save the day? I loved the movie *Lawrence of Arabia* when I was a kid." Affectionately, she brushed her knuckles across Dev's cheek. "You've got the eyes for the part." Her voice dropped an octave. "And you look great on horse-back," she purred, giving Dev a hungry look.

Dev gulped, and Lauren smiled wickedly at the blush creeping up the dark-haired woman's neck.

A little flustered, Devlyn cleared her throat. "Umm… What were we talking about?"

"Abu Dhabi," Lauren reminded her innocently.

"Oh, yeah, Abu Dhabi." Her eyes dropped to Lauren's mouth. The younger woman slowly licked her lips, and Dev's nostrils flared in pure reaction.

"Devlyn?"

"Yeah?" Dev said absently.

"Abu Dhabi?"

Dev's eyes snapped up to meet Lauren's and the younger woman read a touch of embarrassment there, along with naked desire. "Are you going to stop torturing me long enough for me to tell you?"

"Sweet Jesus, were you always this responsive?" Lauren wondered aloud, a little amazed at the instant and powerful longing now coursing through her.

Dev laughed. "Of course! It just used to make you blush."

Lauren bit her lower lip and chuckled soundlessly. "Oh, yeah. I think I'm getting over that now, Devlyn."

The corner of Dev's mouth curled drolly. "No, really?"

"I'll be good, I swear. I *am* interested," Lauren promised. "It's really your fault, you know. If you weren't so beautiful I wouldn't get distracted. But," she squared her shoulders, "I can control myself." A beat. "If you don't take too long." She winked. "Please continue."

Dev gave her a look asking whether or not she was serious, and Lauren crossed her heart. But in truth, she didn't mind a bit. It was comforting to be reminded in a very pleasant way that even critical issues didn't always have to become personal traumas. They couldn't. "I told Ortiz to go back to the embassy and take the next few days off."

A spark lit Dev's eyes and her voice held the no-nonsense timbre that Lauren always associated with her at her most compelling.

Dev said, "If everyone can't play nice, then I don't want my people wasting their time." The fire behind her words dimmed as quickly as it had flamed, as Dev seemed to recall that she wasn't at work. Her expression lightened. "That is why I'm not leaving today, but will just be leaving a little early."

Lauren's eyes widened. "Will that work to get these guys back to the negotiating table?"

Dev chuckled. "Nope. But they'll stop being pissed off at each other long enough to be mad at me. And if negotiations are suspended, then hopefully they won't say anything to each other to make things any worse. It's pretty much a win, win situation." Her grin split her face. "And I'll still get to spend most of vacation with my family," she finished proudly.

Lauren nodded, clearly impressed. "Wow." She gave Devlyn a sound kiss on the mouth, making it crystal clear just how much she appreciated this and the many smaller adjustments Devlyn had made to her life in deference to her doctors, and her family, but mostly for Lauren herself. And the younger woman knew it. She tugged affectionately on Dev's shirt. "You came up with this in the last hour?"

"Well," Dev sniffed. "I *am* the President."

Lauren flopped back on the bed, her smile crinkling her nose and the corners of her eyes. "You're more than that to me."

Dev crawled on top of her, straddling her to pin her to the bed. "Now," she growled and temporarily forgot what she was going to say, dipping her head for a fiery but playful kiss. Which Lauren deepened instantly, drawing a throaty groan from Dev.

After a few leisurely moments, Devlyn pulled away with a loud smack, smiling at Lauren's protesting moan. Two could play at that game. "Now tell me what's in the box. Tell me, tell me, tell me!"

Lauren lifted her head to kiss Dev's chin, then she gave it a gentle nibble. "And here I thought Curious George was just fiction. Forget the box and kiss me again."

"Lauren!" Dev grabbed Lauren's shoulders and began bouncing both women loudly against the mattress. "I've... been waiting—"

Lauren yelped, then burst into helpless laughter as they flopped wildly against the bed like fish tossed onto the shore.

"And waiting, and waiting. All day! I can't wait any more! It's killing me." Devlyn stared at her partner, who was laughing so hard she was shaking Devlyn every bit as much as she was being shaken. "It's not funny!" she protested.

"Stop... Stop!" Lauren squealed between gasps, her face brick red. "We're going to br-br-break the bed!"

Dev stopped bouncing and dropped limply atop Lauren, her weight causing every bit of air to exit the blonde's lungs in an enormous gust. "So you'll show me, right?" Dev asked calmly.

Lauren sucked in a big breath, then spluttered, "I-I-think I'd better."

Dev let loose a sunny smile. "Good." Sweetly, she kissed a very pink cheek and scampered off the bed and onto the floor.

Lauren shook her head and chuckled, amazed as always at the contrast between the devastatingly effective politician and the boisterous playmate that Devlyn could sometimes be. That beloved playmate had been largely absent these past six months, and Lauren was glad beyond words to see the slow but steady return of her long-absent, playful friend. She closed her eyes and said a small prayer of thanks. It was about time.

"Oooo... is that you?" came the disembodied voice from the floor.

Lauren spun around and crawled to the foot of the bed, resting her head on her hands as she peered over the edge to find Devlyn holding up a photograph of her as a child. She wrinkled her face. "Ummm..." For a second, Lauren was tempted to lie.

"You were precious!" Dev grinned at the tiny blonde with braids, grass-stained cut-off denim overalls, and two skinned knees. But probably most endearing of all was the tattered book Dev could see in her hand. It was just so Lauren. "I could just hug you to death. Oh, and your front teeth are missing," she commented enthusiastically, her eyes riveted to the picture.

"Only someone who loves me could think I look adorable in that picture," Lauren said wryly. "I look like a cross between an egghead and a ragamuffin."

Dev reached over and fondly ran fingers through Lauren's wavy locks. "You were perfect."

"I'm glad you think so, because there are several equally horrific photographs in there. And there's one from my first date that you should get a look at now, because I'm burning it the first chance I get."

"You most certainly are not! You'll be lucky if I don't have it blown up to lifesize, framed, and put on display for the White House tours."

Lauren sucked in a breath. "You're pure evil!"

Dev merely snickered before returning her attention to the small pile of items that had been unloaded from the box. "What is all this?"

"Some things of Mama's." Lauren was quiet for a moment as she reflected. "I didn't know she had most of this stuff. Daddy thought I might want it. I guess he finally decided to go through some of the things in their bedroom and pack some away."

Dev's expression turned serious. "That's not an easy thing to do," she stated gently, leaning back against the foot of the bed.

"No," Lauren said soberly. "It wouldn't be."

Eager to regain some of the joy from just a moment earlier, Dev set down the photograph and picked up one of Lauren's Adrian Nash novels. "This is your first, right?"

Lauren nodded, a gentle though bittersweet smile returning. "I was so proud. I sent her and Daddy a copy right away."

"She kept it for a long time," Devlyn pointed out, her finger tracing the author's name emblazoned in shiny gold letters.

Lauren reached for the book and opened it, hearing the spine crack loudly. She let out a deep breath. "She kept it but never read it." She shrugged a little and passed the book back. "I guess that's still something."

Devlyn looked away, unwilling for Lauren to read the anger she was sure showed plainly on her face. *Some people aren't fit to raise a pet,* she thought harshly. *Much less a child.* "What else do we have here?"

Lauren set the book down, then pointed to a small white box. "That was my mom's bracelet."

Dev opened the box and lifted the delicate gold chain, its links sparkling softly in the light.

"She wore it whenever she got dressed up. It was her mother's."

"Mmm…" The slender links felt cool in Dev's hand. "It's pretty."

Lauren's brow furrowed as she looked at the simple but well-maintained piece of jewelry. She wasn't sure why, but she didn't have the slightest urge to wear it herself. Ever. But the idea of simply throwing it away was equally unacceptable. "I think I'll give it to Ashley."

Dev blinked. "Are you sure—?"

Lauren shrugged lightly, though she felt a little nervous when she said, "It would look silly on one of the boys, and she's the only daughter I have, right?"

Their eyes met and held, and Dev thought she might melt into a puddle then and there. She had to swallow thickly before she could speak. "Absolutely," she murmured finally, noting the gray eyes so near to hers were now shining brightly. "She'll be proud to—" The sound of pounding footsteps caused her to pause.

The bedroom door flew open and three screaming, pajama-clad children ran inside and pounced on the bed, all of them scrambling madly to get under the covers. Christopher nearly knocked Lauren to the floor in his haste, but stopped long enough for a quick, "Sorry, Mama."

Devlyn jumped to her feet. "Hey! What's going on?" She helped Lauren off the foot of the bed, and they turned to see the blanket and the three lumps beneath it shaking like leaves in the wind.

"We're afraid!" Ashley squealed, terrified. "He'll get us in our sleep!"

Christopher and Aaron screamed at their sister's words and Lauren and Dev just looked at each other. The women moved to opposite sides of the bed and lifted the blankets back, cringing as more screams nearly pierced their eardrums.

"Shhh!" Dev told them. "What on earth is wrong? Who is coming for you?"

"Don't let him get us," Aaron begged. "Pleeeeeeeze." He pulled Lauren down, climbed into her lap, and held on for dear life.

"Wh—?" Lauren only shrugged at Devlyn, having no idea what was happening. She pressed her lips to Aaron's hair and kissed him firmly. "I would never let anyone get you," she swore. "And… um… Gremlin will protect you too."

Upon hearing Lauren's declaration, both Ashley and Christopher scrambled over to Lauren and pressed themselves against the shocked woman. Their mother might be bigger, but Lauren had just promised her protection, and Gremlin had pointy teeth and breath ferocious enough to slay almost anything. Their mother had said that last part, many, many times.

"What is going on?" Dev demanded, taking care to set Lauren's mother's bracelet on the nightstand.

"Chucky!" the children cried in unison.

"He has a knife dripping blood," Ashley added, her face pale.

Just then, a very sheepish and disheveled Frank Marlowe poked his head into the bedroom. Only his eyes were visible around the door.

Dev arched a sharp eyebrow at her father. "Why don't I remember someone named Chucky and a blood-dripping knife in the movie *Bambi*?"

"Ouch! Ouch! Ouch!" Frank stumbled into the room behind Janet, who dragged the tall man the rest of the way into the room by his ear.

"Explain yourself, old man," Janet said crossly, finally letting go of Frank's ear.

Lauren looked on with wide eyes. "Uh oh," she mumbled, very glad that *she* hadn't done anything to make Janet angry.

Only the faint beams from a silvery moon lighted the room. The children were sound asleep and plastered against Lauren and Dev, the mass of sweaty bodies sticking together.

"How could he do that?" Dev whispered into the dark. She could tell Lauren was awake by the absence of the gentle snores that were now as familiar to Devlyn as her own scent. And though she couldn't see her, she was sure her body was among the mass under the extra blankets the children had insisted they needed. "How could he fall asleep and not disable the voice controls on the television? He could never trust me when I was a child," she continued harshly. "What fool would trust these devil children?"

Lauren sighed and unstuck Ashley's arm from the side of her face, grimacing at the trickle of sweat that trailed down her own throat. "Ugh. I don't know. But I'm burning up," she whispered back, still a little grumpy that her plans to ravage her wife had gone up in smoke. "I think you should have let Janet take the wooden spoon to him."

Dev's chuckles shook the bed. "Don't worry, he's getting his just deserts."

Lauren smiled in the dark. "I don't doubt that. Did you see his face when Janet told him it was time for bed? He didn't want to go with her."

Both women giggled.

"Think we can escape without them knowing?" Lauren shifted a little, able to peel Christopher's leg from hers. "They're dead to the world."

Dev nodded. "Yeah. But we've got to be careful. If we move around too much, one of them will think Chucky is after them and wake up the entire house," she whispered. "If we're lucky we can crash in the boys' room."

"I still have no idea who Chucky is," Lauren told her, continuing to untangle herself. "A knife-wielding doll sounds more ridiculous than scary."

"Oh, no. It's freaky beyond belief." Dev whimpered a little, just remembering. "I saw it on cable television when I was about Ashley's age. I didn't sleep for weeks and I couldn't look at a doll for months. Maybe years."

"Why in the world did your parents let you watch something like that?" Lauren held her breath as she crawled completely out of bed. The wooden floors felt so cool that she sprawled out on her belly and hummed in pure relief. She turned her head when Dev joined her on the floor.

The President lifted her shirt to feel the cool wooden slats against her back. "They didn't *let* me, you goof."

"Let me guess…"

"Yup, Dad fell asleep in front of *Matlock* while Mom was upstairs reading. The remote was *mine!*"

Lauren laughed softly. "How long were you grounded for?"

"The same amount of time that the kids will be grounded for." With a light groan, Dev pushed herself to her feet and offered Lauren a hand up. They both stepped over the soundly sleeping guard dogs on the way to the boys' room.

"And how long was that?" Lauren asked.

"Well, technically I'm *still* grounded." Devlyn kept hold of Lauren's hand as they traversed the dark hallway. "But don't remind Mom, okay?"

Lauren wrapped her arm around Dev's waist and squeezed. "It'll be our little secret."

"Chucky was just horrible," Dev commented after a minute. "Horrible."

"Darlin'?"

"Yeah?"

"You don't have to worry, I'll protect you." Lauren laughed.

"Very funny." A pause. "Promise?"

Lauren's sparkling grin pierced the night. "Absolutely."

DECEMBER 2028

Friday, December 15th

"It's hard to believe this is our last Christmas in the White House," Dev said, handing Lauren a string of gaily-colored garland.

Lauren strategically wedged the garland between two heavy tree boughs, the fragrant needles brushing the backs of her hands.

"Eight years." Dev sighed and stepped around Lauren. Twinkling tree lights reflected in her eyes as she rested her chin on the smaller woman's shoulder and studied their handiwork. "Where did all the time go?"

"I wish I could tell you, honey." Her attention focused on the decoration Aaron had made her five years before. A wistful smile curled her lips. "I feel the same way." She tucked a loose strand of pale hair behind her ear as she took a few slow steps backwards.

Dev shuffled right along with her, their bodies pressed tightly together.

Lauren gave the tall balsam fir a final, critical once-over. "What do you think?"

Dev buried her nose in Lauren's hair. "I think it smells terrific."

Lauren chuckled, and leaned into the loving touch. She rested her arms on the warm ones circling her waist. "I meant the tree."

"I don't care how the tree smells," Dev grumbled playfully, nipping at Lauren's neck.

"Tch." Lauren gave her lover a gentle poke in the side. "You know what I meant, Devil."

"I do," Dev agreed, pulling Lauren over to the sofa and down onto her lap. She reached out with a long arm and clicked off the table lamp, casting the room in blinking shadows. "It looks great." She tilted her head back and drew in a deep breath of pungent, pine-scented air. Her nose twitched happily. "I love Christmas."

Lauren smiled. "Me too."

"I can't believe the kids wimped out on finishing the decorations though." Dev's lower lip began to protrude. "They've never done that before."

"Aww.... Devlyn." Lauren took her hand and gave it a gentle squeeze. "We all spent two hours decorating it last night. Tonight we're just adding the finishing touches. The kids have been looking forward to going with Beth and David to their cabin for weeks now. You can't blame them for not wanting to stay here and string lights."

Dev's lips thinned a little, but she didn't say a word.

Lauren rested her forehead against Dev's, taking a moment to absorb the warmth before she spoke. "Are you sorry we told them about David?" she whispered, her breath mingling with Devlyn's.

"No." Blue eyes fluttered closed and she felt the softest of kisses on their delicate lids. Her quick answer was greeted with utter silence, and she didn't have to open her eyes to know that Lauren was waiting patiently for her to come clean. She opened her mouth again, but let it close without saying a word, this time giving the question the thoughtful consideration it deserved. "Sometimes," she admitted, wrapping her arms around Lauren and pulling her into a firm hug, and feeling Lauren sink into the warm embrace. "Change..." She took a deep breath. "It can be hard for me."

Feeling more than a twinge of sympathy, Lauren nodded. She knew exactly how Dev felt. Their lives hadn't changed dramatically since the family discussion early that autumn, though the conversation alone had reduced most of them to tears. Since then, all the children had shown an interest in getting to know the man who was already a much-beloved uncle to them, and his wife, just a little bit better. It was a heartfelt desire that neither Devlyn nor Lauren could begrudge their friends or their children. Still, family time was such a precious commodity, and the kids were now at ages where their friends commanded more of their free time and interest than their parents, that it was easy to let petty jealousies rear their ugly heads. But she and Devlyn were making a concerted effort to get past that. And, for the most part, it was working.

Dev released Lauren and resettled her on her lap, wiggling a little and quickly getting comfortable again. She glanced up into concerned gray eyes, uncertain until that very second whether she was going to ask the question that had been weighing on her mind. "Telling them about David's sperm donation was the right thing to do, wasn't it?" Even now, after several months, there was still a hint of pleading in her voice. She wanted to be convinced, and Lauren smiled back gently, hoping to reassure her.

"It was, Devlyn." Lauren cocked her head to the side. "And we talked about it for days, honey. Then we talked it over with David and

Beth. We waited until Aaron was old enough to understand, and we told them all together. I honestly don't think we could have done any better. They're smart, curious kids, and there was only so much longer you could skirt their questions without lying."

"I didn't want to lie to them."

Lauren looked at her kindly and brushed dark bangs from Dev's forehead with a gentle hand. "And you didn't. The decision you made not to tell them in the first place was out of love and so was this one." Her heart ached a little as she recalled Christopher's burning anger at not being told from the very beginning, and how for some reason, it had been directed at her as opposed to Dev. "Even if it wasn't easy."

Dev smiled a little. She felt a little better, if for no other reason than Lauren's effort. "No. It wasn't. I still don't see what's so fun about going to the cabin when they could be decorating the tree." She motioned to the half-eaten plate of cookies and the empty boxes that had once held the decorations now strewn all around the living room floor. "Hell, the stockings are hung by the chimney with care in hopes that Saint Nicholas soon will be there! And when you weren't looking, we were all going to shake our presents like we do every year and try to guess what's inside." She put on a bewildered expression. "What could be more fun than this?"

Lauren gave her a look. "David and Beth's new snowmobiles?"

Dev's eyes widened. "Oh, boy." Unconsciously, she licked her lips. "They finally got the two-hundred-forty-horsepower Arctic Cats David's been eyeing since last year?"

Lauren looked skyward and groaned. "Please don't tell me that means the boys are going to be flying as fast as two-hundred-forty horses. My heart can't take it. They're too little to be riding on anything that goes faster than a bicycle," she mumbled, worry coloring her expression.

An indulgent smile touched Dev's lips. "David and Beth are the safest riders and teachers the boys will ever find. C'mon, we talked about this." She patted Lauren's thigh and looked up at her from beneath dark lashes. "They're going to have a blast! Especially with new machines."

"Snowmobiles are dangerous," Lauren protested, picking a little at Dev's pajama pants. Her voice grew soft. "And the boys are just babies."

Ah ha... "Don't be silly," she chided gently. "They're *not* babies. And they'll be fine." Dev rubbed Lauren's back reassuringly. "Just because the machines have the capability of going really fast doesn't mean David and Beth will let the boys drive them at top speed or even solo. They taught me when we were in college, and Beth wouldn't let me drive alone that entire first weekend. I only wish they'd invited us," she added a little indignantly, her eyes narrowing. "I can't believe they're not sharing their new toys with me. Greedy. Selfish."

"Uh huh. What happened to nothing being more fun than this?" Lauren gestured expansively at the mess surrounding them.

"We're talking two hundred and forty horses, Lauren." Dev's voice was patient and slow, as though she were speaking to a dull child. "*Two-hundred and forty!*"

"It's all so clear now," Lauren said dryly. "What was I thinking?"

"Who knows?" Dev shrugged and kicked her feet out in front of her. "Sometimes you make no sense whatsoever." She shook her head in wonder, oblivious to her lover's raised eyebrow. "How could Ash have decided to stay here at the last minute? I swear sometimes I wonder if they switched babies at the hospital. I'll bet that girl is in her room right now curled up on her bed reading one of those sci-fi novels when she could be blazing a trail through fresh powder."

Lauren's other eyebrow crawled up her forehead. "And just what's wrong with that? I can't think of a better way to while away a snowy Friday night."

Dev pulled Lauren a little closer. "I can."

Lauren blinked at the sexy timbre that had suddenly invaded Dev's voice. "Okay," she allowed, nibbling on her lower lip. "You got me there." She sank her fingers into Dev's salt-and-pepper-colored hair, which was still far heavier on the pepper and stopped just above broad shoulders. She began scratching Dev's scalp, grinning happily when she coaxed a mew of pleasure from her spouse.

Dev's eyes closed. "I love it when you do that," she said huskily.

"I know." Lauren leaned and brushed her lips against Devlyn's, but stopped just short of deepening the kiss when she heard a softly muttered, "Ahem."

Dev and Lauren looked up to see Ashley, clad in soft flannel pajamas and her robe, standing in front of the tree. The teen had caught her mothers in similar positions so many times that catching them kissing on the couch didn't faze her in the least. Though she did roll her eyes.

Ashley was nearly as tall as Dev, and a year on the swim team had begun to add muscle tone and definition to her slender, lanky frame. Her hair hung down the middle of her back, and its black glossiness set off her brown eyes, giving her an exotic look, especially when compared to her blue-eyed, blond, All American-looking brothers.

Lauren smiled. "Hi, sugar. All done reading for the night?"

Ashley nodded as she approached the women. "It was a good one. Wanna borrow it?" She held out the book, and her gaze flitted back and forth between Dev and Lauren.

Dev wrinkled her nose. Science fiction was never her favorite genre.

But Lauren nodded, pleased that paperbacks were making a comeback. There was just something about holding a book in your hand, the scent and feel of the paper, that could never be replaced by reading from a screen. "Wayne says the author is really good."

Suddenly, Ashley looked as though she might burst. "Oh. My. God. Wayne knows the author?"

Lauren laughed. "Uh huh."

"He's wonderful," Ashley gushed, the normally quiet face growing animated along with her voice. "He's got a fabulous sense of pathos! I thought the subplot was just the tiniest bit thin. But in Chapter…"

Lauren got up to look at the book, and Dev watched in silence while her wife and daughter tilted their heads together as Ashley pointed out a section of text. Her heart swelled a little at the sight of their obvious bond and the affection that flowed freely between them.

Their words floated over Dev, and she yawned, feeling relaxed and comfortable. Her mind turned toward the many nights she'd be able to spend with her family in the coming months. It was a slightly heady feeling that filled her with excitement and a hint of apprehension. She'd been in public service her entire adult life. Logically she knew what it meant to be a private citizen, or as private a citizen as an ex-president could be, but actually living it was going to be another story.

Dev was just reaching for a cookie that had somehow escaped her earlier chocolate-chip frenzy when she heard the buzz of conversation abruptly stop.

"Wow, Ash," Lauren said, looking a little stunned. "I'm…" She blinked a few times then turned to Dev. "What do you think?"

Dev popped the entire cookie into her mouth and closed her eyes. "Wha-ew-I-fhink-bout-wha?"

"Ashley wants to go on a date."

Dev inhaled the cookie and began choking wildly, sending both Ashley and Lauren over to the sofa to pat her back and generally make sure she didn't die. After she gave a series of gasps and hacks, the cookie finally dislodged itself, the experience leaving Devlyn panting for breath.

"God, are you okay?" Lauren cupped Dev's now-sweating cheeks and searched her face.

Dev nodded. "I'm fine." She coughed a few times. "I just-I-I. A date?" she finally squealed.

"C'mon, Mom," Ashley groaned, taking a seat next to Dev. "Don't act so surprised."

Lauren took the empty seat on Dev's other side and patted her wife's thigh, her eyes never leaving Ashley.

Dev scrubbed her face, a million questions running through her mind. But in typical fashion, she quickly distilled them into their simplest form. "Okay, Ash. Who? When? Where? And how?"

Lauren blinked as Ashley adopted her mother's way of thinking in a flash of an eye and responded in kind. "Alexander. Seven o'clock. Next Friday's Senate Democrat Christmas Gala at the Hay-Adams Hotel. He'll pick me up here."

Dev's hands moved from her face to the back of her neck. "Alexander? Why does that sound familiar?" Dev turned to Lauren. "Wasn't there someone named Alexander on *America's Most Wanted, The New Wave* last week?"

"Mom!"

Lauren smothered a chuckle. "Yes, darlin'. But he was a fifty-five-year-old embezzler from Utah. Ashley is talking about Ambassador Antoine Tremaine's son."

"Ooooh." Dev visibly relaxed and gave her daughter a fond smile. "I remember that boy. We had dinner with his family once." Her smile grew even larger when she remembered the boy's placid nature and his endearingly geeky appearance. "He seemed harmles—err... I mean sweet. Has all those cute freckles like his mother." She winked at Ashley. "Isn't he kind of young for you, Moppet?"

"Devlyn," Lauren interrupted, "We had dinner with them *five* years ago. By now the boy has to be…" She pinned Ashley with a serious look that warned her to tell the entire truth. "How old, Ash?"

Ashley winced, and her voice dropped to barely a whisper. Her gaze dropped to the rug. "Seventeen."

Dev shot to her feet. "Seventeen!"

Ashley shot to her feet as well and stood toe-to-toe with her mother. "I have to start dating sometime. And he's only two years older than I am!" She crossed her arms over her chest defiantly. "It's just the mustache that makes him look older."

Dev gaped. "H-h-he has a mustache?" She turned to Lauren with an incredulous look on her face. "A *mustache*?"

Lauren dropped her face into her hands. "Oh, boy," she mumbled to herself.

"Why are we in the snow-filled Rose Garden in the middle of the night?" Lauren asked, pulling the lapels of her coat together at the neck. She was slowly walking, her arm entwined with Dev's, her breath coming in small clouds that disappeared into the night sky as she spoke.

Dev shrugged and led them over to a small granite bench. She brushed it free of snow then spread out the throw blanket she'd snagged from their residence on the way out the door. "I thought it would be pretty tonight. And I wanted the time alone with you." She sat down, feeling Lauren snuggle up close to her. "Is this okay?"

"Mmm…" Lauren nodded. "Sure. I mean, it is freezing. But I'm fine next to you."

Dev smiled and wrapped her arm around Lauren, pulling her close and sighing when the blonde head rested itself against her shoulder. It didn't take long for Devlyn to speak. "You think we should let Ashley go, don't you?"

Lauren was quiet for a long time before she answered. She knew what she wanted and what Devlyn would prefer. But then there was Ashley. "I think she's a smart, funny, beautiful young lady who is going to have most of the boys," the corner of her mouth quirked, "and some of the girls, buzzing around her for a long time to come."

"That doesn't answer my question."

Lauren let out a slow breath. "Exactly."

Dev whimpered a little. "She's my baby, Lauren. She's not ready to have people with mustaches trying to kiss her."

Lauren chuckled softly. *"You're* not ready to have people with mustaches try to kiss her."

Dev snorted. "And *you* are? I saw the look on your face tonight."

Lauren shifted uncomfortably, well aware of how she felt. "No. I guess I'm not what you'd call 'ready.' But whether *we're* ready isn't the point." She took Dev's hand, and tried to warm it in her own. "By the way, how come when I said the boys were too young to go snow-mobiling, *I* was being silly. But when Ashley wants to go on a date, she's your baby? Hmm?"

"I'm fairly confident the boys aren't going to get pregnant while snowmobiling."

"Devlyn Marlowe!" Lauren smacked Dev's midsection. "She's not going to get pregnant on her first date. Ashley's not like that. For God's sake, we're going to be at that party ourselves!"

Dev frowned. "I know," she admitted, aware she was overreacting but helpless to stop herself. She turned beseeching eyes on Lauren. "I can't believe I even said that. I sound like a lunatic. My parents were totally calm. Why aren't I calm? What did your parents say when you first asked?"

"Mama was in her room asleep and so I only went to Daddy." Lauren tried not to smile. "He looked up from his newspaper, said for me to be back by midnight, no drinking, and if I got pregnant he'd disown me. Then he went back to reading the sports section."

"Oh, God," Dev moaned, throwing her hands into the air. "I'm as bad as your father was."

Lauren's gaze softened. "You're not that bad."

"She's just a girl." A look of total dismay swept across Dev's face. "When she starts dating is when someone is going to break her heart. She's so trusting and sweet, and there is going to be some asshole out there who is going to make her feel bad about herself, and make her cry." She let out a frustrated breath and lowered her voice. "How can I protect her from that if I let her go?"

Lauren nodded and tried for the millionth time to look into the sky past the haze caused by the city lights and see stars. "I'd give anything to protect all the kids forever. But we can't, honey. We all get our hearts broken."

Tears filled Dev's eyes. "I know. But I love her so much I can't bear the thought."

Lauren's chest felt heavy, the thought of Ashley being hurt making her sick as well. "Neither can I. But, baby, I don't think it's something we can realistically stop." Tenderly, she wiped the moisture away from the corner of Dev's eyes. "It's part of growing up."

Dev swallowed a few times. "So you think we should let her go?"

"I think we should consider it," Lauren corrected gently. "She *is* awfully young, and she hasn't exactly had your normal childhood, Devlyn." She lifted her hand to forestall the complaint that was poised on Dev's lips. "I know we've tried. But the girl can't go to Dairy Queen without the Secret Service coming along. She's never babysat, or delivered a newspaper, or a lot of the things that teach kids responsibility on the way to becoming an adult."

Miserably, Dev nodded, reminded once again of what her choice of careers had cost her family.

"So if it were another boy from a family we didn't know or the date was going to be someplace where we couldn't keep an eye on her, then I wouldn't even consider it. Not until she's just a little bit older." Lauren drew in a deep breath. "But—"

"But we can at least make sure she's safe this time," Dev acknowledged. A light bulb suddenly popped on in her head. "Is this the boy she was going on and on about a few weeks ago?"

Lauren smiled. She wistfully recalled the memory of her first crush and the nervous boy trying to give her a kiss in the corner of the school playground. "He's the one. Apparently, he's quishy."

"That had better not be contagious."

Gray eyes rolled. "It means 'cute,' Devlyn."

"How do you know what it means?" Dev demanded. "You're not cooler than I am!"

Lauren snorted. "Am too. But… umm…" She paused and picked a little at Dev's coat, her fingers quickly finding the gap between buttons and resting against the warm flannel. "I looked it up after I heard the kids saying it."

Dev let out a disgusted breath. "Figures the boy would be *quishy*." She tilted her head back, letting it rest against the high back of the stone bench. "Why would she want to start a relationship with someone here in Washington when we're moving to Ohio next month?"

"I don't think it's a relationship, Devlyn. It's just a Christmas party."

"Lauri?"

The blonde peered up until their eyes met.

"What about the fact that he's French? They invented doing things with their *tongues*." She hissed the last word as though it were a curse and then used the muscle in question to lick all around Lauren's mouth, causing the younger woman to burst into giggles.

The licking soon turned into soft but passionate kissing, and for a long while on that cold December night they lost track of time as they necked in the Rose Garden.

Finally, Dev pulled away, her body tingling all over, every bit of the chill chased away by her ardor. "Is she ready?"

Lauren easily picked up the thread of their prior conversation. "Not for what we were just doing, no." She ran her knuckles across Dev's cheek, reveling in the feeling of soft, flushed skin. "But to dip her toe in the dating pool…"

"All right." Dev sighed. "But only because we're going to be there."

Lauren nodded. "And only if she drives to and from the Hay-Adams with us."

Dev smiled. "Good one." Feeling better, she yawned. "I'll have the FBI run the boy's background and do a profile on him tomorrow."

Chuckling, Lauren rose to her feet, tugging the President along with her. "I'm going to pretend you're joking."

"Of course I'm joking."

"Devlyn—"

"Heh."

Saturday, December 22nd

Dev sat behind her desk; her palms were flat against the shiny surface as she just looked at the room. The door to David's office opened and he wandered through as he was finishing a phone call. He expertly clipped the phone onto his belt and regarded his boss. "You're not working?"

She shrugged and leaned back in her chair. "I was just thinking.

And to be honest, there are only a few weeks left here and not a hell of a lot going on. Geoff's transition team has been working like crazy." She shook her head a little. "It feels weird to be in here without anybody running around like a chicken without his head."

"Yeah." David thought about the subdued mood of the entire White House. "I guess they do usually."

Dev ran her fingertips over the polished desktop again. "What do you suppose the chances are that I can keep this?"

"Slim to none."

"I figured." She got up, moved to the couch and gestured for David to join her. "Anything exciting I should know about?"

He dropped down and nudged her with his shoulder, and they both rested their feet on the coffee table. "Haven't the last eight years been exciting enough?"

Dev didn't have to answer. He already knew the answer to that. As much as her job put strains on other parts of her life, she wouldn't have traded it for the world. The ability to make a positive difference in countless people's lives, the raw power of it, the respect, the dazzling thrill of it all that pushed the hard, draining moments into the background and gave her an emotional high that was nearly unequaled, would be hard to give up. Luckily, she didn't have a choice. "So you're really going to stay here, huh?"

The tall man shrugged. "Beth's going back to teaching full time and it would be hard for the new Emancipation Party Chairman to do his job from anywhere else."

"Anywhere else but the center of the universe... or the pits of hell. After eight years, I still can't decide which one Washington is."

They both smiled.

"Besides," David began again. "You're going back into the real world and you won't need me there."

"Hey." Dev turned sideways to face David, her forehead creasing. "You're my best friend. I've always needed you. And I always will." The lines on her face smoothed as she watched her words sink in. "We are a damn fine team, David."

"The best," he agreed, his jaw lifting a little with the admission. "But this is where I need to be to make things happen, and it's time I stepped out from behind your 'skirttails' and made my own mark. For once, I want to speak for myself and have somebody know it's me who's talking."

"You're going to be great, but I'm going to miss my right hand."

David gave her a quietly devoted look. "Not as much as I'm going to miss being it. But I think you can use your own hands on the lecture circuit. And besides, you get to keep Liza. And she'll help keep things on track."

"I can't believe Jane talked her into taking maternity leave. I was seriously worried that if the baby wasn't born when Liza scheduled it—"

"On Sunday morning between three and five a.m.—" David broke in with a smile.

"The least busy time, statistically speaking," Dev laughed, "that the poor woman would have a nervous breakdown."

"Knowing Liza, I'd say that's probably *exactly* when the baby will come."

Dev chuckled. "Very true."

David slapped his knee. "I hope you know I'm going to be calling my old friend and asking her to go stumping for the party's brightest and best."

Dev flashed him a brilliant smile. "I should hope so. But not for the first six months or so. I intend to go home, plant a garden, sit by the fire, and make love to my wife constantly."

"All at the same time? Wouldn't that be dirty and hot?"

Dev grinned. "If I'm lucky."

"And you're going to do this for six months straight?"

Dev actually blushed. "Well, I imagine I won't make it the full six months. I'm not as young as I used to be."

David gazed at her knowingly. "And the chances of you being content sitting around by some fire and gardening your time away are about as good as me becoming Miss America. You, Madam President, are not the sort of woman who will be happy with a life of leisure."

"No," she smiled a little. "I guess I'm not. But I am going to become reacquainted with my kids and parents. And try to make up for some of the many, many late nights I should have spent in bed with my wife but spent behind this desk instead." She nudged him with her foot. "I owe it to them and to myself to at least try."

David nodded. "Understood. So…" He decided on a change of subject. "Have you and Lauren settled on one of the houses you were looking at?"

"I think so. We're flying down to look at our final two choices in Powell over the New Year's weekend. They're both in good locations and close to Mom and Dad. My folks have been wanting to spend more time with the kids for years. And they aren't getting any younger."

"Speaking of someone young, do you know that Aaron asked *me* when he could get a tattoo?"

"What?" Dev screeched.

David shook his head and laughed. "Oh, yeah. Apparently, he mentioned it to Lauren, and she told him when hell freezes over, and over her dead body, and a bunch of other things that made him understand that she was *not* the person to ask to get around going to you."

"Smart woman." Dev nodded. "What did you tell him?"

"I told him that if it were my choice, which it's not," he emphasized that part, knowing that his role with the children was still a somewhat touchy spot between them, "that the answer would be never. But that once he's over eighteen it's up to him to decide."

"David!"

"Well, it's true, Dev."

A dark eyebrow lifted. "Then you'd better manage to get some legislation raising the age from eighteen to twenty-one before Chris gets that old. Hell, twenty-five sounds like a little better age of consent, now that I think about it."

David almost laughed until he realized she was being serious. "Dev," he whined. "That's a state, not federal, issue. You know how I hate state politics." Dev just glared at him, so he tried another tack. "My hands are tied."

She gave him a firm poke in the belly. "Well, Mr. Big Shot Party Chairman." Another poke. "You've got six years, before Aaron is eighteen, to *untie* them."

David tried to hold it back, but couldn't, and a slightly melancholy smile overtook his face. He swallowed thickly, and his voice dropped to a rarely used, soft tone. "You have no idea how much I'm going to miss you and your family, Devil."

Dev's eyes widened a little with alarm. "Jesus, David, you make it sound like we're never going to see each other again."

David let out a quick breath. "That will never happen," he promised.

She bit the inside of her lip as she tried to keep her voice from cracking. "The hardest part about leaving the job is going to be leaving you here." She paused and let every bit of the love and gratitude she felt for him show plainly on her face. "I-I wouldn't be the woman I am today without you, David. I know that most of the country will never realize how much you've done and how tirelessly you've worked. But *I* know. And I won't ever forget. Thank you."

Their eyes met, and David realized he didn't know what to say. He felt her words all the way to the bottom of his heart. Instead of answering, he just took Dev's hand and cradled it in his larger one, then he threaded their fingers together and squeezed gently as they both turned and gazed out the window at the falling snow. The vision was a blurred one for both friends.

After a few minutes, Dev sniffed and wiped at her face. "Now that the mushy stuff is out of the way, call Beth and get her over here, so you can both have dinner with me and the family."

"I'd love to, Madam President."

Monday, December 25th

Christmas Day

Video calls had been exchanged with loved ones, the McMillians had come and gone, and Lauren had successfully sneaked over to her office while Devlyn and the children were enjoying their late morning Christmas naps. It was a lazy, cloudy day, and she had her glasses off and was gnawing on their stems as she took this rare quiet time to dictate some notes for Devlyn's biography.

As usual, Gremlin lay atop her feet, warming them. He lounged there listlessly, the death of his mate the summer before taking most of the spring from his formerly feisty step. Occasionally, Lauren reached down to scratch his ears, her voice never wavering as she continued with her notes.

"Overview. Last chapter. General thoughts.

"In less than a month, Geoff and Brenda Vincent will move into the White House, and the Marlowes, my family, will move out. Devlyn made a lot of sense when she asked where all the

time had gone. I hardly know myself. I swear to God it was just yesterday that I walked into this place, in utter awe, my mouth hanging open like somebody who was in ten feet over her head." Lauren chuckled to herself. *"Which I was. Nowadays, just every now and then, I stop and look around and remember where I am and what the people here are doing, and it's easy to recall just when I had butterflies the size of bats jumping in my stomach.*

"When I look back at my first year in the White House, at how I was concerned that I couldn't deliver an impartial portrait of this American president, I have to laugh. Impartial? Lord, that flew out the window the moment I fell in love with her. The moment that her life story became mine, and vice versa. Still, Devlyn is the most honest person I've ever met. That honesty bleeds into everything she does and to know her deeds is to, at least for the most part, know her. The good and the bad. The mistakes and the triumphs. I've decided to include it all. The hard stuff too, and the stuff that happened behind closed doors and away from the cameras. It won't be juicy gossip like the tabloids crave. Just the real Devlyn.

"All of her.

"The shooting. Not just that it happened, but what it took for her to recover physically and mentally and to put herself back out there again. In harm's way. Every. Single. Day.

"The nights she couldn't sleep while some operation was taking place halfway across the world, knowing that somebody's son or daughter wasn't going to be coming home. Only Jane and I know about the teary phone calls she made to the families the next day. Out of the spotlight. Alone. She *did that. Not some aide or soldier. The President.*

"The laughter from the White House gym as she, and the willing among the Secret Service agents, grunted and sweated and formed relationships that went far beyond work. And how she lives with the knowledge that part of these people's jobs is to take a bullet for her, if necessary.

"The re-election scandal that nearly cost her a second term in office. God, I still can't believe she made sure that "suicide" wasn't listed as the cause of death on Mama's death certificate. I should have wondered why the press never picked up on exactly

what happened. But so much was happening in my own life then that I didn't know whether I was coming or going. I guess I thought I just got incredibly lucky when it came to Mama's death and the press. But it wasn't luck, and three years after Devlyn did it, it exploded in her face. She risked her entire career for me and did it knowing and believing it was wrong. It was one of the times she wasn't the nation's hero. Just mine.

"The days spent bargaining away little pieces of something she believed in, in exchange for the greater good.

"The endless speeches, negotiations, fundraisers, and legislation that she poured her heart into.

"The pride on her face when she knew she'd done something that was truly special." Lauren laughed lovingly.

"Scratch what I said about including it all. Starlight isn't interested in a twenty-volume set. But my editor and I can duke it out over what to include later. For now, I need to focus on the last chapter.

"It won't be the climax. Or even the wrap-up after the climax. Fiction is so much easier that way.

"I don't believe the last chapter of a biography of a living person should dwell too much on their past accomplishments. That implies that the deeds that got their picture on the book cover to begin with are the deeds that were the most meaningful. That things are somehow over because the words 'The End' are printed at the bottom of the page.

"The story isn't over! She is only forty-six years old. She's vibrant and healthy and still hell bent on saving the world, even if she pretends she'll be happy in some house in Ohio with a white picket fence, a hammock, and a good book. She won't be. And that's all right. Because I won't be either. She's not ready to ride off into the sunset; it's just time for a different trail. One that will largely be 'off camera.'

"My goal is not to leave readers wondering about anything, but to leave them knowing that the book may be over, but the story isn't. I truly believe there are a lot of great things still to come from Devlyn Marlowe. The part that still makes me a little giddy is that I'm going to be there to share them with her."

Lauren paused and took a sip of tea. Then she chewed on her

glasses and picked up a stack of papers that sat next to her computer. She riffled through them until she found the sheet she wanted.

"I think if I tie Devlyn's plans for the lecture circuit into some of Chapter Seven, I can show that—"

Her words were interrupted by a phone call, and Lauren disabled the voice system on her computer and smiled when she saw who was calling.

Lauren was just getting ready to end her video call from Wayne when there was a knock at her office door.

"It's me."

"C'mon in, Ashley," Lauren called.

The dark-haired girl opened the door and poked her head inside what once was Lauren's White House apartment. "Are you busy?" she asked, then she caught sight of Wayne's three-dimensional image. "I can come back—"

"No, no." Lauren waved her inside. "We were just finishing up."

Ashley flashed a brilliant smile as she entered the room and made her way to Lauren, not bothering to close the door behind her. "Hi, Mr. Evenocheck!" She gave the man a little wave.

"Hello, sweetheart," he greeted, his voice warm. Then he let loose with a wolf whistle. "You are every bit as gorgeous as both your mothers." He sighed. "What I wouldn't give to be one of the agents guarding your house and to be not so old that you're absolutely right in calling me *Mr.* Evenocheck."

Lauren laughed as Ashley blushed becomingly. Fondly, she wrapped an arm around the girl's slim waist. "Don't let him embarrass you, sugar." Lauren's eyes twinkled. "He enjoys scaring members of the opposite sex."

"You wound me, Lauren," Wayne said in a serious voice, but he winked for Ashley's benefit.

"Oh." Ashley suddenly remembered the book she'd recently finished. She sucked in an excited breath. "Mr. Evenocheck, Mama said you know—"

Wayne chuckled. "His autograph is in the mail, sweetheart. Just don't drool on it." He winked again. "Runs the ink."

"Thanks!" Ashley gave an excited little hop.

"Oops." Wayne looked down at his phone. "That's my mother on my other line. This is her annual call to tell me how another Christmas has been ruined because I haven't given her any grandchildren." He cringed.

"Mr. Evenocheck has a mother?" Ashley murmured to Lauren, earning a muffled chuckle from the older woman.

"It's hard to believe, isn't it?" Lauren whispered back, tickling Ashley's waist with playful fingers.

"I heard that," Wayne complained, but he was smiling. "Merry Christmas to my favorite author and her family." He met Lauren's gaze. "We'll talk again soon, yes?" He lifted his eyebrows in question.

Thoughtfully, Lauren nodded. "Soon."

Wayne disconnected from his end and with a few security codes, Lauren did the same thing. "How was your nap?" she asked Ashley, taking the time to save her file and turn off her machine.

"Nap?"

Lauren glanced at her in question.

Ashley's mouth formed a tiny O. "Oh, right. My nap." She yawned dramatically. "It was great."

Lauren pursed her lips. Something was up.

"Hurry up, Ash!" came a voice from outside the office. "You're supposed to get her off the phone, *not* take all day."

Lauren gave Ashley a puzzled look, then rose to her feet, gently moving Gremlin aside so she could stand without tipping over. "Aaron, is that you? You can come in."

Then she heard it. The familiar pitter-patter of tiny feet. Four, tiny canine feet, to be precise.

Aaron pushed open the door to reveal a pug puppy, who was on a long, loosely held, bright red leash and collar. Over Aaron's shoulder, Lauren could see a smiling Christopher and a sheepish-looking Devlyn peering back at her.

"What in the world?" Her eyes saucered as a tiny replica of Gremlin scampered in, his paws sliding on the hardwood floors. He ran head-first into a chair leg and shook his head briskly. He was stunned, and he staggered backwards a few steps before landing squarely on his butt with a tiny thump.

Gremlin's ears perked up and with a growl, and at a speed that Lauren hadn't witnessed in several years, he bolted for the puppy, his feet slipping and sliding as he went.

"Gremlin!" Lauren cried, afraid of what he might do to the puppy.

But Gremlin came to a screeching stop just in front of the little pug, and his broad, flat nose bumped gently against the puppy's smaller one.

For a tension-filled few seconds both dogs remained stock-still. Then the puppy's entire body started to shake, along with his stumpy tail.

"Aww..." the kids cooed in unison, making their way to the floor with the dog.

Even Devlyn found herself melting a little as Gremlin tentatively poked out his tongue, then greeted the puppy with a sopping, loud lick.

Lauren blinked as her dog warmed to his new task and began cleaning the puppy's entire face while the puppy mewed and whimpered in delight. A smile edged its way onto her face, and she glanced up at Dev—who was doing her best to look innocent. "Is someone going to tell me what's going on?"

"It's a Christmas present," Christopher explained, petting both dogs with a gentle touch that was so characteristic of the boy. "Gremlin's been so sad."

Aaron stood up and handed the leash to his brother. "He still misses Princess, I think. We thought he might need a friend," he grinned, showing off deep dimples, "with breath as bad as his."

"How—?" Lauren shook her head in wonder. "How did you get one that looks just like Gremlin? I'm not even sure he's purebred. We met at the pound!"

"The puppy is Grem's grandson," Ashley told her, her eyes on the puppy. "Uncle David bred his pugly with a purebred pug, and he ended up with one that looks like Gremlin again. We kept it a surprise."

Dev stepped around her children and the dogs and approached the younger woman. "And are you surprised?" she asked, bracing herself in case Lauren reacted badly. She cocked her head to the side and begged in her most sincere voice, "Can we keep him, Mama?" She batted her eyelashes. "Please?"

Lauren's jaw sagged a little as she wondered whether she'd heard right. "Devlyn Marlowe," she paused to kiss her in greeting, "you have complained about my dog every single day since I came to the White House and now you want *another* pug?"

Dev's cheeks tinted and she dropped her voice so that only Lauren could hear. "But Grem is lonely by himself." She gave Lauren a wish-filled look that left her helpless to do anything but smile.

"You're such an old softy," she whispered back, feeling as though she might cry.

"Shh…" Dev looked around in case she was being overheard. "The kids will never listen to another word I say if they figure out what a soft touch I am."

The children began to giggle. "We know and we still love you Mom," Christopher assured her, as he used the puppy's paws to scratch Gremlin's ears.

"Well?" Ashley looked up from her place on the floor with the boys. "Can we keep him?"

Lauren eyed her dog, who was actually smiling, his crooked teeth gleaming in the afternoon light. Then she looked at her children, who were all giving her the same pathetic, puppy-dog eyes that Devlyn had subjected her to earlier. She sighed. "Was there ever any doubt?"

"Yes!" the boys crowed, startling the puppy and sending it scurrying over to Devlyn.

The white dog with black markings cowered at the President's feet and Devlyn reached out a tentative hand to comfort him, ready to snatch it away in case Gremlin's prodigy decided to take after his Grandpa and go for her pinky finger. But to everyone's surprise, the puppy simply licked Dev's fingers, then nuzzled her hand.

Beaming, Dev picked up the puppy and gave him a sloppy kiss. "He loves me!" She turned to Gremlin, a smug look on her face. "See this?" She squeezed the puppy to her face. "He loves *me*. Me, me, me, me, me! What do you think about *that*?"

Gremlin turned his flat nose up at the President and, seeing no reason to break with tradition now, refused to acknowledge he was even being spoken to.

Dev's eyes narrowed at the chubby dog, and her lips curled into her best snarl.

Snorting at Dev and Gremlin's familiar antics, Lauren reached out to pet the puppy to say hello. "Yeow!" The dog snapped at her, his teensy teeth bared in canine fury. She snatched her hand away, rubbing it even though the tiny teeth had missed her. "Hey," she said softly, "I won't hurt you." She tried again, and this time the dog barked, refusing to let Lauren's hand anywhere near not only him but also his new mistress.

Dev.

On Lauren's third try, the puppy sank his teeth into the sleeve of her sweatshirt and refused to let go even when Lauren jerked her hand back. The frantic action yanked the skinny dog right out of Devlyn's arms and left him dangling from Lauren's shirt as she shook her arm wildly and screamed for someone to get him off.

The children were nearly in hysterics by the time Devlyn successfully unhooked the puppy's teeth from Lauren's favorite, orange, Tennessee Volunteers sweatshirt.

"He's possessed!" Lauren wailed to Gremlin. "Can you believe that? Your own flesh and blood is a demon and he likes *her*," she pointed an accusing finger at her mate, "and not me." She held up her now raggedy sleeve for Gremlin to see. "Look what he did!"

Dev petted the puppy possessively, enjoying this more than she could put into words. "Thank you for naming him, honey. Hello, little Demon," she murmured into his soft white fur.

The children hummed their agreement at the name, enjoying the play between their mothers and most especially the comical, sour look on Lauren's face.

In consolation, Gremlin made the supreme effort of getting up and walking the few paces over to Lauren and plopping down on her feet. He was there for her to scratch, should she find it necessary.

Satisfied for the time being, Lauren shook her finger at Devlyn. "Keep Demon away from me. He's tried to bite me twice and he's just a baby!"

"But he's so precious," Dev cooed, kissing the dog again, mindless of his slobber.

"Uck." Lauren made a face. "I won't even do that with Gremlin. Your lips are not coming anywhere near me for days."

"That's okay," Dev murmured, petting her new beloved. She sniffed haughtily, her nose high in the air. "It's enough to know at long last that a pug has chosen me over you. It's only sweeter that he's a relative of Gremlin's."

"Devlyn," Lauren groaned. "I am not keeping a dog that hates me."

Dev arched an eyebrow. "We all want a new member of the family, and now I'll have lots of extra time to spend with him."

Lauren gave her a challenging look, and Devlyn gave her one right back.

"It's either a dog or a baby, Lauren. You choose."

"Hello and welcome to the family, Demon," Lauren said instantly, trying once again to pet him, only to have to snatch her hand away to safety.

Dev sniggered. "That's what I thought."

"Here." Lauren grabbed Christopher by the arm and hoisted him to his feet. He was already a little taller than she was, and she gave him a quick peck on the cheek before pushing him toward his mother. "Take Demon and Gremlin for a walk and let them get to know each other. I need a minute alone with your mom."

"Oooo…" the kids taunted. "Mom's in trou-blllle!"

Dev blinked, then her eyes widened. "I am?" She tried to sneak out with the kids, but Lauren grabbed the back of her shirt and hauled her back into the room, not stopping until they stood alongside the bed.

"Oh, no you don't, Madam President. I said I wanted to talk to you."

"So you did." Dev sighed and flopped down on the bed with her eyes closed. "I'm not really in trouble, am I?" She opened one very blue eye just in case.

The blonde laughed softly. "No. The puppy will eventually like me." She joined Dev on the bed, stretching out, and propping her head on her upturned hand. "Thank you for thinking of Gremlin," she said, her voice soft and sincere. "He's been so sad."

Dev smiled, but just a little. "S'okay. We've sort of come to a truce over the years." She shrugged one shoulder.

"I know. In fact, that was so sweet I'd kiss you now, but you still have puppy slobber on your face."

Dev eagerly wiped her mouth off using her sleeve. "Better?" She presented her mouth to Lauren for inspection.

Lauren smiled warmly and patted Dev's cheek. Then she leaned close to Dev's mouth, stopping bare millimeters away to say, "No."

The smile slid from Dev's face, and Lauren laughed.

"Damn, you're mean." Dev frowned.

"Aww… C'mere, darlin'." This time their lips met in earnest in a soft, slow kiss that they both sank into. "I." Another kiss. "Love." A third kiss. "You."

"Wow," Dev finally said, sharing the same breath as Lauren. "You're in a good mood all of a sudden."

Lauren nodded. "I'm… well." She drew in a deep breath. "I don't know what I am. Excited, I guess." She pulled away just enough to gauge Dev's reaction. "On the phone today, Wayne made me an offer."

"I need to castrate that man."

Gray eyes rolled. "Not *that* kind of an offer." A beat. "At least not this time." She grinned as Dev's eyes turned to slits, but her expression quickly sobered. "He wants me to write another biography when I'm finished with yours."

Suddenly serious, Dev sat up. "Really?"

"Really."

"Wow." Dev licked her lips. "I… um… I thought you were going to take a year or two off and do another Adrian Nash novel."

"That is what I planned."

Dev blinked as she caught the look of hesitation in her lover's eyes. "But that's not what you'd rather do." It wasn't a question.

"I didn't tell Wayne yes or no to anything," Lauren said quickly, searching Dev's face for her reaction. She felt her stomach flip-flop. "I would never do that without—"

"Whoa." Dev reached out and stroked Lauren's arm. "Slow down and tell me what he said." She smiled encouragingly, and Lauren let out a relieved breath.

"Have you heard of Doctor Graham Lock?"

Dev's eyebrows knitted. "He's a scientist researching…" she searched her mind, "cell structure or cell replication… or… um… cancer, right?"

"Yes, to all those things." Lauren licked her lips. "His latest results from his first round of human trials came back a few days ago. The results haven't been released to the public or even to the scientific community, but Wayne was literally talking to the man when the results came back." She held her breath as Devlyn put the pieces together.

"He did it?" The President sucked in a breath. "Holy Christ, he found a cure for cancer?"

Lauren nodded, well aware of how amazing this was to say. "He thinks so."

Devlyn was about to jump off the bed and head to a phone when Lauren grabbed her arm. "Hang on there."

"I need to call Dav—"

"No, you don't," Lauren said firmly, her eyes flashing with determination. "This is 'off the record.'"

Dev's mouth clicked closed. This was the first time in all these years that their positions had been reversed. And she wasn't sure she liked it.

Lauren eased off of Dev's arm, sat up, and tenderly massaged the places where her hands had been. "The results of the trials will be made public in the morning. Today is Christmas. Isn't that soon enough, Devlyn? Please."

Dev sighed, but nodded. "I'm sorry. I just—"

Lauren's eyes softened. "It's okay. It's amazing news. Wayne's been after this scientist for months. The fact that he found out just a tiny bit sooner than the rest of the world was nothing but dumb luck. According to Wayne, the initial trial results are very promising. Even if Dr. Lock isn't one hundred percent successful right now, Devlyn, he's close. He really believes he's going to find the cure for cancer and so do a lot of other people."

"And Wayne wants you to write his story," Dev breathed, seeing the lives they'd laid out for the indefinite future disintegrate before her eyes.

Lauren gazed at her warily, knowing this was a lot to think about. She hadn't even had the opportunity to think about it herself. "Yes. Wayne is after an exclusive contract for an authorized biography with Dr. Lock. Something he could sell to Starlight after the preliminaries are in place."

"It's the opportunity of a lifetime," Dev said quietly, looking into Lauren's eyes.

Lauren kissed her softly. *"You* were my opportunity of a lifetime. Nothing can change that. But this would be… I don't know. It could be…"

Dev nodded, her mind racing. "Where?"

"Sydney, Australia." At the sight of Dev's widening eyes, she quickly added, "Or Ohio. I wouldn't start until late next summer at the soonest. I need to finish your book, and I need a vacation. A long vacation. But, I don't know, maybe… maybe I could travel back and forth to Sydney and do most research by computer."

Dev frowned. "But it would be better to be there in person, wouldn't it? That's how you work, right?"

Lauren swallowed. "In the past, yes. But your lecturing and the kids' schooling and—"

Dev pressed her fingers against Lauren's lips to stop her. "How long?" Carefully, she pulled back her fingers.

"I'm not sure." Lauren's brain shifted into biographer mode. "Nothing too long. His next set of trials is slated for the fall. And then six months to a year is about normal for research and observation, maybe a bit longer," she allowed, "because I'd have to learn a lot just to understand what the man is saying when he speaks. Then another six months or so to tie things together. But that could be done anywhere."

"Mmm…" Dev nodded again, her face serious as she looked away from Lauren and gathered her thoughts, which were racing along at a mile a minute. It would be hard, yes. But plans could be changed. Things could be worked out. And in the end, there was really only one question that mattered. "Do you want it?" She glanced back at Lauren and met her gaze squarely. Her voice dropped to its deepest register. "Because I would want it."

Lauren sucked in a breath and told the truth, "I don't want it more than I want to be with you and the kids."

Dev's heart lurched, and she cupped Lauren's cheek. "Honey, you're stuck with us. That's not even a consideration. The question is whether you want the job?"

Did she? She thought of what Wayne had said and let the tingle of anticipation burn all the way to her toes. Her gaze sharpened. "Yes."

Dev smiled, leaned back against the headboard, and crossed her legs at the ankles. "Then I guess we're going to Australia."

Lauren was at a loss, and her mouth worked for several seconds before she could speak. "Ca-can we do that?" she stammered. "Just like that?"

Dev's smile turned into an outright grin. "You've lived in my world for eight years." Her voice held a strong note of devotion as the words flowed easily from her heart. "I know it hasn't been easy. I think it's my turn to follow you, Lauren."

Tears welled in soft gray eyes, and Lauren's chin began to tremble.

"You came to the White House with an ugly dog and a dozen boxes. When I tag along after you I'm going to bring our kids, security, a nanny, assuming Emma ever decides to come home from her yearly cruise, and most probably my parents, who have always wanted to see the Outback. Can you live with that mess?"

Lauren let out a ragged breath and felt herself fall in love all over again. And it was so sweet. "Hey," she whispered. "That 'mess' is my family." A tear escaped from one eye. Devlyn gently removed Lauren's glasses, then carefully kissed the tear away.

Lauren squeezed Dev to her with all her might. "I love you

Devlyn," she whispered brokenly. "Thank you."

It felt better than anything she'd done as president, and the thought almost surprised her.

Almost.

"I love you too."

When Dev pulled away, Lauren could see the glint of excitement in her eyes, and she knew it was mirrored in her own.

The President grinned impishly. "I wonder what sort of trouble I can get into in Australia? In two terms of office I never made it out there. Though I've always wanted to go." She jumped off the bed, dragging the smaller woman along with her and positioning Lauren squarely in front of her computer. She pushed the chair out of their way so they could both stand in front of the machine. "Fire this thing up and let's look for beach bungalow rentals that will hold big families. And something with another building on the same property or next door for security."

Dev rested her chin on Lauren's head and handed the blonde back her glasses while Lauren enabled the voice commands

Soon the sound of the women's excited chatter about schools for the children, new options for Devlyn, their schedules, and the house they still intended to buy in Ohio filled the room. After a few heady moments, Lauren spun in Devlyn's arms, and wrapped her own arms around Dev's waist. She gazed up at her. "Are we really going to do this?"

The younger woman was radiating excitement, and to Devlyn, she'd never looked more beautiful. A dazzling smile lit Dev's face, making it all the way to her eyes. "Can you think of anything better than starting a new adventure together?"

Lauren shook her head and rose onto her tiptoes to kiss the love of her life. "Not a single thing."

Printed in Great Britain
by Amazon.co.uk, Ltd.,
Marston Gate.

13494360R00205